PRAISE FOR
THE INVASION OF FALGANNON ISLE!

"What makes MacGillivray's romance so special are the eccentric characters, right down to the cat, and Desmond and B.A.'s growing relationship."

—*Booklist*

"This is an entertaining, humorous and heartwarming tale of love, friendship and a bit of magic. The hero's struggle to make peace with his past and the heroine's determination to help him are nicely depicted. The secondary characters are great fun, especially The Cat Dudley, and the peek into the lives of the main character's siblings whets the appetite for their stories."

—*RT Book Reviews*

"In a word, 'Perfection!'"

—Huntress Reviews

"*The Invasion of Falgannon Isle* is a masterful tale woven by an incredibly talented author. The juxtaposition of the modern day intrusions with the timelessness of Falgannon Isle creates a world readers will want to visit, over and over again."

—CK's Kwips & Kritiques

"Ms. MacGillivray creates characters that seemed so alive that I almost believed Falgannon Isle really exists. If it did, I would really love to move there! *The Invasion of Falgannon Isle* is one of my best reads . . . it has many laugh-out-loud moments, wonderful characters, a hint of the paranormal, and a great romance."

—Mystique Books

A TOOTHSOME PREDICTION

Raven laughed, but suddenly clicking noises sounded and the Gypsy woman moved. Her carved hands once more passed over the huge crystal ball, which began to glow a faint luminous blue, the colors within seeming to swirl. The mannequin tilted her head faintly side-to-side, then her eyes closed. When the lids lifted, those amber orbs gazed at Raven with such intensity it was hard to recall the figure was only a carved figure in a box. Finally, another click sounded and a card ejected on the side. Raven stared at the lifelike woman, unable to move.

Shaking off her silliness, Raven reached out and took the card. The Lovers. She stared at the image on the card's face, once more feeling the hand of Fate molding her future. A warning buzzed in her blood as she studied the image, reluctant to turn it over, fearful to read the fortune on the reverse.

Brishen nudged her elbow. "Go on. See the rest of your fortune. The Gypsy, she promises romance to come—a big handsome lover, eh? But what else does she say?"

Feeling one door close on her life and another open, Raven flipped the card over. A bubbly laugh escaped as she saw the words written there:

Beware of the wolf in sheep's clothing.

Other *Love Spell* books by Deborah MacGillivray:

RIDING THE THUNDER
THE INVASION OF FALGANNON ISLE

Deborah MacGillivray

A Wolf in Wolf's Clothing

LOVE SPELL NEW YORK CITY

LOVE SPELL®

August 2009

Published by

Dorchester Publishing Co., Inc.
200 Madison Avenue
New York, NY 10016

ISBN 10: 0-505-52781-2
ISBN 13: 978-0-505-52781-3
E-ISBN: 978-1-4285-0721-0

Visit us online at www.dorchesterpub.com.

To Muriel—

Miss Fuzz and I miss you

and to some very special ladies—

Diane Davis White, Diane Mae Thompson, Monika Wolmarans and Leanne Burroughs—and all who have fought the battle and survived!

A Wolf in
Wolf's Clothing

Chapter One

"Sometimes, Trev, when you least expect it, life grabs you by the short and curlies and gives you a firm squeeze." Trevelyn Sinclair Mershan vented his frustration to the pair of accusing green eyes staring back at him from his rearview mirror, and oddly he felt for an instant as if he gazed at his twin brother. Looking at the reflection was like looking at Jago; they were nearly that identical—on the outside. Inside they were nothing alike. Saint Jago served as the conscience of the three Mershan brothers.

"And me? Well, they might wonder if I have horns hidden in hair." Trev laughed. "They might be right, too."

He down-shifted the powerful Lamborghini Murciélago, burying the tachometer into the red. His fingers flexed around the gearshift, relishing the engine's deep growl of protest; the sound evoked an image of a panther roaring in the night. At one with the darkness surrounding him, he guided the sleek black roadster toward his destination. He was a fool to come here, he knew that only too well. Regardless, he was lured onward, unable to resist.

"Ulysses was tempted by a siren's song. Why should I be any different?" he said with a touch of self-derision.

Once more, he glanced at the mirror. Questions were reflected in his eyes—questions he didn't like. They asked why he raced through the night, compelled toward his goal against his nature. But this was a fool's errand, and he wasn't even going to summon reasons to justify what he was doing. They'd be lies.

As a vice president of Mershan International, so many responsibilities weighed upon his shoulders. Frequently he did deals worth millions of dollars before lunch—hundreds of millions. His signature on a contract often affected thousands of lives. He liked the control.

"Like it? Bloody hell. I get off on it."

And women . . . Well, he never had the need to chase any female. All he had to do was stand still and they were all over him. It was often humorous, the lengths they would go to end up on his arm—and in his bed. A parade of beauties had traipsed through his life, few ever lasting long enough to leave a lingering impression. "Flavors of the month," Agnes Dodd, his sour-faced secretary, was fond of sneering. Yet for the first time in his life, Trev was going after a woman. It rankled.

She wasn't merely a woman, either. Raven Montgomerie was a riddle. Perhaps that was why he'd been unable to put the portfolio aside and go to bed tonight, leaving all this business until the gala tomorrow. The sexy redhead haunted his waking hours. She invaded his dreams—dreams so vivid that he'd repeatedly awoken bathed in sweat, his body cramped with agonizing need. Endless cold showers did little to chase away his persistent hunger. Trev was tired of reading reports and staring at the stack of photographs of Raven, irritated he had a hard time making the words and pictures go together. Most frustrating of all, he refused to face the fact that he hadn't taken another woman to bed since he'd seen her five months ago. His brother Jago would howl with laughter if he ever got wind of that.

"You're bloody losing it, old son." He clucked his tongue in a manner Jago often did when trying to shame him into being good.

Why should Raven have such a hold over him when they'd never even spoken? She was a beautiful woman, true, but then all the Montgomerie sisters were. One of the pampered granddaughters of Sean "Midas" Montgomerie, she'd been raised in the lap of luxury. A silver spoon wasn't good enough for her; only a service of gold graced the table of Colford Hall where she'd been reared.

Lights of the ancient manor came into view as Trev rounded the bend. In response, his muscles tensed and his heart rate jumped. The glimmering windows cast their pale yellow light out onto the rolled lawn. Trev slowed the car to a crawl as he wheeled past the towering, ornate gates before the winding drive, taking in the 14th-century manor house and swallowing back hate. This palace in all its five-story splendor, this epitome of a wealthy English estate, was a picture of obscenity and unfairness to him and to his brothers.

Oddly, Raven Montgomerie eschewed living in residence, opting instead to make her home in a thatched cottage on the far side of the vast estate. Raven doing this simply made no sense. Why live in a small house barely of notice when she could reside in the regal elegance of Colford and have servants waiting on her hand and foot? People would kill to have the life she was born into. Contrarily, Raven chose a path of modest means and generally kept to herself. Trev supposed that, after learning how the other sisters lived, this bent of Raven's shouldn't perplex him to the point of obsession. One of the older sisters, BarbaraAnne, stayed on a small isle in the north of Scotland, while Raven's twin Asha lived in some strange time warp, running several small businesses out in the middle of bloody nowhere Kentucky.

"Lady Contradiction is thy name, Raven Montgomerie. But you're a puzzle I intend to unriddle. Then you'll vex me no more," Trev said softly.

Small muscles that bracketed his mouth deepened at the idea of Raven also being a twin. It gave him and Raven a commonality, an understanding of what it was like to share your physical likeness with another person while your thoughts and feelings were totally different. That alone set Raven above any other woman he'd been with.

Irritation unfurling, he punched the gas pedal and flew down the lane. These narrow roads through the English countryside were like a racecourse, and it was a true challenge to go as fast as he did—a challenge he savored.

A short distance later, he slowed to take a turnoff. Most people would zoom past and never notice the narrow track; its surface was nearly nonexistent, possibly the remnants of an old Roman way. Fortunately the Lamborghini sat low, for several tree branches bowed almost to the ground. One slapped at the car as it passed, making a noise like fingernails on a chalkboard, and Trev grimaced.

"Bloody hell, I really liked this car. Oh well, maybe midnight blue for the next one," he mused. He traded cars nearly as often as he did women. His smirk became a scowl as the gas pan hit a rut in the road. "Hmm . . . definitely midnight blue."

The flicker of lights appeared in the distance, so he shut off the headlights and slowed the roadster even more. He didn't want Raven to spot him coming.

All things weighed, he wasn't sure why he'd picked Raven as the sister to target. Perhaps the predator in him viewed her as the weak link. Possibly it was something more, some influence he didn't even begin to fathom. He enjoyed strong women, females who didn't play coy. A quick assessment of the Montgomerie sisters would peg them all as warrior stock with a natural ability to intimidate men. Not Raven. Haunting vulnerability wrapped her like a mantle, and in a strange fashion this intrigued Trev, evoked a fey response that defied labels, unlike anything he'd ever encountered.

As a rule, softer women failed to hold his attention. He took pleasure in the challenge of the hunt, the clash of wills—yet none of the other vibrant siblings mesmerized him in the manner Raven did. Trev could enumerate excuses why the other sisters failed to conjure his interest. One-by-one he'd crossed them off the list, coming up with various logical reasons to give each a pass and leaving Raven, some might remark, as the last choice. Something told him that wasn't true, though. Raven would never be the last choice. She was the first and only choice.

As a small knoll materialized in the fog, he cut the wheel, switched off the engine and allowed the car to coast across the lawn to a halt under an oak tree. The slight roll in the landscape saw the mound overlooking the thatched house, nestled into the odd crook in the land.

"My, what a perfect location for tonight's bit of work," he said, his voice loud in the still night. "All the better to spy upon you, Little Red Riding Hood."

Pocketing his keys, he opened the car's gull-wing door and then paused with his foot balanced on the frame while his eyes took in Raven's home. The bungalow was two stories, though the second level was likely just a bedroom and bath due to the steep incline of the roof. The only time Trev had been in a thatched house was when he was small, in the months after his father committed suicide. But he'd been too young to remember that time in Ireland the way his older brother Des did. And while Trev had expected to look down his nose at Raven's humble home, instead he was fascinated. An air of warmth and welcome beckoned him toward the cottage, which was aglow with amber lights.

He sat on the hood of the car and studied the whitewashed structure, trying to pinpoint Raven. Playing Peeping Tom was easy. The onetime gardener's cottage was constructed of so much glass. There were two greenhouses, too, one on either side. The first had likely been a hothouse, the other for plants that required a more temperate clime. But Raven was an artist, a painter. The report Julian Starkadder had compiled said she was working toward a one-woman show for a local gallery come spring. The smaller glass room had been turned into a studio. Even from this distance Trev could see the easel, though it was too far away to tell what was currently painted upon the large canvas.

Aside from the two glassed-in spaces, a dining room had been added, also with glass walls. Raven Montgomerie's life was on display, but he figured she never considered that. Some beautiful women loved to put on a show for anyone looking—even Peeping Toms. Still, for someone as gorgeous as Raven, she didn't live her life on the stage she created here; Trev was willing to bet the Lamborghini on that. Raven was far away from people, so she obviously felt no need to hide behind drapes.

"Where the hell are you, Red?" he asked. "Come out, come out, wherever you are."

It was exasperating: all these walls of glass and he couldn't spot her. He knew she was at home. She'd been working on preparation for the gala all day, doing final touches. After supper he'd grown twitchy, so had driven past the banquet hall that her brother, Cian, had rented for Montgomerie Enterprises' big bash. As he spotted her coming out of the building, Trev swung into a parking lot down the road and watched while she slid into her ancient MGB. Keeping a distance, he followed her until she took the turnoff for this cottage. She was still here. His predator's sense confirmed that.

Growing impatient, he pushed off his car and trotted toward the cottage. The MGB was parked at the side of the house, attesting to her presence within. Staying to the shadows, Trev circled around the larger greenhouse toward the back of the dwelling. As he passed the far side, he saw Raven. Her face was framed in the kitchen window, an overhead light nearly a spotlight on her. From her movements, he discerned she was washing dishes.

Her face was more than beautiful; it was arresting, with a hint of feline ethereality. While her jaw reflected the same Montgomerie stubbornness as her sisters, the thinness of her countenance softened the effect. Trev shuddered. His whole body cramped with longing.

"Longing?" he said aloud. The word caused him to pause. With any other woman he'd have said lust. Trevelyn Mershan didn't long for women; he simply wanted to screw them. Once he achieved that aim, they lost any fascination. Longing required more than animal impulse. It spoke of something deeper.

Music floated through the night, and it took a moment to identify the song coming from the kitchen: "Constant Craving"—an oldie by K. D. Lang. Raven's mouth moved as she sang along.

Though Trev couldn't hear her, a shiver slipped up his spine. Yeah, he knew something about constant cravings. Five months of them. Ever since last May, at her grandfather's funeral. He recalled sitting with his brothers at the rear of that small church, watching the seven Montgomerie sisters in the pews at the front, then later while they exited the ornate building. The memory haunted him. So peculiar: beyond her beauty, there was little about Raven that would normally attract him. No, Raven Montgomerie was *not* his taste in women. And yet, he'd known in that breathless instant when their eyes collided, outside the ancient Norman kirk, that in five months' time he'd come for her, though hell should bar the way. She was the key to getting close to the Montgomeries, to finally meting out the long-overdue Mershan vengeance.

An inner voice warned Trev that he and his brothers' objective had damn little to do with his coming here tonight. A ravenous need was rising in him, something dark, dangerous. A force primeval.

Raven had straight auburn hair that flowed down to the middle of her back. The shade was a bit darker than her twin's. Right now, it was swept back in a ponytail, making her lovely face appear even younger. Trev wanted to go inside to her, to pull that black velvet band from around those dark red tresses, feel their heavy weight in his hands, then yank her head back and kiss her—kiss her until . . . until what? Until he woke up Sleeping Beauty.

She was hiding from the world here. She skirted along life's edges, not putting her emotions out there, never taking risks.

"Too bad, Red. Life's for the meat-eaters." Trev smiled, feeling much like a wolf targeting a choice lamb to single out from the flock.

Raven reached up, snapped out the light above and moved away from the casement. It annoyed Trev he could no longer see her. Prickly, impatient compulsion crawled over his skin. He inched closer to the house, daring to go right up to the wall and look into the kitchen window. Inside, Raven was bent over, pouring dry cat food from a big bag into two bowls. The way those stretch jeans molded across her derrière riveted his attention, leading him to envision walking up behind her and running his hands over those curves. So intense was his fantasy, it took him a minute to notice the fat cats at her feet: one grey and one marmalade rubbed against her calves, meowing.

Trev almost laughed aloud as a new creature appeared: a seagull hopped up and began stealing pieces of food from the cats' bowls. Hopped—because the silly bird only had one leg. The scene grew even more surrealistic when a fat black dog wandered in from the greenhouse. Trev blinked thrice, having a hard time believing his eyes. No, it wasn't a dog but a tiny pony!

He shook his head as Raven sighed. "Come on, Marvin," she ordered—though Trev was unsure whether she addressed the bird or the equine. "You know you're not allowed in the main house. Just the greenhouse." Then, leaving the cats and the seagull chowing down, she marched Marvin the Pony to the back of the house.

Halfway out the screen door, the pudgy equine wheeled and tried to dodge between her legs to get back into the kitchen.

"Nooooo-no-no-no-no you don't." Raven leaned over and managed to herd the toy pony, barely taller than her knee, outside. "Marvin, you can't stay in the house. Get it out of your brain!"

Trev watched from the corner of the porch as Raven prodded the pony down a path to a small stable at the far side of the heavily landscaped property, and then inside. He followed, itching to see what she was doing. Clinging to the deep shadows, he stood so he could see into the barn. Raven spread straw for the pony and gave the beast a scoop of corn and fresh water.

Trev liked watching her, liked how she moved. There was a vital strength to the way her muscles shifted and stretched: sinuous, with the angelic grace of a ballet dancer though that body was built for sin. Closing his eyes for a minute, he fought the waves of longing—um, *lust*—that wracked his body in the form of an erection pushing hard against the zipper of his slacks. Swallowing back the agony, he opened his eyes. It had been a long five months.

Trev suddenly felt a tickle to his nose. He rubbed his hand against it to make the sensation go away, but it didn't. Instead, he felt a sneeze coming on. If he sneezed, she'd hear. And if he was arrested for trespassing and being a Peeping Tom, his brother Dev would have to send Julian Starkadder to bail him out. He would never hear the end of it!

Looking down, Trev saw what was provoking the itch: the grey cat now rubbed against his leg.

"Bloody feline," he whispered. This was just great. He was allergic to cats. Not bad, but he needed shots to be around them. Which was the crux of the problem. "Needles," he breathed in revulsion. There was something obscene about sticking pieces of metal into your body.

The sneeze came, but Trev was quick to pinch his nostrils together. Of course, his head felt like a balloon exploding. As he was trying to equalize the pressure, a sharp stab hit his instep. Glancing down again, he saw the stupid, one-legged seagull had arrived.

He frowned. "I thought cats ate birds," he growled.

The blasted seagull looked up at Trev, cocked its head to one side and then the other, as if asking who he was and why he was there. When no reply came, the evil bird began pecking at his foot again—and its damned beak was sharp and hard! Trev gently shook his foot, trying to scoot the bird-brain away, but the cat reared up and rubbed a little higher on his leg. The resulting sneeze—traveling 165 kilometers per hour—came and there was no holding it back.

Raven's head snapped around. "Hello? Is someone there?"

"Bloody hell," Trev muttered under his breath. He dashed back to the house, but nearly tripped as the cat decided this was all a big game and chased around his feet. "Shoo, you mangy feline!"

Raven stepped from the barn, putting her hands on her hips and looking toward the cottage. When she heard nothing more she cocked her head toward the road, staring out into the night. Trev prayed she couldn't see his black car under the centuries-old oak. He doubted it, not through all the autumn foliage.

She finally noticed the bird hopping about. "What are you up to, Atticus? I didn't know birds sneezed." Closing the barn door, she scooped up the seagull, tucked him under one arm, and started back to the house.

Trev faded into the shadows of a different oak, hiding behind its thick trunk. He rotated as she walked, keeping to her blind side. She passed so close that, if he dared, he could reach out and touch her shoulder. With the faint wisps of fog swirling close to the ground, and with the way the shadows caressed her face and body, she seemed exotic, mythical, an elfin creature perhaps with the powers of the *Leanan Sidhe*, a fairy lover conjured to drive a man to torment. Her scent wafted up: lemon and cinnamon, as if she had been baking. These weren't scents he would associate with sex, but nonetheless his mouth watered.

His hand lifted, and for an instant he intended to reach out and touch her—to *take* her. He ached to possess her, to own her, to bring his attraction to this woman down to pure animalistic cravings. Nothing Then perhaps these jumbled feelings she provoked would be banished from him and he could stop acting like a total idiot. But his hand dropped and she passed by.

She stopped at the porch and deposited the bird on the wooden floor. Her hand reached for the back door-knob. Hesitating, she slowly rotated to look directly at the tall oak where Trevelyn hid. She stood, her beautiful face caught in pale yellow shadows thrown by the kitchen light. He could almost taste her fragile femininity.

She stared out into the night, watching, waiting, almost as if she knew he was there. She could sense him, and was perturbed. But . . . there was no way she could see him behind the tree, no way she perceived his presence. Prickles rippled up the back of his neck as he told himself not to get fanciful.

"Who's there?" she asked of the night. But then one shoulder lifted in a shrug and she hurried inside. The seagull hopped to the door and followed through a metal pet entrance.

" 'Tis me—the Big Bad Wolf," Trev whispered. "I hope you're ready, Red, because I'm coming tomorrow. Enough of these games. Tomorrow, Red, I'll huff and puff and blow your house down. . . ."

Whistling an old tune by Sam the Sham and the Pharaohs, he made his way to his car. Pulling his keys from his pocket, he glanced back to the house to see the light in Raven's loft bedroom wink out. " 'You're everything a Big Bad Wolf could want.' "

Chapter Two

"Something's going to happen tonight. Maybe something dangerous," Raven Montgomerie whispered to the wooden dummy staring back at her, lowly enough that no one heard.

She wasn't one to embrace change of any kind. In truth, she worked very hard to create a cocoon, shielding herself from the world and the hurts it could bring. But spellbound by the clockwork fortune-teller, she ran her hands over the polished wooden case, fascinated by the love that had gone into its crafting. The golden oak booth held the life-sized figure, a Gypsy dressed in purple and black and so real in every detail that Raven expected to see her chest rise and fall with breaths. And the Gypsy was . . . familiar.

As she watched her twin brothers Phelan and Skylar, and her longtime friend Brishen, carefully shift the six-foot-tall rectangular box into position, the statue's amber eyes almost seemed to follow her. A poignant quality about the carved mannequin sent a shiver up Raven's spine. Precisely why remained elusive in the same way as her fey belief that tonight was different in some way, the premonition that promised her life would soon take a turn either for the better or the worse. Descended from a long line of Scottish witches, Raven ofttimes heard a voice speak in her mind, warning when an unusual occurrence loomed near. But instead of the usual whispered premonitions, her little internal voice was shouting. It was making her jittery, panicky.

It had been the same last night. She'd almost been certain someone stood outside her house, watching. Silly notion, but one she couldn't shake. Because of that lingering feeling, she hadn't rested at all. What little time she'd drowsed, she had been haunted by the eyes of the painting she was working on. They floated at the edge of her mind, as if she needed only to concentrate hard enough to recall . . . recall *what?*

" 'By the pricking of my thumbs,' " she breathed, audible to herself only, striving for a touch of levity in the words of the Bard. The attempt failed.

Dismissing her rising trepidation, Raven returned her attention to the fortune-teller booth. "Oh, what a find! Just the special focal point I needed for the gala. I was fearful it wouldn't arrive in time. I'm going to hug LynneAnne when she comes back," she said to the three men.

The booth was a gift from her sister, who was currently touring Europe buying items for her business. Raven's older sibling restored vintage merry-go-rounds, and often trekked to backwater towns all over the States, Canada and Europe, searching for neglected painted ponies to purchase and reclaim. On her last trip, LynneAnne discovered this box in a forlorn state, bought and restored it for Raven's birthday—and in time to be the focal point of tonight's gala. Tomorrow Raven would take it home, place it in the conservatory of her thatched house and cherish it endlessly.

"Careful!" She half jumped in alarm when her brothers set the box to rocking. A moment later, the Gypsy was in motion; hands lifted and made passes over the large crystal ball before her. So deft were the mannequin's movements, Raven expected a real person to pop out of the booth and scream, "Surprise—fooled you!" The huge ball glowed and swirled, hypnotizing her.

Shrugging off the sudden dizziness, Raven noticed all eyes were upon her watching the fortune-teller. To cover her odd reaction, she explained, "That mechanical doll is called an automaton—a forerunner to today's robots. If you drop a coin into the slot, she goes through those movements, and a card—a tarot image on one side and a sage fortune on the reverse—appears in the niche at the side. At least, LynneAnne assured me it would."

"It's a mechanical *ofisa*," her friend Brishen explained. "That's Romani for 'fortune-teller booth.' She is a *drabarnoi*—a reader of cards."

"Sort of like a huge Magic Eight Ball," her brother Skylar assessed.

Raven thought for a moment, then nodded. "Actually, that's rather accu—Careful!" she shrieked as the men edged it too close to a table, nearly scratching the wooden finish and upsetting rows of fluted champagne glasses.

"Come on, sis. It's cumbersome, but we're not club-fisted moving men. We're paying attention to what we're doing," Phelan complained. Then he indicated Skylar. "Or I should say *we* are. Brishen's too busy looking down your dress."

Raven picked up the program for the night's affair, which she'd nervously folded accordion-fashion like a fan, and swatted Brishen's muscular forearm. "Stop that. Brothers don't drool over their little sisters."

"Ah." The handsome Gypsy smiled. "But therein lies the problem, sexy Raven. You're not my sister, despite your silly insistence, so at times I claim the right to indulge in a little manly appreciation. Tonight, you're especially gorgeous in that red gown. While Romani mistrust that shade and fear it brings *prikaza*—ill-luck—you'll make your own fortune tonight. All men's eyes will be glued to you. But beware, little one. The women shall hate you for it."

"You're balm to a lady's ego." Raven rose up on tippytoes and brushed a kiss to her friend's cheek. "But save the razzle-dazzle for someone who'll respond. I still think you'd make a good husband for Paganne. She needs someone like you."

Brishen's laugh was booming, a wondrous expression of his joy in life. "Only if your little sister will come live in my *vardo* and share my life with the *kumpa'nia*. I must travel among our caravan to follow my calling, to walk in the footsteps of the heroic Milosh, the greatest—"

"—vampire hunter to ever take up the stake," Raven joined in. It was an old song and dance. Brishen was descended from the legendary Milosh, who two centuries before had been a serious vampire hunter, according to Gypsy lore. Still, she'd never understood how much Brishen truly bought into the idea of hunting vampires in this day and age, and how much was charming shtick.

"Well, you've a problem there. You'll never lure Paganne far from her library or her archaeological digs. She's determined to be the one to locate Boadicea's grave, resolute to prove the Romans murdered her instead of the accepted version of suicide."

Brishen shook his head. "The pretty lass needs to stop dreaming about the past, find a good man and make beautiful babies. Then she'll be happy."

"Don't say that to her," Raven laughed, "or she'll take that Pictish knife our grandmother gave her and carve her initials on your chest."

"Ah, I'd rather she'd carve them on my heart, but I've given up hope. Yet another of the beautiful Montgomerie sisters I've lost. You ladies are hard on a man's libido—and on his tender heart."

Skylar released the straps around it and stood back to admire the fortune-teller. "She's a beauty," he acknowledged. "Has Bette Davis eyes. She's so real *I'd* ask her out."

"She reminds me of someone," Phelan spoke up. "I feel stupid for not knowing who." With a shrug, he reached into his pocket and withdrew two coins. Giving Raven a once-over in her strapless gown, he winked and said, "Seeing you don't have a pocket . . . here, you should have the honor of the first fortune. It's your birthday present after all, sis."

Raven took the two twenty-pence pieces but hesitated, as if by inserting the coins and accepting the fortune-teller's card her fate would be sealed. That tingling sense of change brushed against her mind once more. All three men stared, puzzled by her dithering, but how could she explain the strong presentiment that her life was in the balance and nothing after tonight would ever be the same?

Actually, her brothers knew their sisters' fey ways; they wouldn't laugh. And Brishen—the mighty vampire hunter—would encourage such an impression. Still, sometimes it seemed better to let life just slap you in the face with a piece of wet liver than expend worry in anticipation of what might be.

"Why do you hesitate, little one? The Gypsy . . ." Brishen patted the box, his vivid blue eyes twinkling. "She's a friend of mine. Family. My mother's father's sister's cousin. She'll treat your fate with care. Word of honor."

"Is that a *Roma* word of honor, or a word to a *Gadjo*?" Raven teased.

"Stop avoiding Lady Fate. Stick a coin into the slot. She's yours, so you must be first to have your fortune read."

Raven sighed in resignation, then stepped to the booth. After a deep breath, she carefully dropped the coins into the box and waited. Nothing happened. "Well, bugger. All that foreboding was a waste. You eejits broke her."

She laughed, but suddenly clicking noises sounded and the Gypsy woman moved. The carved hands once more passed over the huge crystal ball, which began to glow a faint luminous blue, the colors within seeming to swirl. The mannequin tilted her head faintly side to side, then her eyes closed. When the lids lifted, those amber orbs gazed at Raven with such intensity it was hard to recall the figure was only a carved figure in a box. Finally, another click sounded and a card ejected on the side. Raven stared at the lifelike woman, unable to move.

Shaking off her silliness, Raven reached out and took the card. The Lovers. She stared at the image on the card's face, once more feeling the hand of Fate molding her future. A warning buzzed in her blood as she studied the image, reluctant to turn it over, fearful to read the fortune on the reverse.

Brishen nudged her elbow. "Go on. See the rest of your fortune. The Gypsy, she promises romance to come—a big handsome lover, eh? But what else does she say?"

Feeling one door close on her life and another open, Raven flipped the card over. A bubbly laugh escaped as she saw the words written there:

Beware of the wolf in sheep's clothing.

"What's it say?" Phelan asked impatiently.

Raven held up the card to allow them to read it. Phelan and Skylar exchanged glances, then rolled their eyes. Skylar sniggered and started *baaa*ing like a sheep.

Brishen smacked his arm. "Silly *Gadjo*. 'Tis never wise to mock one with the powers to show you the way."

"She's a wooden dummy!" Skylar flashed an exaggerated grimace and rubbed the side of his arm. "I mean, seriously—*sheep?* What a howl."

"You miss the point of the foretelling: the wolf." Brishen shook his head as if Raven's brother was lacking in the intelligence department. "Try again, Raven. Perhaps the prediction will become clearer with a second card."

"You don't seriously believe this—," Skylar began, only to have Phelan give him an elbow. He frowned at his brother, ignoring the warning. "Stupid me. I'm asking a veteran vampire hunter."

Brishen scowled back, then stepped to block Raven's brothers' view of the booth. "Ignore Flopsy and Mopsy. Don't be afraid to embrace the unknown, little one."

Raven put the second coin into the slot and watched as the Gypsy's hands passed over the crystal ball again. Likely it was only an illusion, perhaps the way Brishen's body blocked the light, but the swirls within the crystal seemed to take on shapes. As Raven stared breathless and mesmerized, she could almost swear the eddying blue smoke slowly formed a pair of ghostly eyes.

The image struck a chord within her, some stray forgotten shard of memory, another resonance of déjà vu, as if she had stared into those haunting eyes before. Her heart squeezed, and she couldn't breathe as a wall of emotions slammed into her, so strong her knees almost buckled. Forcing her mind to focus on the vision—was it real, or simply a play of shadow and light?—she jumped as the box clacked and ejected the next card.

Prickles crawled up her spine as she reached for it. She again stared at The Lovers. When she flipped to the reverse side, the same fortune was written there:

Beware of the wolf in sheep's clothing.

Raven glanced uneasily to Brishen, as if seeking his laughter to reassure her that this was a prank the three of them were playing on her. His expression was anything but comforting.

Trying to dismiss all these queer imaginings, she gave the three men a forced smile. "What? You, Flopsy and Mopsy stacked the deck?"

Phelan leaned past her and inserted a coin, then pulled out his card when it came. Holding it up, he showed The Wheel. " 'Something comes, bringing change,' " he read.

"Boy, is she good. Don't look now, but 'something comes' all right." Skylar nodded to the front of the hall. "Early guests. Free grub and booze always draws moochers."

"No one driving a Lamborghini could be a moocher," Phelan chuckled. "Dig that gull-wing door! What say we go pretend to be valets and 'park' it for him."

Skylar laughed and nodded, moving to steal a canapé. "See you in a bit, sis. We're off home to change—after we commit grand theft auto."

"Don't you dare! Cian will have a fit if you 'borrow' that

Lamborghini." She was joking, though she was unsure if the twins were. They were daredevils. She still recalled the time they were eleven and Skylar tied a rope around Phelan's chest, then pushed him out of the barn loft to help him learn to fly. Phelan ended up with three cracked ribs, and Skylar couldn't sit down for two days—Mac had spanked him pretty hard.

Brishen gave her forehead a kiss. "Take care, little Raven."

"You're coming back with my brothers, aren't you?" she asked, feeling the need of support.

Her friend since childhood only shrugged. "I know you and your family welcome me here. Some of the other *Gadje* . . ." He allowed the sentence to go unfinished.

"Anyone not welcoming my brother is free to leave." Raven glanced down at the two cards she held and trembled. Feeling ridiculous, she tucked them behind her back.

Brishen gave a soft laugh. "I keep telling you, I'm not your brother. But very well. I'll come, but only to see what happens this night. It shall be interesting, I think. The planets' alignment speaks of a great occurrence, the ending of an old cycle that began a very long time ago and the start of a new one. You feel it, don't you?"

He lifted a strand of her hair and rubbed it between his fingers. "Gypsies believe red hair brings good luck. You may need it before the clock strikes midnight. *He* comes for you, lass."

Raven swallowed the knot in her throat. "Who?"

"Your wolf. He comes, little Raven. My Gypsy blood tells me this." Her friend's blue eyes regarded her with a seriousness that stopped Raven's laughter in her throat. "I don't think anything can stand in his way."

Raven fingered the cards tucked behind her; then she looked through the glass front of the hall, watching her brothers accost the driver of the expensive black car, who had started to get out. He was tall and elegantly dressed. Rarely had she seen a man so suited to wear a tuxedo. The evening breeze ruffled his blue-black hair, pushing a couple curls to fall over a high, intelligent forehead. In a casual gesture he brushed them back and then turned to stare into the front of the building . . . to look at *her*.

Such a thought was silly. The tinted window had a mirror reflection on the outside, similar to one-way glass; Raven doubted the stranger could see her. Nonetheless, it felt as if their eyes locked and held. He had predator's eyes. From this distance it was hard for her to discern their color, but they had force, and a power to mesmerize. Raven's heart slowed, then almost stopped. A breathless sensation hit her. This was a man who wouldn't let anything stand in his way.

Chapter Three

Trevelyn had followed the circular driveway to the front of the massive stone building. In the dusk, radiant with the soft amber lights inside and out, the large hall was rendered magical in appearance, as if Trev had taken the wrong cutoff and ended up in Fairyland. Raven's magic. She'd created this wonderland to see the gala a success.

Trev's jaw muscles flexed. A peculiar sense of being off-kilter pulsed through his blood. Just a keenness for the hunt, he told himself.

No, that was a lie. This was something different. And he didn't think he liked it.

He glanced at his gold Rolex. *Too early.* The crowd coming tonight would, of course, be fashionably late. For his plans to work he needed to blend in and not draw the attention of the rest of the Montgomerie clan. From Julian's reports he knew the family tended to rally protectively around Raven, since her life had taken several bumps over the past couple of years. If they viewed him as a threat to her, they'd close ranks, making Trev's task harder.

It wouldn't matter. He wasn't about to let anything stop him. Still, he was antsy and couldn't wait any longer. Fashion be damned. He was never one to follow the herd.

Catching sight of his face in the Lamborghini's rearview mirror, he pushed two errant curls off his forehead. Without being vain, he knew he was a handsome man—above handsome. The term drop-dead sexy had been applied to him more than a few times. He was a man that women responded to on many levels.

"Poor Little Red Riding Hood doesn't stand a chance," he said to his reflection. And it was the bloody truth. He wouldn't allow her one. Every morning for the past month he'd stared at the gold-embossed vellum invitation to this, the Montgomerie Enterprises charity gala, and it was the last thing he looked at before turning out the light at night. He'd never felt such intense anticipation.

The cell phone chirped, causing Trev to frown. He almost ignored it, wanting to stay focused on what lay ahead, but supposed it might be Desmond or Jago checking in. He'd e-mailed his brothers just before he left the office, letting them know he was on his way to the gala. He also wanted to make sure they, too, had arrived safely at their destinations.

With a sigh, he slapped the speaker button. "Trevelyn," he said, short and to the point.

"Well, who else would I expect to answer your cell, you bloody eejit?" the crabby voice on the other end snapped. Agnes Dodd. The woman *looked* like an Agnes Dodd, too. The bane of his life, she was. And, though he would never admit it, he adored her.

"Can it wait? I'm on my way to that charity affair."

"Affair?" She snorted, which was unladylike, but then Agnes would never bother to behave as a lady. She was a harpy, Medusa's second cousin. She was a sixty-three-year-old pain in the bum. Translation: his secretary.

For years he'd had problems keeping a good assistant. They'd fall in love with him and make cakes of themselves until he was forced to fire them. One had nearly turned into a damn stalker! It was a serious problem. Training a new secretary took time, slowing down office efficiency. He needed a gal Friday who had her mind on business and business only. To see Mershan International running smoothly, and with the minimal amount of high drama, his brother Desmond had stuck him with Agnes. The woman surely ran on steroids, never slept, did five times the work of all the other Mershan secretaries . . .

and tried to be his conscience. Thus the snort. She knew where he was going. And why.

"Save the commentary, Agnes. I presume there's a purpose to your call—or did you get lonely for my voice?"

"Commentary? Me? Just because I think you're up to no good? You and your brothers have schemed for years, haven't you? Plans on paper. Seeing them to fruition in the real world will be another matter. I shan't wonder these Montgomerie women might teach you Mershan men a trick or two." She added, "Never underestimate a woman. Any man who does is a fool. Never thought you three were fools, but maybe I was wrong."

"Agnes." Trev rolled his eyes. "Unless you have something specific to say, I'm ringing off. You can harangue me to your little heart's content when I get back to the office."

"Very well, *Mister* Mershan." She only took that tone when she was ticked with him. "You forgot to sign the bank drafts for the current stock buyouts. I was supposed to make the transfer first thing in the morning. I guess you were in too big a hurry to go hunt down that poor Montgomerie girl and ruin her life."

"Agnes . . . you're fired," he said in a tone that would win Donald Trump's admiration. But it was an empty threat. He'd never admit it to Desmond or Agnes, but she was worth her weight in diamonds. He couldn't function without her.

The woman chuckled. "Silly boy, you can't fire me. Only Desmond can do that—as we both know."

"Agnes, I'm thirty-seven years old. You can't call me a boy."

"When you're as old as I am you can," she countered.

Trev chuckled. Agnes was like the grandmother he'd never had, and she had no scruples against trying to reform her black sheep of a grandson. She had no chance, however. Tonight he wanted Raven Montgomerie. Nothing and no one would stop him from having her.

"Agnes, if you weren't such a sourpuss I'd tell you to put your dancing shoes on and get your bum down here to enjoy the beautiful wonderland Raven Montgomerie has created. Who knows, you might find some lonely millionaire who needs someone to boss him about," he teased.

"Don't try that sweet charm on me, laddie boy. You're up to no good, going to break that poor girl's heart. Shame on you," his secretary chided.

Trev laughed. "Yeah, shame on me, Agnes. Were the bank drafts the only reason for ringing? I can sign them in the morning—but then you already knew that, and you're itching to give me a piece of your mind about tonight."

She sniffed. "Think what you like, dear boy. I've given up hope you will see the error of your ways and redeem yourself through a good woman. Actually, there was a different message I was going to pass on. Dr. Hackenbush—"

"Hacksell," Trev corrected, knowing she got the name wrong deliberately.

"Whatever. He said you missed your appointment. Did you want to reschedule? He said you might consider nasal steroids as an alternative, though they would take time to build up. Considering you're a pantywaist where needles are concerned, I'm assuming you need a shot for something."

Trev sighed, allowing the scissor door of his car to open. "Call first thing in the morn and set up another appointment for eleven a.m. Now . . . good night, Agnes." He cut her off before she could start in again.

Two young men came rushing over, drooling over the car: Raven's younger brothers, Skylar and Phelan. They grinned eagerly as he pushed out of the driver's seat, but it didn't take a rocket scientist to know they weren't thrilled to see *him*; rather the Lamborghini had their full attention.

"Wow, what wheels!" one of the twins said.

"Crazy doors," the second chimed in. "We told our sister that we were coming out to pretend to be valets so we could park your car."

"Park?" Trev arched a brow and chuckled.

The second twin offered a big smile. "She did mention something about jail time and embarrassment to the family."

"Well, we cannot have that." Trev tossed over his keys. A little bribe to get into the boys' good graces couldn't hurt.

The taller twin gaped and then looked at his brother. The one holding the keys said, "You're kidding, right? You don't even know me."

"I know you're Mac Montgomerie's sons. I've seen his picture. You look much like your father." Yes, Trev had seen pictures of Mac—along with the whole Montgomerie Clan. But he wasn't going to mention where.

"I'm Phelan, and this is my brother Skylar." Not returning the keys, Phelan stuck out his hand to shake. He leaned back and nudged his twin with an elbow, prompting Skylar to do the same.

Trev accepted both hands and said, "Trevelyn Sinclair."

Phelan asked, "So, you really mean it—we can take the car for a spin?"

"Sure, enjoy."

"Me first!" Skylar chirped, making a snatch at the keys. Phelan quickly pulled them out of reach. "I'm older."

"I'm prettier," Skylar argued.

His brother laughed. "I doubt Mr. Sinclair cares."

"Call me Trev," Trev spoke up, enjoying their banter. It reminded him of how he himself fussed with Jago. "Go on now."

He didn't have to encourage the boys twice. Phelan was soon carefully reversing the car, taking time to check where everything was located. As he did, another vehicle zoomed up from behind and honked—rudely, considering Raven's brother wasn't completely blocking the road.

With an exaggerated rev of the engine, the silver Lotus then wheeled around the Lamborghini to park. Skylar rolled down the window and flipped the other driver the bird. Trev smiled as the brothers pulled onto the roadway and flew off down the narrow lane. Then, shrugging, he turned his attention back to the building.

The front of the rental hall was huge panes of tinted glass with a hint of reflection, tawny in the golden torchlight all along the stone walk. First-class all the way—Montgomerie Enterprises' style. Trev couldn't help but wonder: His wasn't the only family touched by the scandal that resulted in his father taking his life. How many others had lost fortunes while Sean Montgomerie had held on to everything? His eyes remained fixed on the elegant hall, staring at the wall of partially reflective glass. Raven Montgomerie was in there; he could sense her. Once more on the prowl, he felt his lips spread into a grin.

"A wolfish grin," he chuckled.

A flicker before the windows caught his eyes—a woman dressed in vivid red. Though he couldn't see her face clearly, he knew it was Raven.

"My, what sharp little eyes I have. All the better to see you in that sexy dress, Little Red Riding Hood," he said under his breath. "And my, my my . . . She's even wearing red."

Thunder rolled in the distance, harbinger of a storm. Good. That suited Trev's mood. He loved storms, felt almost as if he could call down the lightning and wrap it around him, draw upon that power to refashion the world.

Unable to contain his expectancy any longer, he walked up the creek-stone walkway and into the building, knowing tonight something important was going to happen. He would *make* it happen. Something dangerous.

Chapter Four

"I'd rather be dancing around a campfire with Gypsies," Raven grumbled, despite the evening being a huge success. A jagged flash of lightning streaked across the night sky, then thunder boomed overhead. She jumped as the whole hall shook.

"But it rains, little Raven. No campfire this night," Brishen teased, helping himself to champagne. He gestured with the flute to encompass the banquet hall, decorated in the splendor that Montgomerie Enterprises' money afforded. "You must dance here in this golden wonderland you conjured. 'Fess up—you're spooked, waiting for your wolf to come."

"Bah, humbug," Raven pretended to scoff. But she hugged herself as her skin turned to gooseflesh. "Teach me to wear a strapless gown," she added. Still, she knew her choice of attire had nothing to do with the shiver; she recalled the tarot cards with the warning on the back, and that strange feeling of premonition hadn't left her all evening.

Pleased with the decorations, she admitted they harmonized to achieve her envisioned design. Netting beaded with delicate amber lights hung overhead, creating a fairyland effect. The placement of antique rocking horses, several carousel ponies and carousel benches "borrowed" from LynneAnne's last shipment from Europe, along with the pièce de résistance clockwork fortune-teller, lent a whimsical, romantic flair. Not that she'd actually set out to conjure this dreamy, sensual tone; that the decor proclaimed the night for lovers made Raven's restiveness surge, made her lonely in the midst of hundreds of people.

Her mind again summoned images of the cards she'd drawn from the fortune-teller box. Butterflies fluttered within her, half scared by the warning, half wanting to embrace that ripple of danger carried on the rising storm. All her life she had played it safe. Now that she'd recently celebrated her thirtieth birthday, an itchy restlessness crawled just under her skin. It drove her to skate on the edge of the razor, to do something dark and dangerous.

Unsettled and not wanting to reflect upon her urges, she said with a fake smile, "This evening is interminable. And there are still several hours to go. Excuse me while I groan."

Sharp of hearing, Brishen grinned. "True, but you come from a race of warrior women— so Paganne keeps telling me. You shall endure. Speaking of your luscious sister, I think I'll go torture myself by slow dancing with her. It'll be fun to see if the maddening woman lets me put my hands on her arse or keeps shifting them back to her waist."

Raven chuckled as he winked, then watched her friend chase her youngest sister around the room, trying to catch up with her. A real smile came to her lips when he immediately placed a hand on Paganne's curvaceous rump and then her sister exaggeratedly moved it. Being a "Meddling Montgomerie" who felt entitled to interfere with her siblings' love lives, she wished Paganne would wake up and see Brishen right before her nose. The handsome Gypsy would be good for her.

"You're someone to dispense advice, Miss Busybody," she admonished herself.

There was no man in her life, and most of the time she didn't feel any yearning to change that. Her solitary lifestyle permitted her to concentrate on painting. With that one-woman show scheduled for next spring, she needed every spare moment for work. And she had her cats, a midget pony and a one-legged seagull for chitchat. With that menagerie, who really needed a man? What good were they? Well, outside of backrubs, having someone to take out the trash and chase prowlers away. Who needed a man to hold her late at night while rain pattered on the windows of her bedroom, or to cuddle before the fireplace as it snowed outside . . . ?

A knot of emptiness twisted within Raven, and with a sigh she glanced around the ballroom. Again, her fey intuition brushed her mind—predicting that her life might soon change? What a silly notion.

"I'm too old to believe in knights in shining armor," she reminded herself.

Yet, each of her sisters had been touched with witch's blood, knew things, felt things. She did, too. "Only, my blood must come from a dyslexic witch." *Wrong-way Raven,* her siblings called her. "Always bobbing when I should weave."

So, why the thrum in her soul that promised tonight would be different?

The gala was beautiful. The theme of Autumn Magic was mysterious and quixotic, and the mood reflected a hint of Halloween, which was only weeks away. She must've bought out every peach sorbet and coral rose in Britain and Eastern Europe, and those and sprays of baby's breath graced the tables with larger bouquets in black wicker baskets placed about. Yes, she'd done a good job organizing the gala, despite having to fight that bitch Melissa Barrington every step of the way.

Raven sent a frown across the room toward the Alfred Hitchcock blonde talking with Cian, the woman's hand clinging to his arm. Raven knew this possessive attitude irked her brother, so why he kept Melissa on she failed to understand. Ever since Cian's divorce two years ago, the woman had slapped a target on his back. Her gaze followed him, relentless as a heat-seeking missile.

Melissa, Raven knew, would love to hold court at Cian's

side at one of these functions, at every Montgomerie Enterprises gala or dinner. His executive secretary, she perceived it as an insult each time Cian asked his sister to take charge as hostess. But Cian continually asked. Raven herself enjoyed decorating, drew great satisfaction from giving each event its own artistic flair—and since she did little else to earn her share of the big dividends her stock paid off every six months, she thought it the least she could contribute. But this time she had a feeling Melissa took greater umbrage than usual. Those calculating, ice blue eyes held a quiet desperation.

"Likely, you're sharpening daggers to stick in my back when no one's looking, eh?" Raven flashed Melissa a big fake smile and received one in return, neither woman fooling the other. "Bitch."

Lightning suddenly streaked overhead, causing Raven to flinch. Its flickering, blue-white brilliance flooded the hall, and the crowd in the center of the room shifted. Dancers swirled, and her vision was drawn to a second table of refreshments being set up. Raven's eyes locked on a man in a black tuxedo. His back to her, he reached out and accepted a glass from the waiter. Magic—dark magic—thrummed through the air, both alarming and exciting.

Beware of the wolf in sheep's clothing.

Raven's breath caught and held as the man started to turn. Everything else receded to a shimmering blur. He was close to six feet tall, with shoulders strong and square, if not a bulky, muscular frame. He had an elegant grace, a power about his carriage, the casual arrogance of a man who knew his worth and position in the world. His hair was black—not dark brown but a true blue-black. The style was short on the sides and the top, but rebelliously long in back, brushing the collar of the tux, so thick and wavy that her fingers itched to touch the locks and stroke them.

An odd image suddenly flashed bright as lightning within her mind: a darkened bedroom, rain pounding on the roof, rumpled sheets around her from making love. In this wakening dream she leaned over a man, could almost see his face in the grayish half-light. Handsome— nay, beautiful—he had a blue-black lock of hair that fell rakishly over his forehead. With a poignant smile Raven reached out and twirled it around her finger, staring into his pale green eyes as in slow motion her mouth formed the words, *"I love you."* She couldn't breathe as she waited for the words to be returned, to *finally* hear them. They didn't come. Instead, the man reached up and took a strand of her hair and used it like a tether to pull her down for a kiss. She closed her eyes against the pain, kissing him with all her passion, allowing it to speak to him and praying she could reach this man and make him understand before it was too late.

Too late?

So intense was the vision, so memory-like, it nearly blotted out the party around her. But then thunder boomed, rattling the glass panes and breaking the strange enchantment, and the image in her mind shattered. Her heart slammed against her ribs. Everything inside her coiled, waiting for the stranger across the room to turn. Willing him to turn, waiting to see if his face was the same.

"Old girl, you're slipping a cog," she whispered.

Still, Raven continued to stare, couldn't look away if her life depended upon it. She was compelled to watch as the man slowly rotated and then lifted his glass to his sensual mouth. And, oh boy, did that mouth conjure the vision back, provoke scenes in her mind! Long deep kisses, those lips on her neck, her breasts . . . A surge of pure, unadulterated lust punched through her body and hit her womb with a hard contraction; her desire was so strong she felt light-headed.

Then he lifted his eyes to focus on her.

I'll cross these waters now,
I need to cross this ocean of time,
to be with you. . . .

The words from the band's song wrapped around her, increasing her dizziness. From this distance, and under the muted amber lights, it was hard to be sure of the man's eye color: not blue, but gray or green maybe. Their force rocked her. Adrenaline buzzed through Raven's blood, leaving her unable to breathe.

The stranger paused before taking a drink, the corner of his too sensual mouth lifting faintly, smugly. The vexing man was clearly aware of her regard, was cognizant of his effect upon her. His look said she was his for the taking. Irritated, Raven was seized by the sudden urge to march over, snatch that glass from his hand and toss its contents into that maddeningly perfect face.

"Strigoi," Brishen growled at her side, breaking her thrall. Until he'd spoken, Raven hadn't been aware the music ended and he'd returned with Paganne in tow.

"Where? Who's a vampire?" her little sister enquired, squinting around at the people. "I took my contacts out. They were itching my eyes. I suppose I need a new prescription again."

"Strigoi," Brishen repeated in a hiss, adding nothing more.

"Vampire?" Raven took her eyes away from the handsome stranger for an instant, wondering who Brishen meant.

Her stranger? Yes, Brishen stared directly at him.

"Have mercy, what's *he* doing here?" Paganne paled, as champagne sloshed in her glass. "Quick, we have to do something. Make him go away, Brishen."

Raven felt as if she'd come in for the middle of a play. "Do you know him?"

"Of course I do!" She squinted again. "At least, I think it's him. He's paler than the last time I saw him, but yep, that's him. Brishen, sic him! Vampire or no, you have leave to drive a stake through his heart."

Raven's head spun with confusion, maybe even with sour disappointment that her little sister knew the stranger. Paganne was so heartbreakingly beautiful that men constantly fell for her, though her dear sister remained blithely unaware of that effect. If Mr. Tall, Dark and Sexy had met Paganne, you could bet he was hot on her trail. And from the looks of him, her sister didn't stand a chance. No woman would.

Lightning flared, frighteningly close, followed by thunder that shook the whole building. Lights flickered and nearly winked out before the power came back up, throwing the room into shadow. Then a second starburst exploded against the inky sky. In that heartbeat of eerie illumination, Raven's eyes once more locked with the stranger's across the room.

Her heart raced as they remained frozen, spellbound in a splinter of time. Regret pierced Raven that this man wanted her sister. Despite that, her rising hunger for him was undiminished. She was mesmerized by the glittering force of his stare and shocked by the peculiarity of experiencing such violent emotions over someone she'd never seen before.

Never seen before . . . ? Some ghostly hand touched her soul, plucking a faint chord of remembrance. *Had* their paths crossed at some point? Or was this simply one of those touches of déjà vu?

"I stake him for you, my lovely Paganne," Brishen vowed, full-throttle in his vampire hunter mode. "I stuff garlic down his vile throat, sprinkle him with holy water, and then stake him like the *mulo* he is."

"Mule?" Strolling up and catching the tail end of the conversation, Cian selected a canapé from the refreshment table and popped it into his mouth.

Brishen shook his head. "A *mulo*. A dead person unclean with vampirism."

Cian chuckled. "Sorry, stalwart Gypsy, you shan't stake any of my guests, unclean or not, until after the auction. If a vampire has the blunt for any of the antiques up for bid tonight, he may buy. After he pays"—he grinned— "*then* you may stake him. How's that?"

"You shouldn't risk this evil menace to walk amongst us, perhaps touch your beautiful sisters with his dead hands," Brishen argued.

Cian snagged a glass of champagne to wash down a second hors d'oeuvre, and gave a chuckle. "Oh, my sisters are more than a match for a mere vampire."

"Dead cert," Paganne agreed. "However, I want that particular mule-thing exorcised from this party. *Now*. Britt's not here yet, is she? I don't want her running into him."

Raven glanced back to the stranger, fretting now that Britt had gotten entangled. What, had the guy tried to work his way through all her sisters? Feeling mixed emotions, she watched him give a slow sexy smile. All the people and their senseless chatter melted into mist. Drop-dead megawatt smiles like his should be illegal. Females were just not equipped to handle how it shorted out their systems. Who was he? How was he involved with her siblings?

Feeling like an idiot for staring, Raven still couldn't break the contact. No man had ever caused this strong reaction within her, this deep yearning for intimacy, this craving of a primitive, elemental nature. Long ago, however, she'd made it a rule never to date anyone who was involved with any of her sisters. The one time she'd allowed an exception, she'd married him—and lived to regret it. Boy, had she regretted *that* mistake.

"How do you know him?" Raven couldn't stop the question from popping out.

Cian looked at her with concern, and touched the back of his hand to her forehead. "Are you all right? You're flushed, a bit glassy-eyed. Perhaps all the preparations for the gala were a bit much?"

Melissa strode up, standing by Cian's side as though she were his wife. She shrugged. "I offered to help, but your sister would have none of it."

Cian arched a brow. "She did a beautiful job, as usual. I love how unique you make it every year, Raven." His tone held a clear rebuff.

"Kill him, Brishen! He's coming this way," Paganne interrupted, inviting a scene before hundreds of people, which was wholly unlike her.

It was upsetting for Raven to think her handsome stranger provoked such aggression. She blinked, even more puzzled: Her sexy stranger hadn't stirred. Instead, a man was moving past him, brushing shoulders as he did. A bit taller, he had a lion's mane of pale blond hair. And he was prideful as a lion, too, Raven knew. He was Lucien Delacroix, the movie director. He had been involved with Britt several years ago, was the director of two of her last films—her *best*, actually—and they'd been involved in a torrid off-screen affair. Then something had happened, Lucien had dumped Britt, and Britt had attempted suicide. To this day, Raven's sister refused to speak about him.

"Bloody hell. Can anything else go wrong tonight?" Raven wondered aloud.

Her eyes shifted back to look for her stranger, and she was surprised to find him gone. A quick search of the room failed to locate him, either. Swallowing her sadness, she forced her mind back to Delacroix. Why was he here? Would Britt have to face him again?

Cian tapped Brishen's upper arm. "Come, mighty vampire hunter. We have an unclean person to eject. How the bloody hell did he receive an invitation? They're stopping anyone without one. I specifically said no gate-crashers. I heard a rumor the regulars down at The Naughty Parrot planned on sneaking in for the free booze, and I wanted none of their antics."

"Evidently, you were not specific enough," Paganne sniffed.

Raven's eyes went to Melissa, observing her for a moment. The little voice in her head was speaking again, and it said Cian's secretary had sent the invitation, despite her contrived look of innocence. Trying not to growl, she glared until the irritating female finally blushed and looked away, guilty.

But, why? Raven could see Melissa doing something to cause *her* a problem, but why attack Britt? She doubted Britt and Melissa had exchanged more than passing words. Why set up such a confrontation tonight, knowing how important it was for Cian to have everything run smoothly?

"So how *did* he get an invitation?" Paganne asked, her eyes tracking Brishen and Cian in their attempt to head off Delacroix. In a deft maneuver, each man took an elbow, wheeled Lucien about and gently escorted him toward the doors.

"Great minds work alike. I'm wondering the same thing," Raven commented drolly, picking up a champagne glass and itching to toss the contents in Melissa's smug face. *One of these days—it's coming,* she promised.

Out of the corner of her eye, Raven spotted the black-haired man walking across the opposite side of the room to examine the fortune-teller's booth. Her stomach muscles tightened as his hand reached out to deftly insert a coin, his beautiful face reflected in the glass while he studied the mannequin's lifelike gestures. Then, placing his hands on either side of the booth, he leaned close, nearly pressing his nose against the glass and staring. Finally, when the mannequin stopped moving, the stranger leaned back.

Beware of the wolf in sheep's clothing?

"Surely not," Raven said to herself. He couldn't have drawn the same fortune.

The stranger turned, his eyes coming straight to her as if he'd been aware she was watching the whole time. Then Raven realized that, while she saw the reflection of his face in the glass, he could see her bright red dress behind him as well. Slowly he lifted the card and turned it until the tarot face showed. Even across the room there was no mistaking The Lovers.

A slight lift of his black brows spoke volumes. But was it a question? A threat? A promise . . . ? Raven shivered, scared also of what the cards signified.

Someone jostled her arm, spilling her drink. "Oh, I *am* sorry. I wasn't looking where I was going," a blonde woman apologized as she snatched up an Irish linen napkin off the end of a table and offered it for Raven to dab at her dress. "Oh, I really am sorry. I'm so clumsy of late. Guess it comes with the territory. I haven't seen my feet in a couple months. Hope this doesn't ruin your lovely dress. I'll pay for the cleaners."

The voice finally broke through Raven's haze. She *knew* that voice. Her whole body flinched, suddenly awash in painful memories of a time in her life that held nothing but black sorrow.

"Ellen," she said—not harshly, not warmly, just with a flat neutrality as far from her emotional state as Raven could possibly get.

The wife of her ex-husband blinked owlishly at her. "My word! Raven, I didn't recognize you. I say! Why, you're . . . you're stunning! I guess I've never seen you done up to the nines."

Raven bit her tongue to keep from blurting that the last time they saw each other Ellen had been on a desk, on her back, getting screwed by Alec, and that it was hard to have a clear view from such an upside-down position. But sheathing her claws, she didn't give the woman the satisfaction.

To be honest, Raven couldn't blame Ellen for wrecking her marriage, because by that point there hadn't been much left. She'd already endured too much of Alec Beechcroft's subtle mental abuse and finally realized he'd married her because she was Sean Montgomerie's granddaughter. When the bastard saw that wouldn't help him professionally, he'd set out to punish her for not giving him what he coveted: power within Montgomerie Enterprises. It had taken Raven only a few months after the wedding to realize what was happening.

No, whatever fleeting emotions she'd felt were already dead by the time Raven caught Alec boffing his secretary, Ellen Lister. But complicating matters, Raven had found she was four months pregnant. That was why she'd gone to the office: to tell him he was going to be a father. She hadn't wanted Alec, but she had wanted the baby. Her baby.

Alec had proved a blackguard. After she filed for divorce, he countersued, actually having the gall to seek alimony, hoping to cause her so much grief that Cian would pay him to vanish. Raven's brother had indeed entertained half a notion of doing precisely that, but Alec demanded a big chunk of ME stock. Raven just wanted him to get to Hell and be gone from from her life, to leave her in peace to build a new future for herself and her child, and giving him stock would have only bound them tighter together.

Alec, of course, saw how much she wanted the baby. He had seized upon her need as a tool, saying he planned on pushing for joint custody. Blackmail, plain and simple. The stress too much for her, Raven suffered a miscarriage. And while Alec showed up in her hospital room, feigning concern, she'd never forget how quickly the scene disintegrated into him yet again berating her into tears and admitting that, while the child would've been an advantage to use against Cian, losing the baby was ultimately for the best—he wasn't cut out to play father to some snot-nosed brat.

Some snot-nosed brat? Their baby? *Her* baby? She had lain there sobbing for a long time after he left; then the family heard her screaming. It had just seemed to come out in one long agonizing wail of pain, and she hadn't been able to stop.

Raven's hands trembled as she went through the motions of drying her gown. She was losing it again. So damn pathetic. After the breakdown, her mind had buried all the ugliness from that period, put it away in a shoebox where she hadn't had to deal. Now, however, the shoebox was dumped and the ugly contents spilled out. Everything seemed to be closing in on her, to where she wanted to open her mouth and let loose with another ear-piercing scream. She told herself to breathe, that she was stronger now . . . but then she absentmindedly glanced at Ellen and spotted her very round belly.

How utterly obscene! Ellen was expecting, was maybe seven or eight months along. Raven swallowed the bubble of hysterical laughter rising in her throat, so wanting to ask Ellen if Alec was looking forward to being a father to *her* snot-nosed brat. It took all her willpower to keep from wrapping her arms across her stomach, cosseting echoes of the phantom presence that once had lived inside her.

As if things couldn't get any worse, Alec strolled up behind his wife. Sensing him, Ellen turned and flashed a radiant smile. Raven told herself to hang on, swallowing hard. Paganne was close by her side, and Brishen would return any minute. He could stake Alec through the heart for practice, then all would be right with the world.

Alec smiled that damn jackal smile of his. Oh, how Raven hated that expression—a reflection of glee at seeing someone weaker than himself to torture. He was five years older now, his sandy brown hair starting to thin. Knowing how vain he was, that brought a smirk. Likely, he spent a bloody fortune on hair regrowth solutions. Leaner, his face was etched with the ugliness in his soul. As Raven stared at him, it almost felt as if she looked at a stranger. No emotions rose within her other than hatred for him . . . and anger at herself for being so stupid to have ever trusted the worm.

"Ah, Raven and little Paganne. Such *adorable* names your mother gave you," he said, meaning just the opposite. He touched his wife's arm in reassurance, and she offered him another sappy grin, oblivious to the undercurrent of emotion rippling around her.

"Poor deluded woman," Paganne muttered under her breath. "She must have an IQ of a turnip."

Alec's eyes narrowed. "What's that you say?"

Paganne offered him a wide smile. "I said, 'Surprising to see you two turn up.' I don't recall seeing your names on the guest list."

Alec shrugged, but his face hardened a trace; he fought against it, but couldn't prevent the expression from manifesting. "What? You think I'm not good enough to attend this quaint little Montgomerie to-do?"

Lifting her glass, Paganne gave a chuckle. "That's one way to put it."

Confused, Ellen glanced at Paganne and then back to Alec. The silly woman obviously hadn't expected a chilly reception. "Now see here—"

"Don't upset yourself, my dear. The Montgomeries aren't happy unless they're letting the world know how important they are, and how the rest of us aren't good enough to clean up after them." He glanced exaggeratedly to either side of Raven and then lifted his eyebrows. "What, no date? Don't tell me you're still pining away for me. Really, Raven, that's so pathetic. After all this time—"

"Darling, let me have your glass. It's empty." The deep voice spoke from behind her, drawing everyone's attention. "How am I supposed to get you drunk and have my wicked way with you if I can't keep your glass filled?"

Afraid to breathe, Raven couldn't even blink as a beautiful male hand took her wrist and removed her empty champagne glass. A kiss was placed to the back of her hand and then she was handed another flute, this time full. Her heart bounced against her ribs as she looked up . . . into those warlock green eyes of her stranger. If she had thought them hypnotic from across the room, that was nothing compared to being up close. She fought to keep from being sucked into their emerald depths.

"I know . . . I'm late, late for a very important date." He waggled his eyebrows playfully and gave her a gentle smile as if trying to court her good graces. When she didn't respond, he kissed her cheek. "Forgive me? Your brothers ran off with my Lamborghini. Then my secretary called, and you know with the deal hanging fire I had to take it." Placing a hand at the small of her back, he rubbed slightly. Possessively, intimately—as only a lover would do. "All right, give me the cold shoulder. I love it when you pout. I promise to make it up to you before the night's over." He picked up her free hand and brushed a butterfly kiss to her bare shoulder.

Paganne's eyes nearly popped out of her head, but her expression wasn't as shocked as Alec's.

Raven's ex, his mouth agape, finally drew the attention of the handsome stranger. Raising one black brow, the stranger glanced down his nose at Alec, giving him a silent "you're not worthy to shine my boots" look. Few men could stare into those green eyes and not blink. Raven suppressed a smile. No one had ever tried this game of ranking with Alec Beechcroft and won. This time, there was no contest. Something about this unusual man whispered he was different, special, born to rule.

Giving a small squeeze of Raven's waist, the stranger leaned forward and stuck out his hand for Alec to shake. "Don't believe we've been introduced. I'm Trevelyn Sinclair."

Alec glanced at Raven, then back to her supposed date, and finally shook. "I'm—"

Trevelyn cut him off. "Yes, I know. Raven's told me all about you."

For an instant, the veneer of the civilized man seemed

to fade and Sinclair stared at Raven's ex-husband with such intense hatred that she could scarcely believe it. His hard expression showed he wanted to knock Alec's teeth down his throat. For one breath, Raven expected him to do just that. But startled by the ferocity she blinked, and the expression was gone. Or maybe it was never there to begin with.

Beware of the wolf in sheep's clothing. The words clanged in her head.

Raven stood trembling. Had she just taken a tumble down the rabbit hole?

Chapter Five

"Go ask Alice . . . I think she'll know . . ."

It struck Trev as humorous that the band was playing the old Jefferson Airplane song, since Raven clearly lacked any clue as to what had just occurred. The poor lass stood poleaxed, as though he'd dropped, wings unfurled, through the skylight. Her face was beautiful, enchanting, endlessly kissable, but she had no poker face, that was for bloody sure. *Mmm.* Images of playing strip poker with Raven flashed through his brain. He swallowed hard, heat crawling up the back of his neck, flames of desire licking at his mind.

The last notes faded away to be replaced by strains of "Thief of My Heart"—and a more perfect cue he couldn't ask for. Never one to pass up an opening, he seized the change in tunes as an excuse to lure Raven away from family and friends . . . and some nonfriends. Feeling like Sir Galahad rescuing a damsel in distress, he flashed Raven a smile and took her wrist to drag her toward the dance floor before her lack of guile gave the whole game away. With a wink he tossed over his shoulder to the staring group, "Pardon us, I hate to miss a rumba with Raven."

Raven followed docilely enough; only, when they reached the center of the hardwood floor she just looked up at him with unblinking brown eyes. Like a doe in the headlights. Drawing her close, Trev slowly placed her hand on his right shoulder then reached for her other and curled it around his neck. He liked the way their bodies fit.

"The rumba is a dance of love," he said. "You're supposed to look at me as if you love me." When she simply stared at him, dumbstruck, he asked, "You do know how to rumba, don't you?"

She nodded.

"Good." Trev chuckled at her bemusement, then warned, "If you don't stop gaping at me they'll wonder what's going on. Or worse . . . cause me to do this."

He stepped closer and brushed his lips lightly against her surprised mouth. She gave a breathy gasp. Adrenaline hit his blood in reply; the response zinged along his nerve net, causing a reaction on par with having stuck his finger in an electrical outlet. He shouldn't have, but he was still too damn keyed up after last night to resist, so he deepened the kiss. Not much. Not like he wanted. Just enough so that he could savor soft lips that tasted like Moët Champagne, a hint of Brie cheese, and Raven— a potent blend that went straight to his head and groin.

And maybe my heart.

Startled by the thought, Trev mentally shook it aside. Likely, the feeling was merely a touch of indigestion; he hadn't eaten supper this evening, too wired with anticipation.

When he pulled back, he had to fight against kissing her again. Typically male, he had never been fixated on kissing but rather had other aims when he took a woman in his arms. Men learned in their teens that a kiss was a tool to befuddle the female brain, ensuring an easier surrender. Yet he could barely recall that they stood in the midst of a crowded dance floor, so much did he crave kissing her again . . . and again.

"Who *are* you?" she finally whispered, her lower lip trembling.

Trev gave a small tilt of his head. "Your knight in shining armor, my lady."

"Chivalry is long dead, Mr. Sinclair, and you aren't wearing armor," she countered.

"Ah, times force change. I no longer don heavy mail and plate, nor carry a clanking sword, and my charger isn't a mighty destrier but a Lamborghini—true. Even so, such minor details would never stop me from riding to the rescue of a damsel in need." He was teasing, hoping to get her to relax.

Her eyes lit, and the change was amazing. Those russet eyes were suddenly alive with intelligence, sparkling shards of amber, and their power was hypnotic. Trev felt as though he'd taken a roundhouse kick to the solar plexus. He couldn't even draw air. Everything nearby shifted focus; everything faded but Raven. Was the woman a bloody witch?

She offered him a Mona Lisa smile. "So you're the one."

"One what?" Trev blinked to shake off the spell. It was a damn potent one.

The laughter, the music, the clink of glasses being served—all was muted, and the party kaleidoscoped into a swirl of color. He'd had only one drink, wanting a clear head to relish every nuance of this meeting and the chase. Despite that restraint, he hadn't been this dizzy since Jago and he had gotten plastered after graduating university. While he enjoyed the occasional scotch to unwind, he preferred being in complete control. Life was too bloody sweet to let alcohol fuzzy up its pleasures or oh so delicious victories.

"The driver of the black Lamborghini. You shouldn't have trusted my brothers with the keys. Giving them that car is on par with giving a case of Ho Hos to a chocoholic."

Trev shrugged. "I know where to come looking for it."

"They haven't returned," she smirked.

"As I said—I know just the place to collect it should they lose their way back." His hands clasped her hips just below her waist and nudged her into dancing. "Rumba, my lady, we're drawing attention standing here."

It didn't take but a couple shifts and steps before their

bodies began to move in sync. The corner of his mouth lifted as he watched her follow his lead. Raven danced with a fluid, sensual grace that was a test of his libido. Somehow, he'd assumed that when he finally got this close the fascination with her would lessen. What a bloody fool!

Usually, with any woman, small things quickly began to grate on his nerves: her laugh was irritating, her neck was too short or too long; she was too tall for him or not tall enough. He actively disliked when he had to bend his neck to kiss a woman. Not a problem with Raven. She was just perfect; tall, but not runway model height. Her body was a little thinner than any of her sisters, but still had their trademark voluptuous curves—and displayed in that vivid red dress, he was quickly adjusting his ideas on what was the perfect woman.

Most redheads couldn't wear red and carry it off with élan, but Raven did, as if she'd stepped off the cover of *Vogue*. Before tonight, he'd always favored blue eyes, yet as her luminous amber ones watched him with an enthralled expression, all those baby blues faded until he couldn't recall why he'd liked them. Or why he'd *thought* he had.

"Well, we're dancing—," she began.

For playful aggravation, he cut her off. "And dancing rather prettily, don't you agree?" His body flexed tightly as he considered how perfectly they moved together, already falling into a pattern of anticipating each other's steps. It conjured visions of them making love in the half shadows.

"I prefer to dance with someone I actually know." Raven gave him a Cheshire cat smile, but he refused to accept that as a reflection of her mood. She was flustered and struggling to cover, was responding to his pheromones: all those little signs of a woman experiencing arousal showed in her breathing as her breasts seemed to rise higher with each inhalation; her luminous eyes widened.

Though there was a timid, almost melancholy air about Raven, Trev didn't miss the flash of spirit. That Montgomerie breeding might be tempered in her; nevertheless, it was still present and likely stronger than even she suspected. Perhaps life had beaten down some of her stubborn mien. In spite of that, he figured it wouldn't take too much to summon that strength back under the proper guidance—and the ravenous urge rose within him to be the man to awaken this sleeping beauty.

He almost laughed aloud. *Wrong fairy tale.* He was the Big Bad Wolf and Raven was . . . *My, what big teeth you have, Mr. Wolfie.* A spasm wracked him as he considered the wolf's response.

"Come, come, you know me. I'm your date for the evening." He couldn't resist.

Raven's perfect breasts lifted with a deep inhale. "Lying isn't a good footing to start off being friends."

"Friends? Yes, we might possibly become friends. But then, friendship is a rather tepid relationship, wouldn't you concur? Say, when compared to lovers?" He figured this might provoke a flare of her Scots blood. Instead, Raven smiled, and the expression caused his heart to twist. He suddenly felt like a Grade-A bastard. But that was too bad. There was no veering from his path.

"Tepid? Perhaps." Wariness flickered in her eyes. "But much safer."

"Safe is boring. Don't you ever yearn to do something that risks all? To throw caution to the wind and dance with the devil?"

"Is that who you are? The devil?"

Trev offered her one of his most dazzling smiles. "Well, only last night I pondered if I had horns hidden in my hair."

Absently, her finger lifted to twirl a curl at his collar. When she realized what she was doing, she nearly jerked her hand back. "Do you?"

"You'll have to take the risk and find out, eh?"

She stared at him. "I'm not sure if you're confident or just arrogant, Mr. Sinclair."

"Both," he responded.

Her soft laugh sent a ripple up his spine to lodge in his brain. "You're a dangerous man, indeed."

"You better believe it. I'm the Big Bad Wolf," he joked.

The blood seemed to drain from her face, her eyes flew wide and she missed a step. "Wolf?" She swallowed hard. "W-why . . . would you say that?"

"I suppose that's how I feel. And while you may be lacking the hood, you're most definitely in red." His eyes skimmed over her body decked out in the strapless scarlet gown, and his hands flexed on her waist. "That dress should be illegal. It'd bring out the wolf in any man."

Raven blushed, and since the heart-shaped, bustier-style bodice of the gown left her shoulders and upper chest exposed, he saw it travel across that smooth flesh to finally flood her cheeks. He groaned as his body responded. It was going to be a long night.

Be careful what you wish for, he thought and then sighed deeply. For a month he'd chafed to have this meeting. Now, the words Agnes had spoken earlier came back to haunt him: *"You and your brothers have schemed for years, haven't you? Plans on paper. Seeing them to fruition in the real world will be another matter. Never underestimate a woman. Any man who does is a fool."* Well, he had certainly underestimated the effect Raven would have on him. It just remained to see how big a fool he really was.

She lowered her lashes, unable to meet his hungry stare. "My sister Britt bought it in France several years ago and never wore it. She insisted I wear it tonight. I'm afraid it's not really me."

"Oh, that dress is very you." Trev leaned forward and whispered against her ear, "The you waiting to be set free."

Raven tensed within his arms, and when he pulled

back he faced a gaze of mistrust. She'd been softening toward him, but switching gears she said, "And I suppose you think you're the one to help?"

Her tone made it obvious his words had been taken as nothing more than a shoddy come-on line. Red Riding Hood was too bloody smart by half. No, she'd never succumb to flashy charms; Casanovas were dead meat under her laser glare. The task ahead of Trev was suddenly a bit trickier, but he'd step up to the challenge. He was spoiled, true—too used to women falling at his feet. Never had he expended the slightest effort to land one in his bed. He doubted Raven Montgomerie had ever allowed a man to maneuver her into an affair. If she had, she'd kept it very quiet; Julian's bloodhounds hadn't found one whiff of a man in her life for five years, not since her divorce. Raven was a picky woman with a lot of baggage and exceedingly high standards. A one-night stand would never be a consideration. Trev wanted to be the man who battered down the protective barrier she'd carefully constructed, the man to push her to abandon caution and follow him into the flames.

"Burn, baby, burn," he whispered under his breath, knowing she couldn't hear over the music. Then, all arrogance gone from his voice, he said, "You'd be surprised what I could teach you, Red."

The music ended. They stood there, bound by the magic rising between them. Raven finally dropped her arms from his shoulders and stepped back. Those huge eyes watched him—wanting, fearing.

Trev snagged her arm, afraid his prey would slip away. "Ah, fair lady, I fear I must hold you close this night, protect you from all manner of evil beasties." *Such as jackass ex-husbands,* he finished silently.

Raven's gaze trailed down to where his hand held her wrist. Resistance flashed in those amber eyes, and she almost pulled away. She clearly didn't like a man controlling her.

Trev stared, a silent challenge of wills crackling in the air around them. She likely had one of the most beautiful faces he had ever seen—but every thought, every flicker of emotion was written clearly upon that stunning countenance. She had no dissimulation, no shield against him. Small wonder she hid from the world; it was safer for her.

Trev nearly growled. Inside him there was a primitive male wolf sensing his mate was nearby and trying to evade. But . . . wolf? Mate? What a horrible thought! He gave himself a mental shake. Wolves mated for life. "Next, the urge will possess me to hike my leg and mark my territory."

Raven blinked in perplexity. "Beg pardon?"

The band started another song. Phil Collins's "Easy Lover" momentarily distracted him, the lyrics sending a shiver up his spine. Yeah, Raven could take his heart and he wouldn't feel it. But dismissing the sensation, he leaned close to her. "I said, I need a drink and why don't you introduce me to your brother?"

She gave him a wicked grin. "Oh, aye. You meeting Cian would be interesting. Two rams butting horns."

Trev kept hold of her hand, followed Raven as she wended her way through the crowd and back to the people clearly waiting for her to return. Well, the games would soon begin! They'd want to grill him, find out how Raven had a man in her life yet kept them totally in the dark. He glanced down to where his fingers were laced with hers, wondering at the last time he had just held hands with a woman. Had he ever?

Her younger sister greeted them with, "You two make a pretty couple out on the dance floor. Like you've been partners for ages." Her eyes roved Trev with the same penetrating intelligence as her sister's. "I never knew Raven was so good at keeping secrets."

Raven blushed. "Trevelyn, this is my brother Cian. Cian, may I present Trevelyn Sinclair."

"Your . . . date," the handsome redhead tacked on.

Offering a faint smile, Cian studied him with pale green eyes. On the surface, the man displayed perfect equanimity, but Trev sensed a territorial wariness as he offered his hand. Trev didn't blame Montgomerie; any man attaching himself out of the blue to his own little sister would naturally draw suspicion. And given Raven's past, Trev imagined his perceived playboy persona didn't sit well.

Cian's hand was firm and dry; the man gave a hard squeeze, signaling a bid for dominance. Trev almost laughed. Undaunted, he returned the grip measure-for-measure, not about to give ground to the grandson of Sean Montgomerie, the man who had driven his father to take his life. At the same time, Trev felt a peculiar surge of grudging respect flood through him, and knew under other circumstances they likely could be good friends. There was an air about Cian that made Trev think of Des. His older brother and Cian were cut from the same fabric: family and business before all else. But Trev shrugged the thought aside. There was no room in his plans for them.

"So, have you come for the auction?" Cian asked, his pale eyes flashing with challenge.

Trev knew Raven's brother meant to intimidate him with all his wealth and power, but it didn't work. As Trev had come of age and started to shoulder some of the burdens of Mershan International, his brother Des had recognized his killer instinct and put him in charge of loans. Yes, Cian was the power behind Montgomerie Enterprises, but Trev had lost track of how many CEOs had come begging him for time or an extension. He wondered if, when the Montgomerie Enterprises house of cards came tumbling down, this man would come begging.

Meeting Cian's stare, Trev returned it with a smile. "No. I came for Raven."

Chapter Six

Yes, he'd come for Raven, and nothing would prevent him from taking her. Trev was stunned how strongly he intended that comment—along the lines of a medieval warrior claiming his lady from a high, well-defended tower. That unforeseen intensity rattled him. But then, understandably, it did the same to Cian. Those dark red brows lifted ever so slightly, the man's pale eyes shifting to Raven, assessing her reaction to this unexpected situation, and then back to Trev.

"I've always admired a man who knows what he wants and lets nothing stand in his way," he finally said. "That goes double for one smart enough to see the treasures my sisters are."

Cian's barb was directed toward Beechcroft, who was still hovering close to the group; but it also spoke to how much Cian adored Raven, was a clear warning Trev would face a bitter enemy if he hurt her. Well, she *would* be hurt—her twin in Kentucky and older sister in Scotland, too. All three Montgomerie girls were roadkill under the wheels of vengeance. When the dust settled, Cian Montgomerie would indeed be the bitterest of foes. The Mershan-Montgomerie juggernaut had been set into motion long ago.

Yes, taking Raven, using her to get next to Cian and the daily operations of Montgomerie Enterprises had been part of Desmond's plans for some time. Currently Jago was in Kentucky, and Des was in Scotland doing his part. They would avenge their father's suicide through seduction, betrayal and corporate overthrow, no matter the cost. Des had worked his whole life to keep their family together, easing the burdens of their sudden grinding poverty. Now, after decades of work and maneuvering, the Mershan brothers were finally set to extract justice.

Oddly, Trev was disquieted by unexpected regret bubbling up within him. Developing a conscience at this late date was a bloody nuisance. It pissed him off royally. No matter the circumstances, he'd prided himself on always being in charge. When had the power slipped through his hands? Perhaps it was when Raven asked if he was the devil, looking up at him with those huge amber eyes. His drive to possess her was a poison coursing through him, one that might possibly see him undone— if he permitted it.

Forcing a slow breath, he vowed to reclaim the advantage. "Yes, only a fool would fail to see what a prize Raven is," he concurred. "But I am no fool. Like a warrior of old, I'll do whatever it takes to win the hand of this fair lady."

Inclining his head in approval, Cian conceded a draw. Trev suppressed a grin and turned to Raven, allowing his eyes to roll over her in a manner of proud possession. He slid his arm around her waist and gently urged her closer to his side. Without doubt, he knew what her family saw: an alpha male silently staking his claim. And though most females would balk at the concept, men would understand. They would believe she was his.

This charade had popped into his mind originally as a means for Raven to save face before Beechcroft; he'd recognized the wound to her pride and wanted to ram his fist into the man's smug, supercilious face. The stratagem had seemed particularly appropriate after receiving that tarot card with The Lovers, even if the fortune had been silly: *The lamb often proves stronger than the wolf.* But one thing about that fortune had given him pause: Raven was, in his mind, the lamb that he'd planned to cut from the flock.

Trev suffered a sudden sense of Fate. In his life, he

never questioned the ebb and flow of the cosmos, never debated metaphysical questions. He was a materialistic person who thrived in the here and now. Never once had he asked the meaning of life, never once wondered if he could fall in love. But—

Shattering Trev's thoughts, Alec Beechcroft spoke. "Have you known Raven long, Sinclair?"

Trev turned to take the measure of the man who'd once been married to Raven, who'd been too dim-witted to realize his fortune. He rarely wasted time on someone so dense, but he warmed to dressing this man down. There was a discordant note about the fellow. Trev had never understood how fingernails on a blackboard could make others cringe, yet he was getting the same effect now from Beechcroft.

Oh, Alec was handsome, but then Trev would expect nothing less of a man who could attract Raven. But he already showed signs of aging. Also, Trev pegged him as so vain that he would count every hair he found on his comb and spend more time before the mirror worrying about wrinkles than his wife did; he likely paid a small fortune on products to minimize the march of time. Trev stared at Alec, not disguising the mix of arrogance, condescension and loathing he evoked.

"Not long," he finally replied.

Taking umbrage at Trev's tone, and the other man took a step closer. "Precisely where did you meet?"

"Alec, really!" Raven snapped. "My love life is hardly your concern. Isn't that right, Ellen? As for everyone else . . . well . . ." She paused just long enough for Trev to fear she was about to give away the game. "Sorry to spring this on you, but . . . it came up rather suddenly."

Trevelyn fought back admiration. She wasn't comfortable lying, but she also had no intention of giving Beechcroft any satisfaction.

Curling her hand around Trev's upper arm, Raven flashed the group a dazzling smile. "Now, if you'll excuse us, I want to show Trevelyn the items up for auction. Perhaps something will take his fancy and he'll bid." She winked at her brother. "I know that'll make Cian happy." She then led Trev around the edge of the milling crowd toward the room arranged with the items displayed for auction.

She smiled and nodded at the guests they strolled past, all eyes upon them, the stares lingering, envious. Trev knew they were a striking couple. Even so, he could tell Raven was unnerved by all the attention and struggling to pretend otherwise. He wanted to shatter her control. Yes, the Big Bad Wolf had come knocking, and there was no more hiding within the cocoon she had spun around her.

"I wish to thank you, Mr. Sinclair," she began as they entered the large display alcove.

He corrected, "Trev or Trevelyn—whichever you prefer."

She stopped before a huge rocking horse, dropped her hand and turned to face him. "The question, I suppose, is which do *you* prefer?"

"Trev is what most people call me," he temporized.

Raven bestowed upon him a sphinxlike smile. "That's not precisely the answer to my question."

"Are you always so precise?" Trev watched Raven place her hand on the black mane of the rocking horse and slowly stroke its length. He swallowed hard, surprised how his whole body tensed at the sensual grace of such a casual gesture. Her hands weren't small or delicate, weren't beautiful hands, but instead showed signs of use. They didn't belong to the image of a pampered granddaughter of Sean Montgomerie, which had lived in his mind for this past year. They were strong hands he could almost feel moving over *him*.

"There's . . . comfort in being precise." She was still stroking the horse, using it as a magician's misdirection with her inquiry. "So, how do *you* like to be addressed?"

While he'd rather Raven were touching him, Trev found contentment in studying her, soaking up the small nuances of being with her and the magic of the night. "Most people tend to shorten names, so Trev works. However, I rather enjoyed the way you said my full name."

Her expression was radiant as she met his eyes. "Trevelyn it is, then. Sounds like a name that would belong to one of King Arthur's knights. Sir Trevelyn upon a quest. *Do* you have a quest, Sir Trevelyn?"

He rocked back lightly on his heels, restless to touch her but restraining himself. "You might say that," he admitted.

"One doesn't meet many Trevelyns. Things which are unique should be treasured," she proposed. Unable to maintain eye contact, she looked back at the horse. "Such as this. Isn't it beautiful? Amazing workmanship. The mane and tail are real horse hair. And the eyes . . . Look closely. They're blue opals, bought rough cut then polished to the proper shape. See how the green inclusions appear to shift and change, like the iris of an eye? In bright light, it's as though these eyes follow you to any angle of the room, almost as if they're alive. The saddle is hand-tooled, and the fittings and stirrups are all sterling silver. It's done in the style of a Victorian rocking horse, but created with the reality and size of a carousel pony. A child's fantasy come to life."

The dappled gray rocking horse with black mane and tail was indeed a wondrous creation, but everything seemed hazy and out of focus as Trev watched her. The fantasy that had come to life was Raven. Her expression reminded him of a child at Christmas, espying a special toy, one too expensive to wish for.

In a flash, Trev saw the beautiful horse sitting before a Christmas tree, the image so strong it shocked him. The past and the future warred for dominance, and the muscles in his jaw flexed as he fought against surging emotion. Raven would never understand, but Christmas in his childhood hadn't seen St. Nick answering any wishes. His mother had struggled hard to provide. Too vividly Trev recalled pressing his nose against a fancy department store window, dreaming St. Nicholas would bring him just a few of the wondrous gifts on display. But Santa Claus never heard the wishes of poor children. What few presents they found under the tree came from Des, even though he was little more than a child himself. Memories caused a fleeting smile to touch his lips, memories of Des leaving the price tags on presents, proud they were new and not hand-me-downs. Even then, they were practical items: jeans, shoes, a new coat. Never anything so frivolous—so *magical*—as this rocking horse.

"I'm sorry to see the horse sold. There's something extraordinary about it. Brishen created it," Raven informed him. But then, as she detected the change in his mood, her eyes darkened.

Instead of shaking her from the safe world she worked so hard to exist in, as the darkness roiling within his soul begged him, he slid his hands into his pants pockets. That also kept him from reaching for her. "Ah, the blue-eyed Gypsy with your sister? Gypsies don't usually have blue eyes."

Her whole face brightened. "Brishen is rare, unique in many ways. How many *vampire hunters* do you know?"

Still in the grips of the old pain, Trev forced himself not to smile in response. He hated the power she held over him, as though she were the sun and had the ability to drive away the black clouds in his heart. "Vampire hunter?" he echoed. He recalled reading a note by Julian regarding Brishen Sagari, but had thought it a joke. "You're kidding."

Raven laughed, and the sound shimmered over his skin and flooded his brain. Trev was beginning to suspect Raven was indeed a witch. Despite piles of pictures and years of reports, he'd undervalued this woman. He was coming to see that his arrogance with females had caused him to be a bloody fool. Agnes would smirk and her eyes twinkle with an *I-told-you-so*.

"I'm never quite sure. At times I think he's just pulling my leg; others strike me that he's dead serious. Those blue eyes come from his mother—who was not Rom, so I was told. I never had the chance to meet her. She died, hit by a drunk driver when Brishen was very small. She must've been a very special woman."

Trev didn't press for details, already aware that Brishen's father had been sent to jail for manslaughter. In Julian's opinion the verdict had been harsher than circumstances warranted, simply because Victor Sagari was a Gypsy. Also because of prejudice, Scotland Yard hadn't applied themselves to solving the hit-and-run death of his wife. Brishen's father succeeded where the detectives failed: he'd tracked the rich bastard to a pub one rainy night. When confronted, the driver had broken a bottle and attacked. Victor was only defending himself; however, it hadn't come out like that in court. A Gypsy in a barroom brawl, out to avenge his wife's death? The jury had deliberated a short period before returning a verdict of twenty-five years' hard time—likely a fate worse than death to a Gypsy used to a life of roaming. Sagari died three years later, stabbed by a fellow inmate. Brishen had been raised by his grandmother in a Romani caravan . . . and Trev and the handsome Gypsy had more in common than people would ever suspect.

Unable to keep the swirling emotions at bay, it was Trev's turn to avoid meeting Raven's curious gaze. Looking away, he pretended to examine the craftsmanship of the pony. "Yes, beautiful work, done with loving detail. He's a very talented artist."

"I pray it goes to someone nice. God, I hope Alec doesn't buy it. I think I'll be sick if he buys it for his wife." Once more she stroked the mane. "It deserves to go to someone who will love it."

To someone who believes in dreams, Trev thought.

"Why not buy it yourself?" he asked, intrigued by what her answer would be. With Montgomerie money, she could buy the building and everything in it.

"Ah, you fell for the myth of Midas Montgomerie's grandchildren. In spite of the reputation of my family's vast wealth, I live on modest means. I hope that doesn't disappoint you." Her fingers flexed around the pony's reins, awaiting Trev's answer. This time she didn't avoid his stare, but pinned him with those probing eyes.

He started to suggest she was Cinderella in reverse, but bit the comment back. Wolves, Little Red Riding Hood, Goldilocks—he was falling into the trap of thinking with fairy-tale metaphors, which was whimsical nonsense for a man on a mission. This night was strange enough without trotting out the Brothers Grimm.

"I don't judge a person by rumors—especially not rumors about their upbringing." Trying to keep his hands from curling into fists, Trev removed them from his pants pockets. "An adult defines him- or herself, and that's what I judge."

"Yes," Raven breathed. "It's how we face life that counts."

Trev couldn't resist. "Or the way we hide from it."

Her eyes flew wide. "Obviously you know a lot about the Montgomeries, Mr. Sinclair," she said, a hint of frosty distrust in her tone. "That's an unfair advantage."

"*Trevelyn*, remember?" He stepped over to the fortune-teller booth. "Is everything here up for auction?" Placing a hand on each edge, he leaned closer to study the mannequin. The poignant quality of the dummy touched him on a level he couldn't explain. The face seemed so familiar. "I want this."

Raven shook her head. "That item is just on display, part of the decorations for the night."

"I still want to buy it. I want it. And what I want, I get." His tone brooked no argument.

"Sorry, it already belongs to—"

"Name your price," he interrupted. "I don't care the cost. Isn't that what this gala is all about—helping the orphanage? With what I'm willing to pay, homeless kids could do very well for several years."

"You're a determined man, Trevelyn Sinclair."

She started to smile, but tensed when he pulled a coin from his pocket. He touched her shoulder and then drew his finger down the length of her arm, seeing gooseflesh rise under his caress. "You don't know the half of it, Red."

She held her breath as he inserted the coin, watched with a mixture of emotions flooding her eyes as he picked up the card. "The Lovers. Same as I pulled before," he mused.

As he turned it to see if he'd drawn the same fortune, she said, "I wouldn't put much stock in these cards, Mr. Sinclair. I'm certain my brothers stacked them for a gag."

"Well, when I buy it, I can stack the deck myself," he teased.

"You can be persistent, but the Gypsy belongs to me. She's a birthday gift from my sister." Raven smiled as she described her sibling: "LynneAnne restores carousel horses. Brishen often helps, since he can sculpt in wood and fashion the precise pieces that she needs to repair them. Not many have that talent. I always thought that special commonality would see romance bloom . . ." She shrugged a bare shoulder.

"Instead, he's chasing after your little sister."

"In a fashion. I don't think his heart is truly engaged, despite his protestations. He's gone through phases of being moon-eyed over one or another of my sisters for years. His first big passion was for Britt, but the romance just never worked out. He was ten at the time, and Britt seventeen. Since then, he's been in love with nearly all my sisters."

"And you?" Trev steeled himself against jealousy.

Raven blushed but didn't reply.

"He's an extremely handsome man. What's the problem? A *Gypso* not good enough for any of the granddaughters of Sean Montgomerie?"

He hadn't meant to sound so harsh, and Raven stiffened. "Hardly. I think the problem is Brishen loves us, but he's not *in* love. There is a difference. I utterly adore him, I love him."

Her saying she loved Sagari sent a sudden surge of hot acid spurting through Trev's system. The painful sensation circled around and finally slammed into his heart, which pounded erratically. Yep, it was jealousy, pure and simple; he was nearly blind with the urge to fist his hands in her hair and then drag her off, caveman-style. It took all his willpower not to follow through.

"But it's the love a sister feels for a brother," Raven continued. "Rather sad, actually, because I think Brishen is likely the one man in the world who'd allow me to be me." She gave Trev a bright expression, but there was gut-wrenching sadness underneath. "Once upon a time I allowed a beautiful man to prey on my trust—or my gullibility, if you prefer. Alec was as handsome as you, though I doubt you'd see that now. But he was. He was a golden boy who seemed to know all the right words, the perfect things to do. He used my faith in people against me. I'll never allow any man to use me like that again."

She drew a long, pained breath before continuing. "See? I told you this dress is not me. And that's the truth. Basically I'm a coward, not well equipped to deal with this world and its harsh realities. People joke the Montgomerie sisters are born of warrior stock. I think that gene is missing in me. So, one night a year I pull on a fancy dress and go dancing at a pretty ball. Then I'm content to go home to my pumpkin. I live alone in a tiny cottage and spend my days in jeans and baggy sweaters. Often, I lose myself in painting for hours on end. Brishen accepts me as I am. Most men wouldn't."

"*Happy* to go home to your pumpkin?" Trev pressed. "Or do you settle for being content? There's a difference, Red."

She spun on her heel without answering and headed back toward the rocking horse. The auction was beginning.

Trev watched her go. "Pumpkins be damned," he said, hungry as a wolf. "Time for me to go into my huffing and puffing act, I suppose. Sorry, Red, but you're in the wrong damn fairy tale."

Chapter Seven

While observing the proceedings of the auction, Trev sipped a whisky neat. He relished the soothing sensation of The Macallan, a scotch that had gained widespread popularity over the last decade. The brand was giving the old guard a run for their money, winning awards left and right. He supposed that was why he appreciated the liquor so much: he had a soft spot for a quality underdog, and the whiskey's sudden prosperity almost paralleled the Mershan brothers' rise to power. Finishing off his drink, he absently placed the glass on the tray of a passing waiter.

At the front of the hall, Cian stood before the lots, giving a little provenance for each in turn—who donated or created it—along with the value of the item, all geared to prod people to open their checkbooks. Some pieces were antiques contributed by other patrons of the orphanage. About a third came from regional artists: the Montgomeries were offering local talent a showcase through the charity.

Raven took a position on the opposite side of each item, beautiful window dressing, but once the actual bidding began, both Montgomeries stepped back and allowed the Christie's auctioneer to take over. A prettily staged show. But the whole affair was sadly ironic, and it rankled Trev. He thought of three little boys who'd been driven into deepest poverty because of Sean Montgomerie's ruthless and uncaring actions. No help had been offered by "Midas" Montgomerie to the Mershan sons. Which only firmed up Trev's drive to take back what had been stolen from them all those years ago.

Focused on tracking Raven, he was surprised when a feminine hand curled around his bicep. Glancing to his right he saw Paganne. She was grinning up at him, her chocolate brown eyes flashing with mischief and a come-hither look. The imp. She was going to probe him while her sister was away, test if she could turn his head.

"I rather admire how you handled Alec. Very neatly done," she remarked.

"Won't that handsome blue-eyed Gypsy get in a dither if he finds you on my arm?" Trev replied. He was unconcerned about the possibility, but wanted to judge Paganne's reaction.

"He excused himself for a smoke. Nasty habit." Raven's sister rolled her eyes. "While the cat's away puffing, he has to expect the mouse might get playful. Still, perhaps if he challenged you to a duel at dawn or even fisticuffs—something romantic and dashing—I might think him truly serious about me. More likely, he'll just call you some Gypsy insult and then threaten to have his gran curse you. And bet on it: she would. Something very dire, too—along the lines of all your hair falling out or your manhood shriveling up. Men tend to take those threats seriously."

"Understandably," Trev replied. "We're touchy about our hair and well . . ." He gave a comical glance downward.

Paganne chewed at the corner of her lip and looked him over, deviltry and curiosity barely contained. "So, where *did* you meet Raven?"

Trev almost chuckled. "I met her at the candy store . . ."

Raven's sister started to laugh but lightly bit her lower lip instead. "Cute. 'You turned around and smiled at her'? I get the picture. Just because the song came out before I was born doesn't mean I haven't heard it. Asha, Raven's twin—But oh, you already know she has a twin, don't you?"

"Yes, I do—lighter colored hair, and presently lives in Kentucky," he replied, getting a kick out of their game.

Paganne's perfectly arched brows lifted in surprise, because she still didn't fully believe he'd known Raven before tonight. "Then, she's told you about the Wurlitzer?"

"A jukebox? Uh, no. I don't think we've progressed that far. We've had other things on our minds." He tried to recall if Julian had mentioned anything in his reports. Nothing. But then he hadn't been going over Asha's bio, gleaning small details with the same intensity that he had Raven's.

"Well, there's one in The Windmill. That's a—"

"A restaurant Asha owns," Trev supplied.

"Yes. It has a Wurlitzer, and the thing is loaded with songs mostly from nineteen sixty-four. When my mum was alive, I spent my summers in Kentucky, thus I've heard 'Leader of the Pack' a time or three." Her huge eyes flashed in challenge. "So, Mr. Tall, Dark and Mysterious, are you going to tell me where your path crossed my sister's? I shall get it out of Raven anyway. She never keeps secrets from me."

The corner of Trev's mouth lifted in a faint taunt. "She didn't tell you about me, did she?"

Paganne tilted her head side to side, weighing that. "Possibly there was simply nothing to tell—until you magically appeared from out of nowhere, like some knight in shining armor. Whatever your reasons, you presented Raven with the way to save face before Jerkoff. That alone earns you a merit badge in my eyes." She turned and poked an index finger into Trev's chest. "Be that as it may, you hurt her and I shall take a knife to you."

Trev couldn't resist. "You mean that Pictish knife your grandmother gave you when you turned twenty-one?"

Astonishment filled her features. Paganne's brown eyes widened and she stared, clearly reevaluating her opinion of him. Her mouth opened to say something, but he could tell she was nonplused. Then those eyes narrowed on him, and it felt as though she could see inside his black heart.

"I'm not sure I like you, Trevelyn Sinclair. You're like

some big alpha wolf that's taken human form, looked my sister up and down and licked your chops, viewing her as your next meal. If that's your game, think thrice. It's a dangerous one."

"They're about to start the bidding on my pony!" Brishen said, returning to Paganne's side. Leaning a little forward, he checked their faces. One black brow lifted, a silent comment about Paganne's grip on Trev's arm.

Wickedly Paganne winked at Trev, and then looked back at the Gypsy. "You jealous?"

"He stands beside you, pretty Paganne, but his eyes stay glued on our Raven." Brishen gave a small nod. "It does you good, for a change, to have a man not fall at your feet."

After Cian introduced the rocking horse, listing all the details that made the item a one-of-a-kind treasure, Raven left the auction area. A tension released in Trev: He'd been afraid he'd pushed her too far earlier and destroyed the progress he'd made getting close to her. But she threaded through the people and straight to his side, linked her arm through his and then tilted forward to frown at her little sister.

Paganne was unrepentant, holding his other arm. "Chill, sis. Just testing. He passes. No rust or dirt on this armor."

"Does anyone want to open the bidding?" the auctioneer called out, running his gaze around the room.

"Hush, jealous women. They've started," Brishen chided. He was joking, but suppressed anxiety was apparent on his face.

A man to the right bid five hundred pounds. Another raised the total to seven. A woman made it eight. Then, to the left, a man called for one thousand. Trev knew without looking who had made the offer; Raven's hand had spasmed on his arm. Those nervous fingers relaxed when a fourth man chimed in offering twelve hundred, which was quickly raised to fifteen from someone in the back.

The very pregnant Ellen Beechcroft nudged her husband, who sang out loudly, "Two thousand!"

Once again, Raven's fingers bit into Trev's muscles. Trev glanced to the side to see her expression. She was maintaining a serene mask, and likely most people didn't notice her agony, but it was clear to him.

The auctioneer glanced around. "Do I hear twenty-one hundred? This item is a dream come true for that special child. Imagine their bright eyes when your little tyke awakens Christmas morn to see this heirloom-quality rocking horse. Priceless!"

The crowd seemed to hold its breath, waiting for the next bid. There was only silence and the storm outside.

Her hand on her basketball-shaped belly, Ellen Beechcroft grinned and hugged her husband, and the pompous bastard puffed up his chest as if he were buying her the Hope Diamond. In an odd way, Trev felt sorry for her. He wondered if she had any idea Beechcroft wasn't buying the horse for their baby, but to show off in front of Raven and her family. The man was grandstanding.

"Any more bids? Come, come! This lifelike horse is handcrafted, with silver fittings for bridle and stirrups. The eyes are deep blue opals, alone valued at twice the current bid. This is a gift for your children today and for their children tomorrow. A truly rare treasure. But, no further bids? Very well. Going once . . ."

Raven vibrated, the tremor moving through her hand and into Trev's arm. At the corner of her eye was an unshed tear.

"Going twice . . ."

Ellen Beechcroft bounced on her feet, giddy with anticipation.

"Five thousand!" Trev called out, causing all heads to turn—including Raven's. She looked up at him, her eyes shimmering. Her expression was so poignant, something inside Trev's chest shifted, and he experienced a tightness he'd never before known.

"The gentleman offers five thousand pounds. Obviously a man who understands dreams." The auctioneer nodded, pleased. "Do I hear six? If I don't hear six . . . going once—"

"Six," Alec Beechcroft barked.

Trev was only warming up. "Seven!"

The auctioneer gave him a nod of approval. "Our lover of dreams says seven. Is there an eight?"

"Eight," Beechcroft growled, glaring at Trev.

"If looks could kill." Trev laughed—then upped the amount. "Ten!"

That elicited a ripple of murmuring through the crowd. People glanced between the two men determined to own the rocking horse.

Beechcroft's face flushed red with anger. His wife's mouth was hanging open, and she glanced uneasily toward Raven and then back to her husband, confused. She clearly wanted the horse, but not quite sure it was worth this rising price.

"Fifteen," Alec countered, plainly set on winning.

But the bastard hadn't run into a Mershan before. Mershans didn't fool around. "Fifty thousand pounds!" Trev called out. *Let Beechcroft trump that.*

The crowd gasped then began a loud hubbub, wondering who Trev was and if Alec would counter. Better sense not being his strong suit, the idiot fully intended on doing just that. He took a step forward and opened his mouth, but his wife caught his sleeve and jerked, hard. Strident words were traded by the couple, and Beechcroft didn't tender a counterbid. The auctioneer looked at him. Alec's mouth compressed into a deep frown, but finally he gave his head a shake.

"Going once at fifty thousand pounds. Twice. *Sold*—to the gentleman who cherishes dreams." The auctioneer touched his fingers to his forehead in a salute. Part of the crowd clapped to say well done.

Raven hugged Trev's arm and leaned against him, almost hiding her face. After a moment she lifted her gaze to him. Tears were still in her eyes, but they were tears of happiness. Again, he became lost in her glistening gaze, to the point everything else simply faded away. As the crystalline droplets streaked down her cheeks, his hand raised to gently cup her exquisite face. Trev brushed the fallen tear away with his thumb pad—craved to kiss them away.

Paganne tugged on his other arm, drawing his attention. "I could kiss you!" she said.

"Forget you—*I'm* going to kiss him!" Brishen stepped in front of Paganne and did just that. He grabbed Trev in a bear hug and then planted a noisy kiss on the side of his face. "Do you know what you just did?"

Trev chuckled, unsure. "Bought a wooden horse, I presumed."

"You just made me the artist of a rocking pony that sold for fifty thousand pounds! That puts me on the map. You might be a *Gadjo*, but you're a damn pretty one. Maybe you have a little Roma blood in your beautiful veins, after all, eh?"

Trev reflected upon what the sale meant to Sagari, though he hadn't considered it during the bidding. Artists and antique dealers coveted high sales, for they set the bar for future asking prices. "You're welcome—but to keep gossip down, please hold the kisses," he joked.

Cian rushed over and took Trev's hand, giving a firm shake of respect; this time there was no power play. "Well, if it were Christmas I'd call you St. Nick. You really gave our stalwart vampire killer a big boost." He handed Brishen a business card. "Lee Grey-Morton, the auctioneer, wants to talk to you once the auction is settled. He has connections to galleries in London and Manchester that might be interested in doing a one-man show for your carousel ponies and rocking horses. He says they're very big in part of the Middle East. Sheiks have deep pockets, and seem to have an appetite for that sort of work."

Raven squeezed Trev's arm. "Trevelyn, I need to go fix my face. Thank you so much for buying the horse. You did a very special deed, Mr. Knight in Shining Armor."

Trev nodded, reluctant to let her escape from the magic of the moment. "Hurry back. I'd like to get a couple slow dances in before the evening is over."

Lee Grey-Morton walked up and introduced himself, shaking Trev's hand and congratulating him on his win. Reaching into his pocket, Trev pulled out a gold business card case, instructing him to bill the office, and that a bank draft would be issued first thing in the morning; the horse could be delivered to that address as well. The gray-haired man turned next to Brishen and began discussing his work, how he thought he could get a show lined up for the Gypsy, and that once there were some sales and attention he might bring the items into a Manchester gallery—or possibly London.

Cian turned to Trev and grinned. "I'm warming to your style, Sinclair. You spiked Alec's guns twice tonight, quite effectively both times. Get Raven to bring you to supper at Colford . . . soon."

"I'd enjoy that," Trev replied with mixed emotions. This had been his objective from the start: get close to Cian Montgomerie to monitor if Cian was aware that someone was quietly buying up Montgomerie Enterprises stock. That part of the plan was heading in the right direction. However, Trev admitted, he now owned a grudging curiosity to see Raven in a family situation, and that had nothing to do with his brothers' goals.

Clearly still stunned, Brishen watched the auctioneer stride away. "I am so *didlo*."

Paganne grinned. "You just made a big splash, having your pony go for a king's ransom. How does that make you crazy?"

Brishen glanced at Trev. "I thank you for the honor—though I know it wasn't the pony you were really bidding on."

"Raven showed me the horse earlier. It's worth the price." Trev hadn't meant to harm the Gypsy with his bidding, only to keep the horse from Beechcroft and to please Raven. "You were happy just a couple minutes ago," he pointed out, seeing Brishen looked crestfallen.

"Oh, aye. Then I went and made a bloody fool of myself by agreeing the auctioneer and his art gallery pal could meet me at my studio to discuss possible future sales."

Trev grinned. "And that deflates you? Sounds like a reason to celebrate."

"No." Brishen tried to summon a laugh. "That makes me the worst kind of idiot. I don't *have* a friggin' studio. And who am I kidding? No *Gadjo* is going to want a Gypsy anywhere near their fancy gallery."

Trev stared at the younger man, understanding his frustration only too well, though he doubted Sagari would believe it. "When are they coming?"

"In a week. A week, a month . . . it makes no difference. I am screwed!" He threw up his hands in resignation.

Trev reached out and patted Brishen on the arm. "A lot can happen in a week." He reflected upon the whole night, and extraordinarily realized he wasn't the same person who'd driven up this evening. He wasn't sure he liked the change, either. It had been too abrupt; it wasn't comfortable to be a stranger to yourself. Still, he was no coward to hide from the fact. "Hell, a lot can happen in a few hours. Life takes strange turns when you least expect it."

Brishen Sagari's brows lifted. "So says the man who drives a Lamborghini."

"Ah, but remember. They say to never judge books by covers."

"True—even if that's how Gypsies are judged, eh?" Sagari's expression grew more intense.

Trev shook his head. "Only a fool would, and I'm no fool," he replied, though Agnes Dodd might dispute it. But his secretary wasn't there to gloat or contradict him.

Distracted, Trevelyn nonetheless felt warning bells go off as he caught sight of Alec Beechcroft on the far side of the room. The man was watching the arched entrance that led to the lounges, the same doorway Raven had gone through only minutes before. The man's fingers flexed around his glass to the point Trev feared it might shatter. His mask of politeness down, revealed was a raw, blistering hatred that seemed ludicrous for a man who had remarried. The way Beechcroft glared it was as though he could see through the wall, and the strength of his malevolent regard sent a chill up Trev's spine.

"Fingernails on a blackboard," he muttered lowly enough that his words didn't carry. Trev could see how having Raven and losing her might push a man to the limit, but the man's feelings were unfounded—and unwanted. "Too bloody bad, berk. You blew your chance. It's past time to step aside and allow another man—a *better* man—into her life."

Lifting his glass, Alec drained the last of amber liquid inside and then slammed it down on a nearby table. He rotated, spoke hurried words to his clinging wife, and then started across the room. When he spotted Cian's back to him, he disappeared into the dim hallway toward the lounges.

Trev turned to Raven's brother, who was in front of him. "If you'll excuse me," he said, trying not to clench his jaw. "I have something urgent that requires my attention."

Paganne grinned over her champagne glass. "I'm beginning to like you, Trevelyn Sinclair. I wasn't sure I would."

Without replying, Trev started after Alec. From behind him he heard Paganne urge, "Sic him!"

Trev crossed the ballroom, not giving any pretence of politeness. Several people tried to stop him and offer congratulations, but he brushed them off with words he wasn't even aware he spoke. He was totally focused on stalking Alec, who was stalking Raven. The whole evening was turning out quite differently than anticipated, and not in keeping with the low-profile entrance into Raven's life he had intended.

"I've proclaimed myself Raven's lover, decided to help a Gypsy with blue eyes, and now I'm preparing to punch out Beechcroft. I hope I don't get arrested. Des would be ever so ticked—and I don't even want to think about Agnes."

Trev slowed his steps as he entered the dim corridor, allowing his eyes to adjust. Toward the other end there were sconces on both sides of the hall, and quaint signs over two doors on either side: *Damsels* on the left, *Knights* on the right.

"Hm, what about wolves?" Trev muttered with a chuckle.

He pulled up short when he spotted Beechcroft. Alec was pacing from the door of the men's room to the ladies' room and back, looking at the floor. The door to the ladies' room opened, causing Beechcroft's head to snap up. Raven stepped through, but she froze when she saw her ex standing there, hands in his pockets.

"So, Alec, lurking around ladies' rooms is your new fetish?" She tilted her chin in a defiant fashion and moved to step past him. "It's positively lower class."

His left arm shot out and grasped the door frame, blocking her from returning to the ballroom. "Really, Raven, you truly expect me to believe Sinclair is your date?" His voice was edged with a demoralizing, patronizing tone. "A man like him wouldn't give you the time of day. He can have any woman he wants. What? Did you hope to make me jealous? Tell me, did you pay Sinclair so you'd have an escort for the evening? It's certainly not for the sex. We both know just how pathetic *that* area of your life is."

Barely hiding her repugnance, Raven shoved at his arm to force him to back off. "You're drunk."

"What's your hurry? Think lover boy is out there pining for you? Likely Paganne is all over him by now. I always wondered if I chose the wrong sister."

"Alec, you really should leave. You weren't invited. Cian hasn't booted you because he didn't want a scene, but—"

"Screw Cian. Screw you, too. But then Miss Semivirgin doesn't like to screw, eh?" He locked his arm so she couldn't budge him. "You love reminding me I'm a nobody, not worthy of a high-and-mighty Montgomerie. I don't move in the same vaulted circles."

Trev's temper flared, burning hot and dangerous. A peculiar slippage of time folded about him, as if a portal between two worlds had opened, allowing the past to bleed into the present. The weight of chain mail felt heavy upon his body, and his hand flexed around the grip of a sword hilt; he was ready to step before his lady and battle for her honor.

Trev stalked over and took hold of Beechcroft's wrist. He only used his index finger and thumb, but he got a good hold. Twisting the man's arm like a lever, Trev soon had the bastard wincing.

"You son-of-a-bitch!" Alec snarled.

Trev gave a smug grin. "Tut-tut. Such coarse language before a lady."

Alec grimaced, attempting to jerk out of his iron grip. "She's no lady, she's my—"

"Wife?" Trev's brows lifted in mockery. "So drunk you don't recall your wife's name is Ellen?"

"Let go, you bastard. That hurts!" Alec threw an awkward punch, but Trev yanked his arm up higher, controlling him.

"That's nothing compared to what I'm about to do, unless you take your drunken arse back to your wife and get the hell out of here."

"I'll have you arrested," Beechcroft threatened.

Trev chuckled. "For what? Go ahead—tell the police how I pinched you with my index finger and thumb. I'll be sure to tell pregnant little Ellen that you were in here claiming Raven was your wife. Should be an interesting evening."

Muttering an obscenity, Alec swung out once more with his right hand, but Trev simply spun him full circle and then slammed him up against the wall. Keeping an arm pressed to Alec's spine, he said lowly against Beechcroft's ear, "Come near Raven again and I'll tie you up buck naked and leave you in the middle of Piccadilly Circus with a sign around your neck saying 'I like rough sex.'"

Jerking Beechcroft away from the wall, Trev positioned him to face Raven. "Now, apologize to the lady before I show you just how dangerous my pinkie finger is."

"You better be sure to get money for this. If you're playing King Kong in the hope of sex, you're shit out of luck. She's a lousy l—"

Increasing pressure on his arm, Trev growled, "Way . . . wrong . . . words. I want only the right three from your sewer mouth, and you bloody well better say them. *Now.*"

Beechcroft was still going to refuse, so Trev applied a little more force. "S-s-sorry!" the jerk finally spluttered through a grimace.

"That's not *three* words, but I guess it'll suffice. Run along now and collect your little wife—then leave."

Trev thrust Beechcroft away to stumble back down the hall. He watched to make sure the idiot was actually going, before he turned back to Raven, who was staring at him with unreadable thoughts, her spine pressed up against the bathroom door. Trev wondered if she was shocked or appalled by his actions. What he'd done was nothing compared to what he'd *wanted* to do to the bastard.

"Did I scare you?" Moving closer, he reached out to

gently cup the side of her face, and then allowed his thumb to stroke over her cheek.

Those unblinking eyes watched him until she finally whispered, "Yes, you scare me."

"I apologize—"

She gave a faint shake of the head. "Oh, not the roughness. You did little more than humiliate him. Alec deserved to have his feathers ruffled. He's not a very nice man. It's *you* who scares me. Who are you, Trevelyn Sinclair? What do you want with me? I'm not some princess in a fairy tale, and you're no knight in shining armor. So, what do you want?"

He leaned closer, intoxicated by her nearness, Raven's essence filling every pore, every drop of his blood. No woman had ever spun such magic to ensnare him. "You're right. You're no princess. You're Red Riding Hood. And what do I want? I've come to huff . . ." He brushed his lips softly against hers. "And puff . . ." He pressed another butterfly kiss to her soft mouth. "And blow your house down."

This time he leaned into the kiss, taking her mouth and claiming it. A small moan vibrated in her throat. The sound sent his blood to speed through him, vibrating with need; he wanted to grab her, pull her body against his, feel her soft curves pressed to the length of his hard muscles—but if he laid hands on that beautiful body he wouldn't be able to stop. Placing his left hand flat on the wall beside her head, he stepped closer, but it also prevented him from touching her the way he wanted. He allowed their bodies to brush, felt the heat of her skin, inhaled her light citrusy perfume and the more intoxicating scent of woman underneath. It was simply spellbinding, too much for his senses.

He broke the kiss and pulled back, forced a slow, deep breath. "Don't you know it's dangerous for a Red Riding Hood to be with the Big Bad Wolf in a darkened corridor?"

"I thought you were the devil," she replied.

He exhaled his tension, his sexual frustration, and snatched up her wrist. "Let's go dance before I do something I regret."

It was a moment of kindness that he offered up, but hurt filled her voice. "Regret?" That sadness made him want to bash Beechcroft all over again. And this time, he wouldn't be so nice.

"Regret but thoroughly enjoy," he promised.

"You're kind—"

"Kind, nothing. Don't let the garbage *that* man said to you take root and grow. It's not the truth, you know. Sex with the right person is a beautiful experience. Sex with the wrong person runs the gamut from being boring to being a nightmare. Alec Beechcroft is the wrong person for you." He glanced down and saw her hands were trembling. "Maybe for everyone."

Raven gave him a sad smile. "It's too late, I fear, to not let his words hurt. Years too late. Alec has a way of going for the throat, and I never learned the skills to protect myself. I think it best I go home. I don't feel well."

"Did you drive here?" Trev asked.

"Yes."

"I'll drive you back." She looked too shaky to get behind the wheel.

Instead of answering, Raven put her hand to her forehead, massaged her temple and watched him, emotions warring in her eyes. That bastard Beechcroft really had made her doubt herself. Worse, Raven was now doubting him.

"You're shook up. You don't need to be driving," Trev explained. Not giving her a chance to refuse, he said, "I assume you have a wrap? Let me fetch it and then I shall see you home."

She nodded weakly. "A velvet wrap and matching purse. Ask Mary in the cloak room."

Escorting Raven to the rocking horse, Trev then crossed

the hall to the entrance where the large coatroom was. A blonde woman nodded when he asked for Raven's wrap. She returned shortly, carrying a red velvet cloak and clutch.

Trev shook his head, accepting it. "Why didn't I guess?"

As he returned, he found Raven before the fortune-teller booth, staring at the mechanical Gypsy with an expression of puzzlement and perhaps a little apprehension. That struck Trev as a dichotomy when compared with her pride and insistence that the clockwork doll wasn't for sale.

"Want your fortune told?" he asked, handing over the clutch.

"No!" Belying how loudly she'd replied, she quickly donned a look of indifference. "I had it told earlier. Silly nonsense."

"Perhaps you should try again. Your fortune might've changed since meeting me." It hurt to see her so wounded. So vulnerable. Raven Montgomerie need a knight champion to protect her from the ugliness of this world, and Trev wanted to be that—for as long as he could.

She looked at him as if weighing her decision. "Or perhaps it hasn't."

"That's supposed to mean . . . ?"

"Nothing." She shrugged. "Perchance it's best not to see the future, especially if we're powerless to change or shape it."

Ignoring her, he reached into his pocket and took out a coin. They both watched the mechanical Gypsy rock side to side, and then her eyes closed. The huge crystal ball shimmered with a bluish fog, causing Trev to ponder how that effect was achieved. A bulb inside the base of the globe could account for the blue tone, but he had no idea how the mist was created.

Raven's hand shot out to snatch the card, as if she were afraid for him to see. Giving a playful grin, he beat her to it and held it out of her reach.

"Tut—my coin, my card," he joked. His brow quirked when the tarot card was once again The Lovers. Same as he'd drawn before. Only, the fortune on the reverse wasn't the same. " 'Beware of the wolf in sheep's clothing,' " he read aloud.

Raven paled. Their eyes locked for a moment, and then she said, "I told you my twin brothers stacked the deck. You got that card before."

"The same card, but the fortune was different." Trev was surprised when all further color seemed to drain from her already wan face. Reaching into the inner pocket of his jacket, he pulled out the first card and read it. " 'The lamb often proves stronger than the wolf.' "

Raven stared at him. Oh boy, she recognized him as a wolf—he could see that thought reflected in her golden-brown eyes. Well, there'd been no disguising that fact, he realized. And when she said nothing, he placed her red velvet cloak about her shoulders.

Something was causing a lump in the collar. Trying to smooth it down, he gently tugged on the material until it was free and then lifted the obstruction to cover Raven's head.

"How about that, Red? You even have a hood."

Chapter Eight

Raven watched the ease with which Trevelyn handled his sleek black roadster. At one with the expensive car, he deftly guided it through the stormy night, almost defying gravity. Shifting gears and spinning the wheel, he easily took the curves down the winding road to Colford Hall. She was used to puttering around in her dilapidated MGB, and now it felt as if she were sailing along in a jet—flying low, as her mum used to call it.

Looking over at the handsome man who set her pulse to pounding, she thought, *All the better to crash and burn*. Though in this instance she meant it figuratively.

The notion might be silly, provoked by the Gypsy's cards and the references to Trevelyn being a wolf, but there was something intensely feral about this man. Oh, he was a wolf all right. A rogue alpha male on the hunt.

That's what terrified her. For some reason he had targeted her, and she hadn't the first clue why. Alec was a bloody bastard, but he was right about one thing: Trevelyn Sinclair could have any woman he wanted. So why did he want her? Rattled, Raven turned to stare out into the night, only to be haunted by his reflection on the rain-streaked window.

Women didn't often run across men like Trevelyn Sinclair; she had never pinpointed the reason, but it seemed that, as the world increased technologically, the more men lost that warrior's edge. A power, a strength, a force vital radiated from him. Oh, Sinclair was dressed to perfection in a tuxedo, but this man belonged on the deck of a ship, screaming orders to buccaneers over cannon fire, or in mail and armor, a knight barded for battle and astride his mighty destrier. There was a sensual, primeval earthiness about him, and dealing with him was way beyond her abilities. Bloody hell, she couldn't even cope with Alec. Trevelyn Sinclair would wreak twice as much havoc if she dared let him close. If she was fool enough to . . .

Oh, temptation slithered under her skin. She wanted him—which surprised her. Prior to meeting this unusual stranger, she'd always believed her emotions would have to be fully engaged before any man would receive an invitation to her bed. Trevelyn Sinclair was possibly the exception to the rule. Making love with him would be dancing in a bonfire: she wasn't sure there'd be anything left when the flame had run its course.

Ill at ease, she pressed a hand to her belly to quiet the butterflies. He made her nervous in ways she didn't even want to consider.

Breaking the silence, Trev asked, "You're quiet. Still upset?" He glanced over at her, staring for several seconds, then turned the radio on low.

"I seem to be thanking you for one thing or another this evening. First, giving me the way to save face before Alec, then buying the rocking horse, rescuing me from the idiot and now taking me home. You were right—I shouldn't be driving. It's raining too hard, the road is too dark and narrow, and concentration would've been difficult for me." And likely she'd have been crying. Showing a modicum of wisdom, she bit that observation back. She was a coward, but that was her secret. She didn't want pity from this man.

He took his eyes from the road and allowed them to linger on her. That green stare had a banked sexual heat, but solicitude also flickered there. His salacious look was hard enough on her system, but coupled with concern, it battered down what feeble defenses she could muster.

"You shouldn't let that creep Beechcroft push your

buttons. He's not worthy of you and knows it—it's precisely what has him so ticked off. You give him power when you react as he wants. Take the power back, Raven. Don't let him win."

"I know. I don't handle confrontations well anymore. I never did, really, but since the divorce . . ." She allowed the sentence to trail off, not wishing to bore him, nor caring to rehash the depressing details. Life would be so much simpler if everyone came with delete buttons like computers. "I suppose I'm the misfit of the family. Runt of the litter. I dislike fighting and shrink from competition, which made it hard growing up a twin and one of seven sisters. My sisters are very . . . hmm . . . forceful. In a nice way, of course. Not me. I'm happiest when I can ignore life and its problems. I'm too trusting for my own good, wound easily, deeply. I 'failed to toughen up,' as they say." Her words were a warning to this man—and a plea.

Her eyes shifted to the elegant hand resting lightly on the gearshift. It was a magician's hand, deft, artful, yet a strong hand you'd expect to see wrapped around the hilt of a claymore. Then she glanced at his much too beautiful face, its strong jaw and luminous all-seeing eyes, and finally the wavy, blue-black hair. Oh, his drop-dead gorgeous looks were enough to fluster her. A woman would have to be comatose not to respond to the carnal aura swirling around Trevelyn. Still, there was something else. He seemed familiar in a way she couldn't begin to fathom; a sense of déjà vu wrapped around her and made every moment seem a step out of time.

He gave her a cool smile, unruffled by her long appraisal. Arrogant and uncaring that she knew it, Trevelyn Sinclair was clearly at home in his skin. "What you need is a champion to fight life's battles for you," he suggested.

"The world has a dearth of paladins," she countered.

If things appeared too good to be true, they generally were. And Trevelyn Sinclair was way too good to be true. But oh, for a weak moment Raven wanted Trev to be just how he seemed. For once she yearned to live the fairy tale where Prince Charming would ride up and rescue her, ready to slay dragons and ex-husbands alike. Long ago, she'd learnt life was not that simple.

No, Raven didn't need any words from any Gypsy tarot echoing through her head to tell her what she already comprehended. She was still half convinced the twins had stacked the deck. It would be just like one of their pranks. But a prank made sense, whereas her suspicions . . . well, she didn't want to consider them.

"Drive on past Colford's entrance," she instructed, as the towering gates grew visible in the rainy distance. "I don't live on the main estate, but in a small cottage toward the far end."

"Yes, I know," he replied, with an enigmatic half smile.

Once more, she suffered questions of how he knew so much about her. Raven admitted, "One wonders why you're familiar with such details of my life. My shoulder blades itch like a target's been painted there."

He gave a soft, throaty laugh that sent a shiver up her spine. "All women have targets. 'Tis the nature of the game. In this case, however, it's nothing quite so baffling. The Montgomeries are frequently splashed across the newspapers—in the business and social sections. This charity gala received a lot of coverage. I just moved to the area. It's a small community, which by nature tends to be incestuous. Gossip is the favorite pastime. Spend an evening down at The Fox and Garter and you'd be surprised how much you can suss out."

"Generalities—not personal minutiae," she argued. "A newspaper reporter wouldn't report me living in the gardener's cottage."

"Depends upon the rag, wouldn't you say? In any case, they don't employ the local font of knowledge as a housekeeper. Mystery solved . . . revealing no mystery at all: the woman who cleans my offices is the daughter of Colford's housekeeper. I also hired her to help me get my things settled in my new flat, and to come in twice a week to tidy up after me. So let's say I've heard quite a bit about the beautiful Montgomerie sisters, especially Raven."

"You hired Jilly?"

He nodded. "Hard worker, but her mouth doesn't come with an off switch, I fear."

"None that I've seen," Raven agreed. "I grew up playing with Jilly. I suppose my ears should've been burning. You must've been bored to tears, since my life is rather humdrum." She could bet Jilly had been entertaining him. Her friend had a penchant for pretty men, and Trevelyn Sinclair was as pretty as they came. Jilly wouldn't resist the challenge.

Trev tilted his head in a shrug. "Let's say what I learnt of Raven Montgomerie little prepared me for the mystery of the woman herself."

Raven's breath caught and held; she was taken aback by his tone, his words. By the truth in them. She tried to draw a steadying breath but found it futile, as if Trevelyn had sucked all the oxygen from the car interior. The potent male pheromones he exuded simply fried her nervous system.

Smart women, ones with strong survival instincts, learned the hard lesson that pretty men quickly develop tricks to deceive, the right things to say or do, the way to batter down all resistance. It didn't lessen the effect, just made an inner voice scream not to trust him. Her foolish heart wasn't listening. Or, worse, in her present mood it didn't care. She'd been living alone in a small world fashioned from a gardener's cottage for the last five years, desperately needing that time and space to heal. Only of late, a restlessness was growing within her, one that might see her willing to toss caution to the wind.

"Maybe I'm suicidal," she muttered, thinking he wouldn't hear.

"Beg pardon?" By the arch of his brow and the twinkle

in his eyes, it was clear he'd heard perfectly. That keen wolf hearing.

"I said, 'Maybe slow the car idle,'" she tried to cover. That was so idiotic she nearly winced in pain, only she couldn't come up with anything else. Ignoring his mildly amused look, she said, "The turnoff is ahead on the left."

A cell phone rang in the holder mounted on the dashboard. Trev glanced to Raven, hesitated a heartbeat, and then reached for it. Instead of hitting the speaker button, he picked the phone up and put it to his ear. "Hello? Hello?" Frowning, he pulled it away from his head and glared at it. "Odd, I could've sworn it was fully charged. Battery's so down there's not even warning beeps."

Raven chuckled. "More likely it's me being near. I do that to watches, cell phones . . ." She shrugged, "Technology and I don't get along."

"Really?" His too expressive face conveyed he didn't believe her.

"I'm serious. I can't wear a watch. It always stops within a few hours. About ten years ago, a jeweler suggested a quartz watch. I purchased one with a lifetime guarantee. Stopped in a week. I sent it in for repairs, they fixed and sent it back. The blasted thing died in two days. I returned it. They said they'd fix it one last time, but not to send it again because I was doing something to abuse the watch, which voided the warranty. The jeweler claimed the crystal was melted. It only ran a day before it stopped. I haven't worn one since. I ruin cell phones, computers, watches, and oddly, even seem to destroy cars over a period of time. I must've replaced the generator on the MGB at least once a year for the past two decades. Did the same with two other cars I owned."

"Well, if the call was urgent, they'll ring back." Putting the phone back into the cradle, Trev asked as he slowed the car, "Is this the turnoff?"

"Yes, go at a crawl. The driveway needs grading again." But, Raven frowned. Trevelyn's question sounded as though he already knew the answer and was just going through a pretense. She dismissed the suspicion, fearing she was growing paranoid.

Trev shifted gears and eased into the turn. Rain slashed at the windscreen, leaving it hard to see anything. Poor man winced when the vehicle dragged over a rut. *Men and their babies,* she thought.

He watched her in the dim dashboard light. "Call me curious, but why do you live all the way out here when you could reside in regal splendor at Colford, servants waiting on you hand and foot?"

What to say? One's divorce and breakdown weren't exactly ideal topics for an interested woman to discuss with a handsome man. Raven nearly cringed when she considered Jilly's mouth not only ran at warp speed, but didn't have any filters. Finally, she decided to answer a question with a question, and in a jesting tone: "You mean, Jilly didn't tell you?"

He shrugged. "Let's say I want to hear it from you."

"The simplified version? I needed space. I come from a large family—which you clearly know—and too many of my sisters and brothers still live there. You'd be surprised: though the manor is huge, it can be hard to find a spot to be alone. My siblings are jokingly called the *meddling* Montgomeries, and boy, do they ever! I wasn't permitted to sit and feel blue without the whole pack of them rushing in like a troop of clowns from Ringling Brothers to insist I must get happy instantly. I require solitude so I can paint. Their continual interruptions left me frustrated, so I found the solution of moving to the old gardener's cottage. I always loved the place. It seemed magical to me. As a child I thought it was straight from a Tolkien book. And now the family is close—but not too close."

"What's the complicated version?" he prompted, sounding truly interested.

Raven forced a smile. "I shan't bore you with it. And . . . it's simply pouring out, so you don't have to walk me to the door."

Swinging the roadster into her driveway, Trevelyn brought it to a halt at the side of the house where she usually parked the MGB, instead of pulling around the circle in front meant for guests. He ignored her suggestion, cut the motor and removed the keys. "I guess I should be thankful your brothers returned the Lamborghini before the night was out."

"Did they burn up all your petrol?" Raven paused. Skittish, she hoped Trevelyn would let her go. Prayed he'd allow her escape. Then she wouldn't have to face decisions.

"They left about half a tank." He gave her a warm grin.

"I'm sure they enjoyed it. Thank you for being so kind. They're spirited but good lads. You might hit them up for a wash and wax job for payment." She was jabbering inanely, her hand trembling as she frantically searched for the door handle. She needed to get out and away from this pheromone-saturated air. It was making her woozy and weak. *Hungry.* "Oh, bugger, how does one open a gull-wing door?"

Trevelyn reached across her lap and caught her arm. Slowly pulling it to him, he placed a soft kiss to the inside of her wrist, his lips searing her flesh like a brand. "Red Riding Hood is to sit while I get out and come around to assist her like a gentleman. I may be a wolf, love, but I am a well-mannered one."

Lightning crawled across the landscape, striking a tree nearby. In that breathless instant, the inky darkness was vanquished by a blue-white glow, an eerie radiance pouring over everything and leeching the color from all but Trevelyn's piercing eyes. Time lengthened as she stared at him, held spellbound and unable to breathe. A force slammed into her chest, as if the electrical bolt had struck her. Dizziness swirled through Raven's brain and body;

she couldn't move, seeing and yet not wanting to believe. She knew these green eyes only too well. For that jagged fraction of a moment her answer was there, a solution to the unspoken riddle tantalizingly before her, almost within grasp.

Then the darkness fell again. Raven's heartbeat thundered in her ears.

Trevelyn was close. Too close. She could smell the faint woodsy notes of his cologne, interlaced with a mysterious, earthier one underneath, the combination guaranteed to fry her mind. Coupled with the heat off his body, it left her intoxicated. The moment lengthened as he merely stared at her, his warm breath fanning her lips, forcing her to inhale and almost taste him. In the dim interior his features were shadowy, but the low parking lights illuminated those hungry eyes. He wanted to kiss her. She wanted that, too, her body twisting into knots with a craving so intense that her womb spasmed with need. It overrode all logic and self-preservation clamoring within her mind. Nothing else mattered but this man.

Mortifying, infuriating, he knew full well how he was affecting her. With a slight lift at the left corner of his mouth, he pulled back. He opened the sports car's strange, futuristic door, and then pushed outside.

Raven almost collapsed against her plush seat, aflutter with pulsating sexual tension. Lifting the hood of her cloak she grumbled, "Stop acting like a blethering teenager. He's a wolf. A bloody wolf. A Red Riding Hood should never trust a wolf. *Never be stupid enough to trust a wolf.* Maybe if I repeat it one hundred times it'll sink in."

Through the windscreen, she watched him walk around the front of the car and come to the passenger door. It opened, and Trevelyn extended his hand for her to take. She looked at it, the beautiful long fingers, the broad palm, fearing if she accepted there'd be no turning back; she'd be giving a piece of her soul to the devil's keeping, and something told her Trevelyn Sinclair wasn't the kind to return what he claimed.

"Then again, learning by rote has never been my strong suit." She swallowed hard and put her hand in his.

Chapter Nine

Rain sheeting down upon them, Trev followed steps behind Raven, who hurried to the front of the cottage and onto the roofed porch. Twice she tried to pull her hand free from his grip, but he held tight, sensing she was in full retreat and tossing up barriers to avoid inviting him inside. An old Scottish adage was: It's easier to leave a cat out than put him out. He had a feeling this fey Scots lass was applying it to wolves as well.

Yes, Raven was resolute in keeping him outside so that she need not confront *putting* him out. In frankness, she had admitted she did not deal well with conflict. This Tolkien world she had built far away from everything was a testament to that. Only, this time, circumstances would force Raven into meeting her hidden desires head-on.

If he'd stayed in the car as she pointedly suggested, she could've escaped without having to handle him.

Well, too bad, Red. I checked that little maneuver.

She was now attempting another gambit. He watched her stop on the small stoop, turn and block him from coming any farther, deliberately leaving him on the steps in the pouring rain. Silly wench, she hoped denying him shelter from the storm would hasten him back to his car. But, pitiful drops of water wouldn't keep him from this woman. Bloody hell, a whole herd of fire-breathing dragons couldn't deter him from Raven. He smiled, and then realized the expression was a first—a smile that seemed to go soul deep.

Standing in her old-fashioned cape with its huge floppy hood, the stoop hardly stopping the slashing rain from soaking her, Raven appeared ethereal, a sorceress, more than a simple being of this world. She was the Fairy Queen, weaving enchantments to trap poor Tamlin's mind, and just like that besotted Scottish fool Trev suddenly welcomed her witchy lures. He would slay all the orcs in Isengard, duel blue-eyed Gypsies, and topple kingdoms for her. He would—

Feeling ridiculous, he closed his eyes and tried to exorcise his mind of these alien thoughts. This night was making him loopy. Fairy tales, wolves and Riding Hoods were morphing him into a blethering moron! Long ago he had accepted that he didn't have a romantic bone in his body—or so he'd thought. If he suddenly cried out, "But soft, what light through yonder window breaks!" he was going home to soak his head.

Oddly, ludicrously, wonderfully, he didn't feel the rain. It was beyond his explaining, but there was some quality about this night that was so elemental, nearly supernatural, that the storm merely seemed part of its extraordinary enchantment. Opening his eyes, he put his foot on the top step and then slowly raised himself up, his stare never leaving Raven's face, cosseted inside that red velvet hood. She was tall, around five seven, and with her on the porch and he on the step, that put their gazes on the same level.

Letting go of Raven's hand, he curled his fingers into his palms to keep from seizing her. He sighed in frustration. It was friggin' tough for a wolf to be gentlemanly.

"Well . . . um . . . you should get out of the rain. It's pouring. Thank you again for everything." She managed a tight little laugh, naively thinking escape was in sight.

But words seemed outside Trev's grasp. Struck a mindless tomfool, he swallowed hard and then slowly reached up with both hands. The moment lengthened, spun out to where the world ceased to turn on its axis. His heart slowed, beating painfully. His fingers took hold of Raven's hood and slowly pushed it off her head, allowing slanting spray to mist upon her long hair. Spellbound, she stared back.

All he could think to say was, "You're beautiful in the rain." And she was. Sadly, her velvet cape would be ruined, though he deemed that a small price. The image of her haunting face, the power of this point in time was forever seared into his memory. He so wanted to kiss her, to taste the cool sweetness of the rain on her lips. Instead, he simply remained frozen in this crystalline moment, wondering if he'd fallen down a rabbit hole.

Raven's lashes lowered. He'd seen reflected in her sad eyes that she didn't believe him—and that made him want to smash Beechcroft in the face all over again.

His immediate goal was to get inside her cozy little bungalow. Only three little steps to the door, they were steps Raven was going to prevent him from traversing if possible. If he could achieve that much, he'd next stamp out the seeds of self-doubt that had taken root within her, would teach her how special and rare she was.

"You are, you know." His thumbs brushed under her chin to gently lift her head. Once more, the urge to kiss her slammed through his entire being, tensing muscles and spreading a strange tightness in his chest. "Very beautiful."

Her eyes remained lowered, and she evaded his probing stare, her voice barely audible over the rain pattering down around them. "Please don't. I told you about me. I'm not the kind of woman a wolf wants. Let me go."

Her hand shook as she opened her small clutch, frantically searching for her keys. They rattled in her grasp and then slipped through her wet fingers. Before they hit the wooden porch, Trev snatched them midair. Her head jerked up, and she held out her hand. Only, he took that step she didn't want him to take; she had to back up or their bodies would brush. He offered her an easy smile and moved past her to the door. Raven had just gifted him with the key to his goal—literally and figuratively.

"A gentleman always sees a lady to the door."

Recovering a bit of equilibrium, she laughed. "Is that what you are? This night you wear many masks. Devil? Wolf? Gentleman? Which is the real Trevelyn Sinclair?"

Her question hit home, more than she could ever suspect. Yes, he was wearing a mask tonight, and one even he didn't recognize. The whole evening was a mockery of what he had foolishly envisioned. Instead of sweeping Raven off her feet, he'd been sucked up in a confusing, whimsical whirlwind of emotion, dreams and hopes he'd never imagined. He'd only had two drinks, and that faint buzz had been burned up in his annoying confrontation with Beechcroft. He was stone-cold sober—and yet was drunk from her presence. It scared the bloody hell out of him.

"You might say a bit of all three." He inserted the key in an antiquated lock, and his mouth compressed into a frown. This was the only defense she employed against the world? It was as if she expected no menace would dare invade the bubble protecting her quaint bungalow on the corner of the vast Colford estate.

He tried to push the door open, but it held fast—and not from the inadequate lock. Behind him Raven suggested, "You have to shove hard. In wet weather it sticks."

Trevelyn chuckled. "Wet weather? Which is nearly every day in jolly ol' England." Putting both hands to the frame, he gave a strong push and the door finally popped and swung inward. Then, in a neat little maneuver he removed the key from the lock and stepped into her warm cottage.

The only illumination was the dim bulb of a floor lamp in the kitchen. The living room was a contrast of shadows and that light. Trev held out his free hand, gesturing for Raven to enter. Poor Riding Hood, she'd have to put the wolf out now that he had deftly slipped within. And she knew it, too. Instead of coming in, she remained beyond the threshold. Those luminous eyes watched him, knowledge that she'd lost the game reflected in their amber brown depths.

Lightning flashed close by, followed by the earthshaking boom of thunder, causing her to jump. Still, she hesitated outside. "I didn't show you the cards *I* drew from the fortune-teller," she said.

"No, you didn't. However, I saw your reaction to mine. The Lovers." He couldn't help it, the side of his mouth tugged upward. A scared doe, she had yet to step over that dangerous threshold. He entreated softly, "Come inside, Raven."

She tried to smile. Failed. Desperation . . . and finally capitulation flashed across her face. "I'm not certain, but it might be safer if I turned and ran."

Chuckling, he shook his head. "You'd risk pneumonia? A walk in the October rain is a sure way to court it. Come inside, Raven. I promise not to bite." As she took a step over the doorsill, giving a resigned sigh, he added, "Unless you ask."

She pulled up short. "All wolves bite, whether you ask or not." Raven looked at him as if he'd fall on her and gobble her up in two chomps, maybe with a side of fava beans and a nice Chianti.

He couldn't resist teasing. "My, what big eyes you have, Miss Riding Hood."

Her mouth pursed as she reached for the doorknob to shut the door. With a lift of her brow she replied, "All the better to see tricky wolves."

As they were closed inside, muting the sounds of the storm, Trev stepped to take her cape. Raven tensed when he placed his hands on her shoulders. "Relax, Red," he promised, "I'm just removing your wet cloak—being a gentleman again."

"I think a gentlemanly wolf is an oxymoron." She

turned her head to glance over her shoulder and see his reaction.

"Possibly," he conceded. "But finding out is half the fun, eh?"

"I don't consider sticking my finger in a light socket fun." Reaching into her clutch she pulled out two cards and held them up. "The ones I drew from the Gypsy. The fortune on the back of each warns me to beware of a wolf in sheep's clothing. I pulled the same card twice."

"With The Lovers on the face," he pointed out. "And since you suspect your brothers stacked the deck, why do you pay any heed?"

"I don't . . . I . . ." Her words faltered as she looked down at the cards.

"My fortune warns the lamb is stronger than the wolf. Perhaps you should put the two together to make one, and take comfort in that," Trev suggested, finally removing her velvet cloak. Carefully, he hung it on a tree next to an antique umbrella stand. He swallowed against a tightness cording his throat, desire coursing through his blood until it was hard to think. Turning back to her, he flexed his hands to cover their trembling.

He resented Raven's sway over him, hated how out of control he was. In his mind, over and over he'd played the movie of what would happen tonight. Just before he dropped off to sleep it unfurled in the same manner: dazzling Raven at the gala, them coming home to an evening of hot sex, using that physical attraction to bind her to him in an elemental, primitive fashion. Contrarily, nothing was going as planned. Instead he felt powerless, humbled and needy.

His hands reached out and lightly cupped her bare shoulders, savoring the coolness of her flesh. Raven shivered but didn't step away. He sensed she was as caught up in this strange magic as he. They remained locked in the moment, the sound of the storm outside enfolding them in a sensual cocoon.

Compelled to break the silence, he asked, "Do you recall the ending to Little Red Riding Hood?"

"Vaguely. Something about two woodsmen killing the wolf. A gory return of granny to the land of the living."

Trev leaned forward and nuzzled the hair by her ear. "Those Brothers Grimm. I never cared for that ending. Instead I rather fancy Charles Pennault's version. Perchance you're familiar with it?"

"I'm not certain. There's dozens of variations. I never cared for the Grimms' tales or any of that ilk. A bit lurid."

"Well, Pennault's version moved along in the same manner, right up to Red saying 'Mr. Big Bad Wolf, my, what big teeth you have.' From that point, the tales diverge." When Raven was silent he went on, "How, you may ask? The child's fable is designed to teach little girls to be scared of wolves. Ah, but then there are various kinds of wolves, no? In Pennault's shorter but more interesting version, Mr. Big Bad Wolf tells Red, 'All the better to eat you with, my dear.' And then he does. *Eat* her."

She stiffened, catching his unspoken meaning. "As I said—lurid."

"Hmm, you think so? Are you sure, Red? Really?" He whispered against her ear, "Imagine you and me, the thunderstorm raging overhead, me teaching you just how delicious lurid can be."

In the hushed silence, he kissed the side of her face and then nipped the shell of her ear until he reached the lobe. When she shuddered he smiled. His tongue flicked that tantalizing morsel. Sucking the delicate flesh into his mouth, he rolled her diamond stud earring against his tongue, savoring the sensations like an epicure tasting his favorite meal.

Raven closed her eyes on a sigh and leaned back against him, clearly relishing their contact. The velvet clutch and tarot cards fell to the floor. Almost as though she feared her legs couldn't hold her weight, her hands reached behind and grasped the sides of his thighs. Her fingers flexed, sharp nails biting into the fabric of his slacks and the leg muscles underneath.

Trev drew a slow breath to rein in the spiraling emotions pulsing through him. Not succeeding. He needed to go gently with this woman; she was unique, extraordinary, and too delicate. Oh, not physically. He had a feeling she could lock those long legs around him and ride until they both dropped in exhaustion, meeting him stroke-for-stroke, offering all she had and taking everything he could give. No, it was the inner woman that troubled his mind. At this late hour in the game, he wasn't sure why everything was shifting like quicksand under him. Desmond's plans were meticulous, years in the forming. But Trev felt like the proverbial fish out of water. His brain was screaming to do a one-eighty, to give Raven a chaste good-night kiss and then politely leave. Not what she expected. He could send roses, call later and invite her for a beautiful candlelight dinner. He could romance Raven as she deserved.

But then the wolf inside him howled; a violent hunger refused to be denied. Twenty-four hours ago it had never entered his mind to be concerned about her, fretful over what would happen to Raven after his revenge. But twenty-four hours ago he never anticipated the power of this dark fire igniting between them.

Need shook him to the core, made him want to toss caution to the wind. But as he placed his hand on her belly and pulled her back against him, letting her feel how hot his passions ran, he was rattled by the thought that she might not be the only one hurt by this affair.

He disliked all these qualms, all this second-guessing; it was too damn much like Jago fussing at him. Bugger all, a conscience was something he'd learn to live without years past. Nothing but a bloody nuisance! Who needed some goody-two-shoes inner voice spoiling all the fun? Well, he wasn't going to permit his supercilious superego to rear its head now. Blocking out his odd musings, he focused on the delicious sensation of his palms moving up her rib cage to almost cup Raven's breasts.

Oh, so tantalizing, that *almost*. She wanted him to shift his caress, waited for it. Her breath caught on a raspy hitch, willing him to move his hands just a little higher. Instead, he held at the brink, his thumbs brushing the soft under-swells as he allowed the heady drug of anticipation to course through them both. Inhaling the scent off her body, he gave over to her witchcraft. His inner voice screamed *he* wasn't taking *her*, that she was claiming his soul, yet he was powerless to stop her. He did not even want to stop her.

Angry with himself for allowing her such sway, he spun Raven around, intent on taking her mouth in a bruising kiss and unleashing the demons clawing at his insides. He'd let her see the full scale of his craving for her. Instead he stopped cold, gut punched by her fragile beauty. He simply stared, grappling to unravel the specifics of how she affected him, reaching with her craft into his whole being to change his core.

What made Raven different than other women? He'd been with some who were more beautiful—well, who were perhaps *as* beautiful. Only, as he looked at Raven's face, he had a hard time recalling any of them.

He'd aimed to take her hard and fast, with them barely half out of their clothes, on the floor or up against the wall. Raw. Primitive. Animalistic. He'd meant to deliberately drag down these spiraling emotions to an animalistic level where he felt more in control. He was a wolf, all right—one that didn't even make a pretence of wearing sheep's clothing. Primeval mating instincts surged in his blood, nearly overpowering him. Still, another force trumped his intent.

Giving her a half bow, he asked, "May I have this dance, my lady?"

Her lips twitched into a fleeting smile. "Back to the knight in shining armor?"

"Safer than a wolf, no?" he teased, trying to ease the sexual tension. Impossible. His body refused to listen.

In a dramatic gesture, he leaned down, snatched up her clutch and the cards and set them on the table. "Dance with me, Raven."

Her eyes were pulled to the tarot cards on the narrow table against the back of the sofa, lingered on the naked man and woman, the lovers intertwined. "There's no music," she said.

Despite Raven's air of weakness, Trev had a notion she would have dealt with him if he had come at her like a steamroller. It's what she expected. Perhaps she might reluctantly embrace that headlong leap into the flames, because if he played the Big Bad Wolf she could surrender to his overwhelming charisma. The choice would be taken from her. But this switch back to manners was confusing Raven, maybe scaring her in another way: She'd have to make a conscious decision to take him into her bed.

He stepped forward and put one hand lightly at her waist, then lifted his other into the proper stance for a waltz. "Can you not hear it?"

Her perplexity deepened. "I don't hear anything."

"Come, come, you're not trying. *There.* Just audible over the rain. Fairy music. Like tiny chimes of a music box. The Wee Ones play for us on this magical night."

Trev was kidding; however, as he encouraged Raven to strain to hear them, he almost did catch the soft tinkles of the notes of a melody. Somehow, it didn't surprise him. Anything seemed possible tonight.

She laughed as he swept her into a series of rocking steps.

"What, you vexsome wench? Surprised I can waltz?" He twirled her through a doorway and into the open area of the larger greenhouse.

"I don't think vexsome is a word."

"See, I've created one especially for you!" Trev spun her across the stone slab floor, and under the canopy of glass as the storm raged all around.

Raven gasped. "You're making me dizzy."

"Dizzy? You think you're dizzy? Woman, you haven't seen dizzy." He dropped her hand and then scooped her into his arms, turning them around and around in circles.

"What are you doing, Trevelyn Sinclair?" Her hands clutched his shoulders, desperate.

He smiled. "Why, I'm sweeping you off your feet."

Their laughter echoed against the glass walls as he kept rotating them, but finally he slowed and their mirth died. In the center of the glasshouse, amidst her ferns and flowering plants, Trev couldn't think of anyplace on earth he'd rather be. Rapt, they stared at each other, silently speaking volumes yet unable to find actual words to set them on the proper course.

"I could kiss you good night, leave, and then call you tomorrow. Ask you out for a date, bring you roses. But . . ."

"But?" she prompted in a breathless whisper.

"I don't want to leave. I want to stay with you and fully explore the magic of this night. It's not a come-on, but I've never experienced an evening quite like this. My instincts drive me to hold on to the last minute of something so rare." The words almost seemed as though someone else had spoken them. Even so, deep down Trev knew he meant every one. Desperate to cling to each second, he didn't want dawn to arrive and banish the darkness, was frightened all these feelings would vanish like a puff of fog in the harsh reality of the morning light.

He wasn't sure if Raven believed him. Such sentiments sounded foreign coming from his lips. While they were dancing at the gala she'd displayed a jaundiced eye to romance and assumed he was handing her a line. Would Raven take a chance now and trust him? For, despite whatever pale aims that propelled them to this byroad, he did mean his words: he didn't want the enchantment of this night to end.

When she didn't say anything, he asked, scared of her reply, "Shall I leave?"

Nibbling the corner of her mouth, Raven reached up and pushed an errant lock off his forehead. Clearly enthralled, her dark eyes traced the lines of his face. Her hand slowly fell to his cheek, which she stroked with her thumb. "Stay, Trevelyn Sinclair."

She wouldn't have to ask twice. He had played the gentleman and given her an out, something he couldn't begin to explain to himself. So be it. There was no turning back for either of them. He tilted his head and very lightly brushed his lips against hers, savored the softness of her mouth. Not giving in to his overpowering hunger, he gently kissed her, feeling the world shift under his feet.

Fingers of lightning arced around the greenhouse, as if the storm fed off the emotions rising within them. Never had he felt anything as wildly moving as standing in the center of this glass room with Raven in his arms, knowing this instant in time was pure and unique. All the emotion was too much to handle, so he just gave over to the magic.

The fingers of her right hand wove into his hair, clutching those curls; her left arm slid over his shoulder. Raven opened her mouth, and her wicked, clever tongue ran over the curve of his lower lip. He thought he couldn't get any harder? What a joke. His erection bucked in agony, and all the blood left his head in a whoosh.

Breaking the kiss, he groaned. "No tongues."

"No tongues?" Confused, she blinked.

He chuckled. "Well, not until I get you in the bedroom."

"Down the hall—and the stairs are on the right, Mr. Wolf." Placing her head on his shoulder, she playfully nipped the side of his neck.

His heart pounding with the force of his desire, Trev carried Raven through the darkened house and up the L-shaped stairs. Oddly, he again felt the slippage of time: he was a conquering warrior carrying his damsel to safety in his bower. A shiver rippled up his spine, as if he'd done this before in some distant age. Only, as he looked down at the woman he held, her hair was black, black as his own, long, wavy and cascading free. It caused him to pause before the bedroom door in an attempt to blink away the intruding images.

"Duck." Raven's voice finally made Trev realize he'd been standing, locked in the strange spell. He gave a shake of his head to realign his thoughts. Still, he frowned. Never before had he been given to flights of fancy. Casting his mind back, he couldn't ever recall experiencing any. Yet, his sense of déjà vu was so strong.

"Duck? I thought I was a wolf," he joked, striving for a sense of normalcy.

Raven's laughter was soft, husky. "No—duck your head. The door's opening is a bit low, as many thatches are."

Turning sideways to protect her feet, he danced through the door, stooping to avoid bumping his noggin; then he spun them to the bed, which they fell upon. Their laughter echoed through the room but faded as awe of the very special moment filled them. They were strangers, yes, but this choice would bind them and make them more. So much more. They'd be lovers, just like the man and woman in the tarot.

Trev wanted to study this cozy bedroom that would be a reflection of her character, this space she'd consider most private. Only, as he watched Raven's huge, unblinking eyes, that curiosity was driven from his mind. The one thing he did take note of, a detail that shouldn't surprise him, given the rest of the house: the back slant of the room's roof was glass. He started to recall a fairy tale about a princess placed upon a glass mountain, but caught himself. There were already too many damn children's stories running around his besotted brain; there simply wasn't room for more!

Despite the thunder overhead, a tranquility filled the room, as though time was held at bay in Raven's small bower. He couldn't envision a more sensual setting. The heat off her body mixed with the scent of her arousal and the faint hint of perfume. It filled his mind, more intoxicating than fifteen-year-old Macallan. Something dark and profound coiled within him as he stared at her where she lay half under him. Something terrifying.

"Allow me, Miss Riding Hood." He inched down the bed to where he could slip off her red satin slippers. Not glass, alas, they were ruined by the rain like her velvet cape. It was hard to hold on to magic, he supposed. One shoe fell to the floor; then he removed and dropped the other. "Hmm. This is similar to unwrapping a Christmas present. Where do I start? The shoes and the cape are damaged from the rain. It'd be a shame to damage this beautiful dress as well. I believe my clever little hands detected a zipper while we were dancing . . ."

Raven reached out and took his left hand between hers. She ran her thumb back and forth over his palm, raising deep prickles on his scalp. Never would he have thought such a simple gesture could be so damn arousing! His groin cramped with the thick blood of his desire. She stroked the backs of his fingers. "Clever? Perhaps. But hardly little. Warrior's hands, yet hands blessed with the grace of a magician or a pianist."

He reached out and ran his thumb across her lower lip. "You know what they say about men with long fingers."

Ignoring his question, she rolled over onto her stomach and exposed her back. "Are they good with a zipper?"

His hands were unsteady as he spread them across her bare shoulders. Moving down the smooth flesh, he located and took hold of the zipper tab, slowly pulling it along the path of her spine. She held perfectly still, didn't draw a breath as he dragged the metal clasp over her waist, but tensed as he placed a kiss to the center of her back. He grinned against her flesh because no strapless bra crossed its perfect curve.

"Oh, fairy godmothers must like Big Bad Wolves," he teased.

Rotating onto her back, Raven placed her arm across her bare breasts, a shield against his hungry gaze, as he peeled the dress down her body. She lifted her hips for him to drag the garment free, which was almost his undoing. Clutching the gown in his hands he stood, forgetting to breathe. Raven was left in French-cut panties and sheer red stockings held up by old-fashioned Victorian garters. Not lacy ones. No, those would little suit Raven's style.

Absently, he draped her dress over the foot of the brass bed and sat down by her legs. Placing a hand on her knee, he glided it up to the garter on her thigh—just a small strip of velvet tied with a string bow. Simple, but oh so sexy.

"Oh, Red, you do like to play with fire."

Still unaware of the power of her allure, of her feminine perfection, Raven gave an uneasy shrug. "I started not to wear them, but Britt insisted the garters went with the dress."

"Oh, they most definitely go. Remind me to send sister Britt a dozen white roses in the morning." Trev ran his finger around the garter, tempted to pull the string. "Nope. I think they'll stay. Hold it for later. Anticipation can be so . . . intoxicating."

Raven reached up, took hold of the end of his tie and gave a tug. "Unwrapping things can be fun."

"It can indeed. You, Red, have permission to unwrap me all you wish."

She started on the studs of his shirt—which popped and went flying across the room. "Oops. Sorry!"

"Never mind. Trifles, sweet witch. Mere trifles."

A shiver crawled over his skin as she pushed his shirt open and placed her cool hands on the plane of his chest. She was nervous, her cold hands a clue to the workings of her mind. He had a suspicion that her beautiful body would betray her thoughts in dozens of ways. As she had said, she never developed that shield against the world. It would be his endless delight to uncover each telling secret.

He leaned forward, hovering just above her, to relish the rise of male dominance feeding off her female surrender—a mating rite as old as the dawn of time. As he lowered himself down, he caught her breath and made it his, then settled his lips upon her mouth. Their kiss hit his bloodstream, more potent than any narcotic.

Being a newly reformed wolf, he planned on taking this slow, no matter the cost to him, wanting this special night to wash away the scars caused by that jerk Beechcroft. He was here wearing a mask, but he could give her *that* much. Desperately he yearned to awaken this Sleeping Beauty—

Grimacing, he gave himself a mental kick. No more damn fairy tales! This was reality, not some child's dream. When all the chips fell, Raven would be hurt by him and his deceit. The very least he could do was put her needs before his own and not trifle with fantasies.

His no longer slumbering conscience once more reared its head, warning him to pull back before it was too late. Raven had known no part in what caused his father's death. She was an innocent. Using this gentle woman was wrong. So very wrong.

Trev raised up, almost panicked by his damnable

second thoughts. Raven stared up at him, a question in her eyes. Her expression nearly tore him apart. Already she allowed the slurs from that idiot ex-husband to creep into her mind . . .

She surprised Trev. Instead of giving into the damage the creep had done, Raven hooked one hand behind his neck and pulled herself up to him. Timidly she placed a kiss to his chest, used her right hand to push off that side of his shirt.

"Raven," he began, struggling for the right words. "We're strangers."

She nodded. "For so long, I didn't take risks. I was a prisoner of doubt. Yes, we are strangers, but I shall take my chances on you." Reaching down, she dragged her hand along the inside of his thigh and then higher to his groin, flexing her fingers around his hard flesh. His metal zipper cut into his erection, which was aching to be free. "You, Mr. Wolf, want me. I want you. Let's let tomorrow handle everything else."

The small clock on the mantel chimed. Trev and Raven held still, breathless, while it rang twelve times. Midnight. A time of possibilities.

"The die is cast, lass. Remember I tried to be the gentleman."

She leaned close and put her hot mouth on his right nipple, her tongue brushing the sensitive nub like a cat lapping cream. He wanted to laugh at her unexpected boldness, but that would require thought that had fled his brain when she put her lips on him. Even his bloody conscience was silent.

"Red, you really shouldn't . . . ah . . . do . . . ah . . . that." He blinked against the light swirling behind his eyes.

Rubbing her hand up and down his zipper, she asked, "You don't like?"

"Like?" Replies were nearly beyond him as her agile tongue flashed out and drew a circle around his nipple.

"I hate . . . mmmmm . . . love it." He frantically kicked off his shoes, and as he reached for his waistband, her hands were there helping, with him every step of the way.

Their eyes locked for an instant as blue-white lightning flashed. No matter what had propelled them to this point, a deep sense of rightness filled him. Perhaps it was a sense of destiny.

As he struggled clumsily out of his pants, Raven laughed at his less than graceful movements. He retorted, "You wicked wench, go ahead and mock me. It's times like these that men wish they had those breakaway pants like Chippendales." Cursing his stupid slacks, he finally flung them to the floor.

Raven lay back on the pile of pillows and watched as he climbed back onto her bed. "It feels rather wicked, me still in my stockings and panties while you are quite gloriously naked. You're a beautiful man, Trevelyn Sinclair."

"Men are handsome, not beautiful," he corrected, stretching out alongside her.

She shook her head and wiggled her toes. "You are beautiful. Much too beautiful to be real—like some warrior prince conjured from a fairy tale."

"I am real." He slid his hand around her full breast, squeezing slightly and then brushing the distended nipple with his thumb. Unable to resist, he shifted so he could take it into his mouth, his tongue tormenting her a bit more skillfully as she'd done him.

Raven gasped, her fingernails biting into his back. "Trev, kiss me. Make love to me . . . *now.*"

Pushing up on his elbow, he judged her expression. "I'd be delighted, but I wanted to take this slow, make it special."

She bit the corner of her mouth and then reached up and traced his lower lip with her index finger. "If we fail that the first time, we have all night to get it right."

He stared at her luminous eyes, knowing he'd jump off the nearest cliff if she asked. "Buckle up, Red, it's about to get bumpy."

Trev kissed her softly, then deeper, their passion quickly flaring white hot. Keeping his weight on his elbow, he eased his other hand between her legs, dragging it tantalizingly up her inner thigh to that next-to-nothing barrier of the thong panties. Pushing the narrow strip of fabric aside, he eased his fingers through silken curls and then finally to insert one into her silken heat. Her hips bucked, but not in protest; rather a restless urging of more. She was tight, so he moved the digit out, back in, and then out again. As her inner muscles relaxed, he added a second finger to stretch her in preparation.

She wiggled her toes again, sending him the silent signal to speed things up. His body vibrated with a chuckle he suppressed. Shifting so that his legs were between hers, he raised his hips just enough to let the tip of his erection nudge against her core. Breaking the kiss, he whispered, "Next time, we will do this slow." He eased into her body, her scorching fire welcoming every inch. "Very slow."

"My, what a big—" Raven gasped as his flesh filled her. "Ah . . . *oh* . . . you have."

He flashed a grin as he laced his fingers with hers and then pushed her hands beside her head. His whole body tightened as he flexed and drove deeper into her. "All the better to . . ."

Her inner muscles relaxed for an instant, then tightened like a fist about his burning erection as he started to withdraw. Trev's spine arched from the pain and the pleasure. Lightning exploded overhead, followed by the deep rumble of thunder, the fury of nature matching the violence of their joining together. With each thrust into her, Trev had the strangest sense he lost another piece of himself.

When she moaned and arched against him, he lost control, his body bucking as he followed her into the maelstrom of her climax. He threw his head back, fighting the blinding agony, that pleasure so intense it seemed to destroy and remake him. He howled his release.

It was a sound suspiciously like a wolf finding its mate.

Chapter Ten

The wind slamming against the house disturbed Raven's slumber.

Utterly peaceful, she fought to stay in that drowsy level where you're still mostly asleep yet your subconscious perversely natters at you, that place where you cannot hide from truth. As she stirred, aches came alive. Mercy, she was sore—and in places she didn't want to think about! But despite the stiff, nagging muscles, surrendering to Trevelyn had been worth it. Oh, *had* it been worth it. He was an amazing lover, taking not only his satisfaction but ensuring she'd reveled in their lovemaking measure-for-measure with him.

In a small protected corner of her heart—a young girl's heart that never seemed to fully die, no matter what roughness life meted out—she held the silly wish that Trevelyn had been her first lover. How different her life might have been! Yes, they'd just met and she knew little to nothing about him, but she was falling hard for him. How could she not? He had played the gallant, rescued her from Alec's barbs and humiliation twice, even snatching Brishen's magical rocking pony from the fate of Alec's "snot-nosed brat" slobbering all over it. The entire evening she had been terrified he would push her into an affair—which had been his intent. It wasn't hard to spot the calculation reflected in those green eyes, if it was difficult to discern to what purpose. Then, oddly, he had done an about-face and given her a choice. She had a feeling even Trevelyn was baffled by his actions.

Raven knew why. Women always seemed to grasp

these things before men did. As he'd stood on the stoop
and lifted the hood from her head, his expression of awe
nearly knocked the breath from her lungs. The sexual
predator she might've handled. The countenance of a
man falling in love? That was another matter. How could
her fragile spirit shield itself from that?

Snuggling closer to Trevelyn, she quietly savored the
new sensations he brought to her, drank in the simple joys
of closeness—like how good his skin smelled. Not cologne. No, this was something deeper—pheromones, she
guessed; a primeval scent that told her Trev was the right
one for her. She hadn't felt this happy or content since . . .
well, for so long now it was impossible to recall.

Rain still beat down upon her cozy cottage, as though
it never intended to stop. It was a different sound now,
driven, slashing, hard, as if switching to sleet. When she
was a child it had rained that way—heavy storms for
days on end, especially in autumn. She supposed it was
a sign of global warming that you never saw those week-
long deluges anymore. But this downpour would certainly spill the creek beyond its banks and make her
driveway a spongy mess.

She yawned and shifted restlessly in her bed, enjoying
the cozy heat from the slumbering body sharing it. Trevelyn might have a rough time getting back to the main
road in that low-to-the-ground roadster, possibly would
be stranded a day or two. That likelihood brought a faint
smile to her lips.

*Well, there were a lot of fates worse than being house-
bound with a wolf.* "One very virile, sexy wolf," she added
in a low purr.

Lightning flickered close, and for a breath the eerie
blue light overpowered the night and filled the room. Then
darkness fell again, followed by the resounding crash of
thunder. Stronger gusts of the storm buffeted the side of
the dwelling, almost rocking the structure on its founda-
tion. A strange popping and cracking caused her to glance

up, as if she had x-ray vision to see through the exposed-beam ceiling to the thatched roof, which needed replacing. Thus far it held the rain at bay, but gale-force winds might spell trouble. A thatched roof and so many glass walls were vulnerable to the extremes of nature.

Recently, Mac, her father, had renewed badgering her to move back to the safety of Colford, citing those very reasons. When she refused, he demanded she install a metal roof on the cottage. Maybe it was risky putting the decision off, but she clung to the old ways of her modest abode and simple life. She wasn't a modern girl by any means. It was extremely odd that she'd done something as progressive—and dangerous—as taking Trevelyn Sinclair for a lover.

She'd been a virgin when she'd married at twenty-two, and hadn't taken a lover since her divorce five years ago. Not that she harbored any lingering feelings for Alec; the debris field of their marriage had left her emotionally bruised and battered. So much so, she'd shied away from any emotional entanglements. One-night stands weren't her nature, and an affair would require putting herself on the line. Thus, it had been easier to remain alone.

Well, she certainly had flung her beloved caution to the wind this time! Panic surged. What had she done? She knew so little about this man, or what would happen next. This night, despite his beautiful words, could very well mean nothing to him, while already she wanted more.

Unlike most people, Raven loved rain and oddly felt more alive in a storm. Some fey invigoration filled her, as though she could call down a tempest's ferocity, absorb and channel it into her being. When she had lived with Alec in London, she'd often walked in rain showers just to get away from him. Their brellie-toting English neighbors deemed her a mad Scot, but she'd paid no heed to their raised eyebrows and shaking heads. Everything smelled so fresh, so new. Rain always gave her hope, as though the world was purifying itself.

Trying to find some inner balance, she lay listening to the downpour against the windowpanes. She usually found solace in that sound. Only, as blasts of air pummeled the tiny house, a disquiet crept in on little cat feet.

Ignoring her gnawing insecurities, Raven scooted up the bed until she was leaning half over Trevelyn. She wanted to watch him sleeping. Trev was an eyeful, begging the artist in her to capture his vital sensuality on canvas. The curls of his hair were wild; her fingers itched to reach out and touch them. She dared not awaken him, however. Not just yet. There was a little darkness left before dawn—not much, but she wanted to hold on to this night for as long as she could. Once the sun rose, the magic would evaporate and reality would return; and then like Cinderella her coach would turn into a pumpkin.

Curious, how fairy tales had popped up in their conversation all night. Perhaps, because the stories were an extension of human fears, dreams and hopes, they'd managed to strike just the appropriate chord. After all, it was easier to deal with wicked witches or evil ogres than boorish ex-husbands and psycho secretaries; and coupled with that was the deepest wish of most women: to live happily ever after with the prince of her heart. . . . Fairy tales were whimsical and little prepared a woman to survive.

Uncertainty bubbling inside her, Raven felt pressed to get out of bed and prepare for intruding realities. Trevelyn was on his stomach, resting quietly, but when she started to sneak free, one of his long arms clamped over her hip, pinning her.

"Where you going?" he mumbled.

The question and his possessiveness tickled her, banishing a few of her qualms over them becoming lovers. "Where do you think? I'm running off to join the circus to be with Jo-Jo the Dog Boy."

He pushed up on one elbow and flashed her a come-hither grin, one that made her heart roll over. "You don't need Poochy Boy when you have a real live wolf-man in your bed." The glint in his eyes told Raven she'd better make her escape now, or in a blink she'd end up flat on her back under him . . . or over him. And while both scenarios were extremely appealing, she needed a few minutes alone. The man was overwhelming, potent and dominating.

"What I need is a trip to the bathroom and then to get something to drink. I'm thirsty." She pushed at his arm until he loosened his grip on her. Snatching up her teal silk robe from a chair, she quickly wrapped it about her and belted it.

"Hurry back, Red. We still have a lot of 'practice makes perfect' to get in before morning," he called after her. "I think you're ready for that lesson in being lurid."

Raven made a quick tour of the house to ensure no leaks had developed and to check on the greenhouses. High winds were always a concern for the huge panels of glass. Her father's recent insistence on the new roof and safety glass would cost a fortune—likely he counted on that to drive her home. Yes, it would be cheaper to live in the Hall. Even so, Raven couldn't bring herself to go back. She loved it here. Something about this cottage suited her soul.

Reaching down, she patted the silver-gray kitty rubbing against her leg. "Maybe after the galley opening. We can muddle through the winter, eh, Pyewacket? Then we can replace the roof."

Her eyes were pulled to the door on the far side of the living room, the one leading to the smaller greenhouse where she painted. She usually loved being in the studio. The sun, hitting there mornings and evenings both, provided light perfect for painting. She was now drawn to the room yet almost scared to go inside.

Her marmalade tabby, Chester, hopped down off the back of the sofa and waddled over, wanting his turn at attention and nudging the gray puss away. Pyewacket gave him an air swat but relinquished the position without true protest. Always sensitive to her moods, the gentle Chester was picking up on her fears. The cats were likely also puzzled by a male presence within their static domain, since none had stayed overnight before.

Ever since that odd vision of the couple making love had flashed into her mind at the party, Raven had experienced a strange niggling at the back of her brain. Like some half-forgotten memory, the fragment was waiting for the key to turn in the lock before, suddenly, all secrets would be revealed. She could recall the couple, the woman's intense longing to hear the words "I love you." The pain when they didn't come. So strange: she had married Alec and thought once—mistakenly—that she loved him, yet in their months together as husband and wife she'd never once experienced such a profound love as this dream brought. But along with that pleasure came the sudden fear that it might be too late.

"What might be too late? I'm bloody losing it." She started toward the door, half dreading what awaited yet still determined to exorcise her ghosts, prove to herself that she was allowing her imagination to run away with her.

Crossing the living room, she put a hand to the knob. The wind shifted directions, whipping against the side of the house until everything shuddered. Like some insidious intruder, it slipped through every crack in the stone walls, whispering and hissing its unstoppable presence. An instant drop in the temperature followed. Still, as Raven stared at the unopened door, she wondered if the chill was actually from her apprehension.

The top half of the door was stained glass, which allowed her to see slightly distorted into the room through the scene of fruit. The studio was unlit, but she easily made out the ghostly shape of a large canvas on an easel, off to the side. The image on that painting was burned in her mind. Not part of what she was preparing for the show, she'd begun the work one night after waking from a troubled sleep. Wanting to avoid falling back into the vivid dreams, fearful of returning to the same painful images, she'd come downstairs to work. When she'd picked up her brush and begun slapping paint to the gessoed canvas, she hadn't the slightest idea what she'd be creating. At first, it was nothing but dark swirls, similar to fog at midnight. As the minutes ticked away, she painted in silence on the upper right part of the canvas and slowly her stokes became a pair of eyes. No face to go with it, just the eyes. Over the past five months, the eyes had come into focus through her periodic brushwork, but she'd never added more than a forehead and a riot of black curls. Later, below, she had produced a warrior on a horse.

Almost daring herself, she pushed open the door and entered. Not bothering to turn on the lights, her bare feet moved silently across the cold stone floor to the square canvas. She hadn't worked on it for a month, being too busy with preparations for the spring show, thus there was a sheet in the way. She stood hesitating, her hand poised, fearful to pull the ghostly material off her oil painting.

"Silly coward. It's only a picture." Her words echoed hollowly in the glass room. Despite her self-chiding, she stood there, too afraid of removing the sheet. Finally, with a deep sigh, she yanked it off.

Lightning, more distant now, signaled another cell was moving toward them. It flickered several times, the flashes unnaturally illuminating the room. Raven's breath sucked in and held. She barely saw the part with the mounted warrior, for the eyes held her spellbound. As nature's fireworks again lit the sky, followed by the loud crash of thunder, she experienced a time slippage. Once more she was sitting in the Lamborghini, staring at Trevelyn's eyes. Now she knew why they were so familiar. She'd painted them months ago.

I love you. The words the woman spoke in the vision. All the worship, the blackest despair over when she hadn't heard them in return now flooded Raven. It was nearly too intense to bear. How spirit crushing, to hold such a rare and wonderful thing in your heart and not have it shared! Extreme emotion washed through her, anguish so severe that she folded her arms across her stomach and choked back a sob, fighting to keep from losing herself in the strange madness.

"Raven!"

The vertiginous images and feelings were shoved back to a dark corner in her mind as her head snapped toward the open door. *Trevelyn.* She swung back to the painting, panicked he'd see. Frantically, she looked around for the sheet and found it fallen to the floor. Chester was sitting in the middle of it, cleaning himself, while Pyewacket had settled down for a nap. She snatched at one corner, trying to dislodge the fat cats, but silly Chester thought it a new game and clung to the sheet, setting his claws. Pye wasn't moving and was dead weight.

"I'm going to make you two sleep with Marvin if you don't get off," she threatened, attempting to pull the sheet away from the obtuse felines.

"Raven! Where are you?" Trev's voice drew closer. Impatient, perhaps a little worried.

With a second to spare, Raven dropped the sheet and grabbed the easel, turning it about-face so it would be hidden from view. Trev came through the door, a plaid blanket around his shoulders like a cape. Despite her concern over the painting, she had to smile.

"Finally, Red." Concern threaded through his voice. "I had a moment's panic, thinking you had decided to escape into the rainy night after all." He spared a quick glance around the studio. "Why didn't you come back to bed?"

"You're wearing a blanket." She knew she looked like a child caught with her hand in the cookie jar. She'd never been good at lying, so had blurted the first thing that popped into her scattered thoughts.

"I most certainly am—and nothing else," he said wickedly, with a waggle of his eyebrows. "But you should come close, Miss Riding Hood, and make sure Mr. Wolf is telling the truth."

Not sparing another glance at the troublesome canvas—how could she, when beautiful Trevelyn was there grinning—she took in his virile perfection partially wrapped in that blue and pink tartan. Drop-dead sexy was a term that just didn't do the man justice. Oh, she wasn't shallow enough to fall for physical beauty alone, but a power, an assurance of his worth in the world resonated within her. She'd be safe in his keeping.

Giving the painting no further thought, she walked to him.

Trevelyn opened the blanket and then closed it around her, enfolding her in his warmth. She stepped against him, slid an arm around his waist, and then lifted her head to brush her lips against his. So tender was the kiss she had to fight against closing her eyes and giving over to the spell he wove. As strong as the urge was, she wanted to watch his face.

Breaking the kiss, she reached up with her right hand and stroked his cheek. "I want to paint you," she whispered in awe. Her mind harkened back to the images on the hidden canvas that bore such a startling likeness to him. In a strange way, she'd already started painting him. Now that Trevelyn had come into her life, she pondered what direction the portrait would take.

Trev chuckled. "You mean . . . *paint* me? Like they used to do to Goldie Hawn on *Laugh-In*? That reminds me, I once saw a couple of pictures on the Internet of a man. He'd held still while someone had tattooed his"— he waggled his eyebrows playfully—"tallywacker to look like a dragon."

"Don't even go there!" Raven interjected. "I'm glad that computers and I don't get along if that's the sort of stuff you find."

He pulled her to his chest, giving her a hug. "Consideration of all the pain aside, it was an amazing piece of artwork. But you could bypass the needles and the agony. Think of the hours of pleasure you'd have laboring to create such a masterpiece."

Raven couldn't help it. Dropping her hand to his chest, she allowed her fingers to follow the lean, muscular contours of his belly and then lower. His erection was riding high against his abdomen; he was already fully aroused. Closing her fingers around the shaft, she brushed the pad of her thumb over the crown. Trev was uncircumcised, but the smooth tip pushed through the foreskin and was soft. In response to her gentle caress, his cock pulsed and lengthened. She was holding fire.

"I don't think a dragon would look right on a wolf," she said, playfully nipping at his chin. "However, the idea of painting on a new medium has possibilities."

Trev's breath was a hiss as Raven slowly worked her hand down his flesh. "You have no idea what you're do—"

He suddenly made a strange face and jerked his head to the side. For a split second she feared she'd done something to cause him pain, but then he let out three rapid sneezes. Glancing down, he frowned at Chester who was rubbing against his leg.

"Mangy cat," he muttered, then gave another *achoo!*

Well, this was a sticky wicket. "You have allergies?" Great. Just great. Mr. Tall, Dark and Perfect walked into her life and was allergic to her cats.

He nodded. "Unfortunately. Not bad though."

She frowned. "You didn't sneeze earlier."

"I generally don't, unless they start rubbing up against me. The doctor said I wasn't allergic to the cat, just the dander. So, if we could relocate to a room minus felines?" Trev's face contorted, and she assumed another round of sneezes was coming. Instead, he hopped on one foot. "Sonofa—! That hurts!"

She glanced down to see Atticus had come inside. "Stop that! Bad bird!" she cried. The seagull was pecking at Trev's bare toes.

"How about we build a fire in the fireplace and roast the pelican," he jested.

Leaning down, she moved to snatch up the silly bird, but he hopped away. "He's not a pelican."

"No, he's a seagull—a fugitive from the movie *The Birds*. He keeps drilling my toes, I'm going to find out how seagull pâté tastes."

"You've no allergy to birds, have you?" she asked.

"I'm rapidly developing one to this menace." Looking down, he shook his foot at the seagull. "Birds aren't carnivores, are they?"

Raven laughed and then kissed his cheek. "That's so funny—the Big Bad Wolf being terrorized by a one-legged birdie."

Trev shot her a doleful look. "You only say that because you aren't tormented—ouch!— by—damn it!—this feathered Norman Bates. I also might point out that my 'dragon' tends to deflate when my toes are being pecked."

Taking his hand, Raven laughed. "A fate to be avoided! Let's get you back to the bedroom, away from this attack of the killer birdie. He can't get up the steps on one leg."

"What about the cats?" he asked. "They have four legs. They can follow."

"Yes, they can and likely will—but I'll close the door."

Leading him from the room, Raven also hustled her teeny herd of critters out of the studio. At the threshold, she paused to glance back at the painting, troubled by how much the eyes resembled Trevelyn's. Her anxiety shifted as she closed the door: a gale-force blast of wind crashed into the house, and for the first time in all her years here, she questioned the dwelling's safety.

Trevelyn used her arm to tow her back into his warm embrace. "Seems something other than the Big Bad Wolf likes to huff and puff," he said. Kissing the side of her head, he cradled her to him in a manner offering solace.

Once more, apprehension surged within Raven. She'd spent the last five years hiding from life; thus it was hard to totally let down her shields. This was all still too new. Despite the sense of rightness about this man, a lot of questions and doubts were attached. And the blustering fury of the windstorm fed her skittishness.

All cautionary thoughts faded as she looked up into his handsome face. Words bubbled up in her, ones she couldn't contain. "Trevelyn . . . I—"

"Blue, black and bloody indigo! I am going to wring his neck!" Trev tried to push Atticus away with his bare foot. "I wonder how seagull under glass tastes."

Raven laughed. "Stop threatening my poor bird. He's only got one leg."

"Ah, I get it. He resents me because I have two—misery loves company." He waggled a finger before her face. "Next time I come, I'm bringing a cattle prod."

The hilarity of the moment died as she stared into Trev's green eyes. Outside, it was already getting lighter, signaling their fairy-tale night was at an end. It was time to face the music. "Next time, Trevelyn? Will there be a next time?"

The playful grin slowly slipped from his face. He looked at her for so long that she dreaded his coming words. Part of her knew this journey they'd started on would transcend one night; a strong sense of Fate was working, weaving a pattern for their future. Another scared side of her nature feared she merely deluded herself.

Fighting a tear, she looked down, unable to meet his haunting eyes any longer. His strong hand reached out, his thumb lifting her chin, forcing her to look at him. His gaze moved over her face as if he beheld some rare mythical being. "I think, quite possibly, I shall have to one day beat Alec Beechcroft to within an inch of his life. He must answer for his sins."

In a quick move, he pushed Raven's bird aside with his foot and swung Raven up and over his shoulder. Once he'd shifted her weight securely, he gave her a swat on her rump.

"Ouch!"

"Ouch all you want. I am a man on a mission."

Raven laughed, trying to grab hold of him to keep from bouncing as he mounted the stairs. "And, pray tell, what mission is that?"

"Why, I am going to paint a masterpiece," he replied, rushing through the bedroom door and shutting it before the felines trailing behind could slip in.

"Paint? With what? On what?"

He tossed her crossways on the bed. Reaching for the belt of her robe, he gave her a wolfish smile. "You, love, shall be the canvas. And the brush will be my tongue."

Chapter Eleven

Bright morning sun flooded through the skylight, its heat warming Raven's arm where it hung over the side of the bed. The rays didn't touch her anywhere else, due to being mostly buried underneath Trevelyn: She rested on her stomach, his heavy male body half covering her, his chest pressed to her back. His large hand was under her, curled around her left breast. There was something reassuring about his solid weight pressing down upon her. So easily could she envision waking in this manner for the rest of her life.

For several heartbeats she was unsure why she had awakened. She yawned, still exhausted because they'd barely slept all night. Finally, the racket outside intruded, and fussing voices moved through her kitchen.

"There's something to be said about locking doors," she grumbled. Trev was dead weight, pinning her to the soft mattress. She gave a backward push with her shoulders, but he only flexed his muscles to keep her pinned to the bed. "Trevelyn! Bloody hell. *Move.*"

"Later, you insatiable woman. Me and the dragon are worn out." He nestled his face into her hair and inhaled slowly as if savoring her scent, clearly refusing to budge.

"Damn it, Trev, let me up. Someone's in the house." She raised her voice enough to maybe break through his sleepy haze.

"A burglar? The devil you say! Don't fret, love, Atticus will soon have the situation in hand." He laughed and finally shifted enough for her to turn under him.

She pushed at his chest. "Please move. That's my idiot brothers. I have to get up. Now."

"Why? They're aware I'm here, Red. The Lamborghini parked out front is a clue." Offering less resistance, Trev allowed her to roll him onto his side. When she slid out of bed reaching for her silk wrapper, he scooted up to lean against the headboard and watch her dress. "Your brothers may be a bit playful, but they're men. They'll see the car and know I'm with you. If we don't come down, they'll clue up and decamp in short order."

"You don't know my brothers. Subtle, they are not. Besides, it might not be just the twins. Mac is apt to be with them. Lately he tends to take his morning constitutional and wind up here, and invites himself to breakfast." Raven quickly snatched up her hairbrush from the vanity and attempted to vanquish the tangles.

"Your father?" Trev crossed his arms over his chest and considered. "Hmm. I concede that meeting your father under these circumstances could be a bit delicate."

"Delicate? Hung by your heels and kissed the Blarney Stone, did you? Oh yeah, that's one way to put it. He'll probably pay Brishen to stake you through the heart." Raven flashed him an impious grin.

"Ah, but I'm not scared. I am the proud owner of a high-priced rocking pony. That makes me virtually stake-proof."

Leaning over the side of the bed, Raven searched underneath to locate her missing slippers where the cats had scooted them. "Best course of action?" she suggested. "You stay up here until I shoo them away."

"Raven."

"Then you won't have to deal with their antics. Afterward—" She captured one shoe but had to push partly under the bed on her stomach to reach its mate.

"Raven!" Trev's tone was sharp.

"What?" She pushed back out and looked up at him.

Trev sat glowering at her. "While your arse is quite adorable, I prefer to look at your face when we're talking. It's less . . . distracting. Now come here."

She mistrusted that predatory glint in those vivid green eyes. Getting to her feet, she held a slipper in each hand. "I am here."

"Don't get cute, Red. Come closer." Trev blinked as he noticed her shoes. "I didn't know Riding Hoods had glass slippers!"

She waved one of the clear plastic shoes with the teal puffball on the vamp at him. "No more fairy tales, please. Midnight has chimed. There are no fairy godmothers. And I'm just a silly female who prefers to hide from the world—nothing that would hold the interest of a Big Bad Wolf. End of story."

Regret flooded through her at this truth. Raven started to back up a step, but Trevelyn lunged at her, much in the manner of a wolf bringing down prey. He grabbed her waist with both hands, lifting her weight easily despite his being slightly off balance, and pulled her crosswise across the bed. Placing a hand on either side of her shoulders, he planted his right knee by her hip and then the left knee opposite, effectively pinning her under him.

Trevelyn was damn sexy, rumpled as he was and wearing a satisfied half grin on his face. Making love to him in the half shadows and flashes of lightning had been a magical and rare occurrence. Only, now they were in the harsh light of day, in the sharp focus of reality, another experience entirely.

She swallowed hard, envisioning making love again in daylight, imagining it only too well: her moving over him in a pagan rhythm, watching his beautiful face as he came inside her. She wanted to reach up and touch his chiseled perfection, wanted to run her fingers over that sculpted chest and smooth her hands along the broad shoulders. He was an artist's dream. Even so, the second she laid hands on him thoughts of everything else would go out the window. Her brothers might stomp through the house with a marching band playing John Philip Sousa and she'd fail to pay heed.

"Raven!" one of the twins called from the bottom of the staircase.

"Trevelyn, let me up," she demanded with rising urgency.

"Nope." He shook his head. "You're having doubts about us, and seizing on *brothers interruptus* as a means of getting some distance. I shan't permit it."

"Let me up, please," she repeated.

"Not until I get a good morning kiss."

"Raven!"

This time the call was from the small landing in the stairwell. Raven glanced to the door and then back up to the man looming over her. "Trev . . ."

He shrugged. "I'm not budging until I get a proper kiss good morning. I refuse to be hidden away in the closet like some philandering milkman until your brothers depart, like last night wasn't special."

She nibbled at the corner of her mouth. In her rush to head off Phelan and Skylar, she hadn't meant to cast that sort of impression. "I'm sorry I made you feel that way. It's just the twins are . . . well . . . a little lacking in decorum at times."

"Apology accepted. Kiss me and then you can go sic Atticus on them."

She hesitated, unsure how to explain why she held back. Recklessly, she had jumped into the fire last night, with no real heed to the consequences. The time to put aside glass slippers and dreams of happily-ever-afters had now arrived. "Trev . . . I . . . Last night was . . ."

"Raven!" It seemed her brothers' last warning.

"Oh, hell." She tried to wriggle out from under Trev, but he leaned back on his haunches, lightly applying his weight on her thighs. The notion of bucking her hips to dislodge him passed through her brain, but then the pulsing thump of his erection bumped against her lower belly. It was never good to toss a lit match into petrol!

He gave a sideways tilt of his head, saying it was her

choice: she could kiss him, or they would sit here waiting for one of her brothers to pound on the door.

She gave a sharp exhale. "Bloody arrogant man."

Trevelyn leaned forward, triumph flashing in his eyes. "Good morning, Raven." He brushed his lips softly against hers.

The contact caused hunger to roar to life, sending all the usual chemical changes to ravage her body. Her breasts tightened and her womb clenched into a hard fist. Blood swirled through her brain, setting her to burning. Ah, this could be damned addictive!

Evidently, the raw power slammed through Trev, too, because he groaned and broke the kiss.

"Raven! We need you!" Skylar called, ruining the moment.

"Perhaps you had better go deal with your idiot, um, adorable brothers," Trev suggested with teasing reluctance.

Raven's mind was fried. "Brothers?" She repeated the word as if the concept was foreign.

Trev forced a painful grin, running his thumb pad across her lower lip. "Remember? Those junior car thieves with champagne taste?"

She nodded, sliding out from under him. "Ah, *brothers*. Yes, good idea."

Rolling off the bed, she didn't even pause to find where her shoes went. Opening the door, she turned back for one last look at the long-legged, sexy man on her bed, as comfortable naked as he was in the expensively tailored tux. "Mercy," she muttered under her breath, and then went to confront her pesky siblings.

Skylar scurried back down the steps and nonchalantly leaned against the newel post as she came outside. He gave her a sunny, innocent expression. "It's not like you to sleep so late, sis. Usually you're up at the crack of dawn, painting away. We hated to wake you, but need you to tell us where the damn box goes."

"Box?" she asked.

"Your clockwork witch in a coffin."

The fleeting jest fell flat as the word *coffin* sent a cold shiver up her spine. Pushing aside the silly notion and rush of strange images suddenly crowding the edges of her mind, she looked to the front of the house. "Wasn't the road mushy after the rain?"

"We used Brishen's horse cart and came the old way. Since no one drives on that part anymore, it was rather immune to last night's deluge. The wagon is not out front, but at the entrance of the big greenhouse. Brishen figured it might be easier to bring it through from there," he explained.

When she entered the kitchen, Phelan was giving the cats fresh water. He glanced up and gave her a genuine smile. "Coffee's on. Want some? I also fed and watered the kitty-babies. They were complaining. The bird is helping himself to their chow."

"Flippin' bird thinks he's a cat," Skylar sniggered.

"No coffee, thanks," she answered, going to the refrigerator and taking out a chilled pitcher of lemonade. "Let me get a drink and then I'll be with you."

"Thirsty, are you?" Skylar smirked.

"Av akai! Av akai!"

At the sound of Brishen shouting, Raven paused pouring the juice. Her friend came through the kitchen archway, hot on the trail of Marvin. She chuckled at the comic sight.

"The pony doesn't speak Gypsy, Brishen. He only knows you are yelling at him."

"I'll give him something to run from," Brishen threatened.

Skylar stopped laughing and broke into a chorus of, " 'Pony boy, pony boy, won't you be my pony boy . . .' "

"I tell the blasted creature to come here. Does he listen? 'Tis *prikaza*—very bad luck—to have a pony in the house, Raven," the Romany warned.

She chuckled and then took a sip of lemonade. "Don't fuss at me. I didn't let him inside."

Brishen paused from herding the little black horse out the back door, to take in her appearance: barefoot, mussed hair, whisker burns, dressed in nothing but the teal robe. He arched a black brow as he reached out and lifted the lapel of the silk wrapper. "A bit under-dressed, aren't we?" Playful admonishment was clear in his tone.

Giving him a glare, she smacked his hand away.

"Morning."

The single word was spoken from behind them, si-lencing all the chatter. Raven's head snapped around to see Trevelyn stranding in the archway, dressed in his tuxedo slacks and shirt, with only half of the studs fas-tened. She blushed when she recalled why most of them were missing.

Trev gave everyone an easy grin, and then came for-ward to lift the glass from Raven's hand. Swallowing a big sip, he offered her a wink. "Thanks. I was thirsty."

"Funny, so were the cats," Phelan commented.

Skylar's lavender eyes flashed with mischief. "Yes, seems to be going around this morning."

Forgetting about the pony on the porch, Brishen lifted his brows dramatically and looked to the twins. They mimicked him by raising their own in intrinsically male communication. Raven frowned, knowing where this was heading. Meddlesome Montgomeries plus one!

Brishen stopped near Trevelyn and very deliberately looked him up and down. "A little overdressed, aren't we?" he asked.

Skylar nudged the Gypsy with his elbow. "Is this where we—in concerned brotherly fashion—drag him outside and beat the *shite* out of him?"

"Not," Trev chuckled good-naturedly, "if you hope to gad about in my car again." He handed back Raven's glass of lemonade.

"Hmm." Phelan pretended to seriously weigh his prospects. "Let's see—a night on the town in a Lamborghini versus our sister's honor. Tough decision. But then, Brishen really couldn't pound on you after you paid a king's ransom for his horse. Sorry, sis, you're on your own."

"A night on the town *each,*" Skylar amended, bouncing on his heels hopefully.

Raven suppressed a giggle. Lamborghini mania knew no bounds. So much for brotherly love!

Trev started to give a laugh, also, but caught a sneeze instead. Looking down, he frowned at Chester depositing reddish cat hair on the leg of his pants. He reached inside his tuxedo jacket and removed a silk handkerchief, ready for a second round, blinking sheepishly. "Sorry."

"Oh, dear. Possible trouble in paradise. You're allergic to cats?" Phelan questioned.

Skylar said, "Deep trouble. Love my sister, love her pussy." His twin delivered a sharp kick to his shinbone, and he added, "—uh, cats."

Trev suppressed a smile, searching his pocket for his keys. "It's a mild reaction. A couple pills will handle it." He was interrupted by the chirping of his cell phone in the pocket of his jacket. Flipping the device open he answered, "Trevelyn. Yes, Julian, I know. On my way now. Sorry, I was . . . detained."

Raven blushed as his eyes skimmed over her. Feeling the need to shoo the audience from the room, she reminded the others, "I believe you three came to deliver my Gypsy?"

Skylar grabbed an oatmeal cookie from the cookie jar on the counter next to the refrigerator. "Lug that thing and forsake our proper duty as your brothers to grill your date on what his intentions are? How can you think we'd abandon you at a time like this?"

"Sorry to miss the prospect of that fun, but I seriously have to run." Trevelyn kissed Raven's temple. "I truly have to dash. Call you later. Gentlemen, have care with the Gypsy in the box. I still intend to buy her."

"Dream on, Sinclair," Raven replied.

Atticus caught Trev on the right shin as he started to leave, giving him a strong peck with his beak. Trev grimaced and stopped. Reaching down, he grabbed the silly seagull's beak in a small pinch. "You and me, bud. I'll hop on one leg and we can duke it out."

Raven scooped up the puzzled gull. No one had dared discipline him before. "Trevelyn, stop threatening my poor bird!"

Trev winked at her. "Yeah, sure—side with him. Later, Red."

After he'd gone, Raven stood wiggling her toes. She finally put down the crazy bird and tucked away her insecurities. His words hadn't exactly sounded like a kiss-off. *Later* did hold the possibility of, well, later.

The three remaining men stared at her, waiting for her to speak.

"Now the floorshow is over, shall we get the fortune-teller inside?" she asked.

The men grumbled, stole more cookies and headed toward the greenhouse.

"Before we move the box off the cart, why don't you decide where it's going? That way we can shift it with purpose instead of dragging it around to suit your whim," Phelan suggested.

"I know precisely where she goes—in the corner where the direct sunlight never reaches. That way she'll be the focal point of the bigger greenhouse but also protected. I wouldn't want her costume or the velvet lining in the box to fade." Trailing after Brishen and her brothers, Raven glanced out the greenhouse to see Trevelyn's black car pull out of the drive and disappear down her little lane. "At least it didn't turn into a pumpkin," she muttered.

Brishen gave her a soft smile, his vivid blue eyes speaking a concern he didn't voice.

She was glad her friend—perhaps best friend in the world—chose silence, because she really didn't need to deal with him and his questions. She had plenty enough rattling around inside her head. The Gypsy just reached out and squeezed her arm.

The twins had the moving straps and were lifting the six-foot-tall box from the back of Brishen's old-fashioned wagon. Skylar flashed her friend a dirty scowl. "You could help them, you know."

Brishen laughed and turned up empty hands. "You only have two sets of straps."

As the twins shifted the large box with ease toward the right side of the long room, Raven instructed, "Turn her catty-corner. Careful."

Phelan rolled his eyes. "Yes, ma'am, anything you want, ma'am."

"Atticus!" Raven snatched up the idiotic creature, who was suddenly hopping toward Skylar, but not before the bird gave her brother a hard peck on the foot.

Skylar glared at the creature. "Raven, that dumb seagull thinks he's a woodpecker."

"He only pecks people he likes," she explained with a shrug.

"Well, I'd rather he'd like someone else."

Phelan set his end of the oak booth down and then rocked it into place. "This how you want it?" he asked.

"Yes, perfect! I have this small window awning I found at an estate sale. I'm going to put it over the top with a small spotlight hidden underneath. That will finish the look." Carefully depositing Atticus to the stone floor, Raven went to touch the magical booth.

The oddest look crossed Brishen's face as he studied the wooden Gypsy up close. "She reminds me of someone. I can almost place who."

"Here, sis." Phelan nudged her and held out two coins. "You need to christen La Belle Fortune in her new home."

After pulling the two cards last night, Raven hesitated to try again. Silly. She wanted the automaton, so at some point she'd have to face asking for a fortune; might as well get it over with now. Accepting the coins, she inserted one, then a second, heard the clicks and then the turning of the gears. A card was ejected with a loud *clack*, then shortly another.

She breathed an inner sigh of relief when the card she pulled was not The Lovers. It was The Moon, a card that signaled trickery and deception. She slowly turned it over to read the accompanying fortune. *Trust the heart to know what it wants.* A second card was the Ace of Cups in the reversed or upside-down position, often meaning a hesitancy to accept things from the heart. The words on the reverse read: *Listen to the past—for there you shall find the answers to what you seek.*

Skylar shrugged. "At least there's nothing about sheep or wolves."

"No need," Brishen informed him. "The wolf already came. The Gypsy . . . she now shows our Raven the path to tame him."

Chapter Twelve

Agnes Dodd looked up from the computer keyboard, glared, and then removed the half-glasses from the tip of her nose, allowing them to dangle at the end of the gold chain around her neck. The pinch of disapproval set her mouth, indicating to Trev that she was working up to her usual dry set-down. The best course of action when that look was on her face was to sidestep. Oh, she'd find a way to deliver her upbraid, but this made her work for it, was merely one move in their perverse game of cat and mouse. Only, as he flashed her his megawatt smile, he pondered who was really the cat and who was the mouse.

He headed her off at the pass by asking, "Where's Julian?"

"Harrumph." Her black eyes flashed, a glacial stare that had Mershan secretaries fainting in terror when Agnes was in residence at corporate headquarters. Playing the game, she ignored his question and picked up her steno pad and pencil. Any other secretary used one of a dozen gadgets that were really baby computers designed for the palm of her hand. Not Agnes. She disdainfully said newfangled things broke too easily. If her pencil point broke she could sharpen it and go back to work.

"Funny." Following him into the office, she finally deigned to reply. "That was the same thing I heard from Lord Starkadder when he came in before lunchtime. 'Where's Trevelyn?'" she mimicked Julian's hint of an accent.

The accent was just one of the mysteries about Julian

Starkadder, who wasn't really a lord as Agnes joked; it tended to shift slightly, making discernment of where he was from impossible. No one knew much about Julian's past, and he clearly preferred it to remain that way.

At times, Trevelyn resented Desmond's closeness to the man. With so much weighing upon his shoulders, Des needed a confidant, a friend. In some ways, his bond with Julian ran deeper than blood ties. Des had been both a brother and a father to Jago and Trev both; thus he supposed it natural that Des was protective, shielding them from the dirtier sides of big business. But Julian was privy to all of Desmond's darker dealings.

"So, where is Julian?"

Agnes's chest rose and fell with her dry, "Ha ha. That one only tells you what he wants you to know. Surely you've learnt that by now."

"Hmm. I wonder if I can enroll in his Handling Agnes 101 class." Trev set his white bag on the desk and then went to pour a glass of ice water from the carafe on the sideboard. "So, other than Julian isn't about, anything else I need to know?"

Agnes wiggled her pencil back and forth, its eraser annoyingly tapping her pad about every third time. "Dr. Hackenbush—"

"Hack*sell*," he stressed.

She gave a one-shoulder shrug. "Whatever. I think a doctor should have more sense than to have 'hack' as part of his name. My opinion, but it just doesn't instill trust. I mean, would you go to a dentist named Dr. Pain—?"

"Agnes," Trev growled in warning.

"Very well. The receptionist for Dr. Hacksell called and asked if you were going to keep your appointment. Judging from your doggie bag, I see you have. Did you get a shot?" she asked, a smile lighting her face.

"Sadistic woman, taking glee in my misery. Where did Des hire you from again? Nazis-R-Us?" He opened the bag and dumped its contents on the desktop.

Agnes continued on as if he hadn't spoken. "The banking issue was handled on my way in. All this moving money from Mershan to Trident Ventures and then to Sinclair, Ltd., is a bloody headache. Aside from that . . . the decorator confirmed he's coming in the morning to measure the office, though I have no idea what to tell him about that." With a clear question in mind, she pointed her pencil toward the corner where the rocking horse sat before a huge window. "Not *de rigueur* for the perfect office image."

"It stays."

"Preparing for your second childhood, me boyo?" she kidded, smug. "You plan to inform Desmond how much you paid for that trinket?"

Trev ruffled through several papers neatly stacked on the side of his desk, seeing nothing urgent. "Mark it down under expenses for the Montgomerie Enterprises takeover."

"Oh, fancy that! I thought it was a hobby horse—a fifty-thousand-pound hobby horse." She couldn't help it, a giggle popped out.

"It's not a hobby horse. Obviously, Agnes, you're missing the finer points of second childhood. Hobby horses are stick ponies. Sometimes they're called cock ponies." Trevelyn had to fight hard to keep from laughing aloud. "Such as in the nursery rhyme, 'Ride a cock horse to Banbury Cross—'"

"Stuff and nonsense, they can be big. You see them in the May Day parades or with Morris dancers. You're just saying that word thinking you'll fluster me. On a cold day in Hell. I'll tell you where you can stick your cock pony, me bucko."

"Agnes, you're not Irish—"

She waggled her eyebrows, clearly pleased with herself. "But you are."

"Only half," he countered.

Giving him a self-satisfied smile, seeing she had him

on the mat, she inquired, "Shall I send Miss Montgomerie the standard dozen red roses?"

"What standard? *You* never send them." He allowed Agnes to wait while he opened his pill vial and took the tablets the doctor prescribed. He hated pills, but could stand them a lot easier than shots. "No. Send her one single white rose."

"White? And only one?"

There was a glint of admiration in the secretary's eyes—but there was a first time for everything, he supposed. "Losing your hearing, Agnes? I know Des will spring for a hearing aid if you need one. Mershan International has a very progressive medical program for its employees."

"Don't spar with Agnes. You're outclassed," Julian Starkadder said from the doorway. He held up two bags. "Not the Ritz, but damn fine sandwiches and slaw from the restaurant down the road. Figured you might be hungry."

Agnes turned to leave, so Trev called after her, "Don't forget about the rose."

She gave him a gentle smile and answered, "I won't."

"Agnes," he called as she started to close the door. "Cancel that."

"Don't send anything at all?" she questioned. "And, don't give me that static about hearing. It's your judgment I'm challenging."

"That will be all, Agnes." His voice held a note of finality, which told her not to push any farther.

She batted her eyelashes and replied, "Yes, boss. Anything else, boss? Want me to shine your shoes, boss?"

"Agnes!" he growled.

She exited, closing the door softly.

"Corned beef on rye?" Julian made no comment on the running battle between Agnes and Trev, but asked as he took the wrapped sandwiches from the brown sack, "Or ham on French bread?"

Trev realized he'd been in such a rush since leaving

Raven's that he hadn't given a moment's thought to food. His stomach grumbled, so he snatched the beef on brown bread from Julian's hand. Biting into it, he gave a nod of approval. "I'm not sure if it's because I'm half starved or if this beef is really that good."

"Been living on love, eh?" Julian asked, pouring some ice water into a glass and then sitting in the chair before the desk. "So, I take it things went well enough last night?"

"You might say that," Trev replied.

"I meant to pop into a tux and crash the party, just to watch the fun, but decided you didn't need the competition." Julian worried the small gold hoop earring in his left ear. "Me being prettier might've turned her head."

"Dream on." Trev gave a laugh, but Julian wasn't entirely off the mark. Women tended to be drawn to the air of mystery swirling around him. The man looked like a throwback to a time of marauding pirates.

"About me being prettier or turning Raven's head?" Julian gave him a lazy grin and reached for the ham on white.

"Either. Both."

Julian paused before taking a bite. "So? Tell me about La Belle Raven."

Trev used the excuse of having a full mouth to avoid giving an answer. He was torn between wanting to tell Julian everything, down to the smallest detail, and sharing nothing. He'd never had a problem talking about women before. Locker room talk, men called it. Oddly enough, he didn't care to tell Julian about her in that fashion.

"So . . . that's how it went." Julian's hazel eyes shifted from red-brown to green as he watched Trev, unblinking. It was damnable how the man seemed to see all and yet keep his own secrets shuttered away behind that redoubtable stare. He wasn't someone to play poker with.

"I don't know what you mean."

"Don't you? You told Agnes to send a single rose—hardly the style of love 'em and leave 'em Trevelyn. Then you cancel that, for which I have several guesses why. And, so far, since I entered the room, you've looked at the phone seventeen times."

"You're daft."

"No, I've counted."

"I repeat—you're around the bend, old chap."

"It's why your brother pays me the big bucks."

"To count how many times I look at a bloody telephone?"

"I'm paid to notice everything around me, especially what concerns the Mershan brothers. You look at the phone and almost make up your mind to call Raven, and then you change it. My guess: Your thinking of ringing her this soon tells me you can't get her out of your mind. The fact you haven't broken down and dialed her number means you're trying to exert a bit of control, distancing yourself from what happened. You're rattled."

"Get stuffed."

Julian chuckled. "Raven's gotten to you, and you don't like that. It wasn't part of your scheme, eh? You're like Des in that. Neither of you accepts things going against your carefully crafted plans. It's your greatest strength— and your biggest flaw."

As Trev continued to eat in silence, Julian wadded up his wrapper and then slowly rose to his feet. Going to the window, he examined Brishen's rocking horse. "I take it that you barfed up fifty-thou for this to impress the Montgomeries—or was it just *one* Montgomerie? Bloody hell, the eyes are black opals!"

"Actually, I was bidding to keep it out of the hands of her ex-husband," Trev confessed. "His very pregnant wife thought it would be a nice addition to their nursery."

"Beechcroft?" Julian looked surprise. "I wouldn't think Cian would allow him within a mile. How did the worm get on the guest list? I really had to pull strings to see that *you* got an invitation."

"By whatever means, he was there. The bastard tried a

few mind games on Raven, and then accosted her outside the lady's lounge." Trev picked up a paper napkin and wiped his mouth. "Since you're at loose ends and killing time while Des is in Scotland, I'd like a deeper investigation of Alec Beechcroft. I mean everything—finances, how much he owes on his home, his business, his car . . . his bookie. Any complaints from neighbors? What's his tab at the local pub? Something about the man sets off warning bells in me. I don't like him."

Julian ran his hand down the horse's mane. "It's called jealousy, my friend. Likely a new experience for you. You've had women parading through your life, but they never mattered. What was it you told Jago? Never say a woman's name while making love because it's too bloody easy to forget who you're with and say the wrong one? Now here's one that has you fretting over an ex-husband—and buying a very expensive rocking horse."

Trev frowned and tossed the napkin down. "Yes, it's jealousy. The creep should be beaten to a bloody pulp for ever putting his slimy hands on her. Only, it's more than that. There's something . . . off. I'm not sure how to explain. Only, his hatred and reactions toward her go way beyond normal."

"So, I'm curious. How did you approach Raven?"

Trev glanced at the phone then his watch.

"Eighteen," Julian sniggered.

"Actually, I presented myself as her date," Trev finally admitted.

Julian spun back. "What?"

"That scumbag Beechcroft was razzing her about being without a date and implying that she either couldn't get one or was pining for him. I spiked his guns. I walked up, apologized for being late, and carried on as though we were lovers."

Julian laughed, shaking his head in disbelief. "Only

you would run a gambit like that. What did the rest of the Montgomeries think of her having a lover no one had seen or heard of? I'm betting they didn't buy it. Especially Cian."

"I don't think he was convinced. Neither was Paganne. Only, they were so pleased over me playing the gallant and ruining Beechcroft's barbs that they allowed the situation to play out."

Julian nodded. "And you cemented things by coughing up a small chunk of change for the orphanage."

Trev avoided meeting Julian's penetrating stare, not comfortable with explaining why he'd bought the horse. "Something like that."

"Care to be more specific?"

Sidestepping the answer, he said, "Actually, I'd like all the information on Beechcroft as soon as you and your associates round it up. Also, get a listing of rentals—barns, workshops and empty buildings that could be turned into a studio."

"A studio for Raven?" Julian hazarded a guess. "She already uses that greenhouse to paint."

Trev steepled his hands and then laced the tips of his fingers. "No, for the man who created the rocking horse—Brishen Sagari. I think he could make it big with a little push. I want to offer him a few choices for a studio. Something that will accept a quick conversion. Immediate occupancy is a must."

"Trevelyn Sinclair, patron of the arts." Julian gave him a level stare. "Tread carefully, *Mr. Sinclair*. You play a more dangerous game here than Jago does in Nowhereburg, Kentucky, or Des on that rock in the Hebrides. Both places are throwbacks, very isolated and likely care a lot less about Internet and such access to instant information. While Hampton Green is a very small village, and a bit backwards in its own way, the Montgomeries move in high society. Someone attached to them will draw

notice. Or is that why you chose Raven as your target?
Because she keeps to herself so much?"

Trev couldn't stop his eyes from going to the telephone.
He hated to admit that reason had never even come into
play when he considered Raven. It wasn't like him to
overlook details like that.

"Nineteen," Julian mocked.

Trevelyn sped the car through the fading twilight. An
odd sense of urgency drove him to bury the tachometer
into the red, almost as if he raced to reach Raven before
sunset. He glanced over at the white, rectangular box on
the passenger seat. The reason he'd changed his instructions to Agnes about sending the rose: he wished to give
it to Raven himself. A florist's delivery was a bit imper-
sonal. Instead, he wanted to watch her expressive brown
eyes light with pleasure at the small gesture when he presented her with the single, perfect bud. He wasn't sure,
but he had a feeling Raven would love white roses. The
artist in her would adore any color, but white was somehow in keeping with her simplistic lifestyle.

All afternoon he'd fought calling Raven. When he'd
left this morn, he'd said he'd ring, and he intended to do
so. Only, what could he say? Raven and he had jumped
headlong into the fires of passion but they were still
strangers, and after a rocky start to the morning he had a
feeling she'd be furiously rebuilding those protective
walls around her life. Not calling her was also—as Julian
pointed out—his means of regaining a measure of control over himself. Which rankled more than he cared to
admit.

Julian was right. He couldn't get Raven out of his mind.

So being an arrogant arse, he'd put it off until the last
minute. When he dialed her number before leaving
the office, there had been no answer. Well, what did he
expect—that she'd spent the whole day hanging by the
phone waiting for his call?

He glared at his reflection in the rearview mirror. "Bloody fool."

The sun was setting behind Colford Hall as he took the turn. A burning sensation filled his stomach, an ulcer flare of hatred. Even so, he didn't slow but zoomed on past. Seeing the hall made him wonder about Des, how he was doing on Falgannon. There was a bloody fortune at stake in Mershan International's takeover of Montgomerie Enterprises, but it was more than the money that drove Des in this desperate toss of the dice; revenge was a demon.

Before, the concept seemed clear cut. Now Raven was more than a series of photographs and a report. She'd become important to him in ways he wasn't prepared to examine.

Trev swung the Lamborghini into her little lane, growling because he had to go slow, which left him alone with his thoughts. He'd gone through most of his life without being too concerned about how his actions affected others. Outside of Des, Jago and his mother—and maybe sourpuss Agnes—there simply wasn't anyone he cared for. Things were different now, at least with Raven.

The house was dark save for two very dim lights. Pulling into the drive, Trev parked behind the red MGB. Poor thing had to be over thirty years old, though Raven seemed to keep it in mint condition. As he recalled, an MGB wasn't too reliable a car. Of course, it was a collector's item. So few were produced, the percentage of "moggies" surviving over three decades had to be rather small.

The car was part of Raven's rescuing things, he supposed. Trev was glad of Julian's extensive research, for it gave him a greater insight into this unusual woman. Her pony had been saved from ill-treatment at a petting zoo. The seagull had flown into the side of the house during a foggy night. Raven had wrapped him in a towel and rushed him to an animal hospital. The vet couldn't save one leg and said the seagull would never fly again, and had recommended the bird be put down. She'd had none of it, and nursed him back to health at home. Both of the cats were foundlings that someone had dropped and left to fend for themselves.

He shut off the car, sat for a moment and listened as he had the first night he'd come to watch her. That night he'd known Raven was inside, felt her presence even though he couldn't see her. That same sense told him there was now a coldness to the cottage, as though it missed the vital spark of her presence.

Climbing out through the gull-wing door, he closed it and walked to the front of the cottage. The doorbell didn't work, so he used the brass knocker. He chuckled as the orange tabby popped up in the window and meowed. "I guess a doorbell is another of those electric devices that fail around Raven, eh, Chester?"

He waited, knocked again, impatience surging. He should've called early in the afternoon instead of being an arrogant jerk. Standing at the door holding the box felt awkward, like he was a prom date coming to call. He glanced to the side of the house and then stepped off the stoop to look up at the bedroom window.

"Screw this." Going back to the door, he curved his hand around the doorknob and found it turned easily in his grasp. Inside he was greeted by The Three Amigos: Chester, Pyewacket, Atticus. All stared at him, though not in a challenging manner. Chester finally padded over and gave a welcoming rub against his leg.

"Raven!" Trev called, though the stillness in the dark house told him what he had already sussed.

Swallowing his frustration, he placed the box down on the hall coat tree and then strolled toward the dim light in the kitchen. Raven's car keys were on the counter, next to a brochure for metal roofing. No other sign of her was about. Pyewacket rubbed against him, which caused Trev's nose to tickle, but then the puss waddled over to the unopened sack of cat food and gave a soft meow.

"Hint, hint? Wanting bribes, are you?" Trev picked up a knife from the wooden rack and cut an opening. There were two ceramic bowls with the cats' names on it, so he poured them each half full. "Hey, Atticus, you don't have one with your name on it?" The bird hopped over and pecked the vamp of his shoe twice, then pushed between the two cats to steal a piece of their chow. "Silly bird, haven't you ever heard it's not nice to peck the foot that feeds you?"

Walking back to the living room, Trev searched for a clue as to where Raven had gone. Nothing. Irrationally, he wanted her here, waiting for him. A jumble of emotions roiled up. He put a hand to his abdomen and rubbed, disliking the sensations.

"Or, maybe I'm just getting an ulcer," he said, trying to dismiss Raven's effect on him.

Seeing a soft glow coming from the larger greenhouse, he followed the light. Raven had placed a canvas window awning over the top of the fortune-teller booth and hidden a banker's lamp under it. With that presentation, it lent an eerie realism to the mannequin that sent a shiver up his spine. There was something about her, especially the—

A hard peck to his foot broke his concentration. "Damn, Atticus! I almost had it."

He hesitated a moment, then shoved his right hand into his pocket, fishing for a coin. Coming up with one, he dropped it into the slot and watched, mesmerized, as the crystal ball began to swirl. The bluish fog shifted, twisted and began to take on a shape. He didn't even draw breath as he waited for it to coalesce into a recognizable form. Even Atticus pecking at his foot didn't break the spell. Then the mechanical works clicked and the Gypsy opened her eyes.

Trev stared, spellbound for an instant, unable to draw breath. Then it hit why she seemed familiar. The eyes were just like looking into Raven's. The face was similar, though the dummy had black hair, long and wavy. The image that flashed into his brain was of Raven as he carried her up the stairs last night.

A card was ejected with a loud snap, drawing his attention away from the carved figure. When he glanced back to make sure his imagination wasn't playing tricks, he found the eyelids on the mannequin shut. Taking the card he stared at it: The World. He didn't know a lot about tarot cards. The Lovers had been easy to decipher. With this one he could only hazard a guess. On his way to work he'd passed a bookstore, an old church that had been deconsecrated. He'd pick up a book tomorrow.

The fortune on the reverse read:

What you seek is at heart's end—if your eyes are wise enough to see.

When his shin was pecked, he winced and glanced down. "Wonder what all that means, Bird-Brain?"

A flash of red, outside in the garden, caught his attention. Thinking Raven might be with her pony, he hurried to the outer door and out into the gloaming. He scanned the large garden. Part was neat and cared for; the other section encompassing nearly an acre was wild, obviously once part of the nursery intended to supply Colford with the shrubbery and plants needed to maintain its regal splendor. The splash of color rippled on the other side of climbing roses, moving away from the house.

Trev followed. Laughter softly echoed through the warm autumnal air. A time that was neither night nor day, the evening here had a supernatural feel. He almost anticipated seeing fairies flit about, dancing on the last rays of the sunset.

"Trevelyn . . ." His name hung and floated on the dust motes. Or perhaps they *were* fairies and he wasn't looking hard enough.

The melodic laughter and the distant flap of red material

lured him on. Again, he caught site of that brilliant hue—either a scarf or a shawl—as it disappeared into a stand of ancient trees. The air was cooler as he moved under their intertwined limbs, most still holding on to some of their foliage. Dry leaves rattled and crunched as he followed a worn path that threaded through the tall trunks. The scent of smoke reached his nose, causing his steps to slow. More laughter was carried on the soft breeze, but this time it seemed to be from several people.

"Trevelyn. Come."

The ancient beeches, oaks and horse chestnuts were closer together here, seeing it darker, damp. Yet, unhesitating, Trev followed the gentle summons.

As he broke free of the wood, he spotted a small circle of painted wagons. Putting his hand on the smooth bark of a silver birch, he paused and allowed himself to study the situation before charging headlong into the group.

Giving a light sneeze, he realized he had company. Glancing down, he saw Chester curled around his ankle. "Brishen's Gypsy camp I take it, Puss?" he asked. The cat looked up with soulful eyes and meowed.

Pushing away from the tree, Trev headed toward the camp. He approached, noticing the flickering of the flames seemed from more than just air currents. As he came alongside a turquoise wagon, he saw two bodies moving around the fire, creating a distortion of shadows. A man and a woman danced before the small bonfire, their bodies swaying to the haunting music.

Trev only had eyes for the woman. She leaned and then spun in rapid movements, graceful, sensual. His muscles clenched, and he felt as if he'd taken a blow to the solar plexus, knocking all air from his lungs. *Raven.* And she was dancing with Brishen.

Jealousy was an acid that burned in his blood. There was such an earthy, primitive power in her lithe body, such a strength and confidence that it seemed at odds with the woman who'd sworn she held nothing to interest a wolf. "Well, this wolf is interested," he muttered. "Damn interested."

"You jealous?" a voice asked to his left. Sitting on the steps of the turquoise wagon was Raven's sister, Paganne. When Trev didn't reply, her impish smile widened. "Good. I see the look on your face that I wanted to see on Brishen's last night. That's the expression I want a man to wear for me. Brishen's lack of jealousy tells a lot, don't you think?"

Trev steeled himself against the conflicting emotions storming through him. "Perhaps it should tell you that he's a reasonable man and is sure of you."

"Ah, but then no man should ever be sure of a woman. He becomes too cocky then and doesn't call when he should."

Trev just stared at the goddess dancing about the campfire, not sure of anything—except that perhaps Raven was unique and he wanted to possess her, to brand her as his. Oh, he could tell himself they were barely more than strangers, or that as they grew to know each other the magic of their relationship would lose its fascination, but that would be lies. All lies. He could almost hear Agnes mocking, *I shan't wonder these Montgomerie women might teach you Mershan men a trick or two.*

Oh, yeah, this wolf's heart was learning to roll over, sit up and beg.

Chapter Thirteen

"I am Magda Sagari. Cross my palm and I will tell you about yourself, Trevelyn Sinclair." The old woman who'd appeared gave a faint smile as she stopped before him.

"You know my name." Trev was faintly surprised.

She tilted her head to one side, regarding him. "No mystery. Raven spoke of you, as did my grandson. I figured her wolf would be tracking her trail."

By the shape of her mouth and chin, Trev knew instantly this was Brishen's grandmother. His heart went out to the woman who had cared for her grandson the best way she'd known how, same as his own mother had fought to survive and keep her sons with her. Magda's frame was small; her head barely came to the middle of his chest. She was thin to the point of being frail, yet there was strength to her.

"When I was young and pretty enough to turn your head, I said cross my palm with silver. Alas, coins these days have little silver, eh? Still, winter comes and my needs are many. Thus, I accept what the *Gadje* use as payment."

Taking his eyes from Raven, where she danced with Brishen, Trev reached for his wallet. Extracting five hundred-pound notes, he laid them in her upturned hand. Her eyes locked on the bills, and then, with thoughts unreadable, returned to his face. He had only meant to lend aid to Brishen's grandmother. Day-to-day existence couldn't be easy lived in this nomadic fashion. Only, he wondered if he might have presented some grave insult by offering so much money.

"The reading is the same no matter the sum. You possess a kind heart. But already you've proved this in buying my grandson's horse. The money will do good for many children, eh? Maybe help my Brishen in the same breath?" The corner of Magda's mouth lifted faintly, as she curled her gnarled fingers around the bills and then stuffed them in the pocket of her intricately embroidered vest. "Are you left- or right-handed?"

"Right."

"Hold out that one." She took his large hand between her small ones, which were twisted with age and arthritis, and then shifted so that the firelight warmed his palm. "My eyes—*harrumph*—are not as sharp as they used to be. Still, they serve me. See? Four lines of your palm reveal who you are. Your heart line"—she stroked her dry thumb pad over the deep crease at the top of his palm—"begins close to your index finger. This says you will fall in love easily when you find the right woman. Hmm. . . . strange. Another line, fainter, comes from closer to your middle finger. These two merge here. It's almost as if you have known or will know two great loves in your journey. Somehow, they twine together like ivy. Only, when love finds you, sadly you're selfish. This holding back of yourself causes emotional trauma."

Trev laughed uneasily. It was clear the woman was simply giving him a show and didn't know the first thing about his past or present. "Two loves would cause trauma for any man," he jested.

"Go ahead, do not listen. One day you shall understand I speak truths this night. The second crease is your head line. Your mind is clear, focused on the tasks ahead. Even so, you allow others to propel the direction of your life, thus steering you headlong into a coming emotional crisis. This line crossing it signifies you'll face a momentous decision—perhaps life-threatening. It's not clear if you'll make the right choice when the time comes. You are divided. Notice how it forks, as if you are looking at two paths, and then they fade almost as though your fate has not been written, or you have already chosen wrong and must fight to get back to where you belong.

"Do you believe in Auld Souls?" Magda rubbed her fingers over the spot in his hand as if to assure her the lines were true.

Trev answered, "I'm not sure what they are."

"A belief held by many: We have lived before, and we repeat cycles trying to atone for mistakes we made in previous lives."

"Reincarnation?" Trev shifted uncomfortably. He'd never spared much thought for such ponderings, being a person too content with the here and now. The past—especially some vague, semipossible past—was only a waste of time, same as playing games of what-if or might-have-been. Contrarily, images crowded his mind, like a damn ready to burst. He didn't care for them.

"Some call it by that name. My people speak of them as Auld Souls. The spirit, the essence of a person endures and can come again and again. Some souls travel similar paths and are drawn to each other. Some are doomed to this endless pattern because they will not change."

Trev tried to laugh. He was too materialistic, too in tune with this life to worry about riddles from another.

"This is your life line," Magda continued. "Its length does not determine how many years you have on this earth, as most assume. It's elongated and arched, but it breaks here. You face a sudden change in lifestyle. Much of what has brought you to this crossroads are the actions of others. Your fate has been shaped by those who hold great sway over you—a father or a brother perhaps. Again, you almost have two lines. You will be forced to make a choice. The question lies before you: Will you choose wisely or repeat errors made in the last life?"

A shiver crawled over Trev's skin, even if the words were little more than a harmless Gypsy con. He couldn't help thinking of Desmond's blind quest for justice.

Magda's eyes held a touch of pity. She believed. She also doubted that he'd heed her wisdom. *Fool.* He heard the word as clearly as if she'd spoken it.

He turned away. Hunger burned bright within him, and Trev cast his eyes about for Raven. She had stopped dancing and gone over to speak to a lovely woman sitting on the steps of another bright blue wagon. This young woman gently rocked a baby that restied upon her lap. Raven lifted the edge of the colorful blanket back and then gently caressed the small head.

"What you seek you will find, Trevelyn Sinclair—if your eyes are wise enough to see," Magda intoned.

Trevelyn's head snapped back, and he stared unblinking at the white-haired woman. Her words nearly mirrored his tarot card.

"Now, give me your other palm and I will reach your fortune that comes from the soul," the Gypsy said, taking his hand. "I see three men. One has a dark heart and means ill. One has a heart of gold, loves, but knows he can never have. And the last . . . ?" She gave him a crooked smile. "One has a heart of the wolf. He hungers to claim his lady, wants to possess her, and he does. But he will lose her if he doesn't give her the one thing she needs above all others."

Trevelyn wanted to dismiss the woman's words as prattle. He couldn't. "And that is?" he asked, hanging on her answer.

She thumped his chest, over his heart. "Already your heart knows these truths, Trevelyn Sinclair." Leaning closer, she tapped his forehead. "Your mind is cluttered with things that should not matter, ancient business unfinished."

"What is it she needs most?" he pressed.

Magda's body lifted with her snort. "You are a rich man. Coins will never give what Raven needs. Won't give what *you* need, either. Will you be wise enough, *Gadjo,* to make the right choice when the time comes? Or are you doomed for eternity to repeat the same mistakes? Auld Souls come again and again. They seek to put right what they did wrong in the past. Don't repeat the same mistakes. Listen to your heart, Wolf."

"You never said what it is she needs most!" Trev groused.

Magda gave a small laugh. "You do not listen with your heart."

"Tell me—what does she need?" Trevelyn felt a desperation pricking at the back of his neck.

"Love. Your fate line is strong. You might have much happiness before you . . . if you break free of the chains that bind your soul to the past and cease allowing others to control your life." The Gypsy's face was rapt, sadness filling her eyes. Then Magda tilted her head with resignation. "Brishen's cousin has come to stay, with her baby. Come, we go see the newest member of my family."

The old woman took Trev's arm and strolled with him to the other side of the encampment. Strange men and women, sitting before their wagons or around the campfire, watched as Trev passed. Their expressions were guarded, some troubled. A couple men gave a reserved nod. The women stared until he neared, then quickly looked away and refused to acknowledge his existence.

"Pay them no heed," Magda remarked. "It's not often we have a *Gadjo* other than a Montgomerie pay us a visit. Raven's grandsire long ago granted us permission to stay in this grove as long as we want, and as often as we wish. We are permitted to cut trees for our use. In return, we save half the wood we split for them to use at Colford. We do other things as well: help train or care for their horses, repair buildings, thatch roofs and such chores that need doing about the vast estate."

Magda's face hardened as she added, "Some in the village never liked old Sean permitting us to stay part of the year. Grumbled we would rob them blind." She paused angrily. "Treat a Roma like trash and you get no esteem in return. Meet us with kindness and respect, and you will get that back measure for measure."

As they approached, Trev noticed Brishen cutting a long lock from the underside of Raven's hair. He looked up from his task, his blue eyes watching his grandmother. With deft fingers he plaited Raven's severed tresses and wove them into a small circle. Then he slipped the tiny bracelet around the baby's chubby wrist.

"My people believe red hair gives luck," the Gypsy explained. "Since Raven is the godmother of my cousin's child, it gives extra protection."

Trev moved closer so he could view the child. The babe was healthy, judging by how strongly it waved its arm, and the head was covered with a riot of thick black curls. "I thought most babies were bald," he remarked.

"Some are. Some come with a full head of hair. My name is Katrina, and this is my son Emile." The beautiful woman with black hair and eyes spoke. She asked, "Would you care to hold my son? Go ahead. He does not break like glass."

Trev shook his head, ill at ease around something so small and helpless. But hesitantly he reached out a hand that seemed huge compared to the child's black head and lightly stroked the thick curls. "Thank you, but I know absolutely nothing about children. No nephews or nieces to practice on. Both my brothers are bachelors."

As he looked down at Raven, who was holding the child to her breast, a flood of emotion assaulted his mind and heart. Trev understood why Des had never married. Since he'd assumed the job of father to two younger brothers, Des had often claimed to have already raised one family. Jago and Trev had been too busy being bachelors. *Or, we just haven't met the right women,* his mind whispered. But Magda had said he'd fall hard when he met her.

"You look natural holding a baby," he told Raven,

moved by the gentle image. Seeing how she cared for her menagerie of misfit pets, it didn't take a huge mental leap to know she would be a loving mother. Watching her stirred instincts he hadn't known existed within him.

A small tremble ran through Raven's body, and then she turned to transfer the boy back to the waiting arms of his mother. "He's beautiful, Trina. You're very lucky. I'll come again soon with more things for you and the child. And please . . . with winter coming, think on what I suggested."

"She will," Brishen replied.

Raven leaned over and kissed the baby's forehead. Her eyes were shut tight, almost as though she squeezed them against pain. Turning away, she pressed her lips together and finally said, "I'm ready to leave now, Trevelyn." And without waiting for him to agree, she started off.

Trev hung back. Reaching into his wallet again, he took out another five bills. He tucked them into the edge of blanket. "A gift for the child. Babies need many things. Let that help."

A hand patted his back. "You are a kind man—for a *Gadjo*." Magda laughed. "Now catch our Raven before she flies away. She needs you now."

Trev nodded. "If ever *you* need anything, please do not hesitate to let me know. I sincerely mean that."

Brishen hopped a step to catch up with him, leaving Magda to trail behind at her own pace. "I'll walk with you since I need to see Paganne back to Colford."

"Very well." Trev could see Brishen had a burr under his saddle, and figured it had to do with Raven. He almost laughed when Brishen opened his mouth then snapped it shut as if deciding not to speak, for they had reached the turquoise wagon and it was too late.

Raven was at the bottom of the wagon steps, waiting for Paganne. Her sister passed over a bulky sweater she carried. In answer to the younger woman's questioning look, Raven replied, "It's okay."

"You're certain?" Paganne gave Trev a glare full of daggers. "I'm back to not liking you again, Trevelyn Sinclair."

He gave her a winning smile. "Me? What did I do?"

Paganne pantomimed opening a cell phone and punching in numbers. Lifting arched brows, she said, "Give you a hint?"

"I was detained," he offered in feeble defense.

"Doing what?" Paganne challenged, not missing a beat.

"Actually, I was at the doctor's this morning, getting some work done and a script for pills and nasal steroids so I can be around felines." He arched a brow and looked down at Chester rubbing against him. "So I don't end up sneezing my head off just to be with your sister."

"You're allergic to cats?" Paganne's chuckle was musical.

He nodded. "Pet dander, but I've heard you don't get that unless you have the pet."

"Granted—good excuse, but what about the rest of the day?"

"Relentless, aren't you?" he teased, though he figured he deserved a little scolding. "A meddling Montgomerie."

Raven scowled. "Paganne, knock it off."

Her sister ignored her and nodded. "I'm nothing compared to my sisters. You'd best be glad B.A. is in Scotland, Asha is in Kentucky and LynneAnne is in France hunting abandoned carousel ponies. You haven't understood the definition of relentless until you've met them."

"I look forward to the pleasure." Trev winked at Raven, but got a bit of the cold shoulder. "To account for the rest of my day . . . I had lunch with my business associate, and then he and I went to look at several locations that would serve as a nice studio for Brishen." He glanced over at the young Gypsy standing to his right. "If you're free tomorrow for breakfast, you and I might go look. See if they suit your needs."

Paganne beamed. "I think I like you again, Sinclair."

But Brishen's face shuttered, and the Romany hung his hand loosely on Paganne's shoulder. "A waste of time."

"Hardly. The places we checked out are quick converts. We could get you in, set up and professional-looking in a couple of d—"

Brishen's tone was polite but unyielding. "I said it would be a waste of time. Even if I find a place, I cannot afford it, and I have no way to make it look convincing in a week's time."

Trev laughed. "Oh, fairy godmothers are not the only ones who can work magic. Sometimes the Big Bad Wolf has a trick or two up his sleeve."

"I believe I missed that particular fairy tale." It was clear Brishen wouldn't allow himself even a shard of hope.

Trev turned his attention to Paganne. "See he's ready in the morning."

"I will." Excitement flashing in her eyes, she bounced up and down. "I will."

"You won't," Brishen countered. "Leave it. Both of you. I thank you for your belief in me, but we Roma learnt long ago to make our own way."

Magda walked over to stand by her grandson, love beaming from her sad eyes. "Trust him, Brishen. This man is of a kind heart."

Trev shrugged when the young Gypsy remained resolute. "Well, I am buying breakfast. If nothing else you get a free meal."

Raven touched his sleeve at his elbow. "Good night, everyone. I will come again soon."

"Magda, I thank you for your time and wisdom. It's been a pleasure." Trev took the Gypsy woman's old hand and kissed the back.

Magda nodded, patting her grandson's arm. "Come again, Trevelyn Sinclair. You will always find a welcome at our *kumpa'nia.*"

As they started off into the wood, Trev reminded Raven, "You left your shawl. Did you mean to?"

Raven glanced up and paused, giving him a half smile. "I didn't bring one. Just this heavy sweater." She held it up.

"A scarf then?"

Puzzled, she shook her head no. "Why?"

"I thought you were wearing either a shawl or a large scarf when I followed you to the camp," Trev explained, taking the sweater and helping her slip it on.

"Followed? You didn't follow me. I've been here all afternoon, helping settle Brishen's cousin and the baby. They just returned to the caravan today. I had stuff for the baby and some clothing I wanted to give Katrina. We're the same size."

"Then, I must've followed Paganne."

Raven shook her head. "No, she came with me. We've been here for hours."

"Someone was in the rose garden when I arrived at the cottage. She was wearing something red. I saw it flickering in the distance, and followed."

"And came here? Not likely. Gypsies generally do not like the color red. They think it brings bad luck. While they love bright colors, they would never carry that hue to camp, especially on the day Trina and the babe arrived. It'd be seen as bringing trouble to an innocent. Maybe your eyes were just playing tricks."

And perhaps the shadows and light called him by name as well? Trev wanted to argue but let it go.

Chapter Fourteen

On the walk back to the cottage, Raven was strangely silent. More importantly, she seemed emotionally distant to Trev. He had a notion she was working furiously to re-erect those invisible bricks in the wall shielding her from the world that caused her pain. And that world presently included him.

Naturally, he felt like an arse for not calling her. It brought back the words of Magda: *"Only, when love finds you, sadly you're selfish. This holding back of yourself causes emotional trauma."* Which is precisely what he'd done. All his life he'd been so controlled, never having to think of anyone outside his family. Women came and went, and none had touched him as Raven did. Which scared the holy hell out of him! Thus, every time he'd reached for the phone today, he'd held himself back, trying to prove he was stronger than his need to hear her voice. He almost preferred that she'd fuss at him instead of this cold shoulder routine.

Without a word, she entered her cottage by the back porch, Chester and he on her heels. As she went through the kitchen door, she actually shut it in his face! He glanced down to the pussy cat, who looked up and meowed, and then the cat shoved himself through the pet door.

"I wonder if that meow was catspeak for 'every man for himself'?"

Just as he put his hand on the knob, the door jerked open. No longer wearing her sweater jacket, Raven stood there with a sheepish expression. "Sorry. I'm just used to being alone, so things like closing the door behind me I do out of habit." Nervously, she moved to the bag of cat food and picked it up, intending to fill the bowls. There, she paused. "Thanks. It was kind of you to feed them."

"You're welcome. They're quite adept at making their wishes known."

Raven set the bag down on the floor and went to the refrigerator. Taking out six lemons, she placed them on the counter and started slicing them—an activity where she didn't have to look at him. Her hands shook visibly, to the point where Trev feared she might cut herself.

He moved close, placed his hands over hers. "Perhaps I should deal with the sharp object."

Giving a brief nod, she stepped back and stuffed her hands in the back pockets of her jeans. After a minute she pronounced, "I'm not very good at this."

" 'This'?"

She tried to smile and be brave, but her expression nearly crumbled. "I've never had an affair before."

"Is that what we're doing?" Trev asked, finished with slicing the lemons.

"I'm sure this is old hat to you . . ." She stopped when she heard the jealousy in her words. "Sorry. Look, I'm not in a fit mood, so I won't be good company tonight."

Trev smiled. "What say we start the evening over?" He went to the living room to fetch the florist's box. Opening the front door, he stepped outside and pulled it closed after him. After counting to ten, he lifted the brass knocker and tapped out a rhythm until Raven opened it.

Puzzled, she stood staring at him, Pyewacket and Chester curling about her legs. Her expression showed she was a little lost as to what he was playing at.

He said, "Good evening, Raven. I'm sorry I didn't call, but things came up. I'm hoping this will make up for my lapse." He held out the white box with the pink ribbon. When she took the box but didn't respond, he chuckled. "This is where you invite me in."

She wore no makeup; her long hair wasn't styled and

just hung about her shoulders and down her back. The simplicity of Raven was real, honest, and it moved him in a way he couldn't quite explain. She stepped back, permitting him to come inside again, but he could see her heart wasn't in the game. Setting the box on the table at the end of the sofa, she slowly untied the bow and lifted the lid. Her hands still trembled as she peeled back the layers of green tissue paper to find the single white bud nestled on a bed of ferns and baby's breath.

"Trevelyn . . . thank you. It's lovely. White roses are my favorite." She picked it up and held the pristine flower to her nose. Her beautiful countenance brightened a small measure, but the touch of melancholia lingered.

Trev sat down on the arm of the sofa and reached for her, drawing her close. "Talk to me, Raven. It's how we'll come to know each other. You were upset I didn't call. I'm very sorry I didn't. However, since I was at the doctor's getting needles poked into me just so I can be around your cats, and then went looking for a studio for Brishen, I think you can forgive me. So, it follows something else is upsetting you."

She gave him a crooked smile and asked, "You didn't really get needles poked into you, did you?"

Trev chuckled. "Alas, I did. He said it was for the allergy workup, but I think he likes to use people as human pincushions. And I'll let you in on a little secret." He leaned closer and whispered, "Needles are my kryptonite."

"You're teasing now."

"I wish I were. When I was eleven they gave the kids in our school gamma globulin shots because there was an outbreak of hepatitis. I took one look at that long needle and fainted dead away. My brother never let me hear the end of that, and even told my secretary, Agnes Dodd, about it. Now the blasted woman never misses a chance to torment me."

A spark finally lit Raven's brown eyes. "You have a brother?"

"Uh . . . yeah. James," he answered. His heart missed a beat at the small deception. Well, it wasn't a total lie. Jago was Old English for James. His eyes searched Raven's face, but it didn't seem she'd caught his hesitation. To distract her he added, "And he's more than a brother—he's my twin."

The hand not holding the rose reached out and cupped the side of his face, Raven's thumb brushing his check. "Mirror or fraternal?" she queried, studying him with those artist's eyes.

"Mirror—though his eye color is a darker green."

She seemed befuddled to learn he was part of a pair. "I've lived my life as a twin, though Asha and I are so different inside. I never stopped to consider what it'd be like to be with a man who also has a double out there. It will take a moment to digest that."

"While you're absorbing the detail, why don't you tell me what is really upsetting you. I see you fighting deep emotions."

"Very well." Raven exhaled a sad sigh. "It was Katrina and her baby."

"I caught you telling Trina to consider a suggestion you'd made. Is there something wrong with the child? He seemed healthy."

"No . . . he's perfect." Raven put her palm to his chest, tapping him lightly. "I'm sorry. This is hard for me to handle, and likely a subject that will bore you stiff. Perhaps it's best if we just drop the subject."

He held her in a loose embrace, yet wouldn't allow her to pull back, either physically or emotionally. "You're not going anywhere until you explain what's troubling you."

She leaned into his arms, almost struggling, edging toward a light panic. Then, her spirit just seemed to crumble. "Talking won't help anything, but you're a stubborn man and won't let it go."

"A fair assessment of the situation," he agreed.

"Back in the summer, Katrina asked if I'd consent to

be godmother for her baby. The request was a natural choice. I've been close to Brishen and Trina since we were children. I have the power and money to help her child, so I happily agreed. Foolishly, I never considered how hard it would be on me."

"Hard? Possibly. It's a grave responsibility to agree to help oversee a child's rearing. You were very kind to step in to the task."

"It wasn't that actually. Holding him, I . . ." Suddenly, Raven broke away and rushed into the kitchen.

Trev pondered what would be best, allowing her a few moments to herself or going after her. "I'm not a bloody wolf for nothing, Atticus," he muttered to the bird who pecked at his instep. Pushing to his feet, he followed.

Raven was doing busywork. Pulling a budvase from a cabinet, she filled it with water for the rose and, after trimming the stem, put the flower in the water. Next came lemonade. Taking a juicer, she squeezed and strained the lemons they'd cut.

Trev stood in the doorway watching, wishing he could put her more at ease. Their relationship was still way too new for them to read each other's moods with any assurance. He knew so much about her, why she did a lot of things in her life, yet so much remained a mystery. Before, with the women who had come into his life, he had never really tried to establish that rapport of friends as well as lovers. From Raven, he suddenly wanted both very much.

"I'm not going anywhere. I can wait until you're ready to talk," he said softly. He leaned his shoulder against the doorframe to reinforce the point.

She tossed a lemon rind into the sink. "You're stubborn, Trevelyn Sinclair."

He nodded. "And arrogant, and sexy, and concerned. And . . . ouch! Being pecked to death by your menace on one leg. Why did you name him Atticus, anyway? It was Atticus *Finch.*"

"It was a sin to kill a mockingbird in that book, as they don't do anything to harm people. That line popped into my head when the vet told me I should put Atticus down. Poor thing had a broken wing and there was no saving his leg. I almost agreed, but then the silly bird looked at me and laid his head in my hand. I had to give him a chance."

Trev pushed away from the doorway and went to her. Putting his hands on her shoulder, he rubbed. "See, that wasn't so hard to share. Now, why don't you take a stab at telling me what's tying you up in emotional knots?"

She stared out the window into the night. Trev allowed her that much distance. Still, he could see her face reflected in the window glass and knew she watched his reflection as well. Perhaps it was easier to speak to him in that removed fashion, because she finally nodded.

"My marriage—I loosely use that term—wasn't one of the better points in my life. Almost immediately, Alec made it clear he had designs on moving up the corporate ladder at Montgomerie Enterprises. I was supposed to be the ticket to the top. When Cian demonstrated that would only happen when hell froze over, everything began to fall apart. By the time I filed for divorce, I simply wanted out of a dreadful mistake, to salvage what was left of my pride and life. Only, I was pregnant. To some, it might have been viewed as a dilemma. I detested Alec by then, so carrying his baby . . . Well, as I sat alone one night, I realized I carried a wonderful miracle inside of me—that quite possibly it was the only good thing Alec had ever done, one positive thing to come from my marriage. I wanted that baby. I could see myself rocking it much as Trina did her son tonight. There's so much in me that I could offer a child. I truly wanted that baby—*my* baby, not Alec's . . . mine. The stress of dealing with him proved too much, however. I lost my baby, and in some way I lost a part of myself. Holding Emile brought back all that sadness."

Trev slid his arms around her waist, cradling her lightly. Jealousy burned bright inside him. He didn't want Raven having another man's baby. Perhaps that feeling was selfish, but he couldn't quash it. "You would be a wonderful mother. It's very sad you lost your child, Raven, but you can still be one. There's a baby waiting for you, for your love."

She shook her head, closing her eyes against the agony etching her face. "The doctors said it was doubtful I could carry a child after the miscarriage, that it would possibly be a risk to try."

"I'm sorry. Life can sometimes be so cruel and unfair." Trev was speaking to Raven, but he was also thinking of his mother in Ireland. She was battling cancer, and had wanted to go home. She hadn't said it exactly, but Trev had heard the unspoken truth that she'd gone home to die. Life hadn't been kind to her, either.

"If you cannot have a child of your own, why not consider adopting? You could fill your home with deserving children. You cannot tell me that if something happened to Katrina—knock wood—you wouldn't step in and love Emile as if he were your own."

She gave a faint nod. "Holding Katrina's son brought all my longings back. I put off considering adoption, allowed myself to coast here, far from everyone, away from worries and decisions. It's easy to get lost in time when your corner of the world is safe and secure." Raven rotated in his arms, looking up at him. "Make me forget the past, Trevelyn. I need to lose myself in how you make me feel."

His hands settled on the columns of her back, feeling the narrowness of her waist and how strong the muscles were. It had been maddening to be so close to her, to touch her yet keep his sex drive in neutral because of concern for her mental state. Now, a switch had been flipped. Desire burned a liquid fire inside him, slammed into his brain, down through his heart and then his groin.

He moved his hands over her rounded hips. Grabbing the curve of that sweet derrière, he lifted her weight and commanded, "Lock your arms around my neck and your legs around my waist."

With a giggle she did as he asked. Finally, she smiled—and the sun came out from behind the dark clouds. "Okay, I'm locked and clinging. What now? We still have all our clothes on, and we're in the kitchen."

"Hang on. A quick change in locale is in order. Making love to you before the fireplace in the living room popped into mind, but I think my allergy pills and spray need to start doing their thing before I get eyeball-to-eyeball with your cats. Besides, I fear that psycho bird would take the opportunity to peck my head." He gave her a rakish smile. "Once the meds do their thing, I will come armed with a whip and chair."

"You know," she suggested impishly. "I think I would rather like walking like this without our clothes on."

Trev damn near stumbled going up the stairs. "Hmm, yeah. Well . . . we could practice that. Only, I don't think we'll actually be doing a lot of walking around. It'd be more along the lines of riding a stationary bicycle."

As he leaned down so he could maneuver them through the low doorway, she flashed him a shy grin. "You remembered to duck."

"A fast learner, I am. I also remember to shut out all invading animals." He kicked the bedroom door closed and then carried her to the bed. Placing her down on it, he turned on the dim bedside light. Despite this being her invitation, he could see Raven was tense. On impulse he asked, "Do you have a deck of cards?"

She seemed puzzled. "Uh . . . playing cards?"

"Yes, I thought we might make things a bit interesting. We could play strip poker. I promise to lose," he kidded.

"I've never played poker. Well, my brothers tried once to teach me, but I never saw the point of the game." She chuckled. "I do have a deck for Old Maid."

"Old Maid? I don't think I have ever played it."

"A child's game, rather simple. The deck is one I used to play with when my sisters and I were very small."

Trev nodded, sitting down on the bed next to her. "I missed that. To tell the truth, I missed a lot of kids' things when I was growing up."

"Why?"

"There wasn't money for silly stuff when I was a child."

"Silly stuff?"

"Anything not necessary to survival. Does that bother you . . . that I wasn't born rich like you?" He was curious about her reply, though seeing how she lived here, the way she sought out the Gypsies for friends, he already had an idea of her answer.

"Ah. That explains your comment about Brishen not being good enough for the Montgomerie sisters."

Feeling the old defensiveness rising in him, Trev grudgingly conceded. "I suppose. Brishen took one look at me and saw the differences between us. From my point of view, I recognized the similarities in our lives."

Taking his hand, Raven linked her fingers with his. "Tell me, Trev. You see how I make my home, the simple lifestyle I embrace. I believe many of the things money can buy don't have much value."

The answer should've reassured his leftover insecurities. Instead, it perversely rankled. "The things I was speaking of were food, clothing—a safe, dry place to sleep. You'd be surprised at the value they can have. You've never known what it's like to go to bed hungry. To wake up even hungrier."

"It was that bad?" Sympathy threaded her words.

He nodded. "Brishen saw the car, the designer tux and the check I wrote and slapped the label 'rich man' on me. And I am, now. Likely, he had it better than I did growing up. The Gypsies are clannish, care for each other. It was just my mother and my brothers. She wasn't a strong woman."

"Where was your father?" Raven asked.

A natural question, it nonetheless set off the emotions smoldering inside him. This woman was the granddaughter of the man who had destroyed his father. Oh, Michael Mershan had put a gun to his head and taken his own life, but Sean Montgomerie's finger was on the trigger. Trev should view Raven as carrying the old man's taint.

But, that was a sobering thought. Would his children and grandchildren be paying for what he, Des and Jago were doing? Where did it stop?

Leaning close to Raven, he pressed a kiss to her lips. Pulling back, he looked into her haunting eyes. "Make *me* forget the past, Raven. I need to lose myself in how you make me feel."

He kissed her again, slowly, gently, relishing her flavor. His sex drive had always been strong, near animalistic, but this gentle contact pushed everything to a new plane. Raven magically soothed the pain and hurt within him. The pleasure, the sensations, moved through him, shifting with a strange warmth that filled every pore. Her hands grabbed the back of his arms, fingers flexing with the need to anchor herself.

Breaking the kiss, he rolled until he could pull Raven atop him. Her long hair cascaded over her shoulders; reaching up he fisted his right hand in the thick red mass. His eyes roamed over this special woman, trying to define what set her above all others.

Raven swallowed hard. "Why do you look at me that way?"

He forced a half smile. "Trying to pinpoint what makes you so unique, Raven Montgomerie."

She shook her head. "Not unique. I'm a copy of Asha. You of all people should understand that."

"You are no more a clone of Asha than I am exactly like my twin. My brother is the conscience . . . and I"— Trev resignedly tapped his chest—"am the Big Bad Wolf. We joked over that last night, but it's very much the truth."

And wolves mate for life.

Was that what he was doing? Choosing his mate? He didn't want to consider that possibility. He wanted to forget. Wanted to forget the shame of his childhood. Wanted to forget all about Des and Des's plans. Wanted to forget what he was doing, how it would affect Raven and her fragile heart.

Taking hold of her upper arms, he pulled her down and kissed her with his emotions unleashed. He wanted to feel the wildness of last night, the fierce power of the storm sweeping all thoughts, questions and worries from his mind.

Giving rein to that, he took hold of the hem of her sweater and pulled it up and over her head with the ease of a magician making a bunny disappear. "If it were only so easy to dispose of everything else we're wearing!" He started to laugh, only the sound strangled in his throat as he stared at Raven, nude from the hips up. Curving his hand around her narrow waist, he brushed his thumbs over her insy belly button and then slowly up her abdomen. "Wicked minx, you're not wearing a bra."

Instead of being proud of her beautiful body, she crossed her arms over her full breasts. "After you didn't call, I wasn't expecting you to come. I dress for comfort when I'm on my own."

He frowned. Her tone sounded almost apologetic. "Hey, why the shyness?"

One shoulder lifted faintly and fell. "I . . ." She looked down, allowing her hair to spill around her in the manner of a veil. He reached up and raised her chin so he could see her face.

"What's going on, Raven?"

"Another one of those boring details from the past I would like to forget."

"Tonight is about forgetting, so out with this one so we can exorcise it, too."

"I'm not very worldly with men."

"I gathered that, when Beechcroft called you Miss Semivirgin. The man is a complete arse."

She nodded. "One of his ways of demoralizing me was to pick at my physical flaws."

"And your breasts are a flaw?" He couldn't help it, laughter popped out.

She finally showed some spunk, and thumped him in the chest. "Don't you dare laugh at me, Trevelyn Sinclair!"

"Not at *you*, love. At the jerk!" He reached out and cupped her breast, feeling its soft heaviness. "When we first danced, I recall having a hard time keeping my eyes from straying to your breasts. My very male brain, which was very turned on, thought they were *perfect*. And they are, Raven. I know it for sure now."

And he proceeded to show her just how perfect. First with his hands, strumming his thumbs across her already distended nipples, the crests tightening more with each caress, and then with his mouth. He pulled her toward him, laving one hard nubbin with his tongue, then the other. Her head lolled back, and she rode the sensations washing over her in a wave.

Feeling as if his brain were on a slow boil, Trev gasped for air. "Do you have any idea how you make me feel?"

Her laughter was musical. She flexed her hips where she sat astride him. "Hmm. Yeah, I think I'm sitting on it."

He waggled his eyebrows. "Wicked lass—help me out of my slacks and I'll give you a full demonstration."

"Oh, you sweet talker." Eyes flashing, Raven unbuttoned his shirt and pushed it off his shoulders as he sat up. She slid from the bed and removed her jeans, hers hitting the hardwood floor just before his slacks. "I take it you're going to be lazy and force me to do all the work?"

Trev held out his arms. "I'm all yours. Do with me as you will."

"I *will* a lot, Trevelyn Sinclair."

The use of the Sinclair name was beginning to feel like fingernails on a blackboard, a constant reminder he wasn't being truthful with her. In a rush to blot out the overwhelming guilt, Trev grabbed Raven's arms and pulled her over him, kissing her with the full force of his need for her. He lifted her, impaling her with one smooth, strong thrust—as if he were aiming straight to her heart.

"Take me, ride me." While those were the words he spoke, if she listened hard enough she might have heard something else.

Love me. Heal me. Save me.

Chapter Fifteen

He ran through the lashing rain, trying to catch her. What a bloody fool he had been! She hadn't asked anything of him, ever. She simply wanted three little words. Words that would cost him nothing. Words that were in his heart. Why hadn't he given her that plain truth? Why had he kept them locked inside him? Damn, damn and triple damn! His selfishness had sent her running out into the night, and in one of the worst storms he'd seen in his lifetime. You love only yourself, Tashian Dumont. You want my love, crave it, but you give naught in return. *Annie's tearful words echoed in his mind as he struggled to dodge the whipping tree limbs.*

Where would she go in this dangerous tempest, and wearing little more than her thin chemise? Nightfall had been warm, as autumn tended to be. A nice soft night. Then the squall had blown in, its icy rain almost daggers against his face. A deep shiver wracked his body. Bloody hell! He had to find her before. . . .

Before it's too late. The words caused his heart to clench in pain.

He couldn't lose her. She meant everything to him. He had to find her—

Trevelyn jerked upright in the bed. His heart lurched and thudded to the point it was painful; never had he experienced the like before. Wondering what had set off this reaction, he rubbed the center of his chest. Then, he noticed his whole body was drenched with sweat. Between the sticky perspiration and his elevated heart rate, he could pass for a bloody marathon runner. Only, he'd been sleeping. Which troubled him. Why this nonsense? He'd never been so affected by nightmares.

He amended that. He hadn't been disturbed by a dream since childhood. As a small boy he'd worried about his mother's black moods. Once, when he was six years old, she'd swallowed a bottle of aspirin. Des had been furious with her, ranting and screaming one minute, crying and begging the next. It wasn't until years later that he understood she had tried to kill herself. The police had come, placed her still form in the back of a station wagon and taken her to the hospital; the southern town had been too small for ambulance service. After they'd gone, Des had packed their meager belongings and warned Jago and him to be ready to leave at a moment's notice. Their mother had spent her life in fear that U.S. Immigration might send the entire family back to Ireland, or other authorities might take her sons away from her. This irrational paranoia had rooted deeply in him, more than in Des or Jago. Trev's dreams during that period had evolved into vague, faceless boogeymen coming to take him from his brothers. Des had driven the demons away, saying he would never allow that to happen. And Des had kept his word.

Desmond. Trev ran his hand over his face. He owed Des so much, for all the sacrifices his brother had made.

Fragments of his nightmare floated into his remembrance, oddly about chasing after someone. Annie. But, he had no idea who Annie was or why he'd been pursuing her. *Tashian?* For some reason that was the name she'd called him. Bizarre, to say the least. He'd never heard the name Tashian before.

He would have dismissed the nightmare, but a lingering panic pulsed through him, spreading anxiety that he'd left something undone with Raven. He glanced to his side to assure himself she was all right. At once a picture of innocence and sensuality, she rested peacefully, curled almost into a fetal position. Fortunately, his dream hadn't disturbed her. The poor lass was exhausted!

Small wonder. He couldn't seem to get enough of her. Not just the physical side, either. Making love with Raven was . . . more. He loved how they came together, all those sensations magnified because of their rare magical bond. He found it hard to define, but he felt whole when he was with her. She was so beautiful, he wanted to touch her, run his hand down the graceful curve of her spine, assure himself she was real, that *this* was real. But if he did that, he'd let loose his desire and there'd be no rest for hours.

Swinging his legs over the side of the bed, he reached for his black slacks and slid them on. A smile touched his lips as he thought about shifting some of his personal belongings here. While he loved the scent of Raven's jasmine-scented shampoo on her, he had a feeling it clashed with his masculine sensibilities. He wondered how Raven, used to her contained little world, would view his intrusion.

"This wolf is in and won't be put out," he whispered with a note of triumph.

A bathroom was to the right of the bedroom, small, clearly a walk-in closet that had been remade into a half bath with a narrow shower; the tiled stall was barely big enough to accommodate two, but he'd found the close space had a distinct advantage when they'd made love under the slow spray. He hoped Raven would sleep longer, and feared his stirring would disturb her, so instead of heading there he decided to go down to the full bathroom just off the landing. He tiptoed to the door and opened it. Their tails twitching, two grumpy kitty faces stared at him. Obviously, Chester and Pyewacket didn't enjoy being kept out in the hall.

"Sorry, lads," he apologized, as he closed the door to prevent them from going in and awakening their mistress.

"We men are on our own for now. I'll toss you some grub after I come down in a bit. In case you get really hungry waiting, it's my duty to inform you that Atticus isn't really a cat, as you three seem to think." They followed on his heels to the bathroom, but he closed the door in their noses. "Sorry, a man needs a bit of privacy now and again—and to be able to take a whiz without sneezing."

He didn't bother to switch on the overhead light since the two nightlights—one at each end of the room— gave off enough illumination. Walking to the vanity, he opened the cold water tap. As the sink filled, he stared into the mirror, finding his vision slightly fuzzy around the edges.

"Damn contacts must be bothering me again." The faintly distorted reflection, looking back at him with accusing eyes, reminded him of Jago. "Yeah, I know. I imagine you're having a hard time in Kentucky since all these plans won't sit well with your conscience after coming face-to-face with Asha. I feel anchorless, buffeted in a stormy sea. Talking to Desmond tonight didn't help, either."

Trev thought back to the call to his elder brother. Sometime before eleven, Raven had decided to make them a light supper. While she'd been puttering in the kitchen, he'd felt the urgent need to hear Desmond's voice and seized the chance. The whole world seemed topsy-turvy since meeting Raven. He'd figured nattering with Des would set things to right again.

Ringing Falgannon Isle had been a bit of a pain. The tiny island in the Hebrides was owned by Raven's oldest sister, BarbaraAnne—affectionately known as B.A.— and the whole bloody island only had three telephones— at the general store, a pub and B.A.'s residence. Trev wasn't sure where Des had put up once he'd landed. His single brief e-mail from the island gave no clue, simply saying that B.A. was different than he'd expected, though he foresaw no problems with the plans on his end.

"Lucky Des. Unlike me, where problems abound, I fear."

The call should've provided Trev a touchstone to ground himself with the purpose that had driven the three Mershans for decades. Perversely, the brief conversation unsettled him more. Des had been laughing when he'd answered the phone in B.A.'s home—had answered it as "Ms. Montgomerie's butler speaking." Trev lacked the ability to describe the impression, just knew that Desmond had sounded different.

"He sounded happy," he told his likeness.

Trev tried to think back on the times Des had been happy. Really happy. There weren't many. Desmond had always been fiercely protective of their mother, driven to see the three Mershan brothers rise above the harsh circumstances of the life they'd been forced into after their father's suicide. Over the years Des had been satisfied, pleased with his successes, even enjoyed the pleasures his vast wealth could afford him. However, had he ever been truly happy? Trev feared the answer was no. Though only on Falgannon Isle a short time, already Raven's sister was changing his hard-as-stone brother.

"Bloody hell and horse feathers. Agnes was right. What a mess we've set into motion." He shut off the tap and leaned down to push his face under the cool water. He kept it submerged until he needed a breath. Pushing up, he snorted the water from his nose and reached for the blue hand towel in the wooden holder on the wall. Looking at his mirrored image again he asked, "What am I to do?"

"What you should do and what you will do is a gap wider than the Thames. In the end, you will choose what you always did: to play the selfish fool." The voice behind him was harsh, yet there was a touch of sadness to it.

His heart lurched, speeding acid through his system. Had Raven somehow found out about Desmond's plans? About his own deceit? Facing her, the accusation in her beautiful eyes, suddenly seemed more than he could bear. He remained perfectly still, his chest heaving yet unable to draw air.

After a moment, he finally asked, "How long have you known?"

His mind cast back, striving to pinpoint when she could have tumbled onto the damning knowledge, yet he failed to isolate any change or distance in her. Their last time making love had been slow and so poignant that it had left them profoundly shaken.

"Know about your selfish ways?" She laughed, the sound discordant. "Oh, I have always known. Oh, perhaps not at the start. Love blinds a person to what is before their eyes. But you soon delivered the lesson, did you not? You think I would forget? Not for one day did I forget."

Frowning at the odd words, he turned to face the music. And blinked in shock. No one was there. The door to the bathroom was still closed. Now that he thought about it, the hinges needed oiling. When he'd come in they squeaked, yet no sound warned that Raven had entered the room.

The commode area was partially shielded. Walking to the swinging, five-foot-tall café doors, he stood for a second, debating. Finally taking hold of each side, he jerked them open. The compartment was empty.

"I wonder if small thatched cottages can be haunted." He sighed and then smiled, hearing a kitty scratching at the doorframe and seeing a gray foot push underneath. "If someone opened it, you can bet those sneeze-makers would be in like a shot. Okay . . . maybe I'm dreaming and not really awake."

Going back to the basin, he leaned down and splashed cold water into his face. His movements stilled when prickles of animalistic instinct crawled up his neck. He wasn't alone. Staying calm, he straightened and reached for the towel to blot his face. Even so, the actions were absentmindedly, while his eyes searched the mirror for any flicker of change behind him. Feeling silly, he was ready to chide himself for allowing hazy vision and a vivid imagination to get the best of him.

" 'Because he knows a frightful fiend doth close behind him tread.' "

Trev recited the line from the *Rime of the Ancient Mariner* in jest, yet his weird presentiment increased, leaving him sure if he turned around someone *would* be standing directly behind him. Only Raven and he were in the house. Regardless, a bristle of awareness spread over his scalp.

"Bugger this." Tossing down the towel, he whipped around. He was alone. Still.

"By damn, a guilty conscience evidently plays tricks," he mused.

Determined to ignore the niggling sensation, he rotated back to the vanity and opened a drawer where Raven kept disposable razors. He didn't want his beard stubble marking Raven's soft skin when he went back to show her how a wolf says good morning. Opening the medicine chest, he removed shaving cream. But as he shut the mirrored door, his eye caught sight of movement behind him. For a couple seconds, he struggled to clear the image reflected in the glass, not believing what he saw in the shadows. If he squinted to focus, he could almost make out a long-haired woman standing in the corner.

"Guilty conscience? Is that what remains after it's too late?" a woman spoke from the darkened corner.

Trevelyn frowned. "Who *are* you? And how did you get inside Raven's house?" Of course, the second answer wasn't hard to fathom since Raven kept forgetting to lock her doors. The whole of Manchester United could troop through without an invitation.

The woman sounded like Raven, but the voice was of a huskier timbre. Was it one of her sisters, Britt or Kat? He'd met Paganne, and LynneAnne was in France, and the other two were accounted for elsewhere.

"I come and go as I please these days. Nae doors or locks keep me at bay."

"Obviously," Trev replied. "But I think it beyond the pale for one of Raven's sisters to join her lover in the loo. Don't you agree?" He was trying to keep hold of his temper, but having his privacy invaded by a stranger wasn't the best start to the day, and coming on the heels of the nightmare, his mood was a tad bit cranky.

The shadows in the mirror shifted and swirled, yet didn't seem to come into sharper clarity. "Sisters?" Her laugh was mocking. "We be that . . . after a fashion."

" 'We be that'? Let me guess—watched *Pirates of the Caribbean* too many times, have we?" He chuckled. "Enough of this." Spinning on his heel, he intended to confront the intruder. Once again, he faced an empty room.

Stalking to the light switch, he flipped it on and sent blinding light to banish the shadows of the tiled room. He blinked against the harshness, refusing to accept that he was by himself. Someone *had* spoken from the shadows.

Though the door of the shower stall was glass, he opened it. Not liking this game one bit, he went to the large tub and slid the door back, the rollers loud in the stillness. He even checked the commode again. Jerking the door to the hall open, he saw both cats tumble inward as though their noses had been pressed to the door, waiting to get inside.

"Some watch-cats you are. Aren't you good for anything other than provoking me to sneeze? Watch—next time I go to the john I'll station Atticus on guard outside the door. I defy anyone to get past him, that mangy, beak-wielding bird."

He turned in a full circle, confused. While fuzzy visions might account for seeing things not there, his contacts wouldn't affect his hearing. Maybe it was the allergy meds? Some made you really sleepy; he knew from the warning labels on the packages. Those might account for the bizarre dream and the awakening stupor.

"Nice and logical. I like that, boys. I'll get Agnes to call Dr. Hackenbush—don't tell her I called him that—and ask. Too bad about the medication, though. I haven't sneezed once tonight." He headed down the steps, the felines hot on his heels. He told them, "I really don't want to resort to needles, so I might have to stoop to giving you lads a bath with a dandruff shampoo."

The cats exchanged horrified looks, as if they understood what he was threatening. They were cute, he had to admit. He'd never had a pet growing up—one of those silly, childhood things lost because of being poor. Still, like any young boy he'd wished for one. Even after Des started bringing in enough money, they'd relocated too often. Never in any place longer than a year before their mother grew fearful and suspicious, she'd move them, simply to find a temporary peace of mind.

"Poor bewildered Mum."

Trev sighed sadly, and then headed to the kitchen. Without too much effort he found kitty treats in one cupboard. Unsure about how many to give the cats, he glanced at the label to read the instructions. "Hmmm, funny . . . my eyes are sharp enough to read print. You'd think they'd have instructions on how many are okay to feed you wee people in cat suits. I don't want Raven mad at me for overdosing you on Armitage Good Girl Catnip Drops. What? Don't they make Good Boy Catnip Drops, or is that some female prejudice against toms?" He looked at the cats. "Hmmm, *are* you toms, or did Raven have you mutilated?"

Pyewacket and Chester glanced at each other, almost in question. When Trev rattled the tin, they stood dancing on their hind legs, however, so he shook out six pieces each and put those in their bowls.

The pussycats soothed for the moment, Trev removed a glass from the dish rack in one side of the double sink and took the lemonade from the refrigerator. He was thirsty, drank half a glass in nearly one swallow. Tart and sweet, he enjoyed the juice. Lemonade was another of those luxuries missing from his childhood. He recalled a kid down the street opening a stand. Trev had wanted a glass of that lemonade; it looked so cool in that glass filled with crushed ice. Pitifully, at the time he hadn't been able to afford it.

"Ah, well, times change." He refilled his glass and strolled back into the main part of the house.

Having inhaled their treats, both cats fell into step behind him. When he stopped, they rushed forward and rubbed against his legs. "Oh, perfect. I feed you goodies and now I'm the middle of a cat sandwich. Well, they do say no good deed goes unpunished."

He liked Raven's home. It was small and modest compared to where she was born, yet he didn't feel like a stranger here. Odd, yes, but the house seemed to welcome his presence, as if he belonged. He was even coming to like her eclectic companions.

Padding into the large greenhouse, he stood watching the pale pink light of day struggle to punch through the surrounding mist. Too fine to be rain, a spray fell silently on the glass overhead, streaking along the incline and down the clear walls. Nothing disturbed the dawn's quietude, save the faint moan of the wind through the half bare branches and the shrubbery rustling against the side of the house.

Trev stood sipping the lemonade and enjoying the tranquil moment. In a bit, he would wake Raven and share this peaceful beauty with her, but for now he was content to watch the sunrise. Questions swirled in his mind. Not having any answers, he did his best to ignore them.

Chester sat down and leaned against Trev's right ankle, while Pyewacket playfully pounced upon his pal's orange striped tail.

Something jabbed his left foot. Hard. Trev winced. "Good morning, Atticus." The bird made some sort of strangled noise and then pecked at his toes. "I think I need to invest in a pair of snakebite-proof boots to be around you."

Trev set his glass on a table and dodged Raven's menagerie to walk to the fortune-teller's booth. Shoving his hand in his pants pocket, he came out with a coin to drop in the slot. So lifelike it was disturbing, the carved mannequin again closed her eyes and tilted her head back and forth while her hands made passes over the glowing ball. While he watched Trev muttered, "Tell me, what must I do to solve this mess before it's too late?"

He felt utterly silly for asking a clockwork doll for the answers. Deep down he knew what he would have to do. It would mean choosing between Raven and Des.

Des was everything to him—best friend, brother, father, hero. Des had dedicated his life to seeing his twin brothers had the best of everything, had worked a man's job when he was little more than a teen. Despite their mother's best efforts, they wouldn't have survived as a family if not for Desmond. They owed Des so much.

Yet, to have Raven in his life Trev would have to betray him.

The box clacked, clicked, and the Gypsy's eyelids popped open. Almost breathless, Trev felt as if he stared into Raven's eyes. The long tarot card ejected into the slot, and he reached for it with a touch of trepidation. The card was The Fool.

"I really need to get a book on tarot divination," he told Raven's critters, who were hovering about his feet.

Turning the card over, he read on the back:

Risk, danger and sorrow come on the heels of deceit, when one selfishly fails to heed what he can see.

Though he would welcome the comfort, somehow he didn't think Raven's brothers had stacked this deck. He flipped back to the face of the card, and studied the man in brightly colored clothes, blithely moving through life . . . and about to walk right off a cliff, too stupid to foresee it.

He glared at the Gypsy. "I do believe you're calling me a bloody fool. This is the third time this morning. Once in a dream, then by a ghost, and now by a wooden fortune-teller. You'd think . . ."

His words died out as something stirred outside, big as a man, dark, and heading toward the front of the house. Trev exhaled and told the animals, "Here we go again. Rod Serling time."

Hurrying to the front door, he was in time to spot the shadow skirting past toward the far corner of the house. Not hesitating, Trev almost ran to the smaller greenhouse on the opposite side of the living room. As he opened the inner door, he was just able to see the person zooming along the glass wall and then out of sight, rounding another corner where tall, columnar cedar trees blocked his view. Scurrying by a huge canvas on an easel, Trev reached the door just as the person disappeared in the direction of the barn.

Still barefoot, Trev didn't slow but jerked open the paned door and followed. There was no flash of red this time, but clearly someone was nearby. What the bloody hell was going on? Last night, he had assumed it had been Raven in the garden and had followed her to the Gypsy camp. She'd insisted that wasn't the case. Now someone was lurking about the property in the predawn hours, and he was going to find out who!

Since Raven had put the pony up last night before going to the Gypsy camp, someone had opened the barn door. It creaked, moved by a breeze as he drew near. Trev approached with slow steps and then halted outside, watching the wooden door rocking back and forth, half expecting someone to jump out when he placed a hand on the wood. He waited a full minute, yet there was no sound. The morning air was chilly and wet, the mist collecting on his bare chest and back. It was too cool to be out running around without a shirt; nonetheless, he wasn't going to take the time to go back to the house.

Cautiously, he pulled the door back and stood poised at the barn entrance, straining to catch even the slightest noise. When all remained quiet, he continued on, pausing to feel for the light switch he'd seen Raven use the night he'd spied on her.

It was an intense light but just a single naked bulb, and it cast a harsh brilliance across the center of the stable that failed to reach the stalls on either side, stairs leading to the loft, or the old horse-drawn sleigh like he'd seen in Currier & Ives drawings. These cast inky shadows, twisting into odd, confusing shapes that increased Trev's trepidation.

The pony was curled up in the corner of his stall, but stirred and gave a soft nicker when Trev neared the slatted door. He liked to ride, but didn't find the time often. Maybe he'd make time; this was something Raven and he could do some sunny afternoon. He considered if Marvin might like to tag along, but figured those short legs probably lacked the "horsepower" to keep up. He started to share that joke with the tiny pony, but then a board overhead creaked as if someone's weight shifted.

Trev looked around for something to use as a club. He was fully trained in savate, and frequently sparred with Julian to keep in shape; Des knew Mershan International often required his brothers to be in unsafe corners of the world, so he'd had Julian teach them the martial art. Despite this, Trev remained uneasy with such a situation. Something in his hands would lend him a greater sense of control. A pitchfork rested against one stall, but he dismissed it. He doubted that he had the stomach to wield it as a weapon.

Glancing up, he moved to the flying staircase that went straight to the loft. At the bottom he stopped once more, waiting to see if he could detect stirring. Pretending he didn't suspect someone was hiding in the loft, he walked past the stairs and toward the tack room. As he stood beneath the planked floor, bits of straw floated down from between the cracks overhead.

Swinging around, he grabbed the staircase railing and vaulted over it to land on the steps.

Heavy footfalls sounded, pounding across the loft floor, and then there was the loud crash of the loft doors being flung open. Next came the sound of the heavy hay pulley bearing weight on its rope as someone used it for a quick descent.

Switching directions, Trev dashed for the front of the barn. He reached the closing doors just a second too late, and to hear the wooden bar across the doors slammed into place. He rammed his bare shoulder against it, but while the double doors rocked they didn't give.

"Bloody blue blazes," he growled. He could try to shatter the crossbar with a kick, but he wasn't sure the wood would break.

Recalling Raven had used a small door to the side on that first night, he hastened around the stall where Marvin was housed and found the door just beyond. He pushed through, but immediately stepped on a sharp object that cut into the ball of his bare foot. Hopping on the other foot, he cursed and made sure nothing was embedded.

The loud scream of his Lamborghini's burglar alarm was going off on the other side of the house, shattering the stillness of the dawn. Ignoring the stinging pain of his injured foot, Trev followed the racket. As he passed, the front door opened and Raven came out, belting her robe. She frowned. "Trevelyn, what's going on?"

"Go back inside. Now!" he barked. Without slowing, he continued on toward the car where it was parked behind Raven's red MGB.

The alarm was screeching, but no one was around. As Trev approached, it was obvious the car rested on four flat tires. As well, it looked as if someone had taken a set of keys and scored the whole side, ruining the paint job.

Fishing in his pocket, Trev pulled out the key ring with the remote control to silence the irritating Gallardo car alarm. Then he walked around the vehicle, looking at the tracks in the wet grass. The footprints moved up to the car, circled around, and then led away. Trev followed them to the driveway entrance. Looking in both directions, he tried to get a fix on which way the intruder had gone, but the roadway was so broken and crumbly it was impossible to tell.

"Trevelyn, what's happened to your car?"

He turned to see Raven standing by the black roadster, her face ashen as she surveyed the damage. Giving up his chase, Trev stalked back. "Bloody woman. I ordered you back inside."

"You'll find, Trevelyn Sinclair, I don't take orders well."

"In an instance like this—owww!" His tirade was cut short as he stepped on a large stone precisely where his foot was cut. Cursing under his breath, he put a hand on her shoulder for balance. When he looked up, Atticus was hopping ironically toward them. "Double damn. Bet he's happy now. I'm on one foot, too," he teased.

"Trevelyn. What just happened?" Raven pressed.

He glanced around, not convinced the intruder was gone. Too vividly he recalled how he'd tracked her that first night, hidden behind the oak trees and stood close enough to reach out and touch her. Well, her safe bubble was no longer safe. Right away, he'd get with Julian and discuss what safety measure could be taken without rattling her too much.

"Let's get inside before Bird-Brain decides to peck at my remaining good foot."

"Can you walk?" Raven asked.

He nodded. "Let me use you for balance, then I can hobble on just the heel."

Taking a cue from him, she remained silent until they

were inside and she'd closed the door. "Come, I need to soak that foot and get the dirt out." As they went through to the kitchen, she stopped and broke into a peal of laughter.

Halting, Trev frowned at her. "It's not nice to laugh at another's injury, no matter how much an idiot you think I am for running around barefoot outside."

"Sorry—I'm not. Really. It's just watching you and Atticus is quite amusing. You hop a step. Then he hops a step." The chuckles came again. Raven pulled a stool from the corner and pointed. "Sit."

"Me or the bird?" Trev asked. "You will find, Raven Montgomerie, that I don't take orders well, either."

That said, Trev sat, watching Raven gather a deep rubber pan, place several things in it and pick that up along with a roll of paper towel. She knelt before him and placed his injured foot in the tub, then poured half a bottle of peroxide over his foot. As the fluid trickled off and filled the pan, she picked up a thing that looked like a huge eyedropper.

"What the hell is that?" It reminded him too much of that damn needle and syringe they used for the gamma globulin shot.

She eyed him knowingly and smiled. "It's a turkey-baster. I'm going to use it to flood the cut, to force dirt out of the wound."

Atticus pecked at Trev's other foot and then twisted his head sideways, looking at him.

Trev glared at the weird creature. "No, Atticus, I am not a turkey."

Raven sniggered. "That's up for debate at the moment. Anyone running around half naked and wearing no shoes on a chilly, damp morning might be considered to have the sense of a turkey. How did you cut your foot— other than being a bloody fool out dashing about shoeless?"

"Four," he muttered.

Raven blinked in confusion. "Four what?"

"Fourth time someone has called me a fool this morning." Seeking to distract her he said, "I'm not sure what I cut my foot on. I stepped on something coming out of the barn—"

"Barn!" she gasped. "Oh, Trevelyn, we have to rush you to hospital. You'll need a tetanus shot immediately."

"Shot!" He shook his head, horrified.

She patted his arm as she rose. "Sorry, there's no way around it. You need a tetanus shot. You've likely had a vaccination at some point in your life, but it may have expired. You shouldn't take any chances. The doctor may give you a second one called tetanus-immune globulin. They did when I jabbed myself on a rusty nail."

"Globulin?" Spots appeared before his eyes.

"Here, let me wrap the foot and then I'll call Colford and get someone to come drive us. I cannot get the MGB around that black monster of yours, which isn't going anywhere with four flats."

Trevelyn recalled the tarot card he'd dropped on the greenhouse floor: The Fool. Seems he *had* blithely stepped off that cliff.

Chapter Sixteen

"So what do you think?" Paganne asked later that morning as she parked her bum atop the high wall. She kicked the heels of her Wellies against the stone side, and excitement flashed in her eyes.

Raven barely spared her sister a glance. Her mind was running through the possibilities of the enormous task of converting this deconsecrated church into a studio for Brishen, who was walking around it with Trevelyn at that very moment. "With a little imagination it could be perfect. But, in a week?"

"Don't be obtuse. Not the church, silly. The *man*." Paganne gnawed on her lower lip, awaiting an answer. When none came she said, "He was there at the cottage yesterday morning when Brishen and the twins delivered the fortune-teller booth. And then at dawn, Colford gets a *one ringy dingy, two ringy dingy* saying that you urgently require someone to drive you and Mr. Tall, Dark and Incredibly Sexy to hospital. Whatever were you doing that sent Trev to emergency?"

"I'm not entirely sure." And Raven wasn't. Trevelyn had answered some questions as to why he'd been out in the mist, half dressed and with no shoes, yet she had a sense he wasn't telling her everything. "Someone was prowling around the cottage at dawn, and he tried to catch whoever it was. The person ran into the barn, Trevelyn went in after them and ended up cutting his foot on a piece of glass. I had to rush him to emergency. They gave him two shots and put four stitches in the wound. Poor baby, the instant he saw the needles he nearly passed out."

Paganne's laugh was musical. "Oh, that's funny! Willing to leap buildings in a single bound to run down evildoers—in his bare feet no less—and yet, faced with a long, pointy object he breaks out in a cold sweat. I love it! I simply love it! The man seemed too damn perfect. I don't trust perfect men because they generally aren't. Now that he has a flaw, I'll cut him some slack."

"More than one. You're forgetting he mentioned he has an allergy to Pye and Chester. The doctor prescribed pills and a nasal steroid, but he's afraid it will come to more needles if those fail to work." Raven chuckled.

"Trevelyn Sinclair is so handsome it makes your teeth hurt, rich, and totally wrapped up in you. I really could hate him. I admit it, I'm jealous. But I like how he is with you—how he's trying to help Brishen. Oh, *we* have the money to set Brishen up with a studio, help Magda and Katrina. But will they accept *our* aid? Don't waste your breath with an answer. You know Brishen's spiel, 'We Roma take care of ourselves.' I have my fingers crossed he'll accept Trev's helping hand with the studio. This break could mean so much for him, if only he doesn't allow his pride to get in the way."

"I'm hoping he listens to reason this time," Raven agreed. She bent over and picked up a weed and began to pluck its petals. *He loves me, he loves me not, he loves me* . . . Not wanting to know, she flung it away.

"'He loves me' was the answer," Paganne smugly informed her. "I counted the petals."

Raven flashed her sister a glare. "Brat. You were always too clever by half."

"Merely an interested bystander. I won't ask if you are falling for him. That he made it to your bed tells me everything. I just don't want you hurt," Paganne stated.

"I've hidden from the world since the divorce. I'm risking a lot on this toss of the dice, but . . ." Raven shrugged, not sure how to explain. "Being with Trevelyn feels right."

"You want to talk about the painting? I've seen it, you

know. I didn't believe you knew Trevelyn Sinclair before he magically appeared at your elbow at the gala. Only, last night I recalled the painting. It's him, isn't it? So, you have known him longer and have been keeping mum." Paganne rocked on the wall, waiting for an answer.

"My, aren't you nosy this morning?" Raven arched a brow, letting her little sister know that she'd crossed a line.

"Very well, I shall keep my mouthy mouth shut. I'm just hoping Trev can get through to Brishen. His carvings are brilliant, and he wants this so bad. Magda needs to be in a true home this winter. She's getting too old for her traveling ways. Part of him knows this. Part doesn't want to admit she's gotten weaker. He thinks he can hold time at bay by ignoring what's before his eyes. He's so damn proud." Paganne's eyes followed Brishen with both love and sadness.

"He's a good man, Paganne. I think he'd give up his Roma ways if you'd have him," Raven said.

Paganne wriggled her shoulders and gave a small kick with the side of her foot. "You're one to talk. He was yours for the taking. So why didn't *you* take him?"

"I love Brishen, but as a brother. Deep down I knew that, and I think he knew it, too. In the long run we would've ended up unhappy," Raven replied.

Her sister gave a nod. "So why should it be different for me? It could be—if he only looked at me the way Trev does you. Sadly, that's the reason in a nutshell. I know someday some lucky woman will breeze into his life and Brishen will look at her in that special way. I didn't want to be married to him when that happens, even if he is too honorable to ever leave me. *Especially* then."

Raven squeezed her sister's thigh in comfort, seeing the tear glittering in Paganne's eye.

The tear she was struggling to fight.

"As I said, you're too clever by half. Did I ever tell you that I am proud to be your sister?"

That brought a smile to Paganne's face. "No. I recall

something along the lines of being called 'you dingy bilge rat,' and a few other choice terms."

"Ah, that was when you cut my hair. I asked you to take off a couple inches, get rid of the split ends, and you turned me into David Bowie. I had to go to school looking like that!"

Paganne chuckled. "You were rather angry."

"I had a right. I'd been scalped."

"The ends were split worse than you thought—but it was still fun." She gave an impish grin, then a small push and dropped down to her feet. "Let's go see if your Trevelyn has magic enough to soothe our proud Gypsy. They haven't resorted to squatting. When men squat and talk it gets serious. I can't see how they can stand to do that for so long."

Trevelyn and Brishen turned as they approached. Handsome, confident men. Alpha males in the purest form. Raven's heart squeezed at the sight of Trevelyn. Yeah, she was falling for him. Falling hard. Everything was moving too fast, but for once she embraced that danger and hoped in the end she'd be a winner.

"Notice those laserlike glances of appraisal? The 'we Tarzan, you Jane' sort of stares? Men!" Paganne sighed, putting a hand to her heart. "It should be illegal for these two to stand next to each other. It's not safe for a woman's hormones."

Raven found the men's expressions hard to read, so she spoke to all three. "At least Brishen isn't gesturing with his hands. When he gets his dander up, he really uses his hands to state his case. Thus, I am guessing you're at least listening to Trevelyn, eh?"

Brishen gave her his inscrutable Roma stare. "We are discussing things."

"So, discuss aloud." Paganne put her hand on Brishen's shoulder and rubbed lightly. "Then we highly intelligent females shall tell you what you need to do."

"Highly intelligent females?" Brishen laughed. He turned

to Trev and informed him, "They call them the meddling Montgomeries—a label well-earned, you will learn."

Paganne poked Brishen in the ribs with her finger. "Stop stalling and tell us. We are dying of curiosity."

Trev stepped closer to Raven. He was using a cane they'd given him at the hospital to keep weight off the ball of his foot for a couple days. "I really think this place has possibilities. The others would serve, but this one has more room and comes with the house attached." He nodded in the direction of the large cottage to the far side. "That was the parsonage. It's part of the property. The price is reasonable. I can set it up for Brishen to either freehold or lease. Whatever he wants."

"The house comes with it?" Paganne asked, delighted. "Oh, Brishen, that would mean—"

Brishen turned to her with a silencing stare. "Don't pressure me, Paganne. This is a big step. Even if I say yes, there's no way to get this place presentable to impress the art people in a week."

"But it doesn't have to be perfect, Brishen," Raven said. "You can tell them you're in the middle of relocating—which is the truth. Skylar and Phelan can help. You know Paganne and I will. And think what wonders your Roma can do in a week."

Brishen's vivid blue eyes examined the outside of the building and then shifted almost unwillingly to the parsonage. Raven knew him well enough to see he was tempted, also recognized the house was tipping the scales. It would be perfect for Magda and Katrina.

"But, a church?" he said. "Somehow that seems casting fate to the wind."

"It's not a church along longer—hasn't been for a long time. Nearly thirty years. It's already seen a theatre troop using it. I'm sorry about pressing you for a decision, but a bookstore owner is hot for the lease. We have to move quickly." Trevelyn reached out for Raven's hand, pulling her close and saying, "Talk to your friend. The price is very reasonable. I'm more than willing to underwrite this venture in whatever manner his stubborn pride will allow."

Raven loved that Trevelyn had wanted to touch her; she'd wished to embrace a lover's familiarity but wasn't sure Trev would approve. Some men didn't. That he'd initiated the contact made it all the more special. When she glanced up, meeting his eyes, she loved what she saw there. Maybe risk-taking wasn't such a scary prospect after all.

"Steeple Hill Studio," Paganne announced. "I think you're a fool, Brishen Sagari, if you don't jump at this chance. Pride is all we have sometimes, but don't allow that to stand in the way of bringing your dream into reality. You've planned for this, worked for it."

He looked miserable. "A week?"

"I can get workers in here today," Trev spoke up. "I'll ring the real estate agent and get my associate working on the bank, et cetera. From what they said, immediate possession wouldn't be a problem."

"We can do it. I'll ring my brothers and they can drive by the caravan to let your family know what's happening." Paganne was already pulling the cell phone from her purse. She punched a button and put it to her ear. After a moment she said, "Damn it, Raven. I'm getting static. Walk away."

Raven laughed. "Sorry. Why don't you movers and shakers make your calls? I'll dash over to the restaurant and get sandwiches for us. Trevelyn and I missed breakfast because of the trip to hospital. I'm positively famished. We were just going to fix a bite of something when the agent called about this property."

"Yeah, some food would be in order. Sounds like a plan." Trev nodded, winking at Brishen. "Give up the fight, Sagari, there's no opposing these two ladies."

The Gypsy sucked in a deep breath and held it. Finally,

he exhaled. "Steeple Hill Studio it is. Let's make magic happen."

Paganne jumped for joy and hugged him. "Oh, I know this is going to work!" Still bouncing, she turned and hugged Trevelyn. "Thank you, thank you, thank you! I'm still not convinced my sister met you in a candy store, but I don't care at the moment. You may have her and do all sorts of wicked things to her—provided you promise not to break her heart."

"Paganne, I swear you act like you were plucked from a neep patch," Raven scolded, buffeting her sister on the back of her head.

Paganne's shoulder lifted and dropped with sangfroid. "I'm a meddling Montgomerie, what can I say? Go fetch food. Lots and lots of food. I'm suddenly ravenous, and we have a lot to do—and your witchy chemistry is messing up my cell."

Trev offered to Raven, "Want me to come with you?"

"Thank you for helping Brishen." She stood on tippy toes and kissed his cheek. "Stay. You don't need to be dashing about with those stitches in your foot. I promise not to be long."

The little bell at the restaurant tingled overhead as Raven pushed through the front door. All eyes turned to the newcomer, assessing her. She met their stares with a pleasant smile, and moved to the counter where she could place her takeaway order. A couple of men nodded in recognition.

The delicious smells from lunch wafted in the air, causing her stomach to grumble. It made her realize how hungry she was. Since Trev had come into her life, food kept taking a backseat. Oh, well, she was living on love.

That thought stopped her. Yes, she was falling in *love* with Trevelyn Sinclair. Loving Mr. Big Bad Wolf. It scared her. Petrified her. Only, what she'd told Paganne was the truth. Being with Trev felt *right*.

"They say wolves mate for life," she said lowly to her-self. "Perhaps I can tame this one."

Her attention was drawn to the far side of the room where a couple sat in a booth; she wasn't sure why. The lunch crowd was starting to trickle in, so the dining area was nearly half full. Why this booth attracted her atten-tion, she couldn't say. Only, some sort of animalistic in-stinct kicked in. A fey sense of warning, as loud as bells clanging in her brain.

She tilted her head for a clearer view. Every booth had high-backed seats that rose to form a barrier, affording each table privacy. She could only see the tops of the heads of the two people sitting there. The one farthest away and facing forward was a man. Facing him was a blonde.

"Curious," she muttered, fighting an odd feeling it was Alec and someone other than his wife.

"What would you like to order?" a waitress asked, dis-tracting Raven's attention from the couple.

"Let's see. Enough for four very hungry people—two of them men," she replied, looking at the menu. "How about six hamburgers with everything, and chips. Four large colas."

The waitress replied that it would be a couple minutes, but already Raven had rotated her focus back to the booth. The man was gesturing with his hand, finger pointed. She'd seen Alec do that very thing many times. He leaned forward on the table to say something to the woman, and his face came into full view. At the same instant, he spot-ted Raven. His expression hardened. He spoke to his com-panion then straightened up, took out his wallet and tossed some bills onto the table.

"Here you go." The waitress placed several sacks beside the register. "I'm putting the condiments and salt packets in the smaller one. I double bagged the colas for you."

Raven took her wallet from her small purse, removed several five-pound notes and handed them to the woman, who seemed familiar. "You're Jilly's cousin Annalee, aren't you?"

"Yes—newly divorced and come home," the woman admitted. "I'm working here until I get a better job offer. Not too much in this town, but I prefer my two daughters to be raised around here. City life is too crazy for me. Drugs, crime . . . it's scary. I remember growing up here and always feeling safe. I want my kids to know that, want me not have to worry about them every minute they're out of my sight."

"You were a legal secretary, weren't you?" When Annalee nodded, Raven took a business card from the holder at the register and picked up the pen next to it. She quickly scratched Cian's name and phone number on the back. "Give my brother a call. I bet he can to help you." Maybe he'd even fire that bitch Melissa if Annalee was qualified enough.

"Thanks, I really appreciate it! This job is giving us enough to get by, but I'd like something a little more stable, if you get my drift." Annalee gave Raven a winsome smile and stuffed the card into her blouse pocket.

Raven picked up the food. Turning to check the booth once more, she saw it was empty.

"Cut and run did you, Alec, before I saw who she was?" she muttered. It was really none of her business—and unsurprising. Alec had cheated on her; she supposed he wouldn't be any more faithful to his second pregnant wife. Raven suddenly felt empathy for Ellen.

About to leave, she suddenly caught sight of a blonde going down a corridor at the back. The sign on the wall said Ladies Lounge. Okay, she was being a snoop, but something about the woman set off an alarm, as if Raven knew her. She likely had Melissa on the brain at the moment, but this pale blonde hair was the same shade. And if Melissa was playing footsy with Alec, Cian would want to know. "Just call me Samantha Spade."

Raven set off down the dimly lit corridor. The swinging door to the ladies' loo was unmoving, but she pushed through anyway. A quick inspection of the two-stall bathroom showed the room was empty.

As Raven came back out, a busboy was pushing a cart down the hallway. She stopped him and asked, "Tell me, is there another exit through here?"

The busboy nodded, wiping his hands on his apron. "Yes, around the corner. It's a back door. We use it for a fire exit."

"Can I go out that way?"

"Sure. It's kept open. No alarms go off or anything."

Raven nodded. "Thanks." She hurried to the end of the hall and turned left, coming out the door at the same instant a gray Beemer peeled out of the paved parking lot. Following, she tried to get a look at the license numbers.

Something hit her shoulder, slamming her up against the building. She nearly lost her grip on her bags of food, and did lose it on the drinks, which fell to the pavement. The soda soaked the sack and spilled onto the concrete. Raven looked up into the cold eyes of her ex-husband.

"Well, well, little Raven is stooping to play super-snoop." Alec held her pinned against the wall, pressing hard on her shoulder. "So pedestrian—so beneath the high and mighty Montgomeries."

Raven swallowed her fear and gave him a smile. "Let go, Alec, or you will be sorry."

"Sorry? More sorry than about Cian and Mac Montgomerie ruining every business opportunity for me? Every place I turn, I get doors slammed in my face. Why? Because Cian and Mac are pulling strings to ruin me. They're fighting your battles, Raven. You're such a little coward. Always were. How utterly pathetic you are."

"If you're having business problems, perhaps you should consider relocating to a more suitable clime," she suggested, trying not to allow him to see her fear. If he saw, he would only become worse. Alec was a bully, and like all bullies fed on fear.

"You'd like that, wouldn't you?"

She gave a small laugh. "Not to see your face ever again? Yeah, you bet. I'd love it. Go away, Alec. We were a mistake. Our marriage was doomed from the start. I just wasn't smart enough to see it. Let's both cut our losses and move on."

"Well, the loss columns don't balance, Raven. You owe me. Your brother owes me—"

Alec's face suddenly contorted with pain. She looked over his shoulder to see Trevelyn had hold of his neck in an odd pinch, and clearly had her ex-husband's free arm twisted up behind his back.

"Let go of me, you bastard," Alec snarled.

"Seems to me that we've danced this dance before—even had the same discussion on my lineage. Bit tiresome, don't you think? Isn't it odd, how a bully loves to shove someone weaker around but becomes a sniveling whiner when the tables are turned?" Trev asked, maintaining his grip. "Let her go and step back. One step, mind."

Alec failed to comply, so Trevelyn increased the pressure, which eventually had Alec whimpering. "You'll be sorry, Sinclair!"

"Doubtful. But I did warn you about my pinkie finger, how dangerous it was. Now, here is the drill: You let go of Raven, then I'll escort you to your car." He nodded toward the Audi just a few steps away. "Finally, if you ever come near her again, you won't like the repercussions. I might be forced to use *both* index fingers. Right now, I want three little words from you: 'Yes, I will.' " Trev twisted his arm a little higher.

"Screw you," Alec snarled.

Trevelyn sighed. "It has to be the hard way then." He swung Alec away from Raven and gave him a small shove toward his car.

Instead of leaving, Alec spun around. "You damn gorilla!" he snarled, and took a wild swing.

Trev easily dodged, and then laughed as he dodged a second punch, too. He said to Raven, "I won't even soil my knuckles on him. My pinkie finger is too good for the likes of this scum. Instead, I'll introduce the jerk to my big toe."

Not learning, Alec came at Trevelyn a third time. "You're crazy. That explains why you want *her.* Only a loon would put up with that bitch."

Trev lashed out with his leg, and his foot caught Alec square in the solar plexus. All the air was knocked from Raven's ex in a whoosh. Alec flew backward into the side of a Dumpster, and then, like a bizarre marionette whose strings had been cut, slid to the ground.

In a leisurely fashion, Trevelyn bent over and picked up his cane. "My last warning, Beechcroft," he growled. "Stay the hell away from Raven. Don't come lurking around her house anymore. If you see her out and about, you shall cross to the other side of the street. Because, next time, I won't be so kind."

He walked to Alec and reached inside the pocket of the other man's suit jacket. Comically, Alec tried to slap Trev's hand away, but Trev slapped back. Pulling out the man's wallet, he ruffled through the bills until he found a couple of five-pound notes. He tossed the rest against the slumped man's chest. "For the drinks you ruined. My lawyer will be in touch with a bill for my tires and the ruined paint job on the Lamborghini."

He walked back and touched Raven's shoulder. "Come on, love. Let's replace the colas and go have lunch. Forget about the idiot. That creep won't bother you anymore."

Raven was shaking. She hated that she was, and tried to cover it by saying, "Big toe, huh?"

"Yep, the toe is mightier than the fist." Trev opened the door for her, and then glanced back at Alec, who was still sitting against the Dumpster. "Just think what it could have done if I didn't have stitches in my foot!"

"Was that some sort of kung fu?" she asked as they went inside.

"Savate. It's French kickboxing. Julian Starkadder taught me. It's a martial art that evolved from street fighting."

"I think I may have to kiss Julian when we are introduced."

Trev gave a big grin. "You kiss him? Over his dead body."

Chapter Seventeen

"Oh, Brishen will be ticked, but I don't care." Paganne laughed with glee as she jerked the tailgate down on the Colford Hall truck. "This stuff was sitting in the attic, gathering dust."

Raven frowned as her sister climbed up into the truck-bed and struggled to drag a heavy desk to the rear of the vehicle. "Paganne, let the men do that. It's one of the things they're good for."

Trev walked up behind her and placed his hand at the small of her spine. "And here I thought you kept me around because I gave good back rubs."

Raven felt a blush crawl over her skin, recalling how Trevelyn had given her a full body massage with almond oil last night. The whole time, she wasn't permitted to move or to touch him in return, while he soothed, stroked and tormented her body with devious fingers. She was so wrung out by the hour-long emotional roller coaster that she'd climaxed the instant he entered her, and kept hitting that shimmering pinnacle over a dozen times before Trevelyn finally reached his release. Hunger for him roared through her blood, twisting her insides into knots of need. Wicked man, he'd made mention of it simply to provoke the reaction!

She smiled up at him, feeling love growing in her heart for her wolf. For the past two days, they'd poured all their energies into turning the neglected building into a studio for Brishen. Like a master wizard, Trev had set wheels in motion. Whatever they needed to put the place to rights, it was done or supplied in a snap.

And the nights were theirs. Those endless hours of

unimaginable pleasure were a contrast to the gentle times of lying in the darkness, talking and getting to know each other. Her heart ached with the need to tell him how much she was falling under his spell, but something within her psyche warned it was too early. She held the secret close, waiting for the perfect time.

"Julian is sending over a roofer this afternoon to make sure everything is solid, and to give an estimate for repairs if needed," Trev informed her. "Perhaps you might like him to swing by your cottage and have a look?"

Ignoring his pointed question, she teased, "Hmm . . . the mysterious Mr. Starkadder again. I truly don't think he exists outside of a bottle. You make a wish, rub the side, and everything magically happens."

Trev laughed. "Other than the bottle, the opinion isn't far from right. Julian is a very resourceful man."

"So, when do I get to meet him? I admit to being curious about this genie without a bottle."

Trev offered her an inscrutable half smile. "Oh, soon, I should think. But I warn you, he's no jinn. He's closer to a bloody pirate."

"A pirate?" Paganne's face lit up with interest and she called down, "You mean like Johnny D?"

Trev chuckled. "Think of Capt'n Jack on steroids, then you'd be getting close. He even has a small gold hoop in his ear."

"Which ear?" Paganne asked.

Trev's body vibrated with his chuckle. "Do you think if it was the wrong ear I'd be leery of him meeting Raven? Julian attracts women in droves."

Paganne sighed in exaggerated disappointment. "Ah, well, no matter how magnetic the personality, I never buy overly popular merchandise. You never know who's handled it."

Two of Brishen's cousins—György and Luca—came out to help Paganne unload the furniture. Brishen was right behind. "What's all this?" he demanded.

Paganne wiped her hands on her jeans. "I raided the attic at Colford. It's full of centuries-old furniture doing nothing there but suffering dry rot and being a magnet for dust. A lot of lemon oil and some elbow grease is called for, but they'll be an impressive showcase for your office."

"Office? I don't have a bloody office."

Paganne took Brishen's hand and hopped down from the truck bed. "You will—shortly."

Brishen shook his head and glared at Trevelyn. "This is your fault. It doesn't end. The contractors haven't stopped coming and going all day. Then a landscaper. Now a roofer is coming." The Gypsy grinned but looked a bit frazzled. "No wonder my people choose to live in wagons. It's a lot less stressful."

Raven watched the men carry the furniture inside, amazed at the buzz of activity and by how much had already been accomplished—most of it because of Trevelyn. She hung back from the group, wanting to share the moment with him. When she got the chance, she reached up and stroked his cheek. "You've done a wonderful thing, Trevelyn. I know he's fussing, but it's because he's scared."

He seemed uncomfortable with her praise. Taking her hand, he pulled her away from the front of the studio. "Come look at the house. They've finished painting the walls. Tomorrow they'll put up storm doors and windows, see the house is snug and secure."

Raven followed him into the empty cottage, which seemed larger inside than it did from out. It'd make a lovely home for Brishen's family. The walls were now soft beige, and the woodwork an off-white. One corner of the front room showcased a charming Victorian fireplace. "Trevelyn, these colors brighten the place up! I cannot wait for Katrina and Magda to see it."

"The backyard is huge and butts up against the woods. I thought they could park their wagon back there, sort of ease Magda into the move," her beloved suggested.

"Magda wants what is best for Brishen. She understands how important this is for him. But it's still thoughtful of you to consider that."

Trev opened the first door at the head of a short hallway. "This is small, but it'd serve as a lovely nursery, and then Katrina could have the bigger room next to it for her bedroom. A door adjoins the two rooms, so it struck me as perfect for her and the baby."

Raven tried not to be affected. Her pain was a waste. She had to get over her sensitivity where babies were concerned. Still, she knew her reaction showed on her face by the sympathy flooding Trevelyn's eyes.

She walked into the room and turned in a circle. "Yes, I believe you're right. The night Katrina returned to camp, I talked to her about moving into a house because of Emile. While she respects the ways of her people, she wants something more for her son. It's pulling at her—keeping faith with the past or reaching out and taking a chance at a different life. I could say a 'better' life, but perhaps in some ways I'm not sure it is."

Trev nodded. "I understand. Really I do. What happened to the father?"

"Killed in Iraq. John was much too young to die. He was only twenty-five."

"Did she get survivor's benefits?"

"Not a shilling piece, as they say. Though he wasn't Roma, they were married by Gypsy ways. The British Government are not recognizing the marriage as legal, hence she's not entitled to any support for her or the child. Cian has been fighting the ruling through legal channels, but I don't hold much hope. My guess? Because she's a Gypsy, no one cares."

"I hate to bring this up, but she'll need stuff for the baby. A bed . . ." He shrugged, clearly out of his depth. "Well, she'll need all those baby things, and I haven't a clue what they are. To spare you I'd go order stuff, but I—"

"You're very sweet for worrying, but there's no need to

order anything. I have everything already. It's packed away at Colford. I'll have the twins fetch the stuff around for Katrina right away."

He reached out, catching her arm and pulling her to face him. "The things for your child?"

She couldn't find the words, so she gave a small nod.

"Are you all right?"

She sucked in a slow breath and nodded. "One of those problems in life you deal with and then move on. You cannot allow the past to control the present. I've done that, lived in the shadows for too long. Now I walk in the sun. The present is all we have. It's precious. We must try to be the happiest we can with what we have."

Trev's face was ashen. "I suppose that's true. But sometimes the past won't let you go."

Raven had a feeling he was speaking about himself rather than her. She wanted to question him further, but she'd noticed at odd moments like this that Trevelyn held himself back. This troubled her, but she hoped as they grew to know each other better he'd be more comfortable letting down his guard.

A horn honked, shattering the solemn moment and drawing her to the window. A dark gray Mercedes pulled off the road at the side of the property and two men got out. "Buckle up, baby, it's about to get bumpy," she muttered.

"What's wrong?"

"Cian just arrived. And Mac is with him."

Trev smiled. "Ah, meet-the-father time. Do you fear he won't approve of the Big Bad Wolf hanging around his Riding Hood?"

"Big and bad, my arse. Come on, Fairy Godfather, and do the pretty before my daddy." Raven took his hand and pulled him from the house.

Cian was the first to greet them. He winked at Raven and then held out his hand to Trevelyn. "Good to see you again, Sinclair." He inclined his head toward the man standing next to him. "I would like you to meet my father. Father, may I present Trevelyn Sinclair."

"Ah, yes, I do believe I've heard the name a few times at the dinner table. You've made quite an impression on several of my children." Mac Montgomerie held out his hand. His incisive eyes moved over Trevelyn, taking his measure as they shook.

"Nice to meet you, sir." Trevelyn sounded properly respectful, yet in the same instant conveyed he wasn't intimidated.

"Raven, you've been remiss. You should bring Trevelyn to supper soon—say, dinner tomorrow?" Mac suggested, but Raven knew it was more than an invitation. It was a command. Mac Montgomerie was soft-spoken; however, only a fool would fail to recognize the steel in his words.

Turning back to Trevelyn, her father said, "Cian mentioned you've just opened a consulting firm in town. May I ask what sort, and why here? We're rather backwater by many standards."

"I sought a quieter lifestyle. Big cities have lost their charm." Trevelyn smiled easily. "As to my firm, I put deals together, make things happen. Connect businesses struggling with other businesses or individuals looking to invest. Broker mergers, takeovers—"

"Hostile takeovers?" Mac's brows lifted slightly, implying a faint disdain.

Raven almost smiled when Trev met her hard-as-nails father's eyes without blinking. Mac was unused to that. Men tended to quail before him, and her father enjoyed that.

Unruffled, Trev went on, "If the case calls for it, yes. I do the research on prospective businesses for clients, which allows them to make informed choices on how to invest their capital. Or, if a business is looking to go on the market, I work up a presentation to make them appear interesting enough to draw buyers."

"Have we met?" Mac asked. "Your face seems familiar."

"Enough with the Spanish Inquisition, Father. Come look at the soon-to-be studio we're working on for Brishen. None of this would be happening without Trevelyn pulling strings with the bank." She gave her father's arm a squeeze to let him know she loved him, even if she wasn't fond of his meddling ways. "Stop tweaking Trevelyn's nose."

Mac gave her a buss on the cheek. "Raven, you're ruining all the fun of being a father. Tormenting suitors is one of the privileges that come with the territory. When I courted your mother, I went to the door and met her father before I was allowed to take her on a date. Nowadays . . ." Mac shook his head and teased, "Well, nowadays, you females are out of control. Ever since women started wearing trousers in public, the world has gone to hell in a handbasket."

Trev's brows lifted in surprise. "Britches are the root of all evil?"

"You're forgetting Mum led the wave on that, too." Raven laughed. "I recall the story she used to tell about you taking her to a restaurant back in the nineteen seventies. It's hard to believe, but there actually were places that refused to seat women if they were wearing slacks. Father and she went to supper at this one place. Mum was wearing a long tunic—"

"Ah, it's *my* story." Mac took over the retelling. "Raven's mother was dressed in a lovely silver mesh tunic that reached just above her knees . . . over black trousers. We're in line, waiting to be seated at our table. As we reach the reservations desk, the owner informs us he cannot allow us seating, and gestures to a big sign at the top of the entrance that said they reserved the right to refuse service to women in slacks. Your bold and brassy mother gave him one of her steely-eyed stares, and right on the spot dropped her trousers, then very deftly picked them up and handed them to the shocked man."

Trevelyn laughed. "And did they seat you?"

"Damn straight they did! The next time we dined there,

the sign was gone and women wearing slacks were permitted entrance. I remain firmly convinced we men lost control of the world the night Raven's mother dropped her trousers in the foyer of that restaurant." Mac reached out and patted Trevelyn's upper arm. "Come show what you've been doing for our fearless vampire hunter."

Raven caught the sleeve of Cian's jacket and tugged, a signal to stay behind. When Trev looked back at her in question, she said, "Run along with my father. I promise he won't bite. I'll be there in a minute. I wanted a word with my brother."

Cian waited until the others were out of earshot before asking, "So what's up, little sister?"

"It has to do with Melissa. Or, rather, might have to do with her." When her brother frowned, she snapped, "Don't give me that look. I couldn't care less that you keep that ice bitch as your secretary. You can even boff her—though I would prefer to think my brother has better taste."

"Who I do or don't see in my private life is none of your business. So butt out, you little meddling Montgomerie." Cian tapped her nose with his index finger to soften his words.

"Put a sock in it, Cian. I'm trying to tell you I think I saw her with Alec a couple days ago."

Cian's brows lifted. " 'Think'?"

"I didn't see the woman's face. Just the back of her head. I went to the restaurant down the street to get lunch for everyone. While I was waiting, I met Annalee—"

Her brother nodded. "She called. I gave her an appointment for an interview next week. She sounds good. I have a receptionist going out for maternity leave soon. From what Annalee said, she could step into the job without too much training. If she works out there, I'll find her a permanent position."

"Like Melissa's job?" Half jest, half seriousness, Raven couldn't resist. "Anyway, while I was waiting for my order, I noticed Alec sitting in a booth with a woman. They were on the far side, and I could only see the back of her head, but I am fairly sure it was Melissa. I figured you'd want to know. I tried to follow her and get the license number, but Alec jumped me."

"Raven, you should have called me about this." Cian looked ticked off, but she knew it was directed more at Alec than herself.

Raven rolled her eyes. "I tried. You were out of town. I left a message with your secretary to have you call me. Hello? I guess Melissa didn't tell you?"

"Sorry. I'll deal with her. The injunction from years ago on Alec may still be in effect. I'll check with our solicitor. I want him to stay away from you."

She nodded, crossing her arms against the sudden breeze that had sprung up. "We had a prowler at the cottage. He slashed the tires on Trevelyn's car and scratched up the paint. Trev believes it was Alec."

"Damn it, Raven! I want you to move back to Colford. I don't like Alec starting up with this nonsense. Not now. Now with . . ." Disgusted, frustrated, Cian stalked away a few paces until he had control of his temper again.

Raven pressed. "Why not now?"

Cian threw up his hands and turned around. "I think Mac may have the right of it. We lost control of you females when Mum dropped her trousers. I'm not sure. Just some disturbing things have been happening around the edges of Montgomerie Enterprises. Stock shifting hands. I cannot run it down, yet, but I'm getting a sense of someone trying to destabilize the corporation."

"Stocks are sold every day, aren't they?" she asked.

"Yes, but these are longtime shareholders doing quiet sales. From what I gather it's been going on for months, not trading on the open market but off-the-grid sales, private stuff done on the Q.T. Don't worry. I'll get to the bottom of it."

"You think Alec might be behind it? He sounded very bitter, saying Mac and you were ruining him financially."

A sense of unease settled over her with her brother's revelation. She'd never taken any interest in the shares she owned of the family corporation. All the children had a percentage, but allowed Cian to vote them as he needed. "Cian, that makes Alec's meeting with Melissa even more important, don't you think?"

"If it was Melissa. Remember the time you got that wild hare about the chauffeur for old lady Brennan? You were convinced he'd done her in and buried her body in their tool shed?"

Raven chuckled, giving him a playful grin. "Well, she did drop out of sight for nearly the whole summer, and there actually was a mound in the dirt floor of that locked shed."

"But it turned out—*after* you called Scotland Yard, mind—that she'd been visiting her sister in Edinburgh, and the mound was where Jacobs had buried her dog who'd died of old age." Cian smirked.

Trevelyn came back, looking between them. "Anything wrong?"

Raven smirked. "Nothing a big toe couldn't cure."

"You deal in business rumors to zero in on investments, don't you?" Cian asked.

Trevelyn nodded. "Coin of the realm. Who is buying—"

"And who is selling?" Cian finished. "Ever hear of Trident Ventures?"

"Not offhand. Why?"

"Oh, the name just popped up in a business deal Mac is doing, and I was seeking information on them." Cian shoved his hands in his pants pockets.

"I can ask around if you like," Trevelyn offered.

Cian nodded. "I'd appreciate it."

They turned at the sound of a truck backfiring. The rickety red vehicle puttered up with *Josephine's Custom Signs* painted in white on the side. In the back was a huge silver tarp covering something.

"Sign-maker?" Brishen nearly groaned as he came

hurrying outside, followed by Paganne. "No one said I needed a sign."

Cian grinned. "Relax, this is well in hand. My contribution to the effort. Wait until you see. I think you'll be pleased."

Josephine—at least Raven took it to be the proprietor herself—hopped out and began unlashing the tarpaulin. She flipped it back to reveal a large sign, already completed and with wrought-iron posts attached. It had a carousel pony on one side of the name, *Steeple Hill Studio*, and a Gypsy wagon on the other. *Brishen Sagari, Owner* was centered near the bottom. They had to move closer to read the underlying small print: *Resident artist and vampire slayer.*

Cian chuckled at his bit of playfulness. "I figured it couldn't hurt to draw some people in with that hook."

Short and squat Josephine grinned at her handwork. "Turned out quite nice, if I say so myself." Pulling out a posthole digger from the truck bed, she grinned. "I'll dig the holes while you big braw men position the sign. You might grab your landscaper over there, and see if he wants to dress this up with a couple small shrubs and such."

Raven stood back with Paganne, watching the men in their lives wrestle the huge sign into the holes Josephine dug. It was one of those special, quiet moments, so perfect, so rare, that Raven's mind captured the images and pressed them into the pages of her memory.

Chapter Eighteen

"If that phone call to Desmond in Scotland left me with more questions than answers, it's nothing compared with my call to Jago in Kentucky," Trevelyn told Atticus. He folded the cell phone and looked down at the bird fussing around his feet. The silly seagull was begging for another chunk of shortbread. Trev broke off a piece and dropped it for the insistent creature before adding, "But then, I suppose if Jago knew I was holding a conversation with a one-legged seagull that thinks he's a cat, my brother would be quite concerned about me as well."

The bird bobbed his head up and down, and then partially raised his one good wing.

"I'm not sure if you're agreeing with me or doing a happy dance because I'm sneaking you junk food. Remember—a bird that pecks toes doesn't get Twiglets or Walkers Salt & Vinegar Crisps." The bird was a *junk food freakaconus*. Having discovered Atticus's weakness, Trev wasn't above slipping him bribes.

The family dinner at Colford Hall had gone surprisingly well, and Trev found himself liking both Cian and Mac. Thus, the start of Sunday found him in a mellow mood. Trev glanced over to the two cats, dead asleep, melted into puddles on the floor of the sunshine-filled greenhouse. The allergy pills and nasal spray seemed to keep his cat problems at bay, so he'd risked making love to Raven before the fireplace last night. After they'd finished putting up Brishen's sign for his studio, everyone decided to call it quits for the day. They still had time before the art people came to look at Brishen's ponies; and as Raven had pointed out, it didn't have to be perfect, just give the impression of Brishen being serious about his work. Brishen even suggested Raven should send over some of her paintings to hang on the walls, to display her work along with his.

Trev had stopped on the way back, picked up a bottle of wine and a couple cheeses, and when they got home, built a fire in the fireplace. Tossing the cushions from the sofa onto the floor, they'd proceeded to spend the whole evening talking and making love. At times, he'd just held Raven close, feeling her heart beat under his hand, savoring the peaceful purity of those moments.

He checked the grandfather clock in the entry now, taking note of the hour again. Their presence was expected at Colford at 1 p.m. for Sunday dinner. Facing a boardroom full of upset stockholders he took in stride. Conversely, being tossed into the middle of the meddling Montgomeries was a daunting prospect. It had been part of the plan, getting him close to Colford and Cian. Now that everything was falling into place, unease was multiplying within him. Thus, the unplanned call to Jago.

Raven had been out chasing the errant pony about the yard, intent on putting him in the barn before she came in to get ready for lunch at the Hall. With her occupied, he'd seized the opportunity, simply wanting to hear his brother's voice. Of course, he hadn't considered the difference in time zones. Kentucky was five hours behind UK time, so while it was elevenses here, over there it was still early morning. Even so, Jago had answered and claimed to not have been woken up. But also, instead of being happy to hear from him, Jago had been oddly short, maybe even irritated.

Everything was different than he'd expected, setting this plan in motion. "It seemed so bloody simple," Trev muttered under his breath. But nothing was simple, and they should have known that going in.

Desmond had worked for years to see this takeover

come about, this vengeance for Sean "Midas" Montgomerie's failed pyramid scheme that caused his father's suicide. He'd worked to take back Colford Hall, the horsefarm in Kentucky and Falgannon Isle—everything the man had used to obtain his ill-gotten empire, and that rightfully should have belonged to the Mershans and other fooled investors. Des had wanted to hand Sean the papers, show him everything he'd built on the blood, sweat and tears of others was about to be snatched from him; but then, as victory was almost in grasp, he'd been dealt a bitter shock: Sean Montgomerie died last May. Des was robbed of the satisfaction—the *closure*—of ruining the man he blamed for his father's death.

Perhaps the Mershan brothers' plans should've died there, too. Only, they were already locked into this juggernaut of destruction. For Des to toss up his hands and walk away would have meant he'd lose all. A multimillion-dollar fortune was at stake. Everything he'd worked for decades to build would go down in flames. For a child who had grown up hungry, facing poverty again was something Des couldn't accept. There was simply no pulling back. For any of them.

Without asking, Trev knew Jago was also having second thoughts. His brother's conscience was likely gnawing at him even before he stepped off the plane in Kentucky. Now . . . now Jago said he was *in love* with Asha. Trev had wanted to laugh at that statement. It'd only been a few days since Asha and Jago met! From the start of the conversation Jago had been grouchy, pushing Trev to tease him about falling under Asha's spell. Jago's response had knocked the wind from Trev's sails.

"No spells, no magic," his twin had stated flatly. "I'm in love with her, and if all these Machiavellian plans don't ruin my chances, I want to marry her."

That rock-hard conviction irritated Trev all to hell. How could Jago be so bloody sure? Knowing his twin, Trev was convinced Jago hadn't even slept with Asha yet. Being perverse, he'd tried to kid Jago, ribbing him about drinking too much Kentucky moonshine. He'd only ended up antagonizing his brother more.

"That saintly conscience of his," Trev told the bird. "Sometimes, my oh so perfect brother irks the bloody hell out of me."

Setting the last part of the biscuit down on a plant stand, he shoved his hands into his pants pockets and watched Raven play catch-the-pony. Marvin, the little devil, was fast for being such a small animal, and clearly enjoyed running circles around her. Currently they were going around and around the sundial at the head of the rose garden.

So many questions ricocheted around inside Trev as he observed the comical scene. He almost hated that Jago could be so sure about his course. Did everything Desmond had done, each and every sacrifice he'd made, mean nothing to Jago? One look at Asha, and Jago could forget the hardships they'd endured, how their mother had suffered—*still* suffered? Trev was angry at Jago.

"And I'm angry at myself, because I'm about to fall into the same trap." Despair haunted the words Trev spoke to the bird.

With a sigh, he realized he'd been fingering the coins in his pocket. His eyes shifted to the fortune-teller's box, and he felt an utter fool for wanting to see what a clockwork doll would say regarding his dilemma. Walking over to it, he leaned close to study the mannequin, which still bore a subtle resemblance to Raven. He fished a coin out of his pocket.

His mind flashed back to that old *Twilight Zone* episode where William Shatner kept putting pennies into a fortune-telling machine. The Mystic Seer spat out vague yet eerily uncanny replies to Shatner's questions, seeing his character increasingly dependent upon the answers and too fearful to take his next step without the prediction.

"Is that what I'm doing?" After a moment, he shrugged. "In for a penny . . ." Dropping the coin into the slot, he watched, mesmerized as the life-sized doll awoke. It was damn spooky how alive she always appeared. "So, pretty Gypsy, do you have any wisdom to share on my predicament?"

With a *click-clack-clunk*, a card was ejected into the tray. Trev picked it up and stared. Death.

He couldn't help it, a shiver ran up his spine. Turning the card over, he read the words written there:

Embrace sacrifice to effect change everlasting. The answers you seek can be found in dreams.

Arms slid around his waist as Raven placed her head to his back and hugged him. "You're playing with my fortune-teller? Learn anything interesting?"

"Interesting? Perhaps, if one understands the meaning of the tarot." He smiled, and pulled her around for a soft kiss. That wasn't enough, so he kissed her again, and then kissed the tip of her nose. "You wouldn't happen to have a divination book around? What's the good of a fortune being told if you cannot understand it?"

"There are likely a couple books at Colford. We can swipe one while we're there."

Trev held up the card for her to see. "The latest bit of nonsense."

"Trev, the Death card doesn't actually mean someone is going to die. That's Hollywood's bit of Grand Guignol, putting forth that impression for impact." Even so, he saw the color slowly leech from her face as she stared. "This card means the death of something, the coming to an end of a phase of life, an abrupt or complete change due to past events or actions."

"So, I'm not going to get pecked to death by a crazy bird?" he teased.

She shook her head. "Many things can die, Trevelyn.

Beliefs, emotions . . . relationships." Her eyelids lowered to veil her thoughts. "Sometimes, a change can be for the better."

Embrace sacrifice to effect change everlasting. Prickles crawled up his spine. He was sorry he'd showed Raven the card, for despite her protests that it held little ominous meaning, it scared her. Fear and worry were clear in her beautiful eyes.

Hoping to divert her, he asked, "So, is the Great Pony Roundup over?"

"For now. I do believe he thinks me chasing him is a big game. I don't mind, but now I'm sweaty. Think I can entice you to come scrub my back?" A sparkle of mischief returned to her eyes.

He inhaled slowly as if considering the offer. "There is a possibility—if you bribe me—that I might be drafted for such a chore."

"A bribe? Such as?" Raven nipped at his chin and rubbed her knee up the inside of his thigh.

He ran his hands down her back, then over her rounded derrière in those tight stretch jeans, then nuzzled the hair over her left ear. "Hmm. I'll wash your back if you wash mine."

Her head dropped back so she could see his face. Waggling her eyebrows playfully, she said, "You mean, tit for tat?"

He laughed as she unbuckled his belt. "Ah, yes. Your tit for my tat. You do have the most wonderful suggestions."

Pulling his belt free from its loops, she danced away. "Last one to the shower has to clean it out afterward."

"Minx." He watched her dashing up the steps, taking them two at a time. He glanced down to Atticus, then picked up the last of the shortbread and tossed it to him. "Guess I'm going to be scrubbing the tub, eh?"

Running after her, he followed suit and took the steps

two at a time. He made it to the large bathroom just in time to see a flash of her bare sweet arse vanishing into the shower. Undressing in record time, he jerked the glass door open. Inside, Raven stood under the cool spray, water hitting her neck, breasts and belly.

The beautiful Celtic water goddess turned her head, watching him enter the stall. With a mysterious smile she picked up the bar of soap and washcloth, and held them up. "I believe you kindly offered to scrub my back?"

Trev tossed the washrag over his shoulder. "Why should a stupid piece of towel have all the fun?" Rolling the bar of soap around in his hands, he quickly created a froth of lather. "I did say I would wash your back—eventually."

Raven turned, curving one arm around his neck. "It's rather distracting to view your wonderful expanse of male flesh." She ran her hand across his shoulder. "Such nice square shoulders—warrior's shoulders. And then this broad chest and taut stomach . . ."

Her hand snaked downward, fingers closing around his rock-hard erection, which pulsed high against his belly. As her thumb circled the tip, the internal temperature of his body spiked, leaving him surprised that the water hitting him didn't turn to steam. Over the past few days, Raven had grown more assured of her skills in lovemaking, and she was bringing every touch, each stroke to bear on his too sensitive body. And he loved it!

"See, I'm making it easy for you to reach my back." She nearly purred as he ran his soapy hands up and down her spine.

He strangled, tongue-tied in getting out the words. "Um, no. You're making it hard . . . *very* hard."

He pulled her flush against him, her breasts pressing against his chest in the unyielding embrace. It was nearly impossible to breathe, but then she always seemed to rob the air from his lungs. She let him take her mouth, kiss her with the ravenous need she set loose. Blood drained from his brain, leaving him dizzy, weak. The bloody woman was impossible on the knees—and even harder on his heart.

He inched backward toward the bench built in one corner. When the backs of his thighs butted against it, he sat down. Under the slow spray, he hefted her until she had a knee planted on either side of his hips and was astride him. He kissed her, ravenous desire searing all worries about the future from his mind. There was only the here and now, and what they made each other feel.

Taking hold of the globes of her perfect behind, he shifted her just enough . . . and then he was inside her hot, welcoming body. She gave a small hiss of pain-pleasure. She was tight, so bloody, wonderfully tight; then her body relaxed to allow him in the rest of the way, and he slipped so deep that the tiny ripple of a coming climax already shimmered through her.

Trev's inner voice whispered that this was where he belonged; with her, he was whole. The physical part of this primitive power between them was mind-blowing, but it was the emotional side that summoned awe. The passion, the need, the love—it allowed him no retreat. It buffeted his wounded soul. Agonizing. Too much. And also . . . it was not enough. It would never be enough.

His arms curved around Raven's back to grip her tightly, allowing him to drive upward. Raven met that flex, rode him with a wildness she could no more resist than he. Her breathy gasps empowered him, drove him.

Enthralled by this dark magic, he tilted back to watch the desire play across her beautiful face. Raven shook as a climax spiraled through her, her raspy keen snapping the last bit of his control. Before she came down from the razor edge of ecstasy, he thrust again and again, catching her internal ripples moving in waves down his flesh and using them against her, pushing her higher and higher into release after release.

Raven's eyes flew wide as her nails scored his back,

but she didn't stop. She wanted more. With a needy moan, her hips moved against him, urging his increasingly aggressive thrusts. There was no civilized man left in him. This was the wolf.

He took her mouth, kissed her with a hunger that was violent. Unable to stop himself, he flexed his hips, plunging deeper into her. Her body tightened, once more her internal contractions fisting about him. The sensations skittered along his shaft, across his skin and to explode white-hot in his mind. He closed his eyes as he surrendered to the dark sea of emotions, the overwhelming passion that fused them together. He gritted his teeth, in near agony as the full force of this mating hit him, his scalding seed empting into her body, pulling her into the swirling vortex with him.

A wolf mates for life. The words thundered in his head as he nearly passed out from his release; their intensity blotted out the soft whisper from his heart that spoke of this bond in an entirely different way.

Chapter Nineteen

No! Please, no!

Trevelyn jerked upright in bed, sitting there, trying to breathe. His heart ached, and once again he was covered in sweat. This happened too frequently of late. He glanced over at Raven to see if he'd awakened her, afraid he had actually screamed the words aloud. Evidently not. She rested on her stomach with a cat curled in the middle of her back. Pyewacket watched him with solemn eyes that almost glowed in the moonlight.

Trev moved his foot to dislodge the fat tub of lard named Chester. The orange tabby had taken out adoption papers on him. Fortunately, the allergy situation was minimal, helped because Paganne found an ionic pet-grooming brush. Trev had once suggested taking a vacuum to the furry beasts as a solution, and both cats and Raven had glared at him like he was the Abominable Snowman. He reached out and stroked the sleep-grumpy Chester. He'd found comfort in the cats. They were small friends in fur suits.

He sat quietly in the predawn, trying to shake off the panic that seemed to be an ever-present companion the past two weeks. At a loss to explain it, a dark apparition followed him everywhere. Even in his happiest moments with Raven, the shade hovered nearby. And these stupid dreams weren't helping—dreams of Tashian and Annie. Dreams of him losing her.

Magda had talked of Auld Souls, doomed to return to correct past mistakes. Before, Trev would have chuckled and said, "Bah, humbug." After three weeks of being haunted by the same dream, he wasn't quite so skeptical. Was it possible? Did such things really happen?

Trev groaned as Chester dragged his fat feline body across his lap and up his chest. The kitty bounced on his paws and crawled to give him a head-butt to the chin. Raven kept saying the cat was expressing love when he did that, something about a scent gland in the forehead and marking Trev as his. "I think she might be having me on. It feels more like two rams butting heads during mating season," Trev whispered to the cat, patting him.

Sliding from the bed, he tugged on jogging pants and headed down to the landing bathroom, Chester right on his heels. Leaning over the sink, Trev filled the basin with cold water and splashed it onto his face. His lingering unease seemed stronger than on previous occasions. Usually when he'd awoken from the dream, he'd come down to cool off or shower and gradually the nightmare faded away, replaced with logic and reality. This time was different. Instead of vanishing like mist, the sense stayed with him.

He'd been busy buying stocks all week. Already, Mershan International—through its front Trident Ventures—owned close to a third of all Montgomerie Enterprises' stock. Cian was aware of some of the sales, but not all. They couldn't keep him in the dark much longer. The clock was ticking.

"Yeah, a time bomb, and it's going to blow up in all our faces," Trev said, suddenly feeling sick. "What to do, Chester, what to do?"

"Would you do it, even if the silly animal told you?" the voice behind him asked, clearly doubting.

Trev jerked up, looking into the mirror. "Ah! What the hell . . . ?" He put a hand to his heart as the face, nothing more than a trick of shadows, seemed to gain color and force, resolving into clarity. Trev blinked his eyes, not believing what he saw. The Gypsy from the fortune-teller's booth stood behind him.

"Bloody, bleeding hell! I know it's All Hallows Eve, but this is a bit much!"

Wondering if Skylar and Phelan weren't playing a prank, for whatever idiotic reason, he spun around. Nothing was there. He looked to the cat. Chester crooked his head sideways and growled, but not at Trev—toward the door.

"Cat, I think we're both losing it." But when Trev turned back to his reflection, he jumped in surprise. The face was still there! "Some days it doesn't pay to crawl out of bed."

"Aye, you sense the heavy hand of Fate. The circle is closing again," the fortune-teller intoned.

Trev laughed, but without much mirth. "Yeah, like a noose around my neck. Bugger all, I'm talking to a wooden dummy! A wooden dummy not really there! I must be friggin' crazy!"

The face moved closer, the shadows created by the nightlights wrapping around her like a shroud. "The Wheel goes round and round. What has been, has now come again. Time runs short. Do not repeat past mistakes. Do not doom yourself and her."

Trev leaned his head forward and gently butted it against the glass—not hard enough to break it, but to blot out these damn waking dreams. Sounding much like the Cowardly Lion in *The Wizard of Oz*, he repeated over and over, "I don't believe in ghosts. I don't believe in ghosts. I don't, I *don't* believe in bloody ghosts."

"Trevelyn . . ."

He opened his eyes to see the face of the Gypsy fading to a silhouette. Then it morphed again and came alive, finally shifting and merging into the face of Raven. She moved forward, putting a hand on his back. Concern flickered in her amber brown eyes.

"Are you ill?" She slid her arms around his waist and gave him a gentle hug.

Feeling her warmth, Trev grabbed on to her like a life-line. Pressing her against him, he kissed her—sort of a Prince Charming-Sleeping Beauty scene in reverse. He wanted her to awaken him from this bizarre nightmare.

His body kicked into overdrive, instantly needing the deep physical contact that kept the world at bay. He wanted to lay her down on the cold tile floor and take her with the wildness in his soul screaming to be released. Despite those compelling emotions, he needed to be away from this room and the strange spell he was falling under.

Scooping Raven into his arms, he carried her back upstairs and placed her widthwise across the bed. He covered her with his heavy body, pressing her into the soft bedding; then lacing his fingers with hers, he pushed them above her head, pinning her. At the same instant he spread her legs with his. One hard flex of his hips and he was inside her.

"My version of 'trick or treat,'" he explained impishly, and then proceeded to drive all thoughts and fears from his mind. There was only Raven.

At sunset, Trev watched Raven light the candles in several pumpkins they had spent the afternoon carving. Britain wasn't big on Halloween and the yearly ritual of trick-or-treating, electing instead to celebrate Guy Fawkes Night. However, Raven had spent time with her mother in Kentucky, and had fond memories of the holiday.

While he'd grown up in the States, Trev's early recollections weren't quite so warm and fuzzy. It hadn't been until he turned twelve that Jago and he owned their first costumes—which was Desmond's doing, of course. Vividly Trev recalled Jago insisting they were too old for such nonsense, but that was just St. Jago trying to save them the money Des worked so hard to earn. Des had seen through the lie. He'd taken them to a costume store and allowed them to pick out whatever they wanted. The rows of masks and racks of costumes had seemed like a fun house in an amusement park at the time.

He hadn't said anything to Raven, but with her witch's intuitiveness, she understood. In her gentle way, she'd set about to make a new Halloween celebration, to replace old memories with special ones. Just a small get-together, she'd promised. Brishen came with Paganne, followed a short time later by Phelan and Katrina. Trev chuckled as a meddling-Montgomerie smile spread over Raven's beautiful lips. Even Julian had received an invitation, though he'd remained mysterious and replied that said he'd see.

As Phelan came into the kitchen, holding the door for Katrina, Raven looked up from spreading orange frosting on a cake. "Hi, you two." After exchanging hellos, Phelan gave his sister a kiss on the cheek and then tried to swipe a fingerful of icing. Raven glowered and gave his arm a swat. "Where's Skylar?"

"Oh, he's out trying to scare up a date." Phelan grinned when everyone groaned at the pun.

Paganne came in the back door, but Marvin nearly knocked her down while rushing inside between her legs. "Come back here, you escapee from a petting zoo!" she shrieked, flashing her sister a dirty look. "Why can't you have normal pets like everyone else?"

Raven waved her spatula. "*I* didn't let Marvin in."

"Blast, neither did I!" Paganne groused. As she passed in hot pursuit, she poked Trev in the belly. "Come on, Mr. Drop-Dead Sexy. You can help."

He laughed. "How can I turn down a request phrased like that?"

Between the two of them, they herded the midget horse into the large greenhouse. Trev then positioned himself at the entrance and, whenever Marvin dashed toward him, stomped his feet and clapped his hands, driving Marvin back toward the door outside. Atticus, mad at being disturbed, flapped his good wing and pecked at the pony going past. After about three rounds of this, Marvin allowed himself to be escorted outside.

"Marvin needs obedience school," Paganne huffed. "Thanks for aiding. I would've been a half hour getting him out. Now . . . don't tell Brishen I told you, but he sold a carousel horse today to one of the London art galleries—not for what you paid, mind, but not a shabby deal, either. Eleven thousand dollars. Also, a buyer from Harrods called and requested three rocking horses for Christmas. If those sell, they'll order more. I know it's because of your help with the studio, so I wanted to thank you for giving him the chance."

"I opened a couple doors. It's Brishen's talent that will win him sales and fans."

Paganne stopped at the door to the living room. "You know, I never believed you knew Raven before the night of the gala, but then I recalled the painting. Still, I just can't imagine my big sister having you around and keeping quiet. . . ."

"Painting?" Trev echoed.

"Yes." Paganne tilted her head in consideration. "You haven't seen it? Perhaps she means it as a surprise and I've just let another cat out of the bag. Sorry! You should know: Never tell me anything you don't want broadcasted. I'm not a social creature, and lack the guile to hide things. I always thought Raven was the same, but I guess I don't know her as well as I thought."

"What painting? Raven showed me several works in progress she's doing for her spring show. None of them have anything to do with me."

Paganne leaned close so she could see Raven chattering to Katrina and Phelan through the doorway. "Come, but don't you dare tell her I showed you."

Hurrying to the small greenhouse studio, Paganne pushed open the door. She jerked her head to silently say, Come on. Trev followed, thinking there was more to Paganne than the quiet archaeologist content with digging in a ruin or with her nose buried in a book. Maybe Raven's meddling-Montgomerie ways were rubbing off on him, for he hoped Julian would show up. He'd be curious to see Paganne and his friend together.

"I won't turn on the lights. Raven would see us, then she'd come snatch me bald, I fear. There's still enough light to see." She looked around. "Um, if I can find it." Then her eyes landed upon a canvas covered with a sheet. Pulling the easel away from the wall and turning it so that light could hit it, Paganne yanked off the sheet with the flair of a magician. "Ta-da! Behold!"

Trev felt as if someone had kicked him. The huge painting was done in shades of deep burgundy, black and pale rose. A man sat astride a horse, dressed in old-fashioned clothing. But it was the unfinished image of a man with wavy black hair. And the eyes . . . ? He looked at them every time he stared into a mirror.

"Amazing work," was all he could say.

"You can see why I now believe you knew her before the gala."

Trev inhaled sharply and shook his head. "I'm sorry, I don't understand. I'm assuming Raven did this recently."

"No, I saw this a couple months before the dance." Paganne ran her fingers over the paint applied to the canvas and board. "See? Oil paint takes time to harden. Judging by this, she hasn't touched this painting since the last time I viewed it. It's amazing. Boy, did she catch you. My big sister is very talented, eh?"

"Yes, she's a very special lady." One that had done a painting of him before they even met.

A cool breeze shifted through the glass room, causing Trev to wonder if he stared at Tashian Dumont.

The Halloween party was fun. They grilled shish kebabs over the bonfire Brishen built, and ate Raven's delicious spice cake with the orange frosting. Julian never showed, but then Trev had been fairly sure his friend wouldn't.

After everyone was full, Brishen entertained them with tales of Milosh and that Gypsy vampire hunter's valiant battles to rid the world of evil.

Getting a slight headache, Trev excused himself to go inside for a couple of aspirin.

At the landing bathroom door, he paused, then switched directions and went up to the small bathroom off Raven's bedroom.

There he found the aspirin, took two but feared they might not bring relief. This was a tension headache. He didn't get them often, but they could be doozies when they put in the rare appearance. As he came down the steps he paused at the bottom, then sensed something was wrong. He glanced toward the smaller glass room, considering the painting and how uncanny it was, and how strange that it had been done, if he believed Paganne, before he and Raven met. When coupled with his dreams . . . yes, it did cause him some disquiet.

There was more, however. He couldn't explain, but he suddenly felt a rising unease about Des and Jago. Glancing at the grandfather clock, he saw it was nearing ten p.m. He didn't know how they would celebrate Halloween, or if they did at all on Falgannon Isle, but it was still early enough to call there. And in Kentucky it would only be a little before five.

Opening the hall closet he took out his leather jacket and reached inside for his cell phone. A noise in the large greenhouse drew his attention, so he looked inside. Atticus was pecking at his reflection in a plate of glass. Going to him, he squatted down and stroked the bird's back.

"Hey, boy, you want another bird to play with? Of course, you might not recognize that's you, since you think you're a cat. I'll talk to Raven about some toys, or see if we can get you a friend." The bird turned his head and rubbed it against Trev's shin. "Silly Atticus."

As he rose, his eyes were drawn to the fortune-teller's

booth. He started to walk on past, but with the foreboding increasing, he was weak. "Just call me William Shatner," he muttered. Retrieving a coin from his pocket, he popped it into the slot.

This time when the large crystal ball filled with swirling blue smoke, it undulated and writhed until it began to take on a form. Slowly, through the mist, Trev began to make out a woman. Her hair was long and wavy—dark, maybe black. At first he thought perhaps it was the woman he kept seeing in his dreams, only some inner sense discounted that. She started to turn toward him, but just as he caught a glimpse of a sad smile, she turned and began walking away. He wanted to cry, "Wait! Please don't go! Stay!" But he didn't. He could only watch as she slowly vanished into the orb.

He blinked thrice before he saw a card had been ejected. Trepidation flooded through his mind and heart as he reached for it. The Wheel of Fortune, in the reversed position. And the fortune read:

The Wheel goes round and round.

He'd borrowed the divination book from Colford, and was learning the meaning of the Major Arcana. Thus he knew this meant unexpected bad luck, difficulties and delays.

Suddenly, he felt in a panic to talk to Des and Jago. His legs were too weak to hold him, so he went to the living room and sat on the sofa.

The phone rang and rang at B.A.'s home on Falgannon. Giving up in frustration, Trev tried the number for the pub, thinking surely someone would be there. Not the case. "Damn, and double damn! I really needed to hear your voice, Des, to know everything is all right on that bloody island!" he muttered.

He glanced at his wristwatch. While they might have

plans for Halloween, maybe he could catch Jago before his brother went out. The call went through, but once more it rang endlessly.

Just as he was ready to hang up, the phone was answered. "Oo-it's Wash-o-rama. You pay it, we spray it. What can I do you for?" came the nasally voice on the other end.

For an instant Trev thought he'd misdialed, but then he caught the playfulness in the man's tone. "Is Jago there? This is his brother Trevelyn calling."

"Ah, *Trevelyn* . . . yes, the hired help is here, and yes, you may speak to him. However, remember this is a business, and we frown upon personal calls, just so you—" The chatter was cut off as the phone was either dropped or snatched away; then in the background came more teasing, "Trevelyn? Bet he wears *shorts*, too. Hey, hey!"

Trev chuckled as it sounded like water was being sprayed. This was the touch of normalcy he was so desperately seeking. The pressure building in his chest began to ease.

"Just for that, I'm going to go find your cat, kidnap him and hold him for ransom."

"Well, while you're torturing him, see if he'll reveal his name." Laughing, Jago finally took the phone. "Hello, brother dearest. I'm rather busy at the moment, so make it short, please."

"Yeah, they're getting ready to put you in a padded cell. I leave you alone for a few weeks and you get into trouble. Oo-it's Wash-o-rama? Kidnapping and torturing your cat? *What* cat? Even more pressing, what the bloody hell is an Oo-it?"

Jago explained, "Oo-it is the nickname for a quirky but strangely endearing character who works at The Windmill here. Whole place is full of them."

"Similar to Falgannon Isle. When I talk to Des, he sounds like he's hip-deep in oddballs. He's also getting a hint of a Scottish burr—and you, brother dear, are acquiring a Kentucky twang," Trev pointed out, loving the peace their banter was bringing to him.

"While you are growing veddy Brit. Consider yourself lucky you didn't go to Falgannon or here and escaped the local color. Your finicky temperament couldn't handle it."

"Oh, I wouldn't say I avoided eccentric people. There's a small band of Gypsies camped on the Colford property. I'd think people living in wagons in this day and age ranks right up there with your out-of-the-ordinary." Trev exhaled in relief that everything seemed all right with his sibling. "How are things going?"

"I detect a note of concern," Jago remarked.

"I wish this was all done," Trev admitted. "The pretense of being Trevelyn Sinclair wearies me. I've been buying Montgomerie Enterprise stock left and right all week, yet keeping it slow enough not to draw attention. We're gaining inroads. Still, I'd prefer the takeover to be a fait accompli. I dislike not being in contact with Des or you. I ring and ring and can't reach either of you. I keep having dreams of the sisters getting together and comparing notes—then all hell breaks loose."

"Between us, I'd prefer we just drop the plans, tell them the truth now, before your dream becomes a reality—a nightmare."

"Knowing what it would do to Des? It'd not just ruin him financially, but . . . well, also what it would do to *him*. This isn't about money. You know that," Trevelyn said. But there was less conviction to his words than three weeks earlier.

"There should be another way. The takeover will happen." Jago sounded half angry, half desperate. "Des has the wheels in motion and there's no stopping them. Only, we can come clean first. Lay all our cards on the table. Do the deal straight on."

"Des wants it this way. We owe him—"

Jago exhaled, obviously struggling for control. It was so unlike St. Jago. "Don't start. Just don't bloody start. I've heard the song and dance, chapter and verse, until I am ready to puke, Trev. This is *not* the way. It can't be the way—"

Trev's phone signaled he had another call. "My other line is ringing, Jago. Let me take it. It's Mershan International's number, so it will be Julian. Hold—"

"That's my phone saying the battery is low." Jago clearly jumped at the excuse to break off the conversation. "I need to recharge it. I'm out for the night, so call me tomorrow. Not early. Remember the time difference."

"No! Wait—"

The line went dead. Frowning, Trev punched the button to take the call from Julian. "What's up?"

"Sorry, Trev, no way to break this to you easily. Your mother has taken a turn for the worse. I'm preparing arrangements for you three as we speak. I'll fetch Des from Falgannon. I just tried to call Jago, but his line was busy—"

"Yeah, we were speaking. His phone battery is down. You won't reach him, and he said he'd be out for the rest of the night, unavailable until tomorrow. Damn!"

"Don't worry. I'll book his flights and have a limo driver go pick him up and get him to the airport. I could pick you up before I go for Desmond, but figured you wouldn't want me landing on Colford's rolling lawn with that big Sikorsky with the M on the side. I've sent a driver for you. He should be there shortly. I don't want you driving. You have a lead foot on the best of occasions, and this is not the best of occasions."

"I'll be waiting in Ireland." Trev snapped the phone shut.

Raven was just walking into the kitchen, carrying dirty plates and glasses. She saw him rushing to the stairs and followed. He grabbed his duffel from the bottom of her closet and rushed around, gathering things. He wasn't sure what. It didn't matter. He had to move or scream.

"Trev, what's wrong? Why are you packing?"

He stood by the closet, considering what to take. Screw it. Julian could buy whatever was needed in Ireland. He closed his eyes and tried to figure out what he was going to tell Raven. "I really don't have time. A driver is on the way to fetch me to the airport. My mother is. . . . not well."

"I can come with you, if you like," she offered, sympathy filling her eyes.

"No!" He flinched when it sounded so harsh. "I'm sorry. I'm at sixes and sevens. I need to get traveling to meet up with my brothers. You . . . you . . . should be here for Brishen's grand opening. He will need your support."

"You don't need me?" she asked.

He paused, knowing he was handling this all wrong. Grabbing her, he pulled her to him. "You have no idea how much I need you. Only, everything is a mess. Let me get settled and see what the situation is, and then I'll call you." He kissed the top of her head, squeezing her tightly. "I *will* call, Raven. I promise."

A knock on the door frame called attention to the fact that they were not alone. "I don't meant to play sister interruptus, but there's a big black limo in the driveway and a man asking for Trev."

Trevelyn gave Raven a pained smile. "Sorry, gotta go."

Raven trailed along with him to the waiting car. The chauffer was there, in a black uniform, right down to the bloody jodhpurs. "The mysterious Julian Starkadder strikes again, eh?" she tried to tease.

"I'll call, Raven." Trev nodded and then started to climb inside. Spinning around, he wanted to tell her what was in his heart, but Raven let out a sob and went running back inside. Shaking, he started to go after her.

The driver stopped him. "We have to hurry, Mr. Mershan. You won't make the flight if you don't leave now."

Trev dropped into the plush seat, closed the door and watched the cottage until it was out of sight. The last thing he saw was Pyewacket in the front window, silently asking where was he going.

"I'm going to Hell, Pye. I'm going to Hell."

Chapter Twenty

Trev walked down the long corridor of the hospital. People came and went from the various rooms: nurses, doctors, orderlies, friends, family and even clergy. Patients were wheeled by on gurneys, going for various treatments or tests. Despite the endless flow of people, they were oddly faceless to him. He was aware of his actions, yet he moved through this shifting throng almost entirely detached from them and the endless misery—too steeped in his own, he supposed.

He approached the nurses' island, seeing several there. One was hurriedly filing charts into a rack, another was on the phone, while two more watched monitors and ignored him. The nurse speaking on the telephone held up her index finger to silence his question. He stood waiting until she got off.

Guilt was eating at him. He should have come here before, but Des had insisted she was doing better. His brother was also adamant that they finish this business with the Montgomeries, so he could present their mother with justice all so many years. Only, Trev wondered if they, once again, had left it too late. Des had been too late to confront Sean Montgomerie. Perhaps it'd be too late for his brother to lay vindication before Katlyn Mershan's feet, give her what she had asked for a hundred times—a *thousand* times: to make the Montgomeries pay for what her family suffered.

Trev closed his eyes against that thought. He worried about his brother's soul. Des needed this closure. If it was denied him . . . well, Heaven help Desmond.

The nurse finally rang off and offered him a professional smile. "May I help you?"

"Katlyn Mershan's room? I'm her son, Trevelyn." He managed to get the words out, though it sounded like someone else spoke.

She nodded. "The doctor is in with her presently. If you'll be having a seat?"

"I would like to speak with him when he's through." It wasn't a request, and that was carried in Trev's voice.

The thirty-something redhead picked up a chart and made a note. "Yes, I'll tell him. Is your father coming soon? She keeps asking for him."

It took everything to keep from breaking into hysterical laughter. Or crying. "My father's dead. Has been for a number of years."

"Oh, that's a pity. She keeps insisting he will come soon. Poor thing."

Trev gave a brief nod. "Yes, a pity."

He took a seat on the small sofa off to the side. Poorly designed, it was about as comfortable as sitting on a fencepost. In a place where people did a lot of sitting and waiting, he would have thought they would try to make people as comfortable as possible. He waited, not sure how long, for time seemed to crawl, but finally the doctor came out of the room. Trev rose and stepped to meet him. Dr. Grimaldi. He read the name on the metal placard on the pocket of the white coat. The idiotic thought strayed through his mind that it was a strange name for an Irishman.

"The nurse said you're Katlyn's son." The small, dark-haired doctor held out his hand.

"One of them. I'm Trevelyn. My two brothers, Desmond and Jago, are on their way. They have to travel farther," Trev explained.

The man looked grim. "Let's hope they don't take too long. No patient has an expiration date stamped on the heel of their foot, but your mother is on borrowed time. The last forty-eight hours have seen a marked decline in her condition, with other complications as well."

"What sort of complications?"

"At first we feared it might be Alzheimer's, but that's been ruled out."

"Alzheimer's?" Trev echoed. "Why would you think that?"

The doctor looked exhausted, bone-weary. Trevelyn imagined working with cancer patients was not an easy road to travel. "She's having trouble recognizing where she is, what year this is. She even thinks the nurses are her servants. She keeps asking when her husband is coming home. It's my understanding your father's dead."

"Yes, he committed suicide nearly thirty-five years ago." And left his family to deal with the aftermath. Trev absently wondered if Michael Mershan had ever considered what he was condemning his wife and sons to face when he pulled that trigger. Fighting the emotional wave crashing over him, Trev closed his eyes against the pain.

"We're not sure. It could be the cancer hitting the brain, but she has become increasingly detached from reality. It possibly could be something else. I suppose in her weakened state, her mind is slipping into memories when she was happy with your father. Well, at this stage the problem is moot. The best we can do now is to keep her comfortable. I'm giving her morphine every four hours—"

"Morphine?" Trevelyn echoed.

"She's in considerable pain and nothing else can help. As I said, we're trying to keep her at ease. A word of caution about expectations—some patients seek their release from this world, some fight it. How long your mother lasts will depend on which path she chooses. So, it could be a day or two . . ." The doctor patted Trev's arm in sympathy. "Or it could be longer."

Trev nodded and then moved into the room to face the

terrible prospect of watching his mother die. Two steps inside saw him reel back in horror. *This has to be a mistake.* That couldn't be his mother. The room was pleasant enough, though sparse. The woman in the hospital bed was resting quietly. But as he moved closer, he saw tubes were running through one side of her nose, which seemed to be connected to some sort of pump at the side of her bed.

At the bedside, he still pondered if this wasn't the wrong room. This woman seemed so old. When he'd visited her, just before he returned to England for the charity gala, she had been happy, active. He could recall the day clearly, coming into the room to find her dancing to the Moody Blues song "The Story in Your Eyes." She'd had the big teddy bear he'd brought her, and she and the bear were rocking to the beat. The scene had made him smile because through the years she'd so often been depressed, only late in life being diagnosed with bipolar disorder.

No, this poor woman couldn't be his mother. Then her head turned, and she opened her green eyes and he knew he stared at Katlyn Mershan. The sounds of buzzing bees filled his head and his knees felt too rubbery to hold him up; the whole room seemed to tilt on its axis.

"Jago?" she asked, her throat sounding parched.

He shook his head, finding words hard to form. "No, Momma, I'm Trevelyn—Jago's evil twin, remember?" He tried for a note of levity. It was that or be carried away by a sea of tears.

"So thirsty. They won't give me . . . anything to drink." She almost seemed to fade away.

He looked around for a carafe of ice water, but saw nothing. Anger exploded within him. "I'll get you something to drink, Momma."

He wanted to lash out at life, at how cruelly it had treated his gentle mother. She hadn't been created to fight the world and try to forge a life for herself and three small sons. By God, she'd tried her best, working long hours at low-paying jobs. Now she couldn't even be blessed with a peaceful death?

He was half Irish, and at times like this it showed. Marching out to the nurses' station, he tried to keep hold of the reins of his black temper. It was damn hard. He really craved to put his fist through something, anything. The woman was again on the phone, and she gave him the one finger hold-until-I-finish signal. He leaned over, jerked the phone away and slammed it into its cradle.

"My mother is thirsty. There's no water in her room. Nothing. I will not stand by while she suffers. I want some fruit juices, a bucket of ice and a carafe of ice water in there, *now*. Am I clear?"

She was startled by his aggressive tone, but she only offered him a sad eye. "We're not deliberately ignoring her, Mr. Mershan. She can't have fluids because of being hooked up to that pump. I can bring her some ice chips. You can feed those to her slowly."

"I would appreciate it," he snapped. Getting hold of his temper, he added, "Thank you."

He stalked back into his mother's room. Finding a chair in the corner, he pulled it to her bedside and sat. "They are bringing some ice chips. That will help with the being thirsty." He reached out and took her hand, careful of the IV cord taped to her arm.

"Thank you." Her fingers trembled in his hand. "Is Michael coming?"

Trev's heart felt as if it would burst. He nodded, tears falling. "Yes, Momma, he's coming."

Trev stood staring out the window of the hotel room Julian had rented for them. Two big beds. Two brothers could sleep while one was at the hospital; that way Katlyn was never alone. Of course, most of the time two brothers ended up at the hospital instead of just one. Being there was hard, but it was better than waiting at the hotel. The endless waiting.

The days seemed to blur into one long nightmare. Trev recalled looking up and seeing Desmond and Jago coming down the hallway, with Julian directly behind. Never had anything felt as good as hugging his brothers. Was that a week ago? Two? Closer to three?

"Bloody hell, I have no idea anymore." Trev took the towel from around his neck, left from drying off after his shower, and wiped his face of tears. "Odd, a person cries until he thinks there are no more tears. Yet there are. There always are." He spoke to his ghostly reflection in the window.

He wanted Raven, wanted to hold her warm body against his. He wanted to cry in her embrace. Wanted to lose himself in the mindless sex that could exorcise all this despair threatening to engulf him. But he'd promised himself he would be strong, for as bad as it was hitting him, he knew it was destroying Desmond. His brother needed his support and strength now, not weakness. Only, he didn't know how much more of this never-ending misery he could take.

He glanced at the phone and then started to turn away. It reminded him of Julian counting how many times he'd wanted to call Raven that first day and hadn't. He'd hurt her by not calling. Only a fool made the same mistake twice.

Picking it up, he punched the numbers. Only then did he recall how late it was—nearly four in the morning. By God, he missed her. He wanted her here. For various reasons, that was impossible. Desmond was like a bear with a thorn in his paw, more determined than ever to go through with the merger and destruction. Trev feared Raven's presence would just give his angry, wounded brother a place to vent all his pain. Trev wouldn't risk subjecting Raven to that.

"Hello?" came the sleepy voice on the other end.

"A call to Lil' Red Riding Hood from the Big Bad Wolf. Will you accept the charges?" He tried to tease, hoping the tears clogging his throat wouldn't be heard.

She sighed, and then yawned. "Hmm. That depends."

"Upon what?"

"Upon if he promises to come home soon."

Home. The word echoed in the hollow of his heart. It struck Trevelyn he'd never really had a home. They had traveled, moved so many times over the years, often never finishing a full year in the same school. Then, later, Jago and he went to college—paid for by Des—and after graduation he'd lived in a string of apartments wherever Mershan International sent him. He'd never had a chance to set down roots, to plan on celebrating New Year's at the start of the year and Christmas at the end in the same place. He suddenly wanted that. Wanted it very much. Wanted it with Raven.

"A few more days." Then he changed the subject because he simply didn't know. His life was one endless hell. Worse, he felt bad for thinking such a thought, because for the hell to end would mean his mother would have to die. "How are the beasties?"

"They miss you. Like I do. Pyewacket sits in the window watching the driveway. Poor Chester goes through the house letting out a mournful howl. He sleeps on your shirt, like your scent gives him comfort. I thought about wrestling it away to see if cuddling up with it would work for me, only he's quite insistent it's his. Bit me the last time I tried to swipe it! Atticus just gives me dirty looks."

Trev tried to think of something to say, but small talk was nearly too much for him. "I miss the guys, too. I'm exhausted. I better go get some rest. I just wanted to hear your voice, wanted you to know I was thinking of you."

"Hurry home, Trevelyn."

"Home sounds like paradise. Night, night, pretty lady."

He no sooner rang off than the phone sounded. He

looked at the damn thing like it was a snake, coiling and hissing. An automaton, he picked it up and punched the button. "Trev."

Julian's voice came over the phone. "You better get back here. Fast."

Trevelyn likely broke several traffic laws getting to the hospital. He pulled up at one entrance and jumped out. No Parking signs were all along the circular drive, but he didn't care. He hurried down the long colonnade, the automatic doors opening as he neared.

An orderly greeted him as he came in. "Hey, you can't park there!" he called. Trev flashed him a look that could kill, tossed him the key to the rental but didn't slow.

A family with three nearly grown children was at the elevator doors, arguing over who got to go in first to ICU to see Gran. He tried to push by them, but the one lady wouldn't move, despite him saying "Excuse me" twice. She glared at him with a *wait-your-turn* flashing in her eyes. Exasperated, he picked up the woman by the waist and set her aside. She fussed and tried to slap his arms. He didn't care.

"Oh, how rude!" She glared at her husband. "Well, aren't you going to do anything, Innis?"

Trev stepped in and pushed the button to the fifth floor. "My mother is dying. You think I'm going to stand on politeness?"

The doors closed on her flummoxed expression, but he didn't give a tinker's damn.

The nurses had gotten used to the Mershan brothers coming and going over the past weeks. All heads turned as they saw Trev running down the long corridor. None admonished him. Only pitying stares met his.

He rushed into the door of his mother's room. Julian was standing just inside, and Jago, their backs blocking his view. Mindless with panic, Trev tried to push past, but Julian caught him.

"Steady, friend," the man whispered.

Desmond was sitting in the chair at their mother's bedside; his murmured responses to Katlyn's soft words didn't carry. His larger hands cradled her smaller one, which was so pale and frail. Almost skeletal. The fingers twitched three times . . . and then no more.

"Momma!" Trev tried to shove past Jago, refusing to believe she was gone. She was just resting. He wanted to tell her how much he loved her, how he understood all she'd suffered just to keep the family together. How valiant she had been.

Jago's strong hand took hold of his arm, pulling him back. "She's gone."

The nurse wove her way through the black-haired men to the other side of the bed to take Katlyn's pulse. She listened for what seemed an eternity, then finally put the stethoscope back around her neck and looked at her watch. "She's passed. Take relief in that she's no longer suffering pain." She reached up and tried to close Katlyn's eyelids, but they wouldn't close. She finally forced them down and held them there for a minute so they would stay.

Des looked up from where he was crying, his expression meant to turn the nurse's blood to ice. "Get your hands off her. Now. Haven't you people done enough to her?"

Trevelyn reached out. "Back off, Des. That nurse has been nothing but kind to—"

Des rounded on him, hitting him hard with both hands to the chest and slamming him up against the wall. "Where the bloody hell were you? Where?"

"Des, stop it," Jago ordered, trying to push between them. "He got here as soon as he could. It was the luck of the draw. She could have died when you or I were off trying to get some rest, too."

Desmond closed his eyes, his pain too much to control. He finally thrust past them and out of the room, going down the hall.

"I drove like a maniac getting here." Trev forced a mirthless laugh. "The rental car is likely stolen—with my permission."

Jago nodded. "I know. As I said, it could have been any of us taking our turn. Don't let Desmond dump his pain on you."

Julian swallowed hard and then spoke. "Please accept my deepest condolences on the passing of your dear mother. She was a lovely lady and a gentle soul, who life treated very unfairly. But she was blessed to have three sons that loved her very much."

Trev couldn't find anything to say, but accepted the hug Julian gave him. Pulling back, Julian patted Jago on the back. Tears streamed down the man's face and he glanced at the nurse, who was still waiting at bedside.

"I'll go after Desmond," he said. "Give him space. He's in love with B.A., so this is tearing him apart inside. I'm hoping that love will be his salvation." With that, Julian spun on his heel and left.

The nurse offered the Mershan twins a sad smile. "If you would like to say good-bye to her, I can step outside."

Trev shook his head. What had been Katlyn Mershan was gone—hopefully to a better place, a kinder place. He watched the nurse pulling the sheet up over his mother's head, and for the second time thought that the dead woman couldn't be his beautiful mother. This had to be some horrible mistake.

Jago ran his hand over his face then looked around him like he was lost. "Bloody hell, this whole damn mess is only going to get worse. Des will go after Montgomerie Enterprises with a vengeance now. He will want them to pay. He won't care he could be destroying all our lives."

A chill ran up Trev's spine, for he feared his brother was right.

Chapter Twenty-one

"February second. It's Candlemas . . . a time of renewal," Raven said aloud, almost giddy. "What a perfect day to get the news."

She buried the tach nearly in the red, hearing her ancient MGB rumble and whine. She didn't care if it was a cantankerous car, if it wouldn't start in rainy weather half the time; she was thrilled it lacked cruise control, an on-board navigational device, had no cell phone or any of the other modern stuff that could break. She loved how the car handled and simply enjoyed driving it. Usually she was mindful that it was getting up in years, but today was different. Everything was different. She was going to have a baby!

The secret inside her was no longer her secret. The doctor and nurse knew, and some lab person, too; probably a bookkeeper and secretary as well. But they were honor bound to keep her happy news to themselves. She would get to do the honors of telling Trevelyn he was going to be a daddy.

She sighed, wondering how he would take it. They had never really talked about children. Not about having them together. He knew she wanted a child, but since she hadn't thought she could get pregnant, the topic had fallen off the list of things to share on the nights they lay awake talking.

She'd fretted about him since his return. The arrogant, playful Trevelyn had gone away on Halloween night. The man who returned nearly three weeks later was increasingly drawn, morose and suffered tormented sleep. She hadn't pushed. Men tended to turn into clams when you demanded they open emotionally.

"Especially big bad alpha wolves," she said aloud. Give them space and they usually come around—that was a lesson she'd learnt by having six brothers.

Only, it was now two months since he'd come back and Trevelyn seemed no closer to opening up about what was tearing him apart. Oh, her heart ached knowing his mother's death was hitting him hard. She recalled how he hadn't told her anything about his mother's passing until late that first night home. Then, in the middle of the night, he'd turned to her and cried.

The news had hurt her, his pain being hers. Still, she'd experienced a mild upset that he hadn't wanted her at the funeral. When he'd sensed her distance and asked what was wrong, she finally voiced that she felt he'd shut her out of his life. He'd said there had been no funeral to speak of, just arrangements for the burial and a brief graveside service with him and his brothers, according to his mother's wishes. In a way, she understood that. She had a feeling that his family had felt it was them against the world in life. In death it would be no different.

Clearly, he was grieving, but she had a feeling something else troubled him as well.

They'd had a wonderful Christmas, putting up an eight-foot-tall tree and decorating it with Victorian Christmas ornaments. She'd loved shopping and seeing that everything was perfect. At times his beautiful eyes seemed haunted, and she knew he recalled Christmases past when things were rough for his family. But those eyes were shining when she'd come down Christmas morning and found Brishen's rocking horse by the tree with a big red bow around it—Trev's present to her. For Boxing Day they'd gone to the celebration at Colford, but Christmas had been just for them. It had been a magic time of love and healing.

Paganne tossed a big New Year's party. Raven thought back on the next-to-nothing blue Vera Wang gown she'd worn. Designer gowns were not her style, but she'd gone shopping with Paganne and come back with the pricey item. There was no back, and it was cut low in the front. "A slip would cover more," she'd commented. Only, she'd had an idea the vivid blue gown might be just the thing to shake Trevelyn out of his black mood.

She deliberately hadn't let him see her in it until she came downstairs. He was on the phone when she paused on the landing and struck a pose. Poor man's jaw dropped. He laid the phone down without hanging up, and walked over to the newel post. His stunned expression was worth the price tag of the gown. Of course, she'd been rather speechless herself. Trev was wearing a gray pinstripe suit and oh, wow! Her knees went weak looking at him.

That night was the first time she'd told him she loved him. She had waited for him to declare it. At times she didn't need the words, because she saw the love in his eyes when he looked at her. Or when she would catch him with Atticus, feeding the bird junk food. He showed it in a hundred ways. Still, a woman needed to hear it.

They were dancing when the clock struck twelve, ushering in a new year. He had stopped dancing and kissed her, soft, exquisitely full of the power of their love. She hadn't been able to keep the words back.

"Trevelyn, I love you," she'd whispered.

He'd kissed her again and then whispered, "I'm not sure I have the right to tell you I love you. But I do."

That odd way of expressing it caused her pause, but the party pushed against them as everyone was opening their party crackers, and finding hats and horns to blow. The moment was lost and she hadn't wanted to ask what he meant afterward. Fearful, she didn't want to know the answer.

Well, the time for hiding was over. She was pregnant!

After losing the baby seven years ago, she'd gone through stages. At first, she hadn't wanted to talk about babies, then later accepted she likely would never have one. Some women were career-minded and could have moved on. But at the back of her mind, she wanted a child. Katrina's Emile had only brought home just how much. Still, she hadn't contemplated the miracle of having Trevelyn's baby. Even to wish for it felt like courting pain.

Parking the MGB at the front door, she breezed into Trevelyn's office.

"Miracles do happen, Agnes," she told his secretary. "So never give up hope."

The woman looked up and removed her glasses, then arched her brows. "What? You train Mr. High and Mighty to take out the trash?"

"Something better."

The woman was too bloody sharp. As she looked Raven up and down, shock filled her eyes. "Oh, my! You're expecting?"

Raven put her finger to her lips. "Mum's the word."

And then they both broke out in laughter over the pun.

Agnes came around the desk and hugged her. "Don't fret about him hearing. He's out with Julian, doing a banking run. They should be back in a few minutes. How far along are you?"

"A little over two months. I've been sick a couple mornings this week and thought I was coming down with the flu."

"You caught something else, eh? You'll have your hands full with that one, but he's worth the fight, I'm thinking."

"I agree."

The room seemed to swirl suddenly, and Agnes reached out to catch Raven. "Come on—you need to have a quick lie down while you wait for His Nibs," the woman insisted.

Raven did feel tired, so she stretched out on the comfy leather sofa in the corner of Trev's office. Lying there, she closed her eyes and played inside the theatre of her mind, running over the various reactions that Trevelyn might display when she told him of the baby.

She must have dozed off. The hands on the wall clock had moved nearly a half hour when she heard the outer door open. Expecting Trevelyn, she sat up.

"I'm here to see Trevelyn Mershan," the woman informed her in a cultured voice.

"You must've come to the wrong address, miss." Agnes's voice was frosty. "This is Sinclair Group, Ltd."

The other woman snapped, "Don't give me that, you biddy."

Then it struck Raven why the voice seemed so familiar. It was Melissa Barrington! What was Melissa doing in Trevelyn's office? Then it hit her: Melissa hadn't asked for Trevelyn Sinclair. She had asked to see Trevelyn *Mershan*.

"Young woman, if you don't leave I shall call the constable and have you remo—"

Melissa's laughter was high and shrill. "I sincerely doubt that. Now, you tell Trevelyn Mershan that Melissa Barrington is here to see him. I've been fired by Cian Montgomerie."

Raven blinked, puzzled. Well, good for Cian! But what was Melissa trying to do? Apply for another job?

"I'm sorry, but Mr. Sinclair isn't hiring at this time. If you leave your name and number, I'll place it on file in case an opening comes up." Agnes rose and moved to the door to show Melissa out.

"You can drop the bullshit. I am *not* applying for a job. I've had enough of these fenhoppers around here. Des Mershan promised a big bonus. I'd like to collect it and be on my way. I tried to call him, but I keep getting 'He's unavailable.'" Melissa warned, "If they're thinking to stiff me on the bonus, they'd better have second thoughts. While I no longer work for Montgomerie Enterprises, I'm sure Cian would pay well to know what Trident Ventures and Mershan International are up to. Don't you?"

Raven felt the floor tilt under her feet as she stood. She had never liked Melissa, so the woman's double-dealing didn't surprise her. She'd warned Cian that Melissa had poison pumping through her. But . . .

She opened the inner door and faced Melissa. "Why don't you tell me, my dear? I'll write you a check now."

Instead of shock hitting her face, Melissa just smiled. The expression sent a cold chill up Raven's spine. "I doubt Little Miss Muffet has that much blunt in her checking account, but I would enjoy enlightening you for free."

Raven exhaled. What was it with people always associating her with fairy tales? "Actually, I'm Little Red Riding Hood, but I'm sure the distinction missed you completely."

Melissa strode forward. "Muffet? Riding Hood? Whatever. Shall we go into the office and sit down while I spin you a modern-day fairy tale? Shocks are absorbed so much better when the knees are bent." She turned to Agnes. "You can run along and do what you need for the Mershans."

Raven walked to Julian's desk and sat in his chair, and waited while Melissa seated herself. Outside, Agnes picked up the phone and hit a red button. "Julian, you and Trevelyn get back here. Now."

Crossing her legs, Melissa smiled. "Once upon a time there were three little pigs—"

"Oh, for God's sake, get on with it," Raven snapped.

The blonde chuckled and smoothed her skirt. "Oh, but I am enjoying this."

"Fine." Raven pushed away from the desk. "But I'm in no mood to play games with you."

Melissa continued as if Raven hadn't spoken. "Their names were Desmond, Jago and Trevelyn. They were rich little piggies, but what they had wasn't good enough. They wanted to be kings of the realm."

Raven walked around the desk and picked up her coat and slid it on.

"Oh, come on." Melissa gave her a warm, cajoling expression. "Well, pooh—you're no fun."

Raven flashed her a fake smile. "Ah, Melissa, I prefer my playmates to have a wee modicum of intelligence. I fear you do nothing but bore me. I shall leave you—and your 'pooh.'" She breezed past the other woman, sailing through the office and past Agnes, who called to her. She didn't slow. She had no idea what was going on. Something was very wrong, but she wasn't about to allow this bitch whatever satisfaction she hoped to gain by hurting her. She'd go home, call Cian and have him deal with the information she'd overheard.

Rain nearly drenched Raven as she pushed into her MGB, shaking to a point where she had a hard time getting the key into the slot on the steering column. Somehow she managed, but then the damn car went into its rainy-day act, refusing to start. Raven kept the ignition cranking, its noise almost catching but then stopping. It took three times before it finally caught. Finally the engine turned over with its familiar purr, and she reversed the car at an angle, planning on pulling out of the lot.

Melissa whipped her white Alfa Romeo around to block the MGB's path. She pulled up so she was facing the opposite direction. Their windows were side by side. Melissa rolled hers down, clearly at the touch of a button. She gave Raven an expression that said she had her pinned in and wouldn't allow her to move until Raven rolled down her window and listened. Raven finally gave up and cranked down the glass.

"Since you don't like to play games, I'll make it short and sweet. You're getting screwed in more ways than one, sweetheart. Your sisters, your family, too. His name isn't Trevelyn Sinclair—it's Trevelyn Mershan. He and his brothers are positioning themselves for a hostile takeover of Montgomerie Enterprises. It's already a fait accompli, I fear. I figure that's information enough. Enjoy unraveling the mysterious Mershans. Ta!"

Raven swallowed, waiting for Melissa to pull forward enough to permit the MGB to get by. She flipped on the wipers, then saw the silver Range Rover come flying down the road. This car Trevelyn had been renting for the past couple weeks pulled in the opposite end of the lot, as Raven's and Melissa's blocked the lower entrance. As Raven released the hand brake and began to ease forward, she glanced in the rearview mirror. Agnes had rushed out and was speaking to Trevelyn. She pointed and gestured.

Raven just wanted to get away from him right now. She needed to get home and call Colford. She'd let Cian deal with the mess.

Melissa smiled wickedly and gunned her little Alfa Romeo, pulled directly behind the Rover, crossways. Totally blocking Trev.

"Thank you, Melissa," Raven muttered. Her rickety MGB would never have outrun the powerful Range Rover. Now Melissa, intent on confronting Trevelyn—likely to get that bonus she'd been promised—had gifted her with a head start.

She shifted the MGB for maximum speed, zooming down the road with the wipers barely keeping the windscreen clear. As she sped along, trapped in her thoughts, a coin dropped. She recalled Trevelyn saying his twin was named James. *Jago.* Jago was Old English for James.

She really shouldn't have been driving. Her emotional state allowed her to lapse into questions. Dangerous, on a wet roadway. As she reached the S-turns just past Colford, she was going too fast and the tires hydroplaned. She tried to steer into the skid, but she ended up spinning the small car around three hundred and sixty degrees. It only came to a stop when the passenger-side tires edged off the pavement and found traction in the grass. Coming to a stop, Raven sat for a minute to gather her breath. Her heart was pounding and spots flashed before her eyes.

Taking a slow, steadying breath, she realized the car had gone into a stall and died.

She turned the key and it cranked but didn't catch. "Not now, you spoiled brat! I have kept you from the junk pile or from being chopped up for parts. I have babied you, spent a small fortune on you. Don't repay me this way. Oh, please." She made the mistake of pumping the gas. The damn thing flooded. She didn't have to know about its temperamental traits; she could smell the petrol.

Closing her eyes, she leaned her head against the steering wheel. "Bugger all." Disgusted with the cantankerous car, she snatched up her purse, rolled up the doctor's report and stuffed it into her leather pocket to keep it dry. On the left side of the steering column was a button, which she pulled to start the emergency flashers.

She set off across the back part of Colford's field, which cut her walking time in half. Her shoes would be ruined and she would look like a drowned rat by the time she got to the cottage, but she didn't care. The rain kicked in, pouring harder.

Her heels sank deep with every step across the spongy grass. "It'd serve Trevelyn Sinclair—" She caught herself and corrected the name. "It'd serve Trevelyn *Mershan* right if I catch pneumonia and croak."

As she stomped across the field, she was working up a proper temper. Muttering to herself, she cast all sort of curses on lying bastards and their brothers. Anything to pass the time, really. She'd always had a problem with high dudgeon: It required too much to keep it fueled. Whatever the offence, after her first flush of anger her temper rapidly faded until she couldn't recall why she'd been upset. This time her rage wasn't going to fade. If anything, she figured this was just the start.

Dark was approaching, but fortunately the house came into sight. Hurrying across the driveway and into the house, she stopped just inside the door, resentment almost giving away to tears. If she started crying, she'd never stop.

Both cats came to greet her, looking at her with odd expressions. "Yeah, I know. I look like a drowned rat. I'm not sure what a drowned rat *feels* like, but I'm pretty sure I feel like one, too."

Slipping off her wet coat, she went to the phone and punched out the number for Colford. It rang and rang before a maid finally answered, relaying the information that everyone was out or getting ready for a benefit for the Historical Trust. She left a message for Cian to call, saying it was urgent that he contact her immediately. Hanging up, she closed her eyes. *Paganne's to-do.* Her sister was chairing a benefit to raise money for the historical preservation of an old manor house being sold, trying to keep the land from ending up in the hands of a developer. Trevelyn was supposed to escort her.

"Well, scratch those plans." Exhaling pain, Raven took a step to go upstairs and get a towel for her hair, because she was dripping all over the hardwood floor.

The distant rumble of a car engine coming down the lane at high speed filled her little cul-de-sac. She watched as the headlights bounced, almost chuckled at Trevelyn's head likely hitting the roof when he bobbed through the potholes. Frozen by the emotional fugue, she stood, observing the lights turn and the silver car zoom down the driveway and park at the side of the house.

Looking down the long greenhouse, she realized Trevelyn could come in that way; that door was the closest. She ran down the long row of the glasshouse in time to lock it. Climbing out of the car, he spotted her there at the double-wide door and frowned. Tilting his head, he stalked around to the front.

With a squeak, Raven rushed ahead of him, getting there just in time and locking it. She wasn't sure precisely why she was barring him from the house. The cats looked at her, wondering what sort of new game she was playing.

When he rattled the knob and then pounded on the door, she jumped. "Raven, open the damn door!" he called, and then pounded on it again.

"Ah, the wolf huffs and puffs," she sniffed. "I do believe he's getting his fairy tales mixed up, boys."

Chester twisted his tail and meowed, wanting her to let Trevelyn in.

"No can do, Chester. He's— Yikes!" She jumped as she heard Trev going down the front steps. "Next stop, glass-house number two. Let's see if Red Riding Hood can beat the very bad wolf."

She didn't slow her pace. She could hear Trev rushing his step alongside the greenhouse. She got to the entrance just a couple of seconds before he did, and set the lock. She backed up almost as if she feared the blasted man might reach through the glass and grab her.

Trevelyn stood there, glaring, the rain pouring down on him. Was he trying to will her to open the door? He very calmly mouthed the words, "Open the door, Raven."

She faked a yawn and then looked at her fingers as if examining them for hangnails or chips. His mouth compressed into a glower, but she just rolled her eyes, then she slowly turned as if going to her paintings.

That same instant, he took off around the far corner heading to the back. Raven ran through the living room, down the hallway and into the kitchen. He made it onto the back porch before she could get out there, but she reached the inside door and shot the bolt.

"Ut, ut . . . Trevelyn's mad, I'm glad, and I know what'd take to please him," she sang in the child's chant. "Sorry, Mr. Wolf, you are *out*. Perhaps you should go back to that apartment Mershan International is paying for. You really should get some use out of it."

"Raven, please open the door so we can talk. I want to know you're all right. I found the MGB sitting out in the middle of the road and you were nowhere about. Scared the bloody hell out of me."

"Go away, Trevelyn Mershan. I have to go get ready for Paganne's benefit. I promised I would be there." Of course she had no intention of going, but he could think whatever he wanted.

"I'll drive you. Your car is still out in the road, remember." He rattled the knob.

She shook her head. "I called Cian. He's coming to pick me up."

He closed his eyelids at the mention of her brother. Obviously, he'd hoped to head her off from getting hold of Cian before he had a chance to warn Desmond and Jago that everything was going to hell in a handbasket. Let him think he was too late.

"Raven, please let me in. There is a lot I need to explain."

"Explain?" Her voice rose two octaves. "'Explain' is where there is mistaken information you wish to correct. I seriously doubt you can explain this pack of lies. Now, bye-bye. See you around, Mr. Mershan."

She flipped out the lights, leaving him standing on the darkened porch, and went back down the hall. She paused to look back, to see if he was still there. He was gone.

Raven scowled, caught between wanting to laugh over her small victory, yet ready to burst into tears. The bastard had lied to her! Then she remembered the New Year's party and him telling her he loved her but didn't think he had the right. Now it made sense! Trevelyn Mershan couldn't tell her he loved her. He was lying! About so much. Was he lying about loving her, too?

Trapped in the thought, movement at the other end of the greenhouse attracted her. "Guess he forgot we already played the game with that door."

Chester ran down the long room and up to the door, meowing, his tail vibrating as he talked at Trevelyn. Reaching for the wall switch, just inside the greenhouse—Raven flipped out the lights. The orange tabby came dancing back, meowing a protest about locking his friend outside.

"Bloody traitor," she fussed at the cat.

She tried not to look at Trevelyn standing in the rain, getting madder by the minute. Of course, he knew he had no right to get angry, so he was trying to control it. She knew him that well; she understood what was going through his mind.

"How can I know him so well, and yet didn't even know his real name?" Feeling sadness about to engulf her, her eyes were nonetheless drawn to him—just in time to see him rear back and kick out with his foot. "Oh, hell. He's unleashed that damn big toe again."

He walked in calmly, the rain from outside whipping around him, as though he were a wizard and had called down the power of the storm and surrounded himself with its ferocity. She watched him coming toward her. Coming for her. And she couldn't seem to move to save herself.

She watched, breathless from his feral beauty, the force élan that swirled about him like a mantle. Whatever his name, she loved him. And she was furious with herself for that. He had lied to her, used her, and she didn't even want to consider whatever shenanigans Des and Jago had been up to. But she couldn't turn off the emotions she felt.

She might want to kill him, but she loved him. The lying bastard. Oh, she wanted to scream at him. He and his wolfish charm had forced his way into her quiet world. She had been content before; happy, safe. Now . . . now she carried his baby. A miracle! Whatever else may come of this, he had given her something she wanted very badly.

Instead of offering contrite words, he grabbed her upper

arms and kissed her. His unyielding mouth took hers, formed her to his will, devoured her. Her fingers curled into fists to keep from reaching out and taking hold of his arms to anchor herself against the windswept emotions buffeting her heart, her soul. The arrogant wolf wasn't going to offer words or reasons, he was going to show her she belonged to him. He'd claimed her as his mate and that was all there was to it. Quite possibly it was—but she deserved his apologies, and he wasn't going to get off so easy.

With everything in her, she resisted him. She held herself stiff as a board. He didn't care. He wanted her to understand he was claiming her and there was nothing she could do to fight him.

Well, Trevelyn Mershan was about to learn she wasn't a lass to give way so easily when something so important was at stake. Their future.

She pulled back and started swinging side to side, struggling to break his hold. Tears rolled down her face, but she barely took notice. At this point, anger propelled her. She finally jerked away from him and took a step to run back to the living room. To do what? To run upstairs to the bedroom and play lock-the-door once more? To what purpose? Big Toe the Lethal Weapon would just have at it again. Nothing would be solved. There was no place she could run. She had a feeling there was no place on the whole bloody earth she could run to and he would not follow. Wolves mate for life.

He grabbed her arms from behind, but she was losing control. Swinging her elbow, she hoped a knock or two would get him to release her. Only, she stepped down on her left foot wrong, nearly twisting it, which caused her right elbow to fly high. The pointed bone made hard contact with his chin, stunning him. He backed up a step, trying to regain his balance to keep them both from falling to the stone floor.

"Oww!" he complained, rubbing his chin with one

hand. "I may have a toe for a secret weapon, but that damn elbow is wicked." He gave his head a shake. "You really rang my chimes."

Raven stopped struggling and looked at his chin. A reddish mark was already forming. She put her fingers over her mouth in horror of what she'd just done. It wasn't her nature to fight physically. She shunned emotional fights, which was why the marriage to Alec had been so hard. And she'd never *attacked* anyone. Well, this had been an accident. She hadn't hit him on purpose. Yet, tears streamed down her face, horrified she'd hurt him.

"Oh, Red, don't cry. Please. Let's sit down and talk. I can explain—"

"Do not ever use the word 'explain' to me again, Trevelyn Mershan. I mean it," she warned, feeling her temper going up on a roller coaster of highs and lows. The doctor had warned she would likely experience wild mood swings due to the chemicals being put out by the baby creating a place to live and thrive in her body.

He managed a laugh. "See, already you're getting used to the Mershan name."

It was the absolutely, positively worst thing for him to say! She saw red, and before she was even aware of what she was doing, she pulled back and let fly with a hard right, catching him in the eye. Then she let out a deep moan, agog that she had just slugged the man she loved, lowdown, lying worm that he was. Her head spun, trying to bring the two opinions into harmony.

"Not working," she fretted, and then burst into a flood of tears.

"Friggin' hell, that hurts. I'm going to have a shiner tomorrow and a few days thereafter."

He touched his finger to the already discolored eye. "Damn it, Raven. If it makes you feel better, hit me again, but stop with the waterworks. I cannot stand to see you crying."

One big long howl came out of her, and she shoved

past him, running outside. She had no idea where she was going or why, only that she needed to run. As her legs carried her out into the darkness, suddenly she understood why she ran. She feared he didn't love her.

Trevelyn yelled from behind. She heard his steps gaining on her, a wolf hunting down his prey. He'd win because wolves always did. She made it into the middle of the field. She saw car lights coming from the old road where it led to Colford, but she didn't care who was coming. She just kept running, heading for the woods. There she could lose herself.

Trevelyn screamed, "No!" and came flying through the air, bringing her down. He cushioned her fall, allowing his body to bear the brunt of hitting the ground.

Raven lay there, crying, feeling odd, almost not understanding why she was running from him in the rain. It was a stupid thing to do, but she almost felt like someone else's thought had pushed her to flee.

The alien panic was leaving her, and reality crashed in. The baby. *Oh, please no!* She tried to push up, but Trevelyn rolled off his back and onto her, pinning her to where she couldn't run.

"Please," she said. "Let me up. Please."

He shook his head. "I cannot let you run into the storm. If you do that, I will lose you. I cannot explain—"

"I'll punch your other eye if you say that stupid word once more." She closed her eyes, trying to calm down. It wasn't her and her feelings anymore. It was what was best for her baby, and all this nonsense was putting their child at risk.

The car lights stopped and doors were opened. Two people came running. Katlynne Montgomerie came rushing up, and knelt by her sister. Behind her was the darkly handsome Iain Kinloch.

Raven said, "I won't run. I need to get back to the house and get warm. It's freezing out here. Trev, please. I cannot be rolling around on the wet ground. I'm pregnant."

His head snapped up. "You're what?"

Katlynne glared at Trevelyn. "I believe, Mr. Mershan, my sister just informed you that you're about to become a daddy. You bloody bastard."

Iain held out his hand to help both of them up. Shaking Trevelyn's, he said, "Congratulations, and welcome to the family. You will find these Montgomerie women have an odd way of breaking the news to you that you're a father. In some instances they wait years to do it—thirteen years to be precise."

Katlynne turned her catlike eyes on the man. "Don't start, Iain. Bloody well don't start."

Trevelyn swung Raven into his arms and started back to the cottage. When she opened her mouth, he silenced it with a quick kiss. "Hush. It can wait. I love you. Know that much. Everything else can wait."

Raven couldn't explain what had possessed her. All unfamiliar dread ebbed away with his declaration that he loved her. Trevelyn was right; all else could wait until she knew her baby was safe.

Raven lay curled on her side, later that night. Trev had insisted she come to the hospital to make certain everything was all right. It was. The staff had wanted to keep her overnight for observation, but Raven refused; she wanted to go home and sleep in her own bed, with her kitties nearby. No one ever rested in hospitals. Once she knew her baby was safe and secure, she wanted to be home where they could both gain the rest they needed.

Even so, she couldn't sleep.

When the clock struck one, Trevelyn tiptoed into the bedroom, pulled back the blanket and slipped into bed. He spooned his body against hers, and then gently placed his palm to the curve of her stomach. Where their child rested.

"You're not asleep," he said in a whisper. "Sleepy?"

Raven shook her head. "Just lying here thinking about

everything you said. About your mother and father. Poor Desmond. Trev, he was so young to witness your father pulling the trigger. Too young to take on the responsibility. So much pain, hurt, anger. Only, in an odd way, all that fashioned who we are and brought us to this point."

"I love you, Raven. Everything else we can work on. A future isn't built in a single day or defined by one mistake. Give me time. I'll make everything right."

"Can you teach me that thing with the big toe?" she asked softly.

He laughed and then nodded. "Anything you want, my love."

Chapter Twenty-two

"Why is there a pile of lumber blocking the entrance to the large greenhouse?" Raven poked her head into the room she had once intended to be a nursery.

She had figured the pain of that time would assail her; it always did. Instead, she felt at peace. It would soon be a nursery again, and this time she would have Trevelyn's baby. Whatever it took, that baby would be born. She could almost see a small black-haired boy, watch as his blue newborn's eyes slowly turned to green.

Trevelyn looked up from measuring the window seat, his eyes running over her, judging her mood. He was a smart man. As such, he knew she was still mad as a hornet. His brothers and he had earned the fury, and they had not yet begun to pay for their sins. He also knew she loved him. *Arrogant wolf.* To him it was a matter of groveling enough and waiting her out until she came around. This was the trouble in dealing with a man who knew her too well—he understood she couldn't keep up with the anger forever.

"What are you doing?" she asked, nearly cringed as it came out harsh.

Turning, he leaned back against the window seat and stretched his long legs out in front of him. "My, aren't we full of questions?"

She flashed him a look that warned him not to push. "I had planned to paint all afternoon, but you keep hammering in here and it's breaking my concentration. Now I find you have half a lumberyard piled up against the greenhouse door. Why?"

"I've started work to remodel the nursery. I woke with

ideas on what I wanted to do, so I called and had the lumber delivered. As to why it's specifically blocking the door . . . I kicked in the lock last night. Your door is rather rare, and will require a new handle and locking system. They are not off-the-shelf stuff. I have a guy coming in Friday that does specialty work like this. He's into Victorian wrought iron and such. It'll cost me an arm and a leg, but your greenhouse door will be put back to pristine condition. Since that's four days away, I have the lumber stopping anyone from getting in through there."

"Also blocks us from getting out," she said.

He chuckled. "Hmm. Let's see . . . There's the front door, the other greenhouse door and the back door. I think we can get out quickly enough if needed."

Crossing her arms, she walked into the room. "What are you doing in here?"

"As I said, I'm remodeling it for a nursery. This was the room you were going to use for the baby you lost."

Raven nodded, secretly pleased that he seemed enthusiastic about the idea of being a father. Trevelyn could afford to pay any number of people, including Brishen's family, to come in and do the work he wanted, to buy the very best. Instead, Trev was choosing to do the work himself. For their child. Because of this care, she offered him a faint smile.

"I wanted to make it new, different, to ease any lingering pain for you." His green eyes watched her, weighing her reaction to his words.

"Surprisingly, I don't feel the pain anymore. I've finally let go of it." She looked around but found no ghostly presence. "It was time. So, what are you planning to do?"

"Yellow paint, I think. Nice and sunny. Brishen's cousin Luca is going to help me build a child-safe baby bed. Then I'm going to add a toy chest, a built-in dresser. I'm even going to fashion my own model. One thing I cannot do myself—I have asked Brishen to build a rocking horse. Everything is going to be perfect for my son."

Bloody arrogant wolf. "What makes you think I won't have a daughter?" She tilted her chin stubbornly.

He reached in his shirt pocket, pulled out a tarot card and held it out for her. "The Sun. The Gypsy gave it to me this morning. Since that is a boy child riding on the white horse, I have a feeling my question was answered. The big sun on the card caused me to think the room would look great in yellow."

She flipped it over and read the words:

The journey ends where the heart begins.

He tilted his head, a challenging look that said there was no use fighting fate. "You can have a daughter next time."

"Next time? What makes you think there will *be* a next time? I'm not sure I want you touching me with a ten-foot pole—"

His laughter stopped her small tirade. The bloody man moved so damn quick she didn't have a chance to evade him. Wrapping his arms about her, Trev pulled her forward to step between his legs, his inner thighs brushing the outside of hers. "Ten-foot? Lass, you exaggerate. Though, humble it may be, I recall you rather like touching my pole."

"Don't try to make me laugh, Trevelyn Mershan. I might hit you again. I'm not in a good mood with you." Raven reached out with trembling fingers and gently touched the black eye she'd given him, fighting her wash of emotion. She was sorry she'd hurt him, but by the same token the man deserved decking. Even so, her body responded to being this near to him.

"Sorry, love, it's too late for second thoughts. A wolf mates for life. You and I are highly intelligent people. We have everything before us. We'll muddle through the mess the Mershan brothers created. We were wrong. Like the broken lock, we'll make repairs to the damage we've done." The teasing nature shifted slowly to a serious expression as he'd spoken. "And you and I have made a baby."

After a moment he added, "I grew up without a father. I didn't turn out too bad, because my brother Desmond loved me. My mother tried to raise me. Sadly, she had mental problems. I think her heart broke the day my father took his life, and there was no putting Humpty Dumpty back together again. She did so much wrong . . . but she loved us. She tried her best. And that is all anyone can do. It's what you shall do for our child. As such, you won't want that baby growing up without a father. So, you see, I have several things riding in my favor. Oh, I know I'll spend a good deal of time making things up to you. But I'll enjoy every damn minute of it."

She frowned, knowing he was right. "So assured of everything. Well, you're overlooking one major detail."

Trev nodded. "No, I'm not. Wait right here." He pushed off the window ledge and dashed into the hall. Returning, he held his black leather jacket with his left hand and was rummaging in the pocket with the other. "Ordering the lumber wasn't the only thing I did this morning while you were asleep." Tossing the coat onto the rocking chair in the corner, he held up a small box. He flipped it open and removed a ring.

When she stood unmoving, he reached out, took her left hand and slid the ring on it.

"Trevelyn, I . . ." she started to say.

"Hush. I know you're still disappointed in me, and will be for days to come, but that's something we'll get beyond—together. The past has held me in its talons for too long. Same as you have let go of the pain this room caused you for years, I'm letting go of the pain and hurt that controlled my life for far too long. I'm reaching for the future—a *happy* future—with both hands. My journey ends where my heart begins, and my heart begins with you."

Raven closed her eyes against all the emotions pushing at her. She also knew the baby was causing part of that turmoil. Damn hormones were making it so hard to think calmly, logically.

"Don't give me an answer now. Wear the ring. Allow a few days for everything to settle down. Give the Mershans a chance to put right everything we have done wrong. Give me a chance?"

Unable to find the words, she merely nodded. He was right. It was simply too early to forgive all. Besides, she had the sudden urge she was going to be sick. The room seemed to spin.

"Trevelyn, I don't feel well," she almost whispered.

He nodded. "It's been hard on you, I know—"

"No, Trev. I do *not* feel well. Like, morning sickness."

He looked like he didn't understand, and then his eyes flew wide. "Oh! Let me get you to the bathroom."

"Won't make it—" Already the dry heaves were starting to hit her. "Sink. Kitchen."

She took off running and barely made it. While she retched her guts out, Trevelyn hovered, asking what he should do. Did she want anything? He opened a can of apple juice, then got out the lemonade, and finally made a glass of ice water. She would have found his flustered panic amusing, if she hadn't felt so wretched.

She snatched at the water, swished it around in her mouth and spat it out. Turning on the tap, she allowed the water to rinse out the sink and then splashed some on her face, waiting to see if the sickness would come or if it had exhausted itself.

"How can you have morning sickness? It's afternoon," Trev fussed.

Raven accepted the paper towel and blotted her mouth. Reaching for the lemonade, she took a swallow, thankful to get rid of the taste in her mouth. "It hits most women in the morning, but a few get it in the afternoon. Some get it both."

"Why don't you have a lie down? You really look pale."

When she nodded weakly, he swept her into his arms and carried her upstairs. She wanted to protest, but he was right. She was suddenly very tired. He placed her on the bed and tucked her up with the quilt. Thoughtfully, he dropped the blind over the skylight, darkening the room.

"Rest, Red. I'll cook supper. Something light, like grilled chicken breasts—"

"Trevelyn, please. No food talk," she begged.

Leaning over, he kissed her forehead. "Relax. Feel better. I'll be downstairs playing in the nursery if you need anything."

Raven waited until he'd left before pulling her hand out from under the cover. Wiggling her finger she looked at the beautiful ring, a very simply cut oval diamond. A ring she would have picked out for herself.

"Bloody arrogant wolf," she muttered and closed her eyes.

Raven dozed for a couple hours. She hadn't meant to, but when Pye and Chester came to cuddle, she got very warm and drifted into peaceful dreams.

A chill moved through the house as if a storm were coming. She shivered as she awoke, so she picked up her shawl at the same moment she heard a car in the driveway. Stifling a yawn, she hurried downstairs to answer the subsequent knocking, which was quite insistent. In the half-light of the February evening, she thought she looked at Trevelyn. Behind him, a taxi pulled away from the drive and headed toward the road. She blinked, confused, and then glanced down the hall toward the back room, hearing hammering there. It was an odd moment. She knew Trev had a twin, yet until this breath she hadn't understood how much they did look alike.

The strange figure tilted his head, likely going through the same instant of assessment, comparing her to Asha. "Peculiar, eh?" he said.

She would have liked him automatically because he was Trev's brother, but she was still half mad at Trevelyn, so that anger automatically extended to this man; and the lingering annoyance was kept alive because of what Jago had put Asha through. "I'm not sure the world really deserves two of you. One's bad enough."

"You can berate me later. I want to see Asha. Make sure she's all right." It was an odd mixture of plea and demand. Well, it was obvious, whatever else was going on, Jago was in love with her sister. That was clear to see.

"Asha?" Her perplexity deepened.

"Yeah, your twin. Looks a lot like you but has lighter hair and doesn't have that beauty mark on her lip that you do," he remarked.

"I know my sister quite well. I just don't understand why you would think she'd be here." She looked him up and down and then gave him a mocking half smile. "I see differences between Trev and you, too."

Jago was clearly trying to control his irritation. "Asha's not here?"

Raven shook her head. "She's in Kentucky."

"She left there, was coming home to you."

"She's not here. Her home is in Kentucky now."

She saw he half-believed her, but he also knew she would lie for Asha if the case required it, and he feared this might be one of those times. She gasped when he pushed past her, heading inside, uninvited. Chester paused for a moment, looked to her but then followed Jago from room to room while he called Asha's name.

Raven stood by the door, glaring at him when he came back down the stairs. "Chester, leave the man alone. That's not Trev," she told the cat. The feline paid no attention. "I think it best you leave, Mr. Mershan."

Ignoring her, he dropped down on the oak bench in the hallway. "She's not here."

"I told you she wasn't, but I guess being a lying Mershan, you expect everyone else to lie, too. Asha is in Kentucky. She rang to say she was coming, but an hour later she called back to say she'd changed her mind and was returning to The Windmill."

He stared at her, trying to decide if she was telling the truth. Reading his mind, she shrugged and crossed to a hall table where a landline phone sat. She picked it up and punched out a number with enough digits to tell him it was overseas.

She smiled patronizingly, and then held the receiver to his ear. Asha's voice was clear across the connection. "The Windmill. Hello? Anyone there?"

Jago took the phone from Raven's hand, punched disconnect and started to dial. He paused when he realized he wasn't sure whom to call. He looked at her. "I need Mershan's corporate helicopter and jet warmed up. That's Julian's department, but I guess he's still on Falgannon. Where is Trev?"

"Trev's right here." Trevelyn spoke from the shadow of the hall doorway.

Seeing his twin, Jago laughed. "No wonder Raven saw 'differences.' That is a beauty of a shiner and bruise on your chin. Run into a door? I wonder if you remembered rule number three in handling a Montgomerie female— to protect your *breall?*"

"My what?"

Jago waggled his eyebrows and glanced downward. "Your prized possession."

Trevelyn laughed. "Ah, that made it through the fray unscathed. Just barely."

"So far," Raven muttered, and then tugged her shawl around her shoulders. "I'll leave you wolves alone, so you can do wolfish things, like sniffing each other's *brealls.*"

The brothers, so alike, broke into gales of laughter. As soon it would subside, they'd look at each other and the belly laughs would come again.

"Wolves," Raven growled, and then spun on her heel and went out to the kitchen to grab something—anything—to put in her stomach. Being empty wasn't sitting well with it.

The two men moved about in the other rooms, talking and phoning. Raven nibbled on a piece of toast with apple butter, watching. Yes, she'd known to expect that Jago was Trevelyn's twin. But even with being a twin herself, she hadn't anticipated how much the two men were alike. Despite that, she smiled. She'd never confused the two despite their continual shifting.

Jago came down the hall, pausing to look in on the nursery. His eyebrows lifted and those dark green eyes shifted to her. "So it seems I'm going to be an uncle?"

She didn't reply, just continued to quietly munch her toast and sip her lemonade, her stomach very happy to have both. She was less thrilled at having to deal with a second Big Bad Wolf. Damn fairy tales never mentioned there were two!

"You might wish to know you're going to be an aunt, too," he informed her.

She nearly strangled on the juice. "Beg pardon? Do you mean Asha—?"

The corner of his mouth twisted up in a quirky smile. "Will be interesting to see our children, to say the least. Twins marrying twins. Trev and I are the only twins in our family, but they seem to run in Clan Montgomerie."

"Run? The joke is they gallop." She looked him up and down. He was tired, about as drawn as Trevelyn. "I'm not sure you deserve my sister. But then I don't worry about her too much. Asha is strong. If you hurt her again, she will fix your little red wagon."

In the eyes is where the difference was most pronounced, Raven decided. Jago's were such a dark green, they almost appeared brown or black until you watched them closely. His incisive stare met hers and was judging her measure for measure. "Yes, she's a wild woman.

And I wouldn't have her any other way. But she's tender-hearted. Asha doesn't like her vulnerable side to show. I'm figuring you actually mirror her. You, too, are easily bruised, but there is a strength in you—judging by that shiner my brother is sporting. Perhaps you just haven't realized it, or perhaps my brother brings it out in you."

"Well, they are fueling the Mershan jet and filing a flight plan into Bluegrass Field in Lexington," Trev informed him. "They will be ready by the time you get there. Brother dearest will scream about the cost, but I think he owes you on this one. One hitch. With Julian on Falgannon there is no one to pilot the Sikorsky, plus we cannot get a driver here for several hours. I'm assuming you won't want to wait, so I'll drive you."

"Thanks for handling things. I am beat."

"Shouldn't you eat something? I can make you some sandwiches," Raven offered.

Jago shook his head. "The jet will be stocked with everything. I can pig out over the Atlantic, if I take a mind. Right now food doesn't interest me. I have this pressing need to get back home. Some odd things have been going on there, and I don't like being away for very long."

Trev came to kiss the side of Raven's head as he stroked her cheek with the back of his hand. "Feel up to a drive into London?"

Raven groaned. "I hate going into London when I feel well. Sorry, but I simply couldn't take riding in a car right now."

He nodded. "Why don't you go back to bed and sleep while I'm gone. I'll fix supper when I get back. Go lie down. I'll lock up."

Jago reached out and hugged her. "Sorry we met under these circumstances. I look forward to getting to know you better once matters are all settled."

Feeling very weak, Raven nodded. "Bring Asha for a visit. It's been too long. I often feel like my twin doesn't need me very much."

"I often feel that way, too." Jago laughed and patted Trevelyn's back.

From the bedroom window, she saw Trevelyn and Jago go out to the silver Rover Trev had been using for the last several weeks. They got into the car and then Trev reversed out of the drive. Since the dome light was on, she had the treat of watching two very sexy men until Trev snapped it off. Her eyes followed the taillights until they vanished into the windy night.

The trees were bowing and twisting in the gusts. A storm was coming, and it looked like a bad one. She suddenly wished she had gone with them. The house seemed so empty without Trevelyn's warm presence. Still, maybe the storm would hold off until he returned, and then they could cuddle in bed and listen to nature.

At her bedside she noticed Trevelyn's stack of tarot cards. Her hand reached out seeing the newest one he'd collected: The Tower. It showed a medieval tower being struck by lightning and the house breaking apart in flames. Unlike Trev, who was still learning the meaning of the cards, she knew them. This card meant ruin, disturbance, and dramatic upheaval, with widespread repercussions. Unlike the Death card that was meant figuratively, this card actually carried the warning of being forced into a major change of job or home.

"Silver lining, I suppose. The divination promises enlightenment and freedom at the end of the troubles," she muttered. Wondering when Trev had pulled the card from the fortune-teller, she turned it over and read:

Sacrifice begets gain. To embrace the future, break free of the chains of the past.

So very tired, she lay down on the bed and then pulled the quilt over her head. She'd drowse a bit, and Trev would be there when she awoke.

Chapter Twenty-three

Gusting winds pulled her from sleep. She'd only meant to doze, but had drifted off and now found it hard to awaken fully. So tired, Raven wanted to roll over and ignore the disturbance, only a discordant note was carried above the racket of the trees bowing to the wind's will. It took a minute to register that a mechanical thrum rose above the coming storm.

Raven reached over and switched on the lamp at her bedside. Nothing. No light. She clicked a couple more times. "Must be a burnt out bulb, guys," she mumbled to her cats.

Getting up, she pushed her feet into her slippers, yawned and reached for her shawl. The kitties stretched, grumpy from being dislodged from their cozy sleep spots. Small wonder. The house was cool, evidently the storm dropping the temperature as it drew closer. With a low rumbling purr, Chester came to the edge of the bed. Pyewacket curled into a tiny ball so he could go back to sleep. Raven stopped by the door and flipped the wall switch, but found the overhead light didn't come on either.

"Bugger, the electricity must be out. Hmm, guess I'd better go tend the fire before Atticus complains. Hope it hasn't burned down too much."

Distant lights flashed across the bedroom wall as a car turned into the lane. Since no one used the old back entrance to Colford, they could only be coming to the cottage.

"Trevelyn's back," she told the cats as she headed downstairs. At Trev's name, Chester followed on her heels.

As she reached the turn in the landing, the high beams slashed through the dark downstairs. The car wheeled into the drive, and in the backwash of their brightness, she caught sight of a silver body as it rolled into the slot where Trev parked behind the MGB. She looked out through the long greenhouse to the stack of lumber, piled high against the door, and could hardly see the vehicle's top.

"That ugly pile of lumber is ruining my view," she grumbled to Chester. "Trev is just going to have to figure out another temporary lock in the morning."

In the dark she made a misstep, her foot coming down too late on the edge of the third to last stair. Losing her balance, she tumbled forward. It was a small distance; ordinarily it wouldn't upset her, but panic spilled through her, because she worried that if she fell she might hurt the baby. The doctor had said with her past history that she'd need to be extra careful until the second trimester.

Despite tripping over Chester and making him squall, she caught the newel post and hung on desperately. Her arms jerked, bearing the blunt force of stopping her descent, but she was able to right herself.

Her palms burned and her hands shook. "Stupid, stupid, stupid. I'm not awake enough to watch where I'm going."

The doorknob rotated a several times, then rattled insistently. When Trev took the Lamborghini into the shop to have the paint fixed, he'd removed the house key from that ring and hadn't bothered to put it on the rental ring. Raven sighed, realizing he'd likely forgot his key. He'd done the same thing a couple days ago.

The brass door knocker sounded. Trev assumed she was asleep and was trying to get her attention. It made her think back to the first day when he'd brought her the single white rose.

"Coming!" She shuffled forward, almost not lifting her feet after the scare of the near tumble. Reaching the door, she released the inner lock and pulled it open. "You know, if you—"

Her words died in her throat. There were only faint embers in the fireplace, and no light came from any other source; however, her eyes were accustomed to the dark and she had excellent night vision due to Bilberry being a daily part of her vitamins and herbs. Though he stood in the inky shadows outside, she instantly knew this man was not Trevelyn.

"Alec . . . ?" Her fuzzy brain was struggling desperately to come awake. She held on to the door and blocked the opening with her body. "What are you doing here?"

For a moment he didn't reply, just remained standing there. Finally, he spoke. "I came to see your pet ape."

Raven nearly reeled from the fumes. He'd been drinking. "Hmm . . . I have a one-legged seagull, a midget pony and two fat cats. Don't recall ever having an ape."

"Don't be coy, Raven. It doesn't become you." He lashed out against the door, shoving it wide. It jerked out of her hand and slammed back against the grandfather clock.

Raven was forced back a few steps, making her scared she might lose her balance.

"Alec, you really shouldn't be here. Cian said the restraining order is still in effect—"

"Screw that whoreson. Your brother is next on my list to visit tonight. I'd really like to bury the hatchet with him. You know—the one that's in my back." He whipped around in both directions. "Why are the damn lights off?"

She slowly closed the door against the blowing wind. "The electricity keeps going on and off. The wind. It'll be back on in a few minutes." Instinct told her she didn't want him to know how vulnerable she was here. Alone. She glanced to the phone on the small table. "Let me call Colford, see if they can bring a small generator over."

He took two steps, was beside her as she lifted the receiver and found no dial tone. If she'd felt vulnerable before, it was nothing compared to this. She had a land-line phone for the house because cell phones were so unreliable around here. Her mind went back to Trevelyn leaving with Jago, trying to remember if he'd taken his. She couldn't recall, but he'd have no reason to leave it.

"Damn, it's like being in a cave. I'll build the fire up to where I can see without falling over the furniture. Then we can talk." She tried to make it sound as if she saw nothing wrong with his sudden appearance, nothing more than an old friend stopping by to have a nice natter.

Alec had never done anything to harm her physically. He chose mind games, generally. But then Alec sounded odd, and while he did drink—and drink more than a few—he had never been a drunk. The man before her couldn't stand still. A faint weaving to his posture revealed he was very intoxicated.

She had to stall. Trevelyn wouldn't be gone much lon-ger. He and his big toe should be arriving anytime. That private jest caused her to smile, drawing comfort from silliness when she wanted to panic.

"What are you smiling at?" Alec snapped.

She pulled the glass screens back, and began feeding newspaper to get the fire going in the hearth again. It hadn't been tended since Trevelyn left, so it was really past time, and more ash than ember. The paper half smothered it. She casually reached out for the poker, al-most waiting for Alec to react. When he didn't, she re-laxed a bit.

"Why don't you sit? You know how lousy I am at build-ing fires. It will take me a few minutes to get this burning right."

"I recall you were lousy at a lot of things," he sneered, finally turning back to look at the rest of the house. "Where is lover boy?"

Her mind grasped for a response. She wasn't about to tell him Trevelyn had driven to London. Though he should be back anytime, she wanted something more imminent-sounding. "He went over to Colford to mooch a couple steaks. I was so busy painting this week that I forgot to run to the butcher. He's coming back to fix supper shortly. You know how men are. They get together and talk, talk, talk. Funny, you men always put women down for talking so much and you really are worse."

"Shut up, Raven. You never knew when to keep your mouth shut. Your boyfriend and I are going to have a long talk. He owes me. Bloody bastard. He's going to pay."

Ignoring him, she broke some kindling and fed it to the burning paper, seeing the flames jump to the wood and catch, the whole while trying to stay calm. Her heartbeat was slamming against her ribs. She wasn't sure why, but this intoxicated Alec truly alarmed her.

"There. You can halfway see your hand before your face." She turned and faced him—and really wished she hadn't.

Alec was horribly drunk. That alone made her uncomfortable, especially on the heels of their last run-ins. But it was the look in his eyes that scared her: of desperation, the kind that makes a man do stupid things. She had to get him out before Trevelyn returned, or get away, herself.

Growing more alarmed, she considered her options. She could just open the door and make a run for Colford . . .

Chester meowed plaintively from the landing. He wanted Trevelyn, plus the ginger tabby had never liked Alec. Raven thought of gentle Pyewacket sleeping upstairs and poor silly Atticus asleep in his nesting box out in the large greenhouse. She could never abandon her defenseless pets to this drunken lout. If she vanished, he could easily focus on them as a means for venting the bile boiling inside.

"Alec, you look tired. Why don't you run along and I'll have Trevelyn call you first thing in the morning. I was sick today, and just don't feel well enough to stay and entertain you." She thought about moving to the door, hoping he would do as she asked.

"Stupid bitch." He laughed. "You didn't even know who you were screwing. He was using you to get to Cian. I'll give him credit—he sure succeeded where I failed, eh? And he didn't even have to marry you to do it. I find it rather humorous. I made all the right moves and got zilch. His name isn't Trevelyn Sinclair, it's Trevelyn Mershan. I doubt you and your little homebody ignorance know who his brother is. Des Mershan—"

"CEO of Mershan International. Of course I know who he is." She wasn't about to allow Alec to start with his old games. She lied, and was damn proud of it: "You think I wouldn't know who my brother-in-law to be is?"

"Brother-in-law?" he echoed in shock.

She flashed her ring before Alec's face. "My engagement ring. What? You assumed Trevelyn and Des were keeping things from the Montgomeries? From me? Oh, wake up and smell the sharp aroma of horseshit, Alec. Are you that idiotic? That naïve? The whole ruse was a smoke-screen cooked up between Mershan International and Montgomerie Enterprises. They're moving toward a big merger, which will triple the stock for both companies."

"Now wait a minute . . . Melissa said Trevelyn Mershan was buying up Montgomerie stock left and right—"

"Of course he was. We're trying to consolidate ownership, get rid of the small shareholders so the bulk of the stock will be jointly held by either the Mershans or Montgomeries. If word leaks out about the merger, stock prices will go sky high and there wouldn't be the huge profit for us."

Alec glared at her, not wanting to believe. "Melissa claimed—"

"Oh, please. That bitch—who is blonde in more than just her hair color—would say anything to get back at Cian. He's been planning on firing her for a year. She knew her time was running out. He's merely waited until he could find a good replacement. He hired Annalee last October, and she's ready to assume the position now. Melissa couldn't be so blank that she didn't realize she was training her own replacement. What do they say about never trusting anything a fired employee says? Don't tell me because she's been doing the rumpy-bumpy with you that you actually believed her?" Raven made her tone mocking, condescending. She wasn't going to give him a chance to get into her mind and wear her down as he had so many times in the past. "Okay, don't listen. But you know me—I have no head for business and I'm a lousy liar. Mershan and Montgomerie will announce a merger in the coming weeks. Des and Cian are just doing the two-step currently, each trying to come out with the most power."

"Then why were the Mershans paying Melissa to get information from Cian?"

Raven shrugged with an air of boredom. "Were they? Or did Melissa just spin that bunch of stuff and nonsense for you? Really, Alec, did your IQ just drop? This whole thing is more than a business merger. Jago Mershan is going to wed my sister Asha, and I expect any day that Des Mershan will announce he's marrying BarbaraAnne. I told Trevelyn that I would marry him this morning. So, there—nothing mysterious or a big revelation to me. Perhaps to you. Look, I'm tired and don't feel well enough to answer all your silly questions. So, please leave."

She marched to the door and opened it, hoping he would take the hint and depart. He did take two steps toward her. Then he stopped and just stared.

"You've changed." Alec looked as if finally really seeing her.

"Seven years does that to people," she replied.

He shook his head. "Not seven years. It's since Mershan came into your life. He did what I could never do. He reached you—woke up Sleeping Beauty."

"Sorry, wrong fairy tale. I'm Little Red Riding Hood." The joke was pure bravado. She swallowed hard, debating if she'd made a mistake in moving away from the poker. Did she stand her ground and run the bluff that she wasn't scared of him, or abandon the ploy and get to the poker as fast as possible?

"My, what big teeth he has—all the better to *eat* you." His mouth twisted in a cynical, lascivious smile. "Tell me, little Raven, did Mershan ever get you on your knees before him, your lovely mouth wrapped around his—"

"Alec!"

His smirk was sour. "One might say, then, that he's a better man than I, because I sure as hell couldn't get the Snow Princess to service me."

"Leave. Now. You're breaking a court injunction by being here. Go now, before this becomes a legal hassle—one you shan't enjoy. Think what being dragged through the courts will do to your professional reputation," she cautioned.

He laughed, mirthless. "I guess you don't know everything about the mighty Mershans after all. I thought *Cian* was bloody relentless. A word from Mac Montgomerie or his pit-bull son, Cian, and I found many doors closed, deals scrapped. Your father and brother left me damn little, Raven. Okay, I screwed Melissa. It was a question of who was using whom. I was trying to suck up some crumbs on the Mershan takeover. But the reach of the Mershans is frightening. Your fiancé has destroyed me, Raven. He was kind enough to give me a choice—take the ten thousand pounds and plane tickets to Canada he so generously provided, or stay in England and face charges of insider trading. Either I go halfway around the world or he promises to see me in jail."

"Then I suggest you go home to Ellen and discuss your options. Now, please leave. I think this conversation is at an end." Raven tried to muster her most commanding tone.

For a minute his mind seemed to waver, and he almost obeyed. But as he took a step, his smile spread. He reached out to lift a strand of her long hair away from her shoulder. "No, first I think I shall leave Trevelyn Mershan something to remember me by."

Oily revulsion spread through her stomach and she felt sick. She didn't hesitate. Using her might to shove past him, she went for the poker, only steps away. It seemed miles. She got her hand around the brass rod, but as she lifted it in defense, he caught the end. Giving it a jerk, he pulled her forward.

"Some warrior woman," he derided. He jerked on the pointed end of the brass poker, nearly yanking her off her feet. "Give me it, Raven, or I shall make you sorry for your dismal defiance."

"I've been sorry since the day I met you. Sorry I once cared what you thought of me. You're a bully, a whiner, and your whole life has been spent blaming everyone else for your sad failings. And that is what you are, Alec, despite all your pretenses. You're nothing but a bloody pathetic failure. Go look in the mirror and see your thinning hair, your receding chin and bemoan the fact that life is passing you by. Bemoan that you don't have a portrait tucked up in the attic to bear your sins like Dorian Grey."

This time when he tugged on the poker, instead of fighting him she put her force to slamming forward. The metal-tipped rod rammed into his chest, hitting him hard. But not hard enough.

She released her grip and turned to run. Alec caught her before she took her second step. He whipped her around and slapped her with the back of his hand, catching her across the side of her face and ear. In stunned agony, she stumbled backward. But instead of trying to break her fall, she struggled to curl her arms protectively over her stomach. Her head crashed into the side of the curio cabinet, pain lancing through her brain.

The last thing she thought was, *Please let my baby be safe*.

The next thing she knew, she slowly became aware of looking at Alec from the wrong end of a telescope. Odd. She vaguely recalled hitting her head and passing out. He seemed too distant to evoke any fear. With a detached curiosity she watched things coming into focus, feeling so far away from everything.

Raven felt her wrist being grabbed more than saw it. Almost floating, removed from all her senses, she just wanted to rest. Why wouldn't he go away and just let her rest?

"Oh, damn! Oh, shit! Oh, damn, Raven! I wasn't really going to hurt you. I wanted to scare you, shake up Mershan when he found you hysterical." He lifted her arm and felt for a pulse at her wrist.

Raven knew he'd never find it. She even tried to tell him that. Doctors and nurses had always remarked they could barely get a pulse from her wrist. Only, she couldn't move. Couldn't speak.

She was so tired. Her mind drifted again and she rested in dreamless blackness.

Finding peace.

Trevelyn drove with a lead foot, hurrying back to Raven. Traffic had been heavy coming and going to London, making the trip take longer than he'd anticipated. He'd promised Raven he'd fix supper, but now considered stopping and picking up something from the café near Brishen's studio. As he drove past, he had an odd feeling he shouldn't delay his return any longer. Instead of stopping at the restaurant, he sped on by.

Jago had talked about what had been going on in Kentucky. Someone had broken into Jago's bungalow and stolen a letter concerning Mershan International and Trident Ventures. Later it was left for Asha to find. That he wasn't there with Asha saw Jago uneasy, worried. Trev understood. He sure as hell didn't like knowing Raven was alone.

The card he'd pulled from the Gypsy this morning flashed into his mind. He didn't need the divination book to interpret it, either. As the first flashes of lightning streaked across the night sky he recalled the tower with bolts of lightning crashing about and fire curling out its windows.

A hundred times over he told himself that Raven was safe, that the card had no real meaning. Yet, from the start, the Gypsy had given them card after card with specific guides to help their choices. No Mystic Seer–vague replies. No Magic 8 Ball's *It's a possibility*. The answers hit so close—too close to dismiss.

Lights of Colford Hall came into view as he rounded the bend. In response, he expected his muscles to tense and his heart rate jump, as decades-old resentment rose within him. There was nothing. He was letting go of the past. Instead of slowing, Trev wheeled past the towering, ornate gates of the winding drive, heading home to the cottage and Raven, to his future.

"I have a sexy woman with ruffled feathers that needs soothing, two cats, a one-legged seagull, a midget pony and a baby waiting for my return," he told the reflection staring back at him from the rearview mirror. "I finally have a home, roots. How lucky can one man get?"

Then he noticed the sky behind Colford seemed odd. Lighter. At first he thought it was some strange cloud formation, but then cold dread poured through him. It was getting brighter. And it was definitely coming from the direction of the cottage.

He downshifted the Rover and took the S-turns as fast as he could. By the time he reached the turnoff, he knew a big fire was coming from the direction of the cottage. The image of The Tower flashed to mind, lightning and belching fire shooting out the windows. He'd cursed not having the Lamborghini's speed and handling on the drive home, but was suddenly glad of the Rover's high clearance and four-wheel drive. The roadster always had to crawl down Raven's little lane. The off-road traction of this utility vehicle permitted him to push the car to its limit.

As he neared the cottage, there was no question in his mind. It wasn't the barn; the gardener's cottage was on fire! He'd gone away leaving his family, his life, his beautiful Red Riding Hood in there. Instantly, his mind cast recriminations: he had asked her to go with him! He should have made her go; then she'd be away from this madness. Instead . . .

He couldn't face *instead* right now.

People were running across Colford's back property, rushing past his car as he pulled up and jumped out. He grabbed the cell from his pocket and punched 999, barely hearing the "Ambulance, fire and police—which do you prefer?" on the other end. He didn't care. He just wanted them here. Now.

"I don't see why we cannot have all three. My fiancée is trapped in a burning cottage on the backside of Colford Hall estate, out on Old Post Road." Seeing Luca and several other Gyspies rushing from the woods, he tossed the phone to Brishen's kinsman. "Give them the information they need."

The whole damn thatch roof seemed to be burning, and the front wall was engulfed. But there were other exits. The back door and both greenhouses— Then he recalled he'd blocked the door to the big one with a pile of lumber.

His knees nearly buckled. He had stupidly barred the door with a stack of boards that was chest-high. She would never be able to get that door open. Much in the manner he'd done yesterday, he went from the front of the house to the small greenhouse. His heart dropped when he reached it. While the glasshouse was untouched by the flames, the door opening into it was.

Lightning sounded, splintering across the inky night, and Trev almost felt as if it struck his heart. The back door was safe from the flames at the moment. Jerking open that screen door, he reached the back door only to see the fire was already in the hallway and the nursery. Raven couldn't get to the kitchen to use it. Which left the big greenhouse door, which was blocked.

Trev was beyond panic. His thoughtless act might have doomed Raven to death.

Chapter Twenty-four

Acrid smoke curled around her nose, choking her, and Raven tried to turn over to hide her face. Damn, she'd forgotten to have the chimney sweep in this year! Not smart. Creosote built up on the inside of chimneys and caused all sorts of problems—such as poor drawing, which could lead to smoke building up and getting back into a house. In the worst cases, the damn black stuff could actually catch fire.

Fire?

That single world sent Raven spiraling through the darkness that had claimed her, fighting to claw her way back to consciousness. Back to Trevelyn.

She tried to sit up. Couldn't. Reaching out, she stirred with the grace of Boris Karloff in the movie *Frankenstein*. Her inner voice screamed a warning, but her head hurt too much to heed what her survival instincts tried to relay to her fuzzy brain. She opened her eyes and looked about.

"My vision is screwy," she muttered to Chester. Only, Chester wasn't on the couch with her.

Attempting to draw a breath, she looked around for the cat. As her senses began functioning, she grew aware heat assailed her. High heat. She squinted, recognizing she was experiencing double vision, which made the fireplace seem double its size. But then she turned her head and saw fire all around her. Even behind.

"Oh, God!" Taking hold of the couch's back, she used it as a crutch to stand. She turned in every direction, but no matter which way she looked, flames danced along the walls, even spreading across the ceiling and the exposed beams. "Out. Must get out . . ."

The oily black smoke roiled through the room, the house. Raven strangled, gasping for air. Finally, her brain began functioning, enough to recall that smoke rises. She needed to drop to the floor and maybe there'd still be breathable air.

Falling to her hands and knees, she gulped hungrily for oxygen. After several mouthfuls, she gathered enough logic to know she had to find an exit. Then, it was just a matter of crawling to a door and safety.

She tried to crawl, but her skirt sent her tumbling forward. She reached down and grabbed the back of the hem and then pulled it up like a diaper, tugging the material in at the waist. The front of the house was engulfed in flames. Searching to her left she saw the flames crawling across that wall, the door already aflame. Her mind screamed, *My paintings,* but knew they were not worth risking her life.

A howl suddenly sounded from upstairs.

"Oh—Chester!" Raven recalled how he'd run back upstairs when he'd seen it was Alec and not Trevelyn. "Bloody hell." Pye was probably up there, too!

Not hesitating, she navigated over to the stairs and then stood. Holding her nose, she dashed up the steps, keeping to the right side of the railing because it hadn't caught fire yet. In the bedroom, she heard Chester crying mournfully. The smoke was heavier up there, so she went to her knees again and followed the cat's voice to the bed. Lifting the dust ruffle she found him underneath, crying and hissing.

"Poor baby." When she reached out to him, he came to her. Thankfully, she clutched the kitty to her chest and then looked for Pyewacket. He'd been asleep on the bed. "Pyewacket!"

A faint terrified mewl sounded from the closet.

There was no way she could crawl with two hysterical cats; they would be impossible to handle. She reached for the pillows, dragging two off with one hand. She squeezed Chester between her thighs as she stripped the pillowcases. "Sorry, Chester." Then she shoved the terrified kitty into the pillowcase. The cat would hate her for days for what she was about to do, but it would mean they'd both be around.

Half scooting, she held Chester tight in the case so he had no room to move. Pushing open the closet door, she found Pye at the very back. The gray kitty backed up when she reached for him. Poor thing was so scared.

"So am I, Pye. Sorry, love." She grabbed him by the scruff of his neck and struggled to get the case about him.

In the tussle, her head brushed a yellow Macintosh hanging on the rack. She tugged until the raincoat fell off the hanger. In the pocket was a silk scarf. She used that to tie both pillowcases together. The cats were fussing, but with them snugged down, they couldn't do much but poke claws through the linen.

Seeing a pair of dirty jeans on the floor, Raven snatched them up and pulled them on as she skimmied out of the skirt. The jeans would provide better protection for her legs. Taking her belt from the loops, she ran it around her shoulder and then under the opposite arm, crossways over her chest, and then buckled that over the tied pillow cases. It would help her hold on to the cats when she needed to crawl. Dragging the Mac over her like a tent, she clutched the cats against her and started the arduous journey back down the stairs.

The damn place was going up like a tinderbox! The ancient wooden beams and thatched roof saw the flames spreading in every direction. It was a matter of minutes before the whole roof would collapse inward. Escape would be hopeless. Taking a deep breath, she headed back down the stairs, dodging the flames that were growing worse with each passing minute.

By the time she descended, there was simply no route out through the back of the house. The whole hallway to the kitchen was solid flame. Even the door to the large greenhouse had fire crawling all over the door frame.

She looked in there, seeing the pile of lumber still blocking the door. The greenhouses wouldn't catch fire like the wooden part of the house was doing. However, they were far from safe, presenting dire threat in a different manner. Glass melted—at what point varied by its composition, some older types doing so at very low temperatures. Some shattered. Some actually softened and bowed as it shifted back to a liquid state. Within minutes the whole place would see the huge panes of glass distorting and falling inward, much like guillotines falling from the sky.

Cracking and popping, pieces of the ceiling started dropping overhead, sprinkling cinders. The whole front wall was engulfed, reaching up to the thatched roof. It would be seconds before the fire closed this final avenue of escape.

"Atticus." She spoke the reminder to herself. The bird slept in his nesting box on the far side of the glasshouse. Bending down, she took a deep gulp of good air and prayed. Gathering the frantic cats in the pillowcases to her breast, she faced the only avenue left, tugged the coat closed over her and the cats, and walked through the midst of the hungry flames.

She fell to her knees in the greenhouse, thankful to have broken through the wall of fire unscathed. Choking, she sucked at the air. Even when she didn't drag in a lungful of smoke, the air was fouled by plastics and burning chemicals. Plus, it was hot. It dried her lungs.

Inside the greenhouse, she struggled past many of her treasures, including Brishen's beautiful rocking horse, her collection of Victorian planters and the fortune-teller's booth. The stone slab floor was hard on her knees, harder because of her bearing the extra weight of the wiggling cats. Even so, she finally reached the far rack of plants where her strawberries grew, along with the baby lavender rose she'd pollinated herself. The delicate petals had just started opening. Everything in her safe little world was being destroyed.

"Atticus!" she cried. *Oh, please be here, you silly bird!* She was crying, but the tears dried instantly on her face. Then his orange beak popped out of the large round hole. As soon as he saw she was under the coat, he came hopping out. The smart bird huddled in the Mac with her, as she tried to think what do. Surely the fire would've drawn people by now, as it would be visible for miles. Trev might even be back.

"Oh, Trevelyn." The damn door was blocked, as if Fate had spoken that her time had come.

She hugged the cats and the bird to her, shaking and nearly mindless with fear. Overhead, *pings* sounded, the metal framework of the greenhouse responding to the intense heat. Once the glass was breached, either by falling, shattering or exploding, the air would rush in and fuel the firestorm. She had to break out before that happened.

Glancing over to the corner, she saw the beautiful clockwork Gypsy. Heartbreakingly, the booth was catching fire. Even if there was a way out, it was too heavy for her to drag.

Then her eyes saw the tarot card on the floor before her. It was impractical, but she reached out and snatched it up. It wasn't a Major Arcana card, but the Two of Swords. It pictured a woman balancing blades, crossed and held upright. A blindfold covered her eyes. Raven didn't miss the meaning: life in a precarious balance, requiring blind courage to face adversity. But bloody hell, she wasn't one of the Montgomerie warrior women. She was just a quiet lass who loved her pets and her home. She was shaking and sick, terrified to the point she couldn't think. There was no saving her beautiful cottage she had worked so hard to create . . . but damn if she was going to lose anything else! Blinking away the tears, she struggled against double vision to read the words on the back.

The path of the future lies before you.

Her eyes looked straight ahead at the pane of sheet glass. Not hesitating, she crawled to the table where one of the huge Victorian planters sat. "Atticus! Stay." She unslung the pillowcases from her neck and placed the cats next to the bird, then draped the Mac over them. "Stay. Please stay," she sobbed.

Pulling up on the table, she lifted the planter in her arms. Damn thing was nearly more than she could hold, and there was no way she could toss it to any effect. But she spun around in the manner of a Scottish shot-putter, and let the planter fly.

Likely already softened from the heat, the eight-foot-tall wall of glass shattered into jagged shards. Several were hanging from the top of the frame, dangerous.

The instant in-rush of air saw the fire triple, almost exploding in a whoosh. Then the shrubbery moved, and suddenly Trevelyn was there. He forced his body through the boxwoods and reached out for her. Instead of taking his hand, Raven spun back for the animals.

Just as she reached them, Trevelyn grabbed her and dragged her away. She nearly leapt from his arms, grabbing at the yellow Macintosh.

"Damn it!" He saw what she was doing and grabbed the pillowcases, while she snatched Atticus to her. Brishen appeared, shoving his way through the dense bushes and taking the cats from Trev. That left Trev free to aid her through the hazard of the hanging glass.

Raven turned back to the house to see Brishen's pony and the Gypsy. The booth was half in flames, but the horse remained untouched.

Trev read her mind and jerked her arm. "Leave it, by God."

She swallowed hard, then nodded. She said good-bye in her mind to all her gentle things, which had sustained her and helped her heal away from the hurts of the world. Most of all, she said good-bye to the Gypsy who had likely saved her life. Giving one last farewell wave . . . she saw the eyes were open and looking directly at her.

Raven gave the mannequin a trembling smile and said, "Thank you."

Then she rotated to face Trevelyn. He would keep her safe from now on.

Overhead, a pane of glass bowed and then dropped from its metal fittings, slicing down toward her. Trev leapt, dragging her out and away, far beyond harm's way. The springy boxwoods cushioned their fall.

Brishen and Luca were there, then, hauling them through the boxwoods and away from the house. Raven finally set Atticus down. The bird flapped his good wing and fussed, but didn't move away from Trevelyn. Even the silly bird knew Trev would protect them.

Raven coughed several times and managed a strangled, "The cats?"

Brishen shook his head, wearing a disbelieving smile. "Safe in the Range Rover."

She looked to her house, nearly consumed by flames.

"What's that ditzy female doing?" Brishen began cursing in Roma and then took off running toward the opposite end of the house. "I'll bloody kill her!"

Raven and Trev twisted to see what their friend was screaming about. At the end of the small greenhouse, Paganne had a shovel and was slamming it against the locked door. Her objective met, she dropped the shovel and dashed inside, ignoring Brishen, who was roaring threats at her. As he reached the house, Paganne came dancing out, carrying a huge canvas still covered with a sheet. Paganne evaded Brishen who tried to snatch her long pigtail and came running toward them.

"I got it!" she cried when she has halfway there. "I got it!"

Brishen was right behind her. "You're *going* to get it, you scatty female! I'm going to paddle you until you cannot sit down!"

Paganne set the painting down against the front of the Rover. "You and which man's army?"

Car lights flashed behind them. The police, fire and ambulance crews followed behind a car with Mac and Cian. It was too late for the firemen to do much more than watch the death of Raven's cottage, however.

Raven allowed Trevelyn to pull her into his arms. He laughed. "Damn, they did send all three."

"And like the cavalry in B-Westerns . . . too late," Paganne complained.

Raven stood numb, while Trev ran his hands over her head, shoulders and back, trying to reassure himself that she was unharmed. She welcomed his touch but didn't want to think. She wanted to lean against him and cry.

Mac came rushing up and hugged her. "Are you all right? Anyone hurt? What the hell happened?"

Yes, what had happened? She tried to think back. She could barely recall anything other than the battle to get out alive. Then she recalled her baby. "Please," was all she could cough out.

The emergency people buzzed about, asking questions, as did the police and firemen. So many questions, and she just couldn't deal with them. Hugging Trev, she watched the final death gasps of her beloved home, willing everyone to allow her to mourn in peace.

Trev held her tight, kissing the side of her head over and over. Slowly she grew aware of his tears falling upon her face.

She was so tired, but there seemed no escaping all the faces looking to her. They needed some answers.

"Alec," she sobbed softly.

Trevelyn pushed her backward to see her face. "*He* was here?" His jaw set as his arms dropped, and he started back to the cars.

Raven grabbed his arm. "Don't leave me," she begged.

She saw the warrior in him wanting to avenge his lady, struggling with his need to be near her. Finally he nodded and pulled her close again.

She closed her eyes against the double vision. "I'm not sure. I think he set the fire."

"Why, for God's sake?" Paganne gasped. "What did he hope to do?"

Raven glanced to the cottage, seeing the roof collapse inward. "I really don't know. There was a struggle. I was knocked out."

Brishen assured Trev, "Take care of our Raven. Leave him to me."

"Stand in line, fearless vampire killer. You can drive a stake through his heart after I finish with him," Cian joked, but there was a true threat in the words.

More coughing hit, and Raven was aware of the medic pushing past Brishen and Cian to check her. "She's suffering a concussion, obviously smoke inhalation—"

Trev supplied, "And she's pregnant."

The medic nodded. "We need to get her to the hospital."

Paganne patted her shoulder. "Take her. We'll deal with the beasties and get them settled at Colford."

Raven agreed, but she didn't relinquish her hold on Trevelyn. Before she allowed anyone to take her away, she watched the final moments of her beloved home and said one more silent good-bye to the beautiful Gypsy.

Trevelyn laid the white rose across Raven, who was still sleeping. It had been two days since the fire, but he still hadn't shaken the panic of how close he had come to losing her.

The nightmare had come again, the first night after the fire. Tashian and Annie, his chasing her through the woods. Trev had seen the whole story. She had wanted to hear the words "I love you" and Tashian had been too confused, too arrogant to give them to a simple Gypsy. A man so far above her, Annie had feared he could never love her, had desperately sensed there was an air of doom that hovered around their love. Tashian's unwillingness to give her the one thing she wanted drove her to despair. She carried his baby but refused to tell him until he offered her the love she so wanted. When he didn't, it confirmed her hopelessness. She'd blindingly fled him during the storm. Tashian found her too late. A tree, struck by lightning, had fallen and crushed her.

Last night, the dream hadn't come. It was as though he'd been finally shown the last pieces of the puzzle. There was nothing else left to reveal.

He leaned over and kissed Raven's cheek. "I love you, Red Riding Hood."

Her eyelids fluttered open, and then a sad smile touched her lips. He had a feeling it would take time until her smiles were no longer haunted.

"Good morning," she whispered, her voice still raw from the smoke inhalation. Seeing the rose, she picked it up and breathed in its scent.

He handed her a glass of juice from the tray. "I've been down to check on Marvin. Little bugger is having a ball in the stable with all the big horsies. I let him into the empty wing in the Hall, and let him dash about. I chased him properly, so he got his 'go inside and aggravate the people' out for the day. The cats feasted on pink salmon for breakfast and demanded extra pets. Atticus is in the conservatory and thinks the bubbling fountain is a birdbath. So, how are you and our baby feeling?"

"Well, I think. Just a little tired."

He took the glass from her when she held it out, signaling she was through. After a moment he said, "I brought you oatmeal with honey and diced apples. I thought that would do well on your gimpy tummy."

Raven scooted up in bed. "Thank you. Sounds perfect."

"Well, the cook—and her foul-mouthed parrot—assured me this was good for a new mum to be. That bird is a howl. He must have been owned by a vulgar seaman at one time." Trev chuckled.

Reaching out, he rubbed her knee, lightly, needing the contact. He watched her eat, waiting to discuss other matters. Finally, when she said she was full, he took the tray and set it aside.

"I want the kitties," she requested.

He nodded. "I'll go round them up. Last I saw them, they were in the kitchen mooching treats from the cook and eyeing the parrot like he'd go well with lemon sauce. Now, why they view the macaw as fit for the dinner table and they ignore that ridiculous seagull, I'll never understand.

"First, I wanted to let you know they caught Alec. He confessed to setting the fire, to cover the fact he thought he accidentally killed you. He'll be going to jail for a long time. Lucky for him, because I was going to hold him down while Brishen staked him."

Raven nodded. "What about Ellen?"

Trev sat down on the bed and pulled her across his chest. Stroking her hair, he marveled at this special woman. His woman. His life. "Only you could worry about the wife of the man who almost killed you, accidentally or not."

"Ellen's only mistake was loving unwisely. And she has a baby, Trev."

He leaned back, tasting emotions he didn't want to revisit: a mother with a small child left alone to raise the little boy. Yes, it was only one, compared to his mother who had struggled with three, but still . . . "I know. Despite the child being Alec's, I can no more condemn it to a life of hardship. I've already spoken to Des. We'll set up a trust for the child and make support payments to help raise it, until we see if Ellen lands on her feet."

Raven nodded, then she glanced up. "Thank you."

He gave her a sad smile. He supposed it would be a long time until his smiles weren't haunted as well. He'd come too damn close to losing Raven. That was going to take time to get over. Maybe a lifetime.

"No need to thank me. While it was Alec's doing, it did feel like a bit of history repeating itself. Your grandfather condemned the Mershans to a life of hardship. I'm not about to play his role again, to have a child grow up hating Trevelyn Mershan because I destroyed his daddy. I break the circle here and now."

"But Alec's actions were his own," she argued. "He made his own choices."

"I guess by the same token, despite what your grandfather did, my father's action was his own. He made his choices. It's still too much alike, that I want to prevent the same cycle of hatred and bitterness. I did ruin Alec. In his mind, I gave him no way out. I am not without blame. Perhaps if I had offered him a good paying job in Mershan, none of this would have happened. I am not the saint Jago is."

"No what-ifs, Trev. No wasting life on them." She snuggled closer. "What's going to happen with the takeover?"

"It will happen. Only, Des has found B.A. is worth more than setting right the past. Instead of a hostile takeover, it will be a kinder, gentler merger. After all, the Mershans are going to marry three of the Montgomerie sisters. Let Des and Cian hammer out the details, I'd like to talk about *our* merger. What do you think—getting married on St. Patrick's day? We could tie green bows around Chester and Pye, maybe even Marvin and Atticus."

She finally gave him a real smile. "I think that's doable."

"You know I found another version of Little Red Riding Hood. I thought you might be interested," he teased.

Her face brightened. "Really?"

"Yes. Basically it's the same story, but with Red and the Wolf getting married and living happily ever after. And there was a line or two missing from the crucial dialogue."

"Oh?" She reached up and ran her finger along his jaw. "Pray tell, what?"

"There is a line where Red faces the wolf and he tells her, 'My, what a big heart I have.'" Trev laughed and then finished his version, the *right* version. "To which Mr. Big Bad then adds—hang on to your hats—'All the better to love you with.'"

He kissed her then, shaking with need for this woman and knowing he was a blessed man indeed.

Epilogue

Two days laters, Raven saw the postcard with a crystal carousel on the entry table of Colford Hall. Picking it up, she carried it upstairs to the suite where Trev and she were staying while the cottage was being rebuilt. She paused inside the room and flipped it over, already knowing it was from LynneAnne in New York, even before she saw the signature. She'd dropped her sister a note a couple weeks before, telling her of the loss of the Gypsy fortune-teller, and could she please keep a lookout for another to replace it.

My darling sister, while I love and adore you, I have no idea what you are going on about. What Gypsy fortune-teller booth? I haven't sent you anything for your birthday . . . yet. Sorry, I have a beautiful shawl I picked up in France, but have been remiss in sending it. You know how I am about sending parcels out. Ms. Procrastination! Anyway . . . I'm not responsible for this clockwork marvel you speak of, but would have loved to see it. Sorry it was lost in the fire. I promise to keep an eye out for anything as wonderful, but I seriously doubt coming across anything of the likes again. Something of that quality would be worth a fortune and in the hands of a collector. But a word of warning: If I find something that unique and marvelous, I am keeping it!

—Kisses and Hugs, LynneAnne.

Raven rushed across to the vanity in search of the memento box to dig out the photographs LynneAnne had sent her just before the mechanical Gypsy was delivered, along with her sister's postcard telling her to expect it. After three steps she paused, recalling the box and the contents were lost in the fire. She tried to recall if she had showed the card and pictures to her brothers, but had a suspicion she hadn't.

Trev came up behind her. Taking her in his embrace, he pulled her back against his chest and asked, "What's wrong? You appear troubled."

"I just got a card from LynneAnne," she replied.

The news caused Trev to chuckle. "Julian gets that same worried look on his face whenever your sister's name is mentioned."

"Julian and *LynneAnne?*" she echoed in disbelief. After a moment's thought she shook her head. "Nope. Someone is having you on. It'd never work. They're exact opposites."

"At one time I thought the same thing about you and me." He put his head against hers and just swayed with her. "What else does my sister-in-law-to-be have to say?"

Raven held the postcard up for him to read, still flummoxed by LynneAnne's insistence that she hadn't sent the Gypsy as a belated birthday present. Of all the things she'd lost in the fire, the Gypsy and Brishen's rocking horse hurt most. She recalled taking the last look at the mechanical woman and seeing flames already licking up the sides of the wooden booth. It hurt. She'd felt as if she lost something rare and special. A friend.

"LynneAnne sent me a note saying she'd found the Gypsy and was sending it as my birthday gift. She enclosed two pictures to show me what she'd found. One showed the whole box. The other was a close-up on the face of the mannequin."

"And you don't have them because they went up in the fire with everything else." It was a statement and not a question.

Raven nodded. "Along with everything but your painting."

"Not *my* painting. That is Tashian Dumont. I just happen to look a lot like him, just as the Gypsy looked a lot like you." He sighed. "I don't have the answers you seek, Raven. I doubt anyone does. The Gypsy—Annie Brightmoor—came to us for a reason. When the circle closed, her time was over. She'd done what she came to do: save us. That's the only thing that makes sense to me."

Raven turned in his arms, hugging this man she loved more than life. "I'll never forget her. I wonder what happened to Tashian and Annie."

Trev kissed the tip of her nose. "Someday, my love, I shall tell you of Annie and Tashian. Just not now. I want to hold you and think of the future. Our future. Allow the past to stay in the past for awhile."

> *I'll cross these waters now*
> *I need to cross this ocean of time*
> *to be with you . . .*
>
> *Don't let me drown tonight*
> *Don't bring me down tonight*
> *Don't wanna lose this feeling*
> *that you belong to me*
> *Shine all your light my way*
> *There's nothing left to say*
> *I'll never stop believing*
> *that you belong to me.*

"Oh, Trev, do you hear that?" The words of the beautiful song that was playing finally caught her attention. "That's Mike Duncan. He writes most of his own stuff, too. Amazing voice. That song was playing the night we met! In fact, it was playing that first time when I looked over and you met my stare."

"I recall." Trevelyn smiled softly. "And I'll never stop believing that you belong to me, Red Riding Hood."

"Kate Angell is to baseball as Susan Elizabeth Phillips
is to football. Wonderful!"

— *USA Today* Bestselling Author Sandra Hill

KATE ANGELL

WHO'D BEEN SLEEPING IN KASON RHODES'S BED?

The left fielder for the Richmond Rogues had returned
from six weeks of spring training in Florida to find someone
had moved into his mobile home. That person was presently
in his shower. And no matter how sexy the squatter might be,
Kason wanted her out.

He had his trusty dobie, Cimarron; he didn't need anyone
else in his life. Not even a stubborn tomboy who roused all
kinds of wild reactions in him, then soothed his soul with
peace offerings of macaroni & cheese and rainbow Jell-O.
The bad boy of baseball was ready to play hardball if need be,
but with Dayne Sheridan firmly planted between his sheets,
he found himself . . .

SLIDING
HOME

ISBN 13: 978-0-505-52808-7

CHRISTIE CRAIG

Macy Tucker was five years old when her beloved grandfather dropped dead in his spaghetti. At twelve, her father left his family in the dust. At twenty-five, her husband gave his secretary a pre-Christmas bonus in bed, and Macy gave him the boot. To put things lightly, men have been undependable.

That's why dating's off the menu. Macy is focused on putting herself though law school—which means being the delivery girl for Papa's Pizza. But cheesier than her job is her pie-eyed brother, who just recently escaped from prison to protect his new girlfriend. And hotter than Texas toast is the investigating detective. Proud, sexy...inflexible, he's a man who would kiss her just to shut her up. But Jake Baldwin's a protector as much as a dish. And when he gets his man—or his woman—Macy knows it's for life.

Gotcha!

ISBN 13: 978-0-505-52797-4

JOY NASH

When a girl with no family meets a guy with too much...

For Tori Morgan, family's a blessing the universe hasn't sent her way. Her parents are long gone, her chance of having a baby is slipping away, and the only thing she can call her own is a neglected old house. What she wants more than anything is a place where she belongs...and a big, noisy clan to share her life.

For Nick Santangelo, family's more like a curse. His *nonna* is a closet kleptomaniac, his mom's a menopausal time bomb and his motherless daughter is headed for serious boy trouble. The last thing Nick needs is another female making demands on his time.

But summer on the Jersey shore can be an enchanted season, when life's hurts are soothed by the ebb and flow of the tides and love can bring together the most unlikely prospects. A hard-headed contractor and a lonely reader of tarot cards and crystal prisms? All it takes is...

A Little Light Magic

ISBN 13: 978-0-505-52693-9

Tracy Madison

A Stroke of Magic

You know how freaky it is, to expect one taste and get another? Imagine picking up a can of tepid ginger ale and taking a swig of delicious, icy cold peppermint tea. Alice Raymond did just that. And though the tea is exactly what she wants, she bought herself a soda.

ONE STROKE OF MAGIC, AND EVERYTHING HAS CHANGED

No, Alice's life isn't exactly paint-by-numbers. After breaking things off with her lying, stealing, bum of an ex, she discovered she's pregnant. Motherhood was definitely on her "someday" wish list, but a baby means less time for her art and no time for recent hallucinations that include this switcharoo with the tea. She has to impress her new boss, the ridiculously long-lashed, smoky-eyed Ethan Gallagher, and she has to deal with her family, who have started rambling about gypsy curses. Only a soul-deep bond with the right man can save her and her child? As if being single wasn't pressure enough!

Available July 2009!   ISBN 13: 978-0-505-52811-7

ELISABETH NAUGHTON

Antiquities dealer Peter Kauffman walked a fine line between clean and corrupt for years. And then he met the woman who changed his life—Egyptologist Katherine Meyer. Their love affair burned white-hot in Egypt, until the day Pete's lies and half-truths caught up with him. After that, their relationship imploded, Kat walked out, and before Pete could find her to make things right, he heard she'd died in a car bomb.

Six years later, the woman Pete thought he'd lost for good is suddenly back. The lies this time aren't just his, though. The only way he and Kat will find the truth and evade a killer out for revenge is to work together—as long as they don't find themselves burned by the heat each thought was stolen long ago . . .

STOLEN HEAT

ISBN 13: 978-0-505-52794-3

To order a book or to request a catalog call:
1-800-481-9191
This book is also available at your local bookstore, or you can check out our Web site **www.dorchesterpub.com** where you can look up your favorite authors, read excerpts, or glance at our discussion forum to see what people have to say about your favorite books.

☐ **YES!**

Sign me up for the Love Spell Book Club and send my FREE BOOKS! If I choose to stay in the club, I will pay only $8.50* each month, a savings of $6.48!

NAME: _____

ADDRESS: _____

TELEPHONE: _____

EMAIL: _____

☐ I want to pay by credit card.

☐ **VISA**   ☐ **MasterCard.**   ☐ **DISCOVER**

ACCOUNT #: _____

EXPIRATION DATE: _____

SIGNATURE: _____

Mail this page along with $2.00 shipping and handling to:

Love Spell Book Club
PO Box 6640
Wayne, PA 19087

Or fax (must include credit card information) to:
610-995-9274

You can also sign up online at **www.dorchesterpub.com**.
*Plus $2.00 for shipping. Offer open to residents of the U.S. and Canada only.
Canadian residents please call 1-800-481-9191 for pricing information.
If under 18, a parent or guardian must sign. Terms, prices and conditions subject to change. Subscription subject to acceptance. Dorchester Publishing reserves the right to reject any order or cancel any subscription.